# PRAISE FOR LAIRD BARRON'S *OCCULTATION*:

"With sharp prose and wise, original stories, Barron has repeatedly proven himself one of the strongest voices in the field. This collection is a must read."
—Sarah Langan, author of *Audrey's Door*

"Laird Barron is one of those writers who makes other writers want to break their pencils. I'm serious. His work is that good. Worse than that, he's an original (damn him!), and the finest writer to join the ranks of the dark fantastic in a long, long time."
—Norman Partridge, author of *Dark Harvest* and *Lesser Demons*

"For my money, Laird Barron is far and away the best of the new generation of horror writers."
—Michael Shea, World Fantasy Award-winning author of *Polyphemus*

"…one senses that he has the potential to change the expectations of the next generation of readers by elevating the genre to a new standard of excellence."
—Lucius Shepard, author of *Trujillo*

"If you think there aren't any new Richard Mathesons or Harlan Ellisons out there, you need to read Laird Barron."
—Stewart O'Nan, bestselling author of *A Prayer for the Dying*

"Laird Barron is one of the dynamic new voices in contemporary horror fiction… Barron has all the tools to become a classic himself."
—S. T. Joshi, author of *An H. P. Lovecraft Encyclopedia*

"Laird Barron is a writer who has a real sensitivity to the atmospherics necessary to first rate dark fantasy/horror and the talent to make that atmosphere alive on the page. He is one of the leading writers of his generation."
—David G. Hartwell, coeditor of the *Year's Best Fantasy* series

"Laird Barron's fiction is rich with images that are horrifying and shocking in their otherness, and in their beauty…"
—Paul Tremblay, author of *The Little Sleep*

# PRAISE FOR LAIRD BARRON'S *OCCULTATION:*

"I can't do it: I can't sum up Laird Barron in a single, pithy sentence. He isn't the future of horror: he's where horror is right now. His fiction is a heady mix of elements from the long and varied traditions of horror (including Lovecraft, yes, but Shea and Klein and Straub, as well) blended with material from sources as varied as Wallace Stevens' elliptical poems, Cormac McCarthy's violent apocalypses, and Martin Cruz Smith's blunt thrillers. It's a moving target, returning to favorite themes and motifs, then leaping out into bold new territory. It's intelligent and gripping, and the proof of the integrity of its author's intentions is branded on every last sentence."

—John Langan, author of *House of Windows*

"Reading 'The Imago Sequence' in *The Magazine of Fantasy & Science Fiction* was one of the most thrilling experiences of my life, one that led to a frantic search for every other Laird Barron story I could get my paws on. He has revitalized the weird fiction tradition with works that showcase enormous talent, originality and energy. Above all, his slim yet steadily growing oeuvre reveals an author who combines genius with a determination to work his guts out so as to perfect his art. For me, Laird Barron is the most exciting writer to come along since Thomas Ligotti. Seek ye his books!"

—W. H. Pugmire, author of *The Fungal Stain and Other Dreams*

"Another brilliant engagement with weird fiction from a writer fast becoming a modern master."

—Jeff VanderMeer, author of *Finch*

THE
# BEAUTIFUL
# THING
## THAT AWAITS US ALL

### AND OTHER STORIES

Other books by Laird Barron:

Collections
*The Imago Sequence and Other Stories*
*Occultation and Other Stories*

Novels
*The Light Is the Darkness*
*The Croning*

# THE
# BEAUTIFUL
# THING
## THAT AWAITS US ALL
### AND OTHER STORIES

# LAIRD BARRON

NIGHT SHADE BOOKS
SAN FRANCISCO

Night Shade books may be purchased in bulk at special discounts for sales promotion, corporate gifts, fund-raising, or educational purposes. Special editions can also be created to specifications. For details, contact the Special Sales Department, Night Shade Books, 307 West 36th Street, 11th Floor, New York, NY 10018 or info@skyhorsepublishing.com.

Night Shade Books™ is a trademark of Skyhorse Publishing, Inc.™, a Delaware corporation.

Visit our website at www.nightshadebooks.com.

10 9 8 7 6 5 4 3 2 1

Library of Congress Cataloging-in-Publication Data is available on file.

ISBN: 978-1-59780-467-7

Jacket art and design by Claudia Noble
Interior layout and design by Amy Popovich

Printed in the United States of America

"Blackwood's Baby," first published in *Ghosts by Gaslight: Stories of Steampunk and Supernatural Suspense,* edited by Jack Dann and Nick Gevers, Harper Voyager, 2011.

"The Redfield Girls," first published in *Haunted Legends,* edited by Ellen Datlow and Nick Mamatas, Tor, 2010.

"Hand of Glory," first published in *The Book of Cthulhu II,* edited by Ross E. Lockhart, Night Shade Books, 2012.

"The Carrion Gods in Their Heaven," first published in *Supernatural Noir,* edited by Ellen Datlow, Dark Horse Books, 2011.

"The Siphon," first published in *Blood and Other Cravings,* edited by Ellen Datlow, Tor, 2011.

"Jaws of Saturn" is original to this volume.

"Vastation," first published in *Cthulhu's Reign,* edited by Darrell Schweitzer, DAW Books, 2010.

"The Men from Porlock," first published in *The Book of Cthulhu,* edited by Ross E. Lockhart, Night Shade Books, 2011.

"More Dark," first published in *The Revelator,* edited by Matthew Cheney and Eric Schaller, 2012.

*For Jessica*

# CONTENTS

# INTRODUCTION

## BY
## NORMAN PARTRIDGE

LAIRD BARRON.

If you've an imaginative turn of mind, the name itself conjures images. A man alone. In a castle… or perhaps a manor house. A solitary gent with a few years on him; a man who's carved his place in the world.

Of course, we're talking Scotland. Yes. The man lives in a stone manor on the moors. There he sits, staring at a crackling fire in a huge fireplace. His hunting dogs wait at heel, ready for the bones the master has stripped bare during a long evening meal. The animals are wise enough to hold their place until the word is given. Of course it will be (and soon), for the man loves his dogs as he loves little else.

But something more than love fires this man's engine. Just look above the carved mantle, at the claymore mounted on a pair of hooks that might just as easily be found in an abattoir. There's a spatter of tarnish on the weapon's hilt, but none at all on the blade. And so the claymore speaks of stories that will not cross the man's lips this night… or any night.

Laird Barron.

It's a name that conjures images, if you've an imaginative turn of mind. That's no surprise—if you know the words of the man who owns it.

If you know the work he has set down on the page.

\* \* \*

I first read Laird's work in *The Magazine of Fantasy & Science Fiction*. Cruising the Internet at dialup speed, I'd found that folks were talking about his stories on several message boards. The word around the campfire was that Laird was pretty damned good. In fact, several people in the business were pointing to him as The Next Big Thing.

Often, that kind of attention turns out to be a curse. Sure, it garners a bucketful of buzz, but it definitely sets the bar high when it comes to expectations. So while a young writer's opportunities may increase exponentially with spotlight attention, there's a price to pay if he doesn't live up to the hype. In a way, it's kind of like being the poor sap who caught the brass ring in the Aztec empire. You know, the one who gets everything he wants, only to be trotted to the top of a pyramid a year later, where his heart is carved bloody and beating from the rat-trap bones of his chest.

Of course, that didn't happen with Laird.

He was nobody's one-hit wonder.

He proved that with each new story he published.

But an image like the one I just boiled up? It's a little hard to let go. So let's play *picture if you will* for just a minute. Say Laird slipped through an eldritch wormhole in space and time, and found himself being dragged by several Aztec warriors to the top of a pyramid for a dose of *sacrificial dagger and heart excision* action.

Let me size up that situation.

Let me put it simply.

I just can't picture Laird Barron going gently into that good night.

I'd pay green money to see those Aztecs try to do their stuff, though. Especially if that wormhole and pyramid came complete with a requisite number of slithering things.

Now, that'd be something to see.

Or read about—in a Laird Barron story.

\* \* \*

When I think of Laird's work, I always circle back to the first piece that caught my attention. Originally published in *F&SF*, "Old Virginia" was a knockout, pure and simple. A piece of situational suspense set in a contained environment—not unlike *The Thing*, really, when you looked at the story in those terms—but Barron brought so much more to this particular tale that it was scary. It's a concise marvel, complete with sharp characterization, enough dread and darkness to fill up a novel, and just enough sense of the coming reveal to convince the reader he's forever playing catch-up.

Anyway, I finished the story and immediately read it again, intent on discovering just how Laird managed all that in a scant eighteen pages. I still don't think I've figured out the answer to that one, though I've read the story several times since.

But one thing I have figured out: "Old Virginia" always ends up near the top of the list when I think about the best stories I've read in the last ten years.

It's that good.

And so is Mr. Barron.

\* \* \*

Of course, Laird has come a long way since then. His Night Shade collections, *The Imago Sequence and Other Stories* and *Occultation and Other Stories*, earned him a pair of Shirley Jackson awards. His recent novel, *The Croning*, has earned rave reviews. It's my bet that in 2013 you're going to see the latter on several Best Novel award ballots in the field of the fantastic.

Turns out there's another Laird Barron novel, *The Light Is the Darkness*, that I've somehow missed. But finding out that I've got an unread Barron book in my future is kind of like coming up against a king-sized Yuggothian fungi and discovering that you've got one more very serious bullet in your clip.

One more thing: On my bookshelf, you can find Laird between Neal Barrett, Jr. and Ambrose Bierce.

That's a pretty fine place to be.

\* \* \*

The man himself?

I know what I've read online and in interviews. Laird's a native Alaskan.

He came up tough and has often said that he survived his youth. He's worked in construction and as a commercial fisherman. He raced sled dogs in three Iditarods. If you read Laird's blog, you'll find he occasionally recounts these experiences with an honesty that's both self-aware and (in today's world) astonishingly rare. His truths are often unvarnished. Or, as my old man used to say: "He doesn't gild the lily."

Like most writers, Laird is a creature of his experiences and influences. In the larger scheme of things (and in the territory of Alaska) his experiences may not be unique, but when it comes to writers of the fantastic they're pretty close to it. To stretch the point enough to put it in Lovecraft*ese*: "The grist for Mr. Barron's mill is of a singular variety." But like the best writers, Laird has discovered ways to twist his influences and reinvent them, and (ultimately) make them his own.

I'll go out on a limb and say that Laird has an appreciation for the sardonic, too. You'll see that when you read his story "Vastation." You may also discover it in distant corners of the Internet, where Laird sometimes shows up as The Man with the Lee Van Cleef icon. And you'll find it, too, in a series of posts done last year by Laird's friends: "The Secret Life of Laird Barron."

Google that.

You'll find out that you can have a pretty good time, laughing in the dark.

* * *

But let's stick with Laird's influences for a moment… and the fuel that drives his creative engine. Here's a taste of an interview I conducted with Mr. Barron for my blog:

PARTRIDGE: The first time I read Lovecraft's "At the Mountains of Madness," I was on a backpacking trip in Northern California with nothing around but redwoods. It was an unsettling experience, to say the least. You're from Alaska, and you certainly dipped deep into the dark fiction well while living in a remote environment. Do you think that gave you a different view as a reader, and how did it mold you as a writer?

BARRON: I was born and raised in Alaska, a number of those years spent in wilderness camp as my family migrated with the snow. We raised huskies for travel and freighting purposes, as well as racing in mid-distance competitions and the Iditarod. Money was tight, but books we had and I read voraciously, often by kerosene lamplight. The Arctic isolation, the vast, brooding environment, contributes to a dark psychology that might dilute with time and distance, but never truly dissipates from the spirit. I've siphoned and filtered that energy, channeled it into the atmospherics of the stories I write.

* * *

As you're about to see, those atmospherics come through loud and clear in Laird's fiction. Sometimes. At other times, they're transmitted as little more than a whisper... the kind of whisper that can cold-cock you as surely as a slaughterhouse hammer.

Again, you'll find several examples in the stories ahead. It's not my intention to steal thunder from these tales. But here's one example that's a favorite of mine, cribbed from my aforementioned blog interview with Laird:

BARRON: Touching again on the geographical influence of Alaska, I'll give you a less abstract example of how the primordial energy of that area affects people from varied backgrounds. In the winter of 1993 I was racing a team of huskies across the imposing hills between the ghost town of Iditarod and the village of Shageluk. It was near sunset, thirty or forty below Fahrenheit, lonely wilderness in all directions, and the team trudged along due to poor trail conditions. I was tired, all attention focused upon directing the dogs and keeping the sled from crashing as we negotiated the treacherous grades.

Periodically, I noted old, old pylons made of sawn logs erected off the beaten path. Markers. Initially, I didn't have much reaction, but as darkness drew down around us, the dogs' ears pricked up and a general sensation of nervousness radiated from the team. Within a few minutes I was very much overcome by a sense of dread, a profound and palpable impression of being watched by an inimical presence. Later, I queried several of the villagers about the markers (which indicated trails to hunting and burial areas) and they told me that the region was absolutely unsafe to travel after dark due to aggressive spirits. In the years since, former racers, some of them hard-bitten ex-military men, trappers and hunters, have expressed identical experiences of the approach to Shageluk.

As I learned, it's simply something almost every racer goes through if they find themselves in that stretch around dusk. Not a damned thing happened, but I haven't shaken the creepiness of those vibes in the seventeen years and it inspires me whenever I contemplate the antagonism between man and wild, the modern and the ancient, or what is known versus what is hidden.

* * *

That's a key, right there. Let's turn it in the lock.

*What is known versus what is hidden.*

In many ways, that's Laird Barron's stock-in-trade. Shivers born of something just out of sight. Terrors kindled by insensible fears suddenly made sensible by a universe that's as crazy as its inhabitants. Lovecraftian gods and monsters going nose-to-nose with men cursed by the particular horrors of their kind—blood born of wants and needs, scars born of life and experience, hearts that carry a certain measure of darkness. And every man jack among them is about to take a world-class beating from the universe, because everyone here pays a price.

So, earthy cosmic horror? You bet. It's here. Laird Barron's bringing it. In "Blackwood's Baby," a story that opens with sentences that ram at you like measuring jabs. In the quiet depths of a dark lake with "The Redfield Girls." In "The Siphon," a perfect madhouse of a story. And in the tale I'd pick as my personal favorite of this particular compilation: "The Men from Porlock." Lock 'n' load, because that one mates Lovecraft with the best of Sam Peckinpah. It's *The Wild Bunch* versus The Old Ones, and it's a magnificently brutal tale that would make HPL cry for his momma.

No doubt.

But the trailers are over. Time for the main feature to begin. You can come along for the ride. To paraphrase Laird: "You get to be part of the legend."

All you have to do is step right up.

All you have to do is turn the page.

—*Norman Partridge*
*Lafayette, California*
*October 6, 2012*

# BLACKWOOD'S BABY

Late afternoon sun baked the clay and plaster buildings of the town. Its dirt streets lay empty, packed as hard as iron. The boarding house sweltered. Luke Honey sat in a chair in the shadows across from the window. Nothing stirred except flies buzzing on the window ledge. The window was a gap bracketed by warped shutters and it opened into a portal view of the blazing white stone wall of the cantina across the alley. Since the fistfight, he wasn't welcome in the cantina although he'd seen the other three men he'd fought there each afternoon, drunk and laughing. The scabs on his knuckles were nearly healed. Every two days, one of the stock boys brought him a bottle.

Today, Luke Honey was drinking good strong Irish whiskey. His hands were clammy and his shirt stuck to his back and armpits. A cockroach scuttled into the long shadow of the bottle and waited. An overhead fan hung motionless. Clerk Galtero leaned on the counter and read a newspaper gone brittle as ancient papyrus, its fiber sucked dry by the heat; a glass of cloudy water pinned the corner. Clerk Galtero's bald skull shone in the gloom and his mustache drooped, sweat dripping from the tips and onto the paper. The clerk was from Barcelona and Luke Honey heard the fellow had served in the French Foreign Legion on the Macedonian Front during the Great War, and that he'd been clipped in the arm and that was why it curled tight and useless against his ribs.

A boy entered the house. He was black and covered with the yellow dust that settled upon everything in this place. He wore a uniform of some kind, and a cap with a narrow brim, and no shoes. Luke Honey guessed his age at eleven or twelve, although his face was worn, the flesh creased around his mouth, and his eyes suggested sullen apathy born of wisdom. Here, on the edge of a wasteland, even the children appeared weathered and aged. Perhaps that was how Luke Honey himself appeared now that he'd lived on the plains and in the jungles for seven years. Perhaps the land had chiseled and filed him down too. He didn't know because he seldom glanced at the mirror anymore. On the other hand, there were some, such as a Boer and another renowned hunter from Canada Luke Honey had accompanied on many safaris, who seemed stronger, more vibrant with each passing season, as if the dust and the heat, the cloying jungle rot and the blood they spilled fed them, bred into them a savage vitality.

The boy handed him a telegram in a stiff white envelope with fingerprints all over it. Luke Honey gave him a fifty cent piece and the boy left. Luke Honey tossed the envelope on the table. He struck a match with his thumbnail and lighted a cigarette. The light coming through the window began to thicken. Orange shadows tinged black slid across the wall of the cantina. He poured a glass of whiskey and drank it in a gulp. He poured another and set it aside. The cockroach fled under the edge of the table.

Two women descended the stairs. White women, perhaps English, certainly foreign travelers. They wore heavy, Victorian dresses, equally staid bonnets, and sheer veils. The younger of the pair inclined her head toward Luke Honey as she passed. Her lips were thinned in disapproval. She and her companion opened the door and walked through its rectangle of shimmering brilliance into the furnace. The door swung shut.

Clerk Galtero folded the newspaper and placed it under the counter. He tipped his glass toward Luke Honey in a sardonic toast. "The ladies complained about you. You make noise in your room at night, the younger one says. You cry out, like a man in delirium. The walls are thin and she cannot sleep, so she complains to me."

"Oh. Is the other one deaf, then?" Luke Honey smoked his cigarette with the corner of his mouth. He sliced open the envelope with a pocket knife and unfolded the telegram and read its contents. The letter was an invitation from one Mr. Liam Welloc Esquire to partake in an annual private hunt in Washington State. The hunt occurred on remote ancestral property, its guests designated by some arcane combination of pedigree and longstanding association with the host, or by virtue of notoriety in hunting circles. The telegram chilled the sweat trickling down his face. Luke Honey was not a particularly superstitious man; nonetheless, this missive called with an eerie intimacy and struck a chord deep within him, awakened an instinctive dread that fate beckoned across the years, the bloody plains and darkened seas, to claim him.

He stuck the telegram into his shirt pocket, then drank his whiskey. He poured another shot and lighted another cigarette and stared at the window. The light darkened to purple and the wall faded, was almost invisible. "I have nightmares. Give the ladies my apologies." He'd lived in the boarding house for three weeks and this was the second time he and Clerk Galtero had exchanged more than a word in passing. Galtero's brother Enrique managed the place in the evening. Luke Honey hadn't spoken to him much either. After years in the wilderness, he usually talked to himself.

Clerk Galtero spilled the dregs of water on the floor and walked over with his queer, hitching step, and poured the glass full of Luke Honey's whiskey. He sat in one of the rickety chairs. His good arm lay atop the table. His hands and arm were thickly muscled. The Legion tattoos had begun to elongate as his flesh loosened. "I know you," he said. "I've heard talk. I've seen your guns. Most of the foreign hunters wear trophies. Your friends, the other Americans, wear teeth and claws from their kills."

"We aren't friends."

"Your associates. I wonder though, why you have come and why you stay."

"I'm done with the bush. That's all."

"This place is not so good for a man such as yourself. There is only trouble for you here."

Luke Honey smiled wryly. "Oh, you think I've gone native."

"Not at all. I doubt you get along with anyone."

"I'll be leaving soon." Luke Honey touched the paper in his pocket. "For the States. I suppose your customers will finally have some peace."

They finished their drinks and sat in silence. When it became dark, Clerk Galtero rose and went about lighting the lamps. Luke Honey climbed the stairs to his stifling room. He lay sweating on the bed and dreamed of his brother Michael, as he had for six nights running. The next morning he arranged for transportation to the coast. Three days later he was aboard a cargo plane bound for Morocco. Following Morocco there would be ships and trains until he eventually stood again on American soil after half a lifetime. Meanwhile, he looked out the tiny window. The plains slowly disappeared into the red haze of the rim of the Earth.

* * *

Luke Honey and his party arrived at the lodge not long before dark. They'd come in two cars and the staff earned its keep transferring the mountain of bags and steamer trunks indoors before the storm broadsided the valley. Lightning sizzled from the vast snout of fast approaching purple-black clouds. Thunder growled. A rising breeze plucked leaves from the treetops. Luke Honey leaned against a marble colonnade and smoked a cigarette, personal luggage stacked neatly at his side. He disliked trusting his rifles and knives to bellhops and porters.

The Black Ram Lodge towered above a lightly wooded hillside overlooking Olde Towne. The lodge and its town lay in the folds of Ransom Hollow, separated from the lights of Seattle by miles of dirt road and forested hills. "Backward country," one of the men had called it during the long drive. Luke Honey rode with the Brits Bullard and Wesley. They'd shared a flask of brandy while the car left the lowlands and climbed toward the mountains, passing small, quaint townships and ramshackle farms tenanted by sober yeoman folk. Wesley and Bullard snickered like a pair of itinerant knights at the potato pickers in filthy motley, bowed to their labor in dark, muddy fields. Luke Honey didn't share the mirth. He'd seen enough bloody peasant revolts to know better. He knew also that fine cars and carriages, horses and guns, the gloss of their own pale skin, cursed the nobility with a false sense of well-being, of safety. He'd removed a bullet from his pocket. The bullet was made for a .454 rifle and it was large. He'd turned it over in his fingers and stared out the window without speaking again.

After supper, Dr. Landscomb and Mr. Liam Welloc, co-proprietors of the lodge, entertained the small group of far-flung travelers who'd come for the annual hunt. Servants lighted a fire in the hearth and the eight gentlemen settled into grand oversized chairs. The parlor was a dramatic

landscape of marble statuary and massive bookshelves, stuffed and mounted heads of ferocious exotic beasts, liquor cabinets and a pair of billiard
tables. Rain and wind hammered the windows. Lights flickered danger-
ously, promising a rustic evening of candlelight and kerosene lamps.

The assembly was supremely merry when the tale-telling began.

"We were in Mexico," Lord Bullard said. Lord Bullard hailed from Es-
sex; a decorated former officer in the Queen's Royal Lancers who'd fought
briefly in the Boer War, but had done most of his time pacifying the "wogs"
in the Punjab. Apparently his family was enormously wealthy in lands and
titles, and these days he traveled to the exclusion of all else. He puffed on
his cigar while a servant held the flame of a long-handled match steady.
"Summer of 1919. The war had just ended. Some Industrialist friends of
mine were visiting from Europe. Moaning and sulking about the shut-
downs of their munitions factories and the like. Beastly boring."

"Quite, I'm sure," Dr. Landscomb said. The doctor was tall and thin. He
possessed the ascetic bearing of Eastern European royalty. He had earned
his degree in medicine at Harvard and owned at least a quarter of everything there was to own within two counties.

"Ah, a trying time for the makers of bombs and guns," Mr. Liam Welloc
said. He too was tall, but thick and broad with the neck and hands of the
ancient Greek statues of Herakles. His hair and beard were bronze and
lush for a man his age. His family owned half again what the Landscombs
did and reportedly maintained ancestral estates in England and France.
"One would think there are enough territorial skirmishes underway to
keep the coins flowing. The Balkans, for example. Or Africa."

"Exactly. It's a lack of imagination," Mr. Williams said. A bluff, weather-
beaten rancher baron attired in Stetson boots, corduroys and impressive
buckle, a starched shirt with ivory buttons, and an immaculate Stetson
hat. He drank Jack Daniel's, kept the bottle on a dais at his side. He'd
come from Texas with Mr. McEvoy and Mr. Briggs. McEvoy and Briggs
were far more buttoned down in Brooks Brothers suits and bowlers; a
banker and mine owner, respectively. Williams drained his whiskey and
poured another, waving off the ever-hovering servant. "That's what's killing you boys. Trapped in the Renaissance. Can't run an empire without a
little imagination."

"Besides, Germany is sharpening its knives," Mr. Briggs said. "Your friends will be cranking up the assembly lines inside of five years. Trust me. They've the taste for blood, those Krauts. You can't beat that outta them. My mistress is Bavarian, so I know."

Lord Bullard thumped his cigar in the elegant pot near his foot. He cleared his throat. "Harrumph. Mexico City, 1919. Bloody hot. Miasma, thick and gray from smokestacks and chimneys of all those hovels they heap like ruddy anthills."

"The smog reminded me of home," Wesley said. Wesley dressed in a heavy linen coat and his boots were polished to a high gloss. His hair was slick and parted at the middle and it shone in the firelight. When Luke Honey looked at him, he thought *Mr. Weasel.*

"A Mexican prince invited us to a hunt on his estate. He was conducting business in the city, so we laid over at his villa. Had a jolly time."

Mr. Wesley said, "Tubs of booze and a veritable harem of randy strumpets. What was not to like? I was sorry when we departed for the countryside."

"Who was it, Wes, you, me, and the chap from York… Cantwell? Cotter?"

"Cantwell."

"Yes, right then. The three of us were exhausted and chafed beyond bearing from frantic revels at the good Prince's demesne, so we ventured into the streets to seek new pleasures."

"Which, ironically, constituted the pursuit of more liquor and fresh strumpets."

"On the way from one particularly unsavory cantina to another, we were accosted by a ragtag individual who leaped at us from some occulted nook in an alley. This person was of singularly dreadful countenance; wan and emaciated, afflicted by wasting disease and privation. He smelled like the innards of a rotting sheep carcass, and his appearance was most unwelcome. However, he wheedled and beseeched my attention, in passable English, I must add, and clung to my sleeve with such fervor it soon became apparent the only way to rid myself of his attention was to hear him out."

"We were confounded upon learning this wretch was an expatriate American," Mr. Wesley said.

"Thunderstruck!"

"Ye Gods," Dr. Landscomb said. "This tale bears the trappings of a penny dreadful. More, more, gentlemen!"

"The man's name was Harris. He'd once done columns for some paper and visited Mexico to conduct research for a story he never got around to writing. The entire tale of his fall from grace is long and sordid. It's enough to say he entered the company of disreputable characters and took to wickedness and vice. The chap was plainly overjoyed to encounter fellow speakers of English, but we soon learned there was much more to this encounter than mere chance. He knew our names, where we intended to hunt, and other details I've put aside."

"It was uncanny," Mr. Wesley said.

"The man was obviously a grifter," Luke Honey said from his spot near the hearth where he'd been lazing with his eyes mostly shut and thinking with mounting sullenness that the pair of Brits were entirely too smug, especially Lord Bullard with his gold rimmed monocle and cavalry saber. "A spy. Did he invite you to a séance? To predict your fortune with a handful of runes?"

"In fact, he did inveigle us to join him in a smoky den of cutthroats and thieves where this ancient crone read the entrails of chickens like the pagans read Tarot cards. It was she who sent him into the streets to track us." Lord Bullard fixed Luke Honey with a bloodshot stare. "Mock as you will, it was a rare experience."

Luke Honey chuckled and closed his eyes again. "I wouldn't dream of mocking you. The Romans swore by the custom of gutting pigeons. Who am I to argue?"

"Whom indeed? The crone scrabbled in the guts, muttering to herself while Harris crouched at her side and translated. He claimed the hag dreamed of our arrival in the city for some time and that these visions were driving her to aggravation. She described a 'black cloud' obscuring the future. There was trouble awaiting us, and soon. Something about a cave. We all laughed, of course, just as you did, Mr. Honey." Lord Bullard smiled a wry, wan smile that accentuated the creases of his face, his hangdog mouth. "Eventually, we extricated ourselves and made for the nearest taproom and forgot the whole incident. The Prince returned from his business and escorted us in style to a lavish country estate deep in the central region of the country. Twelve of us gathered to feast at his table, and in the morning he released boars into the woods."

"Twelve, you say?" Mr. Williams said, brows disappearing under his big hat. "Well, sir, I hope one of you boys got a picture to commemorate the occasion."

"I need another belt to fortify myself in the face of this heckling," Lord

Bullard said, snapping his fingers as the servant rushed over to fill his glass. The Englishman drained his glass and wagged his head for another. "To the point then: we shot two boars and wounded another—the largest of them. A prize pig, that one, with tusks like bayonets and the smoothest, blackest hide. Cantwell winged the brute, but the boar escaped and we were forced to spend the better part of two days tracking it through a benighted jungle. The blood trail disappeared into a mountain honeycombed with caves. Naturally, honor dictates pursuing wounded quarry and dispatching it. Alas, a brief discussion with the Prince and his guides convinced us of the folly of descending into the caverns. The system extended for many miles and was largely uncharted. No one of any sense attempted to navigate them. We determined to return home, satisfied with the smaller boars."

"Eh, the great white hunters balked at the precipice of the unknown?" Luke Honey said. "Thank God Cabot and Drake couldn't see you fellows quailing in the face of fear."

Lord Bullard spluttered and Mr. Wesley rose quickly, hand on the large ornamented pistol he wore holstered under his coat. He said, "I demand satisfaction!" His smile was sharp and vicious and Luke Honey had little doubt the man yearned for moments such as these.

Dr. Landscomb smoothly interposed himself, arms spread in a placating manner. "Gentlemen, gentlemen! This isn't the Wild West. There'll be no dueling on these premises. Mr. Wesley, you're among friends. Please, relax and have another drink. Mr. Honey, as for you, perhaps a bit of moderation is in order."

"You may be correct," Luke Honey said, casually sliding his revolver back into its shoulder holster. He looked at Mr. Williams who nodded approvingly and handed him the rapidly diminishing bottle of Jack Daniel's. Luke Honey took a long pull while staring at Mr. Wesley.

Mr. Wesley sat, folding himself into the chair with lethal grace, but continued to smile through small, crooked teeth. "Go on, Arthur. You were getting to the good part."

Lord Bullard wiped his red face with a handkerchief. His voice scarcely above a mutter, he said, "An American named Henderson had other ideas and he convinced two Austrians to accompany him into the caves while the rest of us made camp for the night. The poor fools slipped away and were gone for at least an hour before the rest of us realized what they'd done.

We never saw any of them again. There was a rescue mission. The Mexican Army deployed a squadron of expertly trained and equipped mountaineers to investigate, but hard rains came and the tunnels were treacherous, full of rockslides and floodwater. It would've been suicide to persist, and so our comrades were abandoned to their fates. This became a local legend and I've reports of peasants who claim to hear men screaming from the caves on certain, lonely nights directly before a storm."

The men sat in uncomfortable silence while the windows rattled and wind moaned in the flue. Mr. Liam Welloc eventually stood and went to a bookcase. He retrieved a slim, leather-bound volume and stood before the hearth, book balanced in one hand, a crystal goblet of liquor in the other. "As you may or may not know, Ian's grandfather and mine were among the founders of this town. Most of the early families arrived here from places like New York and Boston, and a few from California when they discovered the golden state not quite to their taste. The Black Ram itself has gone through several incarnations since it was built as a trading post by a merchant named Caldwell Ellis in 1860 on the eve of that nasty business between the Blue and the Gray. My grandfather purchased this property in 1890 and renovated it as the summer home for him and his new bride, Felicia. Much of this probably isn't of much interest to you, so I'll not blather on about the trials and tribulations of my forebears, nor how this grand house became a lodge. For now, let me welcome you into our most sacred tradition and we wish each of you good fortune on the morrow."

Dr. Landscomb said, "I concur. As you know, there are plenty of boar and deer on this preserve, but assuredly you've come for the great stag known as Blackwood's Baby—"

"Wot, wot?" Mr. Wesley said in mock surprise. "We're not here for the namesake of this fine establishment? What of the Black Ram?"

Mr. Liam Welloc smiled, and to Luke Honey's mind there was something cold and sinister in the man's expression. Mr. Liam Welloc said, "There was never a black ram. It's a euphemism for…Well, that's a story for another evening."

Dr. Landscomb cleared his throat politely. "As I said—the stag is a mighty specimen—surely the equal of any beast you've hunted. He is the king of the wood and descended from a venerable line. I will note, that while occasionally cornered, none of these beasts has ever been taken. In any event, the man who kills the stag shall claim my great grandfather's Sharps model-1851 as a prize. The rifle was custom built for Constantine Landscomb III by Christian Sharps himself, and is nearly priceless. The victorious fellow shall also perforce earn a place among the hallowed ranks of elite gamesmen the world over."

"And ten thousand dollars, sterling silver," Mr. Wesley said, rubbing his hands together.

"Amen, partner!" Mr. McEvoy said. "Who needs another round?"

It was quite late when the men said their goodnights and retired.

* * *

The rain slackened to drizzle. Luke Honey lay with his eyes open, listening to it rasp against the window. He'd dreamed of Africa, then of his dead brother Michael toiling in the field of their home in Ingram, just over the pass through the Cascades. His little brother turned to him and waved. His left eye was a hole. Luke Honey had awakened with sick fear in his heart.

While the sky was still dark he dressed and walked downstairs and outside to the barn. The barn lay across the muddy drive from the lodge. Inside, stable hands drifted through the silty gloom preparing dogs and horses for the day ahead. He breathed in the musk of brutish sweat and green manure, gun oil and oiled leather, the evil stink of dogs swaggering in anticipation of murder. He lighted a cigarette and smoked it leaning against a rail while the air brightened from black to gray.

"There you are, mate." Mr. Wesley stepped into the barn and walked toward Luke Honey. He wore workmanlike breeches, a simple shirt, and a bowler. He briskly rolled his sleeves.

Luke Honey didn't see a gun, although Mr. Wesley had a large knife slung low on his hip. He smiled and tapped the brim of his hat and then tried to put out the Brit's eye with a flick of his flaming cigarette. Mr. Wesley flinched, forearms raised, palms inverted, old London prizefighter style, and Luke Honey made a fist and struck him in the ribs below the heart, and followed that with a clubbing blow to the side of his neck. Mr. Wesley was stouter than he appeared. He shrugged and trapped Luke Honey's lead arm in the crook of his elbow and butted him in the jaw. Luke Honey wrenched his arm loose and swiped his fingers at Mr. Wesley's mouth, hoping to fishhook him, and tried to catch his balance on the rail with his off hand. Rotten wood gave way and he dropped to his hands and knees. Light began to slide back and forth in the sky as if he'd plunged his head into a water trough. Mr. Wesley slammed his shin across Luke Honey's chest, flipping him onto his back like a turtle. He sprawled in the wet straw, mouth agape, struggling for air, his mind filled with snow.

"Well. That's it, then." Mr. Wesley stood over him for a moment, face shiny, slick hair in disarray. He bent and scooped up his bowler, scuffed it against his pants leg and smiled at Luke Honey. He clapped the bowler onto his head and limped off.

"Should I call a doctor, kid?" Mr. Williams struck a match on the heel of his boot, momentarily burning away shadows around his perch on a hay bale. A couple of the stable hands had stopped to gawk and they jolted from their reverie and rushed to quiet the agitated mastiffs who whined and growled and strutted in their pens.

"No, he's okay," Luke Honey said when he could. "Me, I'm going to rest here a bit."

Mr. Williams chuckled. He smoked his cigarette and walked over to Luke Honey and looked down at him with a bemused squint. "Boy, what you got against them limeys anyway?"

The left side of Luke Honey's face was already swollen. Drawing breath caused flames to lick in his chest. "My grandfather chopped cotton. My father picked potatoes."

"Not you, though."

"Nope," Luke Honey said. "Not me."

\* \* \*

The lord of the stables was named Scobie, a gaunt and gnarled Welshman whose cunning and guile with dogs and horses, and traps and snares, had elevated him to the status of a peasant prince. He dressed in stained and weathered leather garments from some dim Medieval era and his thin hair bloomed in a white cloud. Dirt ingrained his hands and nails, and when he smiled his remaining teeth were sharp and crooked. His father had been a master falconer, but the modern hunt didn't call for birds any more.

The dogs and the dog handlers went first and the rest of the party entered the woods an hour later. Luke Honey accompanied the Texans and Mr. Liam Welloc. They rode light, tough horses. Mr. McEvoy commented on the relative slightness of the horses and Mr. Welloc explained that the animals were bred for endurance and agility.

The forest spread around them like a cavern. Well-beaten trails criss-crossed through impenetrable underbrush and unto milky dimness. Water dripped from branches. After a couple of hours they stopped and had tea and biscuits prepared by earnest young men in lodge livery.

"Try some chaw," Mr. Briggs said. He cut a plug of hard tobacco and handed it to Luke Honey. Luke Honey disliked tobacco. He put it in his mouth and chewed. The Brits stood nearby in a cluster talking to Dr. Landscomb and Mr. Liam Welloc. Mr. Briggs said, "You in the war? You look too young."

"I was fifteen when we joined the dance. Just missed all that fun."

"Bully for you, as the limeys would say. You can shoot, I bet. Everybody here either has money or can shoot. Or both. No offense, but I don't have you pegged for a man of means. Nah, you remind me of some of the boys in my crew. Hard-bitten. A hell-raiser."

"I've done well enough, in fact."

"He's the *real* great white hunter," Mr. Williams said. "One of those fellers who shoots lions and elephants on the Dark Continent. Fortunes to be won in the ivory trade. That right, Mr. Honey?"

"Yeah. I was over there for a while."

"Huh, I suppose you have that look about you," Mr. Briggs said. "You led safaris?"

"I worked for the Dutch."

"Leave it be," Mr. Williams said. "The man's not a natural braggart."

"Where did you learn to hunt?" Mr. McEvoy said.

"My cousins. They all lived in the hills in Utah. One of them was a sniper during the war." Luke Honey spat tobacco into the leaves. "When my mother died I went to live with my uncle and his family and those folks have lots of kin in South Africa. After college I got a case of wanderlust. One thing led to another."

"Damned peculiar upbringing. College even."

"What kid doesn't dream of stalking the savanna?" Mr. Briggs said. "You must have a hundred and one tales."

"Surely, after that kind of experience, this trip must be rather tame," Mr. McEvoy said.

"Hear, hear," Mr. Briggs said. "Give up the ivory trade for a not-so-likely chance to bag some old stag in dull as dirt U.S.A.?"

"Ten thousand sterling silver buys a lot of wine and song, amigos," Mr. Williams said. "Besides, who says the kid's quit anything?"

"Well, sir, I *am* shut of the business."

"Why is that?" Mr. Briggs said.

Luke Honey wiped his mouth. "One fine day I was standing on a plain with the hottest sun you can imagine beating down. Me and some other men had set up a crossfire and plugged maybe thirty elephants from this enormous herd. The skinners got to work with their machetes and axes. Meanwhile, I got roaring drunk with the rest of the men. A newspaper flew in a photographer on a biplane. The photographer posed us next to a pile of tusks. The tusks were stacked like cordwood and there was blood and flies everywhere. I threw up during one of the pictures. The heat and the whiskey, I thought. They put me in a tent for a couple of days while a fever fastened to me. I ranted and raved and they had to lash me down. You see, I thought the devil was hiding under my cot, that he was waiting to claim my soul. I dreamt my dear dead mother came and stood at the entrance of the tent. She had soft, magnificent wings folded against her back. White light surrounded her. The light was brilliant. Her face was dark and her eyes were fiery. She spat on the ground and the tent flaps flew shut and I was left alone in darkness. The company got me to a village where there was a real doctor who gave me quinine and I didn't quite die."

"Are you saying you quit the safaris because your mother might disapprove from her cloud in heaven?" Mr. Briggs said.

"Nope. I'm more worried she might be disapproving from an ice floe in Hell."

\* \* \*

In the afternoon, Lord Bullard shot a medium buck that was cornered by Scobie's mastiff pack. Luke Honey and Mr. Williams reined in at a remove from the action. The killing went swiftly. The buck had been severely mauled prior to their arrival. Mr. Wesley dismounted and cut the animal's throat with his overlarge knife while the dogs sniffed around and pissed on the bushes.

"Not quite as glorious as ye olden days, eh?" Mr. Williams said. He took a manly gulp of whiskey from his flask and passed it to Luke Honey.

Luke Honey drank, relishing the dark fire coursing over his bloody teeth. "German nobles still use spears to hunt boars."

"I wager more than one of those ol' boys gets his manhood torn off on occasion."

"It happens." Luke Honey slapped his right thigh. "When I was younger and stupider I was gored. Hit the bone. Luckily the boar was heart shot—stone dead when it stuck me so I didn't get ripped in two."

"Damn," Mr. Williams said.

Mr. Briggs and Mr. McEvoy stared at Luke Honey with something akin to religious awe. "Spears?" Mr. Briggs said. "Did you bring one?"

"Nope. A couple of rifles, my .45, and some knives. I travel light."

"I'm shocked the limeys put up with the lack of foot servants," Mr. Briggs said.

"I doubt any of us are capable of understanding you, Mr. Honey," Mr. Williams said. "I'm beginning to think you may be one of those rare mysteries of the world."

\* \* \*

An hour before dusk, Scobie and a grimy boy in suspenders and no shirt approached the hunters while they paused to smoke cigarettes, drink brandy, and water the horses.

Scobie said, "Arlen here came across sign of a large stag yonder a bit. Fair knocked the bark from trees with its antlers, right boy?" The boy nodded and scowled as Scobie tousled his hair. "The boy has a keen eye. How long were the tracks?" The boy gestured and Lord Bullard whistled in astonishment.

Mr. Williams snorted and fanned a circle with his hat to disperse a cloud of mosquitoes. "We're talking about a deer, not a damned buffalo."

Scobie shrugged. "Blackwood's Baby is twice the size of any buck you've set eyes on, I'll reckon."

"Pshaw!" Mr. Williams cut himself a plug and stuffed it into his mouth. He nudged his roan sideways, disengaging from the conversation.

"I say, let's have at this stag," Mr. Wesley said, to which Lord Bullard nodded.

"Damned tooting. I'd like a crack at the critter," Mr. Briggs said.

"The dogs are tired and it's late," Scobie said. "I've marked the trail, so we can find it easy tomorrow."

"Bloody hell!" Lord Bullard said. "We've light yet. I've paid my wage to nab this beastie, so I say lead on!"

"Easy, now," Mr. Welloc said. "Night's on us soon and these woods get very, very dark. Crashing about is foolhardy, and if Master Scobie says the dogs need rest, then best to heed his word."

Lord Bullard rolled his eyes. "What do you suggest, then?"

Scobie said, "Camp is set around the corner. We've got hunting shacks scattered along these trails. I'll kennel the hounds at one and meet you for another go at daybreak."

"A sensible plan," Mr. McEvoy said. As the shadows deepened and men and horses became smoky ghosts in the dying light, he'd begun to cast apprehensive glances over his shoulder.

Luke Honey had to admit there was a certain eeriness to the surroundings, a sense of inimical awareness that emanated from the depths of the forest. He noted how the horses flared their nostrils and shifted skittishly. There were boars and bears in this preserve, although he doubted any lurked within a mile after all the gunfire and barking. He'd experienced a similar sense of menace in Africa near the hidden den of a terrible lion, a dreaded man eater. He rubbed his horse's neck and kept a close watch on the bushes.

Mr. Landscomb clasped Scobie's elbow. "Once you've seen to the animals, do leave them to the lads. I'd enjoy your presence after supper."

Scobie looked unhappy. He nodded curtly and left with the boy.

Camp was a fire pit centered between two boulders the size of carriages. A dilapidated lean-to provided a dry area to spread sleeping bags and hang clothes. Stable boys materialized to unsaddle the horses and tether them behind the shed. Lodge workers had ignited a bonfire and laid out a hot meal sent from the chef. This meal included the roasted heart and liver from the buck Lord Bullard brought down earlier.

"Not sure I'd tuck into those vittles," Mr. Williams said, waving his fork at Lord Bullard and Mr. Wesley. "Should let that meat cool a day or two, else you'll get the screamin' trots."

Mr. McEvoy stopped shoveling beans into his mouth to laugh. "That's right. Scarf enough of that liver and you'll think you caught dysentery."

Lord Bullard spooned a jellified chunk of liver into his mouth. "Bollocks. Thirty years afield in the muck and the mud with boot leather and ditchwater for breakfast. My intestines are made of iron. Aye, Wes?"

"You've got the right of it," Mr. Wesley said, although sans his typical enthusiasm. He'd set aside his plate but half finished and now nursed a bottle of Laphroaig.

Luke Honey shucked his soaked jacket and breeches and warmed his toes by the fire with a plate of steak, potatoes and black coffee. He cut the meat into tiny pieces because chewing was difficult. It pleased him to see Mr. Wesley favoring his own ribs whenever he laughed. The Englishman, doughty as he was, seemed rather sickly after a day's exertion. Luke Honey faintly hoped he had one foot in the grave.

A dank mist crept through the trees and the men instinctively clutched blankets around themselves and huddled closer to the blaze, and Luke Honey saw that everyone kept a rifle or pistol near to hand. A wolf howled not too far off and all eyes turned toward the darkness that pressed against the edges of firelight. The horses nickered softly.

Dr. Landscomb said, "Hark, my cue. The wood we now occupy is called Wolfvale and it stretches some fifty miles north to south. If we traveled another twelve miles due east, we'd be in the foothills of the mountains. Wolfvale is, some say, a cursed forest. Of course, that reputation does much to draw visitors." Dr. Landscomb lighted a cigarette. "What do you think, Master Scobie?"

"The settlers considered this an evil place," Scobie said, emerging from the bushes much to the consternation of Mr. Briggs who yelped and half drew his revolver. "No one logs this forest. No one hunts here except for the lords and foolish, desperate townies. People know not to come here because of the dangerous animals that roam. These days, it's the wild beasts, but in the early days, it was mostly Bill."

"Was Bill some rustic lunatic?" Mr. Briggs said.

"We Texans know the type," Mr. Williams said with a grin.

"Oh, no, sirs. Black Bill, Splayfoot Bill, he's the devil. He's Satan and those who carved the town from the hills, and before them the trappers and fishermen, they believed he ruled these dark woods."

"The Indians believed it too," Mr. Welloc said. "I've talked with several of the elders, as did my grandfather with the tribal wise men of his era. The legend of Bill, whom they referred to as the Horned Man, is most ancient. I confess, some of my ancestors were a rather scandalous lot, given to dabbling in the occult and all matters mystical. The town library's archives are stuffed with treatises composed by the more adventurous founders, and myriad accounts by landholders and commoners alike regarding the weird phenomena prevalent in Ransom Hollow."

Scobie said, "Aye. Many a village child vanished, an' grown men an' women, too. When I was wee, my father brought us in by dusk an' barred the door tight until morning. Everyone did. Some still do."

Luke Honey said, "A peculiar arrangement for such a healthy community."

"Aye, Olde Towne seems robust," Lord Bullard said.

Dr. Landscomb said. "Those Who Work are tied to the land. A volcano won't drive them away when there's fish and fur, crops and timber to be had."

"Yeah, and you can toss sacrificial wretches into the volcano, too," Mr. McEvoy said.

"This hunt of ours goes back for many years, long before the lodge itself was established. Without exception, someone is gravely injured, killed, or lost on these expeditions."

"Lost? What does 'lost' mean, precisely?" Mr. Wesley said.

"There are swamps and cliffs, and so forth," Dr. Landscomb said. "On occasion, men have wandered into the wilds and run afoul of such dangers. But to the point. Ephraim Blackwood settled in Olde Towne at the time of its founding. A widower with two grown sons, he was a furrier by trade. The Blackwoods ran an extensive trap line throughout Ransom Hollow and within ten years of their arrival, they'd become the premier fur trading company in the entire valley. People whispered. Christianity has never gained an overwhelming mandate here, but the Blackwoods' irreligiousness went a step beyond the pale in the eyes of the locals. Inevitably, loose talk led to muttered accusations of witchcraft. Some alleged the family consorted with Splayfoot Bill, that they'd made a pact. Material wealth for their immortal souls."

"What else?" Mr. Williams said to uneasy chuckles.

"Yes, what else indeed?" Dr. Landscomb's smile faded. "It is said that Splayfoot Bill, the Old Man of the Wood, required most unholy indulgences in return for his favors."

"Do tell," Lord Bullard said with an expression of sickly fascination.

"The devil takes many forms and it is said he is a being devoted to pain and pleasure. A Catholic priest gave an impromptu sermon in the town square accusing elder Blackwood of lying with the Old Man of the Wood, who assumed the form of a doe, one night by the pallor of a sickle moon, and the issue was a monstrous stag. Some hayseed wit soon dubbed this mythical beast 'Blackwood's Git.' Other, less savory colloquialisms sprang forth, but most eventually faded into obscurity. Nowadays, those who speak of this legend call the stag 'Blackwood's Baby.' Inevitably, the brute we shall pursue in the morn is reputed to be the selfsame animal."

"Sounds like that Blackwood fella was a long way from Oklahoma," Mr. Williams said.

"Devil spawn!" Luke Honey said, and laughed sarcastically.

"Bloody preposterous," Lord Bullard said without conviction.

"Hogwash," Mr. Briggs said. "You're scarin' the women and children, hoss."

"My apologies, good sir," Dr. Landscomb said. He didn't look sorry to Luke Honey.

"Oh, dear." Lord Bullard lurched to his feet and made for the woods, hands to his belly.

The Texans guffawed and hooted, although the mood sobered when the wolf howled again and was answered by two more of its pack.

Mr. Williams scowled, cocked his big revolver and fired into the air. The report was queerly muffled and its echo died immediately.

"That'll learn 'em," Mr. Briggs said, exaggerating his drawl.

"Time for shut eye, boys," Mr. Williams said. Shortly the men began to yawn and turned in, grumbling and joshing as they spread their blankets on the floor of the lean-to.

Luke Honey made a pillow of the horse blanket. He jacked the bolt action and chambered a round in his *Mauser Gewher 98*, a rifle he'd won from an Austrian diplomat in Nairobi. The gun was powerful enough to stop most things that went on four legs and it gave him comfort. He slept.

The mist swirled heavy as soup and the fire had dwindled to coals when he woke. Branches crackled and a black shape, the girth of a bison or a full grown rhino, moved between shadows. It stopped and twisted an incomprehensibly configured head to survey the camp. The beast huffed and continued into the brush. Luke Honey remained motionless, breath caught in his throat. The huff had sounded like a chuckle. And for an instant, the lush, shrill wheedle of panpipes drifted through the wood. Far out amid the folds of the savanna, a lion coughed. A hyena barked its lunatic bark, and much closer.

Luke Honey started and his eyes popped open and he couldn't tell the world from the dream.

* * *

Lord Bullard spent much of the predawn hours hunkered in the bushes, but by daybreak he'd pulled himself together, albeit white-faced and shaken. Mr. Wesley's condition, on the other hand, appeared to have worsened. He didn't speak during breakfast and sat like a lump, chin on his chest.

"Poor bastard looks like hell warmed over," Mr. Williams said. He dressed in long johns and gun belt. He sipped coffee from a tin cup. A cigarette fumed in his left hand. "You might've done him in."

Luke Honey rolled a cigarette and lighted it. He nodded. "I saw a fight in a hostel in Cape Town between a Scottish dragoon and a big Spaniard. The dragoon carried a rifle and gave the Spaniard a butt stroke to the midsection. The Spaniard laughed, drew his gun and shot the Scot right through his head. The Spaniard died four days later. Bust a rib and it punctures the insides. Starts a bleed."

"He probably should call it a day."

"Landscomb's a sawbones. He isn't blind. Guess I'll leave it to him."

"Been hankerin' to ask you, friend—how did you end up on the list? This is a mighty exclusive event. My pappy knew the Lubbock Wellocs before I was born. Took me sixteen years to get an invite here. And a bribe or two."

"Lubbock Wellocs?"

"Yep. Wellocs are everywhere. More of them than you can shake a stick at—Nevada, Indiana, Massachusetts. Buncha foreign states too. Their granddads threw a wide loop, as my pappy used to say."

"My parents lived east of here. Over the mountains. Dad had some cousins in Ransom Hollow. They visited occasionally. I was a kid and I only heard bits and pieces... the men all got liquored up and told tall tales. I heard about the stag, decided I'd drill it when I got older."

"Here you are, sure enough. Why? I know you don't give a whit about the rifle. Or the money."

"How do you figure?"

"The look in your eyes, boy. You're afraid. A man like you is afraid, I take stock."

"I've known some fearless men. Hunted lions with them. A few of those gents forgot that Mother Nature is more of a killer than we humans will ever be and wound up getting chomped. She wants our blood, our bones, our goddamned guts. Fear is healthy."

"Sure as hell is. Except, there's something in you besides fear. Ain't that right? I swear you got the weird look some guys get who play with fire. I knew this vaquero who loved to ride his pony along the canyon edge. By close, I mean rocks crumbling under its hooves and falling into nothingness. I ask myself, what's here in these woods for you? Maybe I don't want any part of it."

"I reckon we all heard the same story about Mr. Blackwood. Same one my daddy and his cousins chewed over the fire."

"Sweet Jesus, boy. You don't believe that cart load of manure Welloc and his crony been shovelin'? Okay then. I've got a whopper for you. These paths form a miles wide pattern if you see 'em from a plane. World's biggest pentagram carved out of the countryside. Hear that one?"

Luke Honey smiled dryly and crushed the butt of his cigarette underfoot.

Mr. Williams poured out the dregs of his coffee. He hooked his thumbs in his belt. "My uncle Greg came here for the hunt in '16. They sent him home in a fancy box. The Black Ram Lodge is first class all the way."

"Stag get him?"

The rancher threw back his head and laughed. He grabbed Luke Honey's arm. There were tears in his eyes. "Oh, you are a card, kid. You really do buy into that mumbo-jumbo horse pucky. Greg spotted a huge buck moving through the woods and tried to plug it from the saddle. His horse threw him and he split his head on a rock. Damned fool."

"In other words, the stag got him."

Mr. Williams squeezed Luke Honey's shoulder. Then he slackened his grip and laughed again. "Yeah, maybe you're on to something. My pappy liked to say this family is cursed. We sure had our share of untimely deaths."

The party split again, Dr. Landscomb and the British following Scobie and the dogs; Mr. Welloc, Luke Honey and the Texans proceeding along a parallel trail. Nobody was interested in the lesser game; all were intent upon tracking down Blackwood's Baby.

They entered the deepest, darkest part of the forest. The trees were huge and ribboned with moss and creepers and fungi. Scant light penetrated the canopy, yet brambles hemmed the path. The fog persisted.

Luke Honey had been an avid reader since childhood. Robert Louis Stevenson, M. R. James, and Ambrose Bierce had gotten him through many a miserable night in the tarpaper shack his father built. He thought of the fairy tale books at his aunt's house. Musty books with wooden covers and woodblock illustrations that raised the hair on his head. The evil stepmother made to dance in red hot iron shoes at Snow White's garden wedding while the dwarves hunched like fiends. Hansel and Gretel lost in a vast, endless wood, the eyes of a thousand demons glittering in the shadows. The forest in the book was not so different from the one he found himself riding through.

At noon, they stopped to take a cold lunch from their own saddlebags as this was beyond the range of the lodge staff. Arlen trotted from the forest, dodgy and feral as a fox, to report Scobie picked up the trail and was hoping to soon drive the stag itself from hiding. Dr. Landscomb and the British were in hot pursuit.

"Damn," Mr. Williams said.

"Aw, now that limey's going to do the honors," Mr. Briggs said. "I wanted that rifle."

"Everybody wants that rifle," Mr. McEvoy said.

Mr. Williams clapped his hands together. "Let's mount up, *muchachos.* Maybe we'll get lucky and our friends will miss their opening."

"The quarry is elusive," Mr. Liam Welloc said. "Anything is possible."

The men kicked their ponies to a brisk trot and gave chase.

\* \* \*

An hour later, all hell broke loose.

The path crossed a plank bridge and continued upstream along the cut bank of a fast moving stream. Dogs barked and howled and the shouts of men echoed from the trees. A heavy rifle boomed twice. No sooner had Luke Honey and his companions entered a large clearing with a lagoon fed by a waterfall, did he spy Lord Bullard and Mr. Wesley afoot, rifles aimed at the trees. Dr. Landscomb stood to one side, hands tight on the bridle of his pony. Dead and dying dogs were strewn everywhere. A pair of surviving mastiffs yapped and snarled, muzzles slathered in foam, as Scobie wrenched mightily at their leashes.

The Brits' rifles thundered in unison. Luke Honey caught a glimpse of what at first he took to be a stag. Yet something was amiss about the shape as it bolted through the trees and disappeared. It was far too massive and it moved in a strange, top-heavy manner. Lord Bullard's horse whinnied and galloped blindly through the midst of the gawking Americans. It missed Luke Honey and Mr. Williams, collided with Mr. McEvoy and knocked his horse to the ground. The banker cursed and vaulted from the saddle, landing awkwardly. His horse staggered upright while Mr. Wesley's mount charged away into the mist in the opposite direction. Mr. Briggs yelled and pulled at the reins of his mount as it crow-hopped all over the clearing.

"What the hell was that?" Williams said, expertly controlling his horse as it half-reared, eyes rolling to the whites. "Welloc?"

Mr. Liam Welloc had wisely halted at the entrance and was supremely unaffected by the debacle. "I warned you, gentlemen. Blackwood's Baby is no tender doe."

Mr. McEvoy had twisted an ankle. He sat on a rock while Dr. Landscomb tended him. Scobie calmed his mastiffs and handed their leashes to Mr. Liam Welloc. He took a pistol from his coat and walked among the dogs who lay scattered and broken along the bank of the lagoon and in the bushes. He fired the pistol three times.

No one spoke. They rubbed their horses' necks and stared at the blood smeared across the rocks and at the savaged corpses of the dogs. Scobie began dragging them into a pile. A couple of flasks of whiskey were passed around and everyone drank in morbid silence.

Finally, Mr. Williams said, "Bullard, what happened here?" He repeated the question until the Englishman shuddered and looked up, blank-faced, from the carnage.

"It speared them on its horns. In all my years… it scooped two dogs and pranced about while they screamed and writhed on its antlers."

"Anybody get a clear shot?"

"I did," Mr. Wesley said. He leaned on his rifle like an old man. "Thought I nicked the bugger. Surely I did." He coughed and his shoulders convulsed. Dr. Landscomb left Mr. McEvoy and came over to examine him.

Mr. Liam Welloc took stock. "Two horses gone. Five dogs killed. Mr. McEvoy's ankle is swelling nicely, I see. Doctor, what of Mr. Wesley?"

Dr. Landscomb listened to Mr. Wesley's chest with a stethoscope. "This man requires further medical attention. We must get him to a hospital at once."

Scobie shouted. He ran back to the group, his eyes red, his mouth twisted in fear. "Arlen's gone. Arlen's gone."

"Easy, friend." Mr. Williams handed the older man the whiskey and waited for him to take a slug. "You mean that boy of yours?"

Scobie nodded. "He climbed a tree when the beast charged our midst. Now he's gone."

"He probably ran away," Mr. Briggs said. "Can't say as I blame him."

"No." Scobie brandished a soiled leather shoe. "This was lying near the tracks of the stag. They've gone deeper into the wood."

"Why the bloody hell would the little fool do that?" Lord Bullard said, slowly returning to himself.

"He's a brave lad," Scobie said and wrung the shoe in his grimy hands.

"Obviously we have to find the kid," Luke Honey said, although he was unhappy about the prospect. If anything, the fog had grown thicker. "We have four hours of light. Maybe less."

"It's never taken the dogs," Scobie said so quietly Luke Honey was certain no one else heard.

* * *

There was a brief discussion regarding logistics where it was decided that Dr. Landscomb would escort Mr. Wesley and Mr. McEvoy to the prior evening's campsite—it would be impossible to proceed much farther before dark. The search party would rendezvous with them and continue on to the lodge in the morning. Luke Honey volunteered his horse to carry Mr. Wesley, not from a sense of honor, but because he was likely the best tracker of the bunch and probably also the fleetest of foot.

They spread into a loose line, Mr. Liam Welloc and Mr. Briggs ranging along the flanks on horseback, while Luke Honey, Scobie, and Mr. Williams formed a picket. Mr. Williams led his horse. By turns, each of them shouted Arlen's name.

Initially, pursuit went forth with much enthusiasm as Lord Bullard had evidently wounded the stag. Its blood splattered fern leafs and puddled in the spaces between its hoof prints and led them away from the beaten trails into brush so thick, Luke Honey unsheathed his Barlow knife and hacked at the undergrowth. Mosquitoes attacked in swarms. The light dimmed and the trail went cold. A breeze sighed, and the ubiquitous fog swirled around them and tracking soon became a fruitless exercise. Mr. Liam Welloc announced an end to the search on account of encroaching darkness.

Mr. Williams and Luke Honey stopped to rest upon the exposed roots of a dying oak tree and take a slug from Mr. Williams' hip flask. The rancher smoked a cigarette. His face was red and he fanned away the mosquitoes with his hat. "Greg said this is how it was."

"Your uncle? The one who died?"

"Yeah, on the second go-around. The first time he came home and talked about a disaster. Horse threw a feller from a rich family in Kansas and broke his neck."

"I reckon everybody knows what they're getting into coming to this place."

"I'm not sure of that at all. You think you know what evil is until you look it in the eye. That's when you really cotton to the consequences. Ain't no fancy shooting iron worth any of this."

"Too early for that kind of talk."

"The hell it is. I ain't faint-hearted, but this is a bad fix. The boy is sure enough in mortal danger. Judging what happened to them dogs, *we* might be in trouble."

Luke Honey had no argument with that observation, preoccupied as he was with how the fog hung like a curtain around them, how the night abruptly surged upon them, how every hair of his body stood on end. He realized his companion wasn't at his side. He called Mr. Williams' name and the branches creaked overhead.

An unearthly stillness settled around him as he pressed his hand against the rough and slimy bark of a tree. He listened as the gazelle at the water-hole listened for the predators that deviled them. He saw a muted glow ahead; the manner of light that seeped from certain fogbanks on the deep ocean and in the depths of caverns. He went forward, groping through coils of mist, rifle held aloft in his free hand. His racing heart threatened to unman him.

Luke Honey stepped into a small grove of twisted and shaggy trees. The weak, phosphorescence rose from the earth and cast evil shadows upon the foliage and the wall of thorns that hemmed the grove on three sides. A statue canted leeward at the center of the grove—a tall, crumbling marble stack, ghastly white and stained black by moss and mold, a terrible horned man, or god. This was an idol to a dark and vile Other and it radiated a palpable aura of wickedness.

The fog crept into Luke Honey's mouth, trickled into his nostrils, and his gorge rebelled. Something struck him across the shoulders. He lost balance and all the strength in his legs drained and he collapsed and lay supine, squashed into the wet earth and leaves by an imponderable force. This force was the only thing keeping him from sliding off the skin of the Earth into the void. He clawed the dirt. Worms threaded his fingers. "Get behind me, devil," he said.

The statue blurred and expanded, shifting elastically. The statue was so very large and its cruel shadow pinned him like an insect, and the voices of its creators, primeval troglodytes who'd dwelt in mud huts and made love in the filth and offered their blood to long-dead gods, whispered obscenities, and images unfolded in his mind. He threshed and struggled to rise. A child screamed. The cry chopped off. A discordant vibration rippled over the ground and passed through Luke Honey's bones—a hideous clash of cymbals and shrieking reeds reverberated in his brain. His nose bled.

*Fresh blood is best,* the statue said, although it was Luke Honey's mouth that opened and made the words. *Baby blood, boy child blood. Rich red sweet rare boy blood. What, little man, what could you offer the lord of the dark? What you feeble fly?* His jaw contorted, manipulated by invisible fingers. His tongue writhed at the bidding of the Other. A choir of corrupt angels sang from the darkness all around—a song sweet and repellent, and old as Melville's sea and its inhabitants. Sulfurous red light illuminated the fog and impossible shapes danced and capered as if beamed from the lens of a magic lantern.

Luke Honey turned his head sideways in the dirt and saw his brother hoeing in the field. He saw himself as a boy of fourteen struggling with loading a single shot .22 and the muzzle flash exactly as Michael leaned in to look at the barrel. Luke Honey's father sent him to live in Utah and his mother died shortly thereafter, a broken woman. The black disk of the moon occulted the sun. His massive .416 Rigby boomed and a bull elephant pitched forward and crumpled, its tusks digging furrows in the dirt. Mother stood in the entrance of the tent, wings charred, her brilliant nimbus dimmed to reddish flame. Arlen regarded him from the maze of thorns, his face slack with horror. "Take me instead," Luke Honey said through clenched teeth, "and be damned."

*You're already mine, Lucas.* The Other cackled in lunatic merriment.

The music, the fire, the singing, all crashed and stopped.

Mr. Williams leaned over him and Luke Honey almost skewered the man. Mr. Williams leaped back, staring at the Barlow knife in Luke Honey's fist. "Sorry, boy. You were having a fit. Laughing like a crazy man."

Luke Honey clambered to his feet and put away the knife. His scooped up his rifle and brushed leaves from his clothes. The glow had subsided and the two men were alone except for the idol which hulked, a terrible lump in the darkness.

"Sweet baby Jesus," Mr. Williams said. "My uncle told me about these damned things, too. Said rich townies—that weren't followers of Christ, to put it politely—had 'em shipped in and set up here and there across the estate. Gods from the Old World. There are stories about rituals in the hills. Animal sacrifices and unnatural relations. Stories like our hosts told us about the Blackwoods. To this day, folks with money and an interest in ungodly practices come to visit these shrines."

"Let's get away from this thing," Luke Honey said.

"Amen to that." Mr. Williams led the way and they might've wandered all night, but someone fired a gun to signal periodically, and the two men stumbled into the firelight of camp as Mr. Liam Welloc and Mr. McEvoy were serving a simple dinner of pork and beans. By unspoken agreement, neither Luke Honey or Mr. Williams mentioned the vile statue. Luke Honey retreated to the edge of the camp, eyeing Mr. Liam Welloc and Dr. Landscomb. As lords of the estate there could be no doubt they knew something of the artifacts and their foul nature. Were the men merely curators, or did they partake of corrupt ceremonies by the dark of the moon? He shuddered and kept his weapons close.

Dr. Landscomb and Lord Bullard had wrapped Mr. Wesley in a cocoon of blankets. Mr. Wesley's face was drawn, his eyes heavy-lidded. Lord Bullard held a brandy flask to his companion's lips and dabbed them with a handkerchief after each coughing jag.

"Lord Almighty," Mr. Williams said as he joined Luke Honey, a plate of beans in hand. "I reckon he's off to the happy hunting grounds any minute now."

Luke Honey ate his dinner and tried to ignore Mr. Wesley's groans and coughs, and poor Scobie mumbling and rocking on his heels, a posture that betrayed his rude lineage of savages who went forth in ochre paints and limed hair and wailed at the capriciousness of pagan gods.

There were no stories around the fire that evening, and later, it rained.

* * *

Mr. Wesley was dead in the morning. He lay stiff and blue upon the lean-to floor. Dr. Landscomb covered him with another blanket and said a few words. Lord Bullard wept inconsolably and cast hateful glances at Luke Honey.

"Lord Almighty," was all Mr. Williams could repeat. The big man stood near the corpse, hat in hand.

"The forest is particularly greedy this season," Mr. Liam Welloc said. "It has taken a good Christian fellow and an innocent child, alas."

"Hold your tongue, Mr. Welloc!" Scobie's face was no less contorted in grief and fury than Lord Bullard's. He pointed at Mr. Liam Welloc. "My grandson lives, an' I swear to uproot every stone an' every tree in this god-forsaken forest to find him."

Mr. Liam Welloc gave Scobie a pitying smile. "I'm sorry, my friend. You know as well as I that the odds of his surviving the night are slim. The damp and cold alone...."

"We must continue the search."

"Perhaps tomorrow. At the moment, we are duty bound to see our guests to safety and make arrangements for the disposition of poor Mr. Wesley's earthly remains."

"You mean to leave Arlen at the tender mercy of... Nay, I'll have none of it."

"I am sorry. Our duty is clear."

"Curse you, Mr. Welloc!"

"Master Scobie, I implore you not to pursue a reckless course—"

"Bah!" Scobie made a foul gesture and stomped into the predawn gloom. Mr. McEvoy said, "The old man is right—we can't just quit on the kid."

"Damned straight," Mr. Briggs said. "What kind of skunks would we be to abandon a boy while there's still a chance?"

Dr. Landscomb said, "Well spoken, sirs. However, you can hardly be expected to grasp the, ah, gravity of the situation. I assure you, Arlen is lost. Master Scobie is on a Quixotic mission. He won't find the lad anywhere in Wolfvale. In any event, Mr. McEvoy simply must be treated at a hospital lest his ankle grow worse. I dislike the color of the swelling."

"Surely, it does no harm to try," Mr. Briggs said.

"We tempt fate by spending another minute here," Mr. Liam Welloc said. "And to stay after sunset.... This is impossible, I'm afraid." The incongruity of the doctor's genteel comport juxtaposed with his apparent dread of the supernatural chilled Luke Honey in a way he wouldn't have deemed possible after his experiences abroad.

"Tempt fate?" Mr. Briggs said. "Not stay after sunset? What the hell is that supposed to mean, Welloc? Boys, can you make heads or tails of this foolishness?"

"He means we'd better get ourselves shut of this place," Mr. Williams said.

"Bloody right," Lord Bullard said. "This is a matter for the authorities."

Mr. Briggs appeared dumbfounded. "Well don't this beat all. Luke, what do you say?"

Luke Honey lighted a cigarette. "I think we should get back to the lodge. A dirty shame, but that's how I see it."

"I don't believe this."

"Me neither," Mr. McEvoy said. His leg was elevated and his cheeks shone with sweat. His ankle was swaddled in bandages. "Wish I could walk, damn it."

"You saw what that stag did to the dogs," Lord Bullard said. "There's something unnatural at work and I've had quite enough, thank you." He wiped his eyes and looked at Luke Honey. "You'll answer for Wes. Don't think you won't."

"Easy there, partner," Mr. Williams said.

Luke Honey nodded. "Well, Mr. Bullard, I think you may be correct. I'll answer for your friend. That reckoning is a bit farther down the list, but it's on there."

"This is no time to bicker," said Mr. Liam Welloc. "Apparently we are in agreement—"

"Not all of us," Mr. Briggs said, glowering.

"—Since we are in agreement, let's commence packing. We'll sort everything out when we return to the house."

"What about Scobie?" Mr. Briggs said.

"Master Scobie can fend for himself," Mr. Liam Welloc said, his bland, conciliatory demeanor firmly in place. "As I said, upon our return we will alert the proper authorities. Sheriff Peckham has some experience in these matters."

Luke Honey didn't believe the sheriff, or anybody else, would be combing these woods for one raggedy kid anytime soon. The yearly sacrifice had been accomplished. This was the way of the world; this was its beating heart and panting maw. He'd seen such offerings made by tribes in the jungles, just as his own Gaelic kin had once poured wine in the sea and cut the throats of fatted lambs. If one looked back far enough, all men issued from the same wellspring and every last one of them feared the dark as Mr. Liam Welloc and Dr. Landscomb and their constituency in Ransom Hollow surely did. Despite the loathsome nature of their pact, there was nothing shocking about this arrangement. To propitiate the gods, to please one's lord and master was ever the way. That expert killers such as the English and the Texans and, of course, himself, served as provender in this particular iteration of the eternal drama filled Luke Honey's heart with bitter amusement. This wry humor mixed with his increasing dread and rendered him giddy, almost drunken.

Mr. Wesley's body was laid across the saddle of Luke Honey's horse and the company began the long trudge homeward. The dreary fog persisted, although the rain had given out for the moment.

"I hope you don't think I'm a coward," Mr. Williams said. He rode beside Luke Honey who was walking at the rear of the group.

Luke Honey didn't speak. He pulled his collar tight.

"My mama raised me as a God fearin' boy. There's real evil, Mr. Honey. Not that existential crap, either. Last night, I felt somethin' I ain't felt before. Scared me spitless." When Luke Honey didn't answer, Mr. Williams leaned over and said in a low voice, "People got killed in that grove, not just animals. Couldn't you feel it coming off that idol like a draft in a slaughter yard? I ain't afraid of much, but Bullard's right. This ain't natural and that kid is a goner."

"Who are you trying to convince?" Luke Honey said, although the question was more than a little self-referential. "The hunt is over. Go back to Texas and dream away the winter. There's always next year."

"No, not for me. My uncle made that mistake. Next year, I'll go to British Colombia. Or Alaska. Damned if I know, but I know it won't be Ransom Hollow." Mr. Williams clicked his tongue and spurred his mount ahead to rejoin the group.

Later, the company halted for a brief time to rest the animals and allow the men to stretch their legs. The liquor was gone and tempers short. When they remounted, Luke Honey remained seated on a mossy boulder, smoking his last cigarette. His companions rode on, heads down and dispirited, and failed to notice his absence. They disappeared around a sharp bend.

Luke Honey finished his cigarette. The sun slowly ate through the clouds and its pale light shone in the gaps of the foliage. He turned his back and walked deeper into the woods, into the darkness.

* * *

The shrieks of the mastiffs came and went all day, and so too the phantom bellows of men, the muffled blasts of their weapons. Luke Honey resisted the urge to cover his ears, to break and flee. Occasionally, Scobie hollered from an indeterminate distance. Luke Honey thought the old man's cries sounded more substantial, more of the mortal realm, and he attempted to orient himself in their direction. He walked on, clutching his rifle.

Night came and he was lost in the endless forest.

A light glimmered to his left, sifting down through the black gallery to illuminate a figure who stood as if upon a stage. Mr. Wesley regarded him, hat clasped to his navel in both hands, hair slick and shining. His face was white. A black stain spread across the breast of his white shirt. He removed a pair of objects from inside his hat and with an insolent flourish tossed them into the bushes short of Luke Honey. Dr. Landscomb stepped into view and took Mr. Wesley by the elbow and drew him into the shadows. The ray of light blinked out of existence.

The objects were pale and glistening and as Luke Honey approached them, his heart beat faster. He leaned close to inspect them and recoiled, his courage finally buckling in the presence of such monstrous events.

Luke Honey blindly shoved his way through low-hanging branches and spiky undergrowth. His clothes were torn, the flesh of his hands and face scratched and bleeding. A rifle fired several yards away. He staggered and shielded his eyes from the muzzle flash and a large animal blundered past him, squealing and roaring. Then it was gone and Scobie came tearing in pursuit and almost tripped over him. The old man swung a battered lantern. He gawked at Luke Honey in the flat yellow glare.

Scobie's expression was wild and caked in dirt. His face was nicked and bloody. He panted like a dog. He held his rifle in his left hand, its bore centered on Luke Honey's middle. In a gasping voice, he said, "I see you, Bill."

"It's me, Luke Honey."

"What's your business here?"

"I came to help you find the boy." He dared not speak of what he'd so recently discovered, an abomination that once revealed was certain to drive the huntsman into raving madness. At this range Scobie's ancient single shot rifle would cut Luke Honey in twain.

"Arlen's gone. He's gone." Scobie lowered the weapon, his arm quivering in exhaustion.

"You don't believe that." Luke Honey said with a steadiness born of staring down savage predators, of waiting to pull the trigger that would drop them at his feet, of facing certain death with a coldness of mind inherent to the borderline mad. The terror remained, ready to sweep him away.

"I'm worn to the bone. There's nothing left in me." Scobie seemed to wither, to shrink into himself in despair.

"The stag is wounded," Luke Honey said. "I think you hit it again, judging from the racket."

"It don't matter. You can't kill a thing like that." Scobie's eyes glittered with tears. "This is the devil's preserve, Mr. Honey. Every acre. You should've gone with the masters, got yourself away. We stayed too long and we're done for. He only pretends to run. He'll end the game and come for us soon."

"I had a bad feeling about Landscomb and Welloc."

"Forget those idiots. They're as much at the mercy of Hell as anyone else in Ransom Hollow."

"Got anything to drink?" Luke Honey said.

Scobie hung the lantern from a branch and handed Luke Honey a canteen made of cured animal skin. The canteen was full of sweet, bitter whiskey. The men took a couple of swigs and rested there by the flickering illumination of the sooty old lamp. Luke Honey built a fire. They ate jerky and warmed themselves as the dank night closed in ever more tightly.

Much later, Scobie said, "It used to be worse. My grandsire claimed some of the more devout folk would drag girls from their homes and cut out their innards on them stone tablets you'll find under a tree here or there." His wizened face crinkled into a horridly mournful smile. "An' my mother, she whispered that when she was a babe, Black Bill was known to creep through the yards of honest folk while they slept. She heard his nails tap-tapping on their cottage door one night."

Luke Honey closed his eyes. He thought again of Arlen's pitiful, small hands severed at the wrists and discarded in the brush, a pair of soft, dripping flowers. He heard his companion rise stealthily and creep away from camp. He slept and awakened to the old man kneeling at his side. Scobie's face was hidden in shadow. Luke Honey smelled the oily steel of a knife near his own neck. The man reeked of murderous intent. He wondered where Scobie had been, what he had done.

Scobie spoke softly, "I don't know what to do. I'm a man of God."

"Yet here we are. Look who you serve."

"No, Mr. Honey. The hunt goes on an' I don't matter none. You're presence ain't my doing. You bought your ticket. I come because somebody's got to stand up. Somebody's got to put a bullet in the demon."

"The price you've paid seems steep as hell, codger."

Scobie nodded. He remained quiet for a while. At last he said, "Come, boy. You must come with me now. He's waiting for us. He whispered to me from the dark, made a pact with me he'd take one of us in return for Arlen. I promised him you, God help me. It's a vile oath and I'm ashamed."

"Oh, Scobie." Luke Honey's belly twisted and churned. "You know how these things turn out. You poor, damned fool."

"Please. Don't make me beg you, Mr. Honey. Don't make me. Do what's right for that innocent boy. I know the Lord's in your heart."

Luke Honey reached for Scobie's arm, and patted it. "You're right about one thing. God help you."

They went. There was a clearing, its bed layered with muck and spoiled leaves. Unholy symbols were gouged into the trees; brands so old they'd fossilized. It was a killing ground of antiquity and Scobie had prepared it well. He'd improvised several torches to light the shallow basin with a ghastly, reddish glare.

Scobie took several steps and uttered an inarticulate cry, a glottal exclamation held over from his ancestors. He half turned to beckon and his face was transformed by shock when Luke Honey smashed the butt of his rifle into his hip, and sent him stumbling into the middle of the clearing.

Luke Honey's eyes blurred with grief, and Michael's shade materialized there, his trusting smile disintegrating into bewilderment, then inertness. The cruelness of the memory drained Luke Honey of his fear. He said with dispassion, "My hell is to testify. Don't you understand? He doesn't want me. He took me years ago."

Brush snapped. The stag shambled forth from the outer darkness. It loomed above Scobie, its fur rank and steaming. Black blood oozed from gashes along its flanks. Beneath a great jagged crown of antlers its eyes were black, its teeth yellow and broken. Scobie fell to his knees, palms raised in supplication. The stag nuzzled his matted hair and its long tongue lapped at the muddy tears and the streaks of drying blood upon the man's upturned face. Its muzzle unhinged. The teeth closed and there was a sound like a ripe cabbage cracking apart.

Luke Honey slumped against the bole of the oak, the rifle a dead, useless weight across his knees, and watched.

# THE REDFIELD GIRLS

## 1.

Every autumn for a decade, several of the Redfield Girls, a close-knit sorority of veteran teachers from Redfield Memorial Middle School in Olympia, gathered for a minor road trip along the hinterlands of the Pacific Northwest. Traditionally, they rented a house in a rural, picturesque locale, such as the San Juan Islands or Cannon Beach, or Astoria, and settled in for a last long weekend of cribbage, books, and wine before their students came rushing into the halls, flushed and wild from summer vacation. Bernice Barber; Karla Gott; Dixie Thiess; and Li-Hua Ming comprised the core of the Redfield Girls. Li-Hua served as the school psychiatrist, and Karla and Dixie taught English—Karla was a staunch, card-bearing member of the Dead White Guys Club, while Dixie preferred Neruda and Borges. Their frequent arguments were excruciating or exquisite depending on how many glasses of merlot they'd downed. Both of them considered Bernice, the lone science teacher and devourer of clearance sale textbooks, a borderline stick in the mud. They meant this with great affection.

This was Bernice's year to choose their destination and she chose a rustic cabin on the shores of Lake Crescent on the Olympic Peninsula. The cabin belonged to the Bigfish Lodge and was situated a half mile from the main road in a stand of firs. There was no electricity, or indoor plumbing, although the building itself was rather comfortable and spacious and the caretakers kept the woodshed stocked. The man on the phone told her a lot of celebrities had stayed there—Frank Sinatra, Bing Crosby, Elizabeth Taylor, and at least one of the Kennedys. Even some mobsters and their molls.

Truth be told, Dixie *nagged* her into picking the lake. Left to her own devices, she would've happily settled for another weekend at Ocean Shores or Seaside. Dixie was having none of it: ever fascinated with the Port Angeles and the Sequim Valley, she pushed and pushed, and Bernice finally gave in. Her family homesteaded in the area during the 1920s, although most of them had scattered on the wind long since. She'd lived in Olympia since childhood, but Dad and Mom brought them up to the lake for a visit during the height of every summer. They pitched a tent at a campsite in the nearby park, and fished and swam in the lake. Dad barbequed and told ghost stories, because that's what one did when one spent a long, lonely night near the water. Bernice and her husband Elmer made a half-dozen day trips over the years; none, however, since he passed away. Lately though, she thought of the lake often. She woke in a sweat, dreams vanishing like quicksilver.

The night before the Redfield Girls were to leave on the trip, there was a storm. She was startled by loud knocking on the front door. She hesitated to answer, and briefly lamented not adopting another big dog for protection after her black Lab Norman died. Living alone on a piece of wooded property outside of town, she seldom received random visitors—and certainly not in the wee hours. A familiar voice shouted her name. Her teenage niece Lourdes Blanchard had flown in unannounced from Paris.

Bernice ushered Lourdes inside, doing her best to conceal her annoyance. She enjoyed kids well enough. However, she jealously coveted those few weeks of freedom between summer and fall, and more importantly, her relationship with Lourdes was cool. The girl was bright and possessed a wry wit. Definitely not a prized combination in anyone under thirty.

Bernice suspected trouble at home. Her sister Nancy denied it during the livid, yet surreptitious phone call Bernice made after she'd tucked the girl into bed. Everything was fine, absolutely super—why was she asking? Lourdes saved a bit of money and decided to hop the international flight from Paris to Washington State, determined to embark upon a fandango of sorts. What was a mother to do? The child was stubborn as a mule—just like her favorite Auntie.

"Well, you could've warned me, for starters," Bernice said. "Good God, Nance, I'm leaving with the Redfield Girls tomorrow—"

Nancy laughed as the connection crackled. "See, that's perfect. She's been clamoring to go with you on one of your little adventures. Sis? Sis? I'm losing the connection. Have fun—"

She was left clutching a dead phone. The timing was bizarre and seemed too eerie for coincidence. She'd had awful dreams several nights running; now, here was Lourdes on her doorstep, soaked to the bone, thunder and lightning at her back. It was almost as bad as the gothic horror novels Bernice had been reading to put herself to sleep. She couldn't very well send Lourdes packing, nor with any conscience leave her sitting at the house. So, she gritted her teeth into a Miss America smile and said, "Guess what, kid? We're going to the mountains."

2.

The group arrived at the lake in late afternoon. Somehow, they'd managed to jam themselves, and all their luggage, into Dixie's rusted out Subaru. The car was a hundred thousand miles past its expiration date and plastered with stickers like FREE TIBET, KILL YOUR TV, and VISUALIZE WHIRLED PEAS. They stopped at the lodge and picked up the cabin key and a complimentary fruit basket. From there it was a ten-minute drive through the woods to the cabin itself. While the others finished unpacking, Bernice slipped outside to sneak a cigarette. To her chagrin, Lourdes was waiting, elbows on the rail. Her niece was rapidly becoming a bad penny. Annoyingly, the other women didn't seem to mind her crashing the party. Perhaps their empty nests made them maudlin for the company of children.

"Aunt Dolly died here. This is where they found her." Lourdes squinted at the dark water thirty or so yards from the porch of the cabin.

"That's great aunt to you." Bernice quickly pocketed her lighter and tried to figure out how to beat a hasty retreat without appearing to flee the scene. "To be accurate, it probably happened closer to the western side. That's where they lived."

"But, she was the *Lady of the Lake?*"

"Aunt Dolly was Aunt Dolly. She died an awful death. Cue the violins."

"And the ghost stories."

"Those too. Nothing like enriching cultural heritage by giving the tavern drunks a *cause célèbre* to flap their lips about."

"Doesn't it make you sad? Even a little?"

"I wasn't alive in 1938. Jeez—I never knew the gal personally. How old do you think I am, anyway?"

Lourdes brushed back her hair. She was straw blonde and lean, although she had her mother's eyes and mouth. Bernice had always wondered about the girl's fairness. On the maternal side, their great grandparents were a heavy mix of Spanish and Klallam—just about everybody in the immediate family was thick and dark. Bernice had inherited high cheekbones and bronze skin and black hair, now turning to iron. She owned a pair of moccasins she never wore, and a collection of beads handed down from her elders she kept locked in a box of similar trinkets.

A stretch of beach separated them and the lake. The lake was a scar one mile wide and ten miles long. The water splashed against the rocks, tossing reels of brown kelp. Clouds rolled across the sky. The sun was sinking and the water gleamed black with streaks of red. Night came early to the peninsula in the fall. The terrain conspired with the dark. For the most part, one couldn't see a thing after sundown. The Douglas fir and Western redwoods rose like ancient towers, and beneath the canopy all was cool and dim. Out there, simple homes were scattered through the foothills of Storm King Mountain in a chain of dirt tracks that eventually linked to the highway junction. This was logging country, farm country; field and stream, and overgrown woods full of nothing but birds and deer, and the occasional lost camper.

An owl warbled and Bernice shivered. "Anyway. How'd this gnat get in your ear?"

"I read about it a long time ago in a newspaper clipping—I was helping Grandma sort through Grandpa's papers after he died. As we drove up here, I started thinking about the story. This place is so…forbidding. I mean, it's gorgeous, but beneath that, kind of stark. And…Dixie was telling me about it earlier when you were getting the key."

"That figures."

The younger woman pulled her shawl tight. "It's just so…awful."

"You said it, kid." Bernice called her niece "kid" even though Lourdes was seventeen and on her way to college in a couple of weeks. Depending upon the results of forthcoming exams, she'd train to be a magistrate, or at the least, a barrister. They grew up fast in Europe. Even so, the divide was too broad—Bernice was approaching fifty and she felt every mile in her bones. Chaperone to a sardonic, provocative little wiseacre seemed a hollow reward for another tough year at the office.

"There's another thing...I had a really bizarre dream about Aunt Dolly the other day. I was floating in a lake—not here, but somewhere warm—and she spoke to me. She was this white shape under the water. I knew it was her, though, and I heard her voice clearly."

"What did she say?"

"I don't remember. She was nice...except, something about the situation wasn't right, you know? Like she was trying to trick me. I woke in a sweat."

Bernice's flesh goose pimpled. Uncertain how to respond, she resisted the temptation to confide her own nightmares. "That is pretty weird, all right."

"I'm almost afraid to ask about the murder," Lourdes said.

"But not quite, eh?" They must be sharing a wavelength. What wavelength, though?

"I wish Mom had mentioned it."

"It's quite the campfire tale with your cousins. Grandpa Howard used to scare them with it every Halloween—"

"Way insensitive."

"Well, that's the other side of the family. Kissinger he isn't. Nancy never told you?"

"Frank discourages loose talk. He's a sensible fellow. Mom follows his lead." It was no secret Lourdes disliked her father. His name was Francois, but she called him Frank when talking to her friends. She'd pierced her navel and tattooed the US flag on the small of her back to spite him. Ironically, his stepsons John and Frank, thought Francois was the greatest thing since sliced baguettes.

Fair enough, if she hated him. Who knew what Nancy was thinking when she married the schmuck. Except, Bernice *did indeed* know what her sister had been thinking—Francois was a first rate civil engineer; one of the best in Paris. After Bill died, Nancy only cared about security. Her two boys were in middle school at the time and Bill had been under the weight of a crippling mortgage, the bills for his chemotherapy. Bernice suspected she only got herself pregnant with Lourdes to seal the deal. It shouldn't irk her that Nancy had made the smart choice. When Bernice lost Elmer, she'd gone the other direction—dug in and accepted the role of widow. Eleven years and she hadn't remarried, hadn't even gone on a date. It was wrong to begrudge Nancy, but Lord help her, she did, and maybe that was why she resented poor Lourdes just a tiny bit—and maybe she was envious because she and Elmer put off having their own children and now it was far too late.

Lourdes said, "That's why you brought us up here, right? To tell the tale and give everyone a good scare?"

Bernice laughed to cover her mounting unease. "It hadn't occurred to me. I brought a bag of books and sun block. We've got our evening cribbage tournaments. Hope you don't get too bored with us biddies."

"Dixie promised to go hiking with me tomorrow."

"Tomorrow?" Bernice detested hiking. The hills were steep, the bugs ravenous. She'd allowed her gym membership to lapse, and piled on almost fifteen pounds since spring. No, hiking wasn't a welcome prospect. And to think she wasn't even consulted in the change of program. Dixie's treachery would not go unremarked.

"Tomorrow afternoon. Then she's driving us into Port Angeles for dinner at the Red Devil."

"That's a bar. Your parents—"

"The place serves fish and chips. Dixie says it's the best cod ever. Besides, there's no drinking age in France."

"Cripes," Bernice said. Her desire for a cigarette was almost violent, but she restricted herself to a couple of *Virginia Slims* a day, and only in secret. Lights came on in the cabin. Dixie stuck her head out a window to say dinner was up.

### 3.

Li-Hua made stir fry and egg rolls over the gas range. She preferred traditional southern Chinese cuisine. A tough, sinewy woman, she'd endured a stint in a tire factory during the Cultural Revolution before escaping to college, and eventually from Hainan to the United States where she earned her doctorate. For years, Karla nagged her to write a memoir that would make Amy Tan seem like a piker. Li-Hua smiled wisely and said she'd probably retire and open a restaurant instead.

They ate garlic bread on the side and drank plenty of red wine Karla and her husband Chuck had brought home from a recent tour of Wenatchee vineyards. Normally the couple spent summer vacation scuba diving in Puget Sound. As Karla explained, "We went to the wineries because I've gotten too fat to fit into my wetsuit."

After dinner, Dixie turned down the kerosene lanterns and the five gathered near the hearth—Bernice and Li-Hua in the musty leather seats; Karla, Dixie, and Lourdes on their sleeping bags. The AM transistor played soft, classical jazz. Karla quizzed Lourdes about her dreaded exams, the pros and cons of European track education versus the American scattershot approach.

Bernice half-listened to their conversation, wineglass balanced on her knee, as she lazily scrutinized the low, split beam rafters, the stuffed mallard and elk head trophies, and the dingy photographs of manly men posing beside hewn logs and mounds of slaughtered salmon. Darkness filled every window.

"You want to tell this?" Dixie said. "Your niece is pestering me."

"I know. She's been bugging the crap out of me, too."

"Oh, be nice, would you?" Karla said. She stirred the coals with a poker.

"Yeah, be nice," Dixie said while Lourdes didn't try hard to cover a smirk. Her cheeks were flushed. Dixie and Karla had given her a few glasses of wine. "Hey, they do it in France!" Dixie said when confronted.

"Go for it, then." Bernice shook her head. She was too drowsy and worn down to protest. She always enjoyed Dixie's rendition of the tale. Her friend once wrote an off the cuff essay called "Haunted Lake." It was subsequently published in the *Daily Olympian* and reprinted every couple of years around Halloween.

"If you insist."

"Hey, guys," Li-Hua said. "It may be bad luck to gossip about this so close to the sacred water."

"Come on," Dixie said.

Li-Hua frowned. "I'm serious. My feet got cold when you started talking. What if the spirits heard us and now they're watching? You don't know everything about these things. There are terrible mysteries."

"Whatever," Bernice said. She refused to admit the same chill creeping up her legs, as if dipped in a mist of dry ice. "Let nothing but fear...."

"Okie-dokie. What's so special about the lake?" Karla dropped the poker and leaned toward Dixie with an expression of dubious interest.

"She's cursed." Dixie was solemn.

"That's what I'm saying," Li-Hua said.

"I get the feeling you Northlanders brought a lot of superstitious baggage from the Old World," Karla said, indicating Dixie's pronounced Norwegian ancestry.

"It's more than white man superstition, though. In the winter, thunderstorms boil down the valley, set fire to the high timber, tear the roofs off houses, and flood a hundred draws from here to Port Townsend." Dixie nodded to herself and sipped her drink, beginning to get into her narrative. "The wind *blows*. It lays its hammer on the waters of the lake, beats her until she bares rows of whitecap teeth. She's old too, that one; a deep, dark Paleolithic well of glacial water. She was here an eon before the Klallam settled along the valley in their huts and longhouses. The tribes never liked her. According to legend, the Klallam refused to paddle their canoes across Lake Crescent. This goes back to the ancient days when the Klallam were paddling just about everywhere. They believed the lake was full of demons who would drag them to the bottom for trespassing."

A gust rattled the windows and moaned in the chimney. Sparks flew around the grate and everybody but Dixie glanced into the shadowy corners of the room.

"Man, you're getting good at this," Bernice said dryly.

"Keep going!" Lourdes said. She'd pulled her sweater over her nose so that only her eyes were revealed.

"I'd be quiet," Li-Hua said.

Dixie chuckled and handed her glass to Li-Hua. Li-Hua poured her another three fingers of wine and passed it back. "Oh, the locals *adore* stories—the eerie ones, the true crime ones, the ones that poke at the unknowable; and they do love their gossip. Everybody, and I mean everybody, has a favorite. The most famous tale you'll hear about Lake Crescent concerns the murder of poor waitress Dolly Hanson. Of all the weird stories, the morbid campfire tales they tell the tourists on stormy nights around the hearth, *The Lady of the Lake Murder* is the one everybody remembers.

"A tawdry piece of business, that saga. In the mid-'30s, the bar had grown into a popular resort for the rich townies and renamed Lake Crescent Lodge, although most of the locals stubbornly referred to it as Singer's Tavern. A few still do. According to legend, Dolly, who was Bernice's aunt, of course, had just gotten divorced from her third husband Hank on account of his philandering ways—"

"—And the fact he beat her within an inch of her life whenever he got a snootful at the tavern," Bernice said.

"Yes, yes," Dixie said. "On the morning of the big Singer's Christmas party of 1938, he strangled Dolly, tied some blocks to her and dumped her in the middle of the lake. The jerk went about his way as the resident merry widower of Port Angeles until he eventually moved to California. People suspected, people whispered, but Hank claimed his wife ran off to Alaska with a salesman—or a sailor, depending on who's telling the tale—and no one could prove otherwise."

"Some fishermen found her in 1945, washed up directly below the lodge. That lake is deep and cold—there aren't any deeper or any colder in the continental US. The frigid alkaline water preserved Dolly pretty much fully intact. She'd turned to soap."

"Soap? Like a soap carving, a sculpture?"

"Yes indeed. The cold caused a chemical reaction that softens the body, yet keeps it intact to a point. A weird sort of mummification."

"That's freaky," Lourdes said.

Dixie chuckled. "Say, Bernie—wasn't it Bob Hall who identified her? Yeah…Hall. A barber by trade, and part-time dentist, matched her dental records. The young lady's teeth were perfectly preserved, you see. That was curtains for old two-timing Hank. He was hanged in '49. That's just one incident. Plenty more where that came from."

"More murders? More soap mummies?" Karla said.

"I suppose there could be more corpses. Deep as she is, the lake would make a pretty convenient dump site. Folks are given to feuds here in the hills. A lot of people have disappeared from this end of the peninsula over the years. Especially around the lake."

"Really? Like who?"

"All kinds. There was the married couple who bought a washing machine in Sequim and were last seen a mile or so from where we are right now. Those two vanished in 1955 and it's still a mystery where they went. Back in 2005, an amateur detective supposedly found the lid to the washer in two hundred feet of water near a swimming hole called The Devil's Punch Bowl. The kid got pretty excited about his find; he planned to come back with more equipment and volunteers, but he hasn't, and I doubt he will. It wouldn't matter anyway. Then there's Ambulance Point. An ambulance racing for the hospital crashed through a guardrail and went into the drink. The paramedics swam away from the wreck, but a logger strapped to a gurney in the back of the ambulance sure as hell didn't. Every year some diver uncovers the door handle to a Model A, the bumper from a Packard, the rims to something else. Bones? Undoubtedly, a reef of them exists somewhere in the deep. We won't find them, though. Like the old timers say: the mistress keeps those close to her heart. Some say the souls of those taken are imprisoned in the forms of animals—coyotes and loons. When a coyote howls or a loon screams, they're crying to their old selves, the loved ones they've lost."

Lourdes's eyes were wide and gleaming. "You actually wrote an essay about this?"

"Yep."

"You must email it to me when I get home!"

"You got it, kiddo."

Bernice was getting ready to turn in for the night when Dixie laughed with Lourdes and said, "That's a great idea. Bernie, you in?"

"On what?"

"A séance."

"I've studied the occult," Lourdes said with a self-conscious flush. "I know how to do this."

"Black magic an elective across the pond, is it?"

"No, me and some friends just play around with it for fun."

"She looks so normal, too," Bernice said to Karla and Li-Hua.

Li-Hua shook her head. "Forget about it. No way."

"I'm game," Karla said. "I attended a couple of séances in college. It's harmless. What night could be better?"

"Think of the memories," Dixie said. "When's the last time we've done anything wild?"

"Yeah, but you go to El Salvador while we effete gentry glut ourselves and sail around on yachts during summer vacation," Karla said. "Don't the locals believe in ghosts and such? Surely you see funky goings on?"

"From a distance. I'm not exactly brave."

"Pshaw. No way I could stomach the dozen inoculations you've gotta get to enter those countries. Nope, I'm white bread to the core."

"Well, I'm with Li-Hua. I'm tired and it's silly anyway." Bernice stood and went out to the porch. The wind ripped across the water and roared through the trees. She shielded her eyes from a blast of leaves and pine needles. Her hair came free of its barrette and she wondered how crazy that made her appear. Getting in a nightcap smoke was out of the question. She gave up, all but consumed with irritability. Her mood didn't improve when she slammed the door and threw the bolt and discovered Dixie, Karla, and Lourdes cross legged in a semicircle on the floor.

Li-Hua had crawled into her bunk and sat in shadow, her arms folded. She patted the covers. "Quick, over here. Don't bother with them."

Bernice joined her friend. The two shared a blanket as the fire had diminished to fading coals. "This is simply…" she struggled for words. On one hand, the whole séance idea was unutterably juvenile—yet juxtaposed with her recent bout of nerves, the ominous locale, and the sudden storm, it gained weight, a sinister gravity. Finally, she said, "This is foolish," and was immediately struck by the double meaning of the word.

Ultimately, the ritual proved anticlimactic. Lourdes invoked the spirits of Aunt Dolly and others who'd drowned in the lake, inviting them to signal their presence, which of course they may or may not have done as it was difficult to discern much over the clattering shutters and the wind screeching in the eaves. Dixie, head bowed, almost fell over as she nodded off, eliciting chuckles from all present.

Things began to wind down after that. The cabin was quite warm and cozy and the wine did it's trick to induce drowsiness. Again Bernice had decided not to mention her recent bad dreams that revolved around drowning and the ghost of her aunt bobbing to the surface of the lake like a bloated ice cube, then skating across the water, her face black as the occulted moon. Dixie would've laughed and said something about zombie ballerinas, while Karla raised an eyebrow and warned her to lay off the booze. Worst of all, Li-Hua was likely to take it seriously. *So, you've returned to face your childhood demons. Good for you!* No, no, no—far better to keep her mouth shut.

She fell asleep and dreamed of sinking into icy water, of drifting helplessly as a white figure crowned in a Medusa snarl of hair reached for her. In the instant before she snapped awake tearing at her blankets and gasping for air, she saw her sister's face.

4.

Unhappily—so far as Bernice was concerned—they did indeed embark upon a hike along the cluttered beach directly after breakfast. The Redfield Girls had the shore to themselves, although there were a few small boats on the lake. The sky was flat and gray. It sprinkled occasionally, and a stiff breeze chopped the surface of the water. They picked their way until reaching the farthest point on the north side where a stream rushed over jumbled stones; shaggy bushes and low-hanging alders formed an impenetrable screen between shore and deep forest.

The women rested for a bit in a patch of golden light sifted from a knothole in the clouds. Bernice pulled off her shoe and poured out pebbles and sand, and scowled at the blister already puffing on her ankle.

"Don't tell me you thought we'd let you lead us to God's swimming hole and then hibernate all weekend." Dixie sat beside her on a log.

"That's precisely what I thought."

"Silly woman. Hiking is f-u-u-n!"

"Look at this damned thing on my foot and say that again."

Lourdes and Karla skipped pebbles across the water and laughed. Li-Hua came over and stared at Bernice's blister. "Maybe we should pop it? Let me."

"What the hell are you talking about?"

"You know, to drain the pus."

"For the love of—that's not what you do with a blister," Bernice said. She quickly stuck her shoe on before Li-Hua got any more ideas.

"Yeah, that's crazy talk. You just want to try one of your ancient herbal remedies and see if it works, or if her foot swells like a melon."

Li-Hua shrugged and grinned. She didn't think much of Western medicine, this prejudice exacerbated by complications stemming from her hysterectomy conducted at Saint Peter's Hospital. Her own grandmother had been an apothecary and lived in perfect health to one hundred and three.

"My husband knew an old fisherman who lived here." Li-Hua's husband Hung worked for the state as a cultural researcher. He'd assisted on a demographical study of the region and spent several weeks among the Klallam, and Norwegian and Dutch immigrants who'd lived nearby for decades. "Job Nilsson had a ramshackle cabin over one of these ridges. After Hung interviewed him, we brought him cases of canned goods and other supplies every winter until he passed away. It was sad."

"Yeesh," Dixie said. She'd gone to El Salvador and Nicaragua on many humanitarian missions. "I never knew, Li-Hua. You guys are wonderful." She sprang from her perch and hugged Li-Hua.

"Job wouldn't talk about the lake much. He stopped fishing here in 1973 and went to the river instead. He believed what the Klallam said—that demons were in here, swimming around, watching for intruders. He said most white people believed it was mainly ghosts of those who drowned haunted this place, but he thought that was wrong. Only a few corrupted souls linger here on Earth. Or a few who get lost and forget who they are. The rest go to their reward, or punishment."

"Uh-huh," Bernice said. This conversation brought back the creepy feelings. She was frightened and that kindled the helpless anger, again.

"The spirits are great deceivers. They delight in causing pain and fear. Of course, the spirits are angry about the houses, the motor boats, the trash, and seek to lure anyone they can and drown them."

Bernice shook her head. "Last night you groused at us for telling tales. Now look at you go…."

"The cat is out of the bag."

"Huh. Maybe you should put it *back* in the bag."

"That it? The codger was superstitious?" Dixie lighted a cigarette and Bernice's mouth watered.

"His brother Caleb drowned in the Devil's Punch Bowl. Four people saw him fall into the water and disappear. The body was lost, but Job claimed to meet something pretending to be his brother a year later. He was walking along the beach and saw him lying under a pile of driftwood. Job ran toward his brother's corpse, but when he reached it, Caleb sprang from the weeds and slithered into the water, laughing. Job was terrified when he realized the figure didn't really resemble his brother at all. And that's why he stopped fishing here."

"I hope he gave up on moonshine too," Bernice said.

Lourdes was the one who spotted the rowboat. It lay grounded on the beach, partially obscured by a tangle of driftwood just below their cabin. The women gathered around and peeked inside. Nothing seemed amiss—the oars were stowed and only a pail or two of rainwater slopped beneath the floorboards.

"It's a rental," Dixie said. "The lodges around here rent skiffs and canoes. Somebody forgot to tie it to the dock."

"I don't think so," Bernice said. The boat was weathered, its boards slightly warped, tinged green and gray. "This thing looks old." Actually, ancient might've been more accurate. It smelled of algae and wood rot.

"Yeah. Older than Andy Griffith," Karla said.

"Maybe it belongs to one of the locals."

"Anything's possible. We'll tell the lodge. Let them sort it out." Dixie tied the mooring rope to a half-buried stump and off they went.

## 5.

They stopped at the Bigfish to report the abandoned boat and use the showers, then drove into Port Angeles for dinner at the Red Devil. When they returned a few hours later, the moon was rising. Bernice and Karla lugged in wood for the fire. Li-Hua fixed hot chocolate, and they drank it on the porch.

"The boat's still here," Lourdes said, indicating its dark bulk against the shining sliver of beach.

"Ah, they'll come get it in the morning," Bernice said. "Or not. Who cares."

"I know!" Dixie clapped for attention. "Let's take it for a spin."

"A spin? That would imply the existence of an outboard motor," Karla said.

"Yes, but we'll just use the manual override. It comes with oars."

"I've stuffed my face with entirely too much lobster to take that suggestion seriously."

"Don't look at me," Bernice said. "I mean it, Dix. Stop looking at me."

A few minutes later she and Lourdes were helping Dixie shove off.

Li-Hua and Karla waved from the shore, steadily shrinking to a pair of smudges as Dixie pulled on the oars. "Isn't this great?" she said.

Bernice perched in the bow, soon mesmerized by the slap of the oar blades dipping into the glassy surface, their steady creak in the metal eye rings. The boat surged forward and left the rising mist in tatters. She was disquieted by the sensation of floating over a Hadal gulf, an insect prey to gargantuan forms lurking in the depths.

Dixie slogged midway to the far shore, then dropped the oars and let the boat drift. "Owwwie! That did it. Shoulda brought my driving gloves." She blew on her hands. "No worries. Bernie, ol' chum, how about 'bailing' us out here?"

"Dream on. This is your baby."

"Omigod, we'll be doomed to cruise these waters for eternity!"

"I'll do it," said Lourdes. The boat tipped precariously as she and Dixie switched places. "So, what do I do?" Dixie gave her a few pointers, and in moments they listed homeward, lurching drunkenly as Lourdes struggled to find her rhythm.

"We're going to capsize," Bernice said, only half joking as their wake churned and spray from the oars wet her hair.

"Uh oh," Dixie said.

"What uh oh?" Bernice said. The cabin was growing larger. She looked down again and water was rapidly filling the boat. Dixie was already ankle deep and bailing like mad with a small plastic bucket. "Good grief! It's the plug." All boats were fitted with a plug to drain bilge water when dry-docked. She scrambled aft, catching an oar in the shin. She plunged her arm to the elbow, felt around, searching for the hole, and found it, plug firmly in place.

Bubbles roiled about Lourdes's feet. "Guys...." She dropped the oars. Rowing was impossible now as the boat wallowed.

"Oh crap on a stick! I think it's coming apart!"

"We gotta swim for it," Dixie said. She'd already kicked off her shoes. "C'mon Bernie—get ready."

The shore was about seventy yards away. Not so far, but Bernie hadn't swum a lap in years. Her arms and legs cramped with fear, and the darkness swelled and throbbed in her brain. She tasted the remnants of dinner as acid.

Dixie leaped. Lourdes followed an instant later. She stumbled, and she belly flopped. Water gushed over the rails and the boat was a stone headed for the bottom. Bernie held her nose and jumped—the frigid water slammed her kidneys like a fist. She gasped and kicked, thrashing as if through quicksand, and her clothes dragged, made, abruptly, of concrete. In those moments of hyperawareness, she had time to regret all of the cigarettes and booze, to lament spending her days off lying around the yard like a slug. The moon hung too low; it merged with the lake until water and sky reversed. She floundered, trying to orient herself in the great, dark space.

"Lourdes!" She swallowed water and it scorched her sinuses and throat. "Lourdes!" Her voice didn't project, and she began to cough. There was Dixie bobbing like a cork a few yards away, but no sign of her niece. The blaze of moonlight was eclipsed by red and black motes that shot from the corners of her eyes as she gulped air and dove.

On the first try, she found Lourdes in the freezing murk. The girl was feebly making for the surface. Bernice caught the girl's arm, began to tow her along. A distinct point of light flickered at her peripheral vision. It rose swiftly from blackness, so pale it shone as it tumbled toward her, rushed toward her, and gained size and substance. Bernice gazed upon the approaching form with abject wonder. Perhaps she'd fallen into the sky and was plunging toward the moon itself. Terror overcame her—she screamed and a gout of bubbles exploded from her mouth. She brought Lourdes to the surface in one convulsive heave, and then hands hooked beneath her arms and brought her away with them.

Later, in the fetal position upon the small, sharp rocks of the beach, and after Karla shoved the others aside and administered first aid until she spluttered and vomited and breathed on her own, Bernice tried to summon an image of the form she'd seen down there, to perfect its features, and couldn't. Even now, safely ashore and encircled by her comrades, the blurry figure was etched in her mind, and evoked a stark and abiding fear. It had come close, radiating a cold much sharper than the chill water. She squeezed her eyes shut, and rubbed them with her palms in a futile attempt to exorcise this image that had leaked from dreams into the physical world.

Dixie and Li-Hua implored her to go to the clinic. What if she was hypothermic? Bernice shrugged them off—after she regained her senses and hacked the water from her lungs, she felt fine. Weak and shivery, but fine. Lourdes was okay, too, probably better, insomuch as youth seemed to bounce back from anything short of bullet wounds. She huddled with Bernice, eager to relate her tale of near disaster. Her pants cuff had snagged on the rail and she banged her shoulder. Thank the stars for Aunt Bernice and Dixie!

"Guess I owe you one, too," Bernice said as Dixie wrapped her in a blanket and led her to the cabin.

"Not me," Dixie said. "No way I coulda dragged your carcass all the way in on my own. You should've seen Karla go—that old broad can *swim!*"

6.

Karla and Li-Hua suggested pulling stakes and heading home early in light of the traumatic events. Lourdes disappeared outside and Dixie lay in her bunk, inconsolable for cajoling her friends to accompany her on the rickety boat and then nearly getting them all drowned. "I really fouled up," she said. Her voice was rusty from crying into her pillow. "What a jerk I am."

"We should sue the pants off the lodge for owning such a damned leaky boat!" Karla had huffed and puffed her indignation for a good hour.

"We took the boat without asking, didn't we?" Li-Hua said.

"That's beside the point. It's outrageous to keep a death trap lying around. Somebody should give them what for."

Bernice forced herself to rise and go for a walk down to the beach where she smoked a cigarette and watched the sun rise while the moon yet glowed on the horizon. She stubbed the butt of her cigarette on the sole of her shoe. Her eyes were twitchy and dry and her hair was stiff. She shook her fist at the lake, and spat.

Lourdes stepped from the bushes screening the path and came to stand beside her. The girl's expression was different today, more sober; she'd aged five years overnight. The patronizing half smile was wiped from her face. "That is the coldest water I've ever jumped into," she said. "I dreamt about this before."

"You mean the boat sinking?" Bernice couldn't look at her.

"Kind of. Not the boat; other stuff. We were somewhere in the woods— here, I guess. Me, you, some other people, I don't remember. You kept telling the story about Dolly."

"Except I didn't tell the story. Dixie did. She's always been better at talking."

"I got it wrong. Dreams are funny like that. Mom thinks I'm a psychic. Maybe I'm only a partial psychic."

"Your psychic powers convince you to fly over here?"

Lourdes shrugged. "I didn't really analyze it. I just wanted to come see you. It may sound dumb, but on some level I was worried you might be in trouble if I didn't. Looks like I had it backwards, huh?"

Bernice didn't say anything for a while. She watched the water shift from black, to milk, to gold. "I've always had a bit of the sight, too," she said.

"Really?"

"Sometimes, when I was a child, I dreamed things before they happened. Nothing big. I sure couldn't pick lotto numbers or anything. It came and went. I don't get it so much these days."

"Wow. Thanks for telling me. Mom doesn't want to know anything. I confided in her once. Frank put his foot down."

They fell silent and lighted cigarettes. Bernice finished hers. She hesitated, then patted Lourdes's shoulder, turned and walked back to the cabin.

After breakfast at the Bigfish, their mood thawed, and by midafternoon everyone agreed to stay—anything less was an unreasonable waste of what promised to be fine weather and several as yet corked bottles of wine.

Indeed, the remainder of the visit was splendid. By day, they set up a badminton net and a crude horseshoe pit and played until the light failed. Karla and Li-Hua shot two memory cards of photos. Bernice taught Lourdes cribbage and gin rummy. She even managed to power through a book about dream symbolism by candlelight while her companions slept. The book wasn't particularly illuminating in regards to her specific experiences. Nonetheless, she slept with it clutched to her breast like a talisman.

On the final evening, Bernice went with Lourdes to the woodshed to fetch an armload of dry pine to bank the fire. They lingered a moment, saying nothing, listening to the crickets and the owls. From inside came the raucous cries and curses of the latest debate between Dixie and Karla.

Lourdes said, "I haven't thanked you. I was in trouble the other night."

Bernice laughed softly. "Don't worry about it. Nancy would've killed me herself if I'd let you sink. You have no idea how many years she spent freezing by the pool while I had my swim lessons when we were kids."

"That's Mom."

"Yes, well…" Bernice cleared her throat. "I think I was hallucinating. Lack of oxygen to the brain."

"Oh?"

"I've been meaning to ask. Did you happen to see anything odd in the water?"

"Besides you?"

"Watch your lips, kid." Bernice smiled, but her hand tightened on the frame of the shed. The pit of her stomach knotted. Last night she'd been under the lake again, and Nancy was with her, glimmering dead white, hands extended. Only, it wasn't Nancy. She'd simply given the figure a face. "No biggie. I sucked in a lot of water. I think a fish swam by. Panicked me a bit."

Darkness had stolen across the water and through the trees, and Lourdes was hidden mostly in shadow, except for where lantern light came from the windows and revealed her hair in halo, a piece of her shoulder, but nothing of her expression. She said, "I didn't see any fish." She was silent for a moment, and when she spoke again her tone was strange. "There was something wrong with that boat."

"I'll say. Probably rotted clean through."

"What I mean is, it wasn't right. It didn't belong here."

Bernice tried to think of a witty response. She wanted to scoff at what Lourdes was hinting. "Oh," she said. "The *Flying Dinghy* of Lake Crescent, eh?"

Lourdes didn't say anything.

7.

Three years passed before the Redfield Girls returned to Lake Crescent. This was Dixie's year to choose and she invited Lourdes, who agreed to join them. Bernice and Li-Hua declined to accompany their friends on the trip, a first since the women had established the yearly tradition. Bernice begged off because the week prior she'd fallen while cleaning her gutters and suffered a broken ankle. It was healing nicely, although it was wrapped in a cast and not fit for bearing any kind of weight. Li-Hua's excuse was that Hung remained in China on a business trip and someone had to keep an eye on their rambunctious teenage sons, Jerrod and Jules.

Bernice knew better. While Dixie and Karla had quickly gotten over the close call with the rowboat, she and Li-Hua shared a profound antipathy toward the lake; its uncanny emanations repelled them. As for Lourdes, an invitation into the circle was irresistible to a girl of her youth and inexperience, albeit she expressed reluctance to abandon Bernice. In the end, they had a few glasses of wine and Bernice told her to go—no sense watching an old fuddy duddy lie about all weekend listening to her bones knit.

Bernice spent the whole weekend at home, pruning rose bushes, and riding around on Elmer's sputtering mower. Sunday morning news predicted a storm. She worked straight through lunch and finished putting away the tools and hosing cut grass stems from her ankle cast minutes before storm clouds blocked out the fading sun. Thunder cracked in the distance and it began to rain. She hobbled to the pantry, searching for flashlights and spare batteries. The power died a few minutes later, as it always did during storms, and she grimaced with smug satisfaction as she lighted a bunch of candles (some of the very same she'd purchased on Saturday!) in the kitchen and her bedroom. She boiled tea on the camp stove Elmer had always kept stashed in the garage, and retired to bed, intent upon reading a few chapters into a pictorial history of the Mima Mounds. The long, long afternoon of yard work put her under before she'd read two pages.

Bernice woke in complete darkness to the wind and rain falling heavily on the frame house. A lightning flash caused the shadows of the trees to stretch long, grasping fingers down the wall and across her blanket. Something thumped repeatedly. She grabbed the flashlight and crawled from bed and went into the living room, leaning on the cheap rubber-tipped cane she'd gotten at the hospital. The front door was wide open. The elements poured through, and all the papers she'd left stacked on the coffee table were flung across the floor. She put her shoulder against the door and forced it shut and threw the deadbolt for good measure.

She fell into an easy chair and waited with gritted teeth for the pain in her ankle to subside. While she recovered, the fact the door had been locked earlier began to weigh heavily on her mind. What was it that brought her awake? The noise of the door banging on the wall? She didn't think so. She'd heard someone call her name.

The storm shook the house and lightning sizzled, lighting the bay windows so fiercely she shielded her eyes. Sleep was impossible and she remained curled in her chair, waiting for dawn. Around two o'clock in the morning, someone knocked on the door. Three loud raps. She almost had a heart attack from the spike of fear that shot through her.

Without thinking, she cried, "Lourdes? Is that you?" There was no answer, and in an instant her thoughts veered toward visions of intruders bent on mischief and the spit dried in her mouth. Far too afraid to move, she waited, breath caught, straining to hear above the roar of the wind. The knocks weren't repeated.

## 8.

Bernice didn't fly to France for Lourdes's funeral. Nancy, mad with grief, wanted nothing to do with her sister. Why hadn't Bernice been there to protect Lourdes? She'd allowed their daughter to go off with a couple of people Nancy and Francois scarcely knew and now the girl was never coming back. As the weeks went by, Nancy and Bernice mended fences, although Francois still wouldn't speak to her, and the boys followed suit. Those were dark days.

She'd gone into a stupor when the authorities gave her the news; ate a few Valiums left over from when she put Elmer in the ground, and buried herself in blankets. She refused to leave the house, to answer the phone, scarcely remembered to eat or shower.

Li-Hua told her more about the accident when Bernice was finally weaned off tranquilizers and showed signs of life once again.

The story went like this: Dixie had driven Karla and Lourdes to Joyce, a small town a few miles west of Lake Crescent. They ate at a tiny diner, bought some postcards at the general store, and started back for Olympia after dark. Nobody knew what went wrong, exactly. The best guess was Dixie's Subaru left the road and smashed through the guard rail at mile 38—Ambulance Point. Presumably the car went in and sank. Rescue divers came from Seattle and the area was dredged, but no car or bodies were found. There were mutters that maybe the crash happened elsewhere, or not at all, and conjectures regarding drift or muck at the bottom. Ultimately, it amounted to bald speculation. The more forthcoming authorities marked it down as another tragic mystery attributed to the Lake Crescent curse.

Bernice took a leave of absence from work that stretched into retirement. Going back simply wasn't an option; seeing new faces in Dixie and
Karla's classrooms, how life went on without missing a beat, gutted her.
Li-Hua remained in the counselor's office. She and Hung had come very
late to professional life and neither could afford retirement. Nonetheless,
everything was different after the accident. The remaining Redfield Girls
drifted apart—a couple transferred, three more called it quits for teaching, and the others simply stopped calling. The parties and annual trips
were finished. Everybody moved on.

One night that winter, Li-Hua phoned. "Look, there's something I need
to tell you. About the girls."

Bernice was lying in bed looking at a crossword puzzle. Her hands
trembled and she snapped the pencil. "Are you all right, Li?" Her friend
had lost too much weight and she didn't smile anymore. It was obvious
she carried a burden, a secret that she kept away from her friend. Bernice
knew all along there was more to the story surrounding the accident and
she'd pretended otherwise from pure cowardice. "Do you want me to
come over?"

"No. Just listen. I've tried to tell you this before, but I couldn't. I was
afraid of what you might do. I was *afraid*, Bernie." Li-Hua's voice broke.
"Karla called me on the night it happened. None of it made sense; I
was groggy and there was a lot of shouting. People sound different when
they're scared, so it was a few seconds before I recognized her voice. Karla
was panicked, talking very fast. She told me they'd lost control of the car
and were in the water. I think the car was actually underwater. The doors
wouldn't open. She begged me for help. The call only lasted a few seconds.
All of them started screaming and it ended. I dialed 911 and told the
operator where I thought they were. Then I tried the girls' cell phones. I
just got recordings."

After they disconnected, Bernice lay staring into the glow of the dresser
lamp. She slowly picked apart what Li-Hua had said, and as she did,
something shifted deep within her. She removed the cordless phone from
its cradle and began to cycle back through every recording stored since
the previous summer, until she heard the mechanized voice report there
was an unheard message dated 2am the morning of the accident. Since the

power had been down, the call went straight to voice mail.

"My God. My God." She deleted it, and dropped the phone as if were electrified.

9.

Once her ankle healed, she packed some things and made a pilgrimage to the lake. The weather was cold. Brown and black leaves clogged the ditches. She parked on the high cliff above the water, the spot called Ambulance Point, and placed a wreath on the guard rail. She drank a couple of mini bottles of Shiraz and cried until the tears dried on her cheeks and her eyes puffed. She got back into the car and drove down to the public boat launch.

The season was over, so the launch was mostly deserted except for a flat-bed truck and trailer in the lot, and a medium-sized motor boat moored at the dock. Bernice almost cruised by without stopping—intent upon renting a room at the Bigfish Lodge. What she intended to do at the lodge was a mystery even to herself. She noticed a diver surface near the boat. She idled in front of the empty ticket booth, and watched the diver paddle about, fiddling with settings on his or her mask, and finally clamber aboard the boat.

She sat with the windshield wipers going, a soft, sad ballad on the radio. She began to shake, stricken by something deeper than mere sorrow or regret; an ancient, more primitive emotion. Her knuckles whitened. The light drained from the sky as she climbed out and crossed the distance to where the diver had removed helmet and fins. It was a younger man with golden hair and a thick golden beard that made his face seem extraordinarily pale. He slumped on the boat's bench seat and shrugged off his tanks. Bernice stood at the edge of the dock. They regarded each other for a while. The wind stiffened and the boat rocked between them.

He said, "You're here for someone?"

"Yeah. Friends."

"Those women who disappeared this summer. I'm real sorry." The flesh around his eyes and mouth was soft. She wondered if that was from being immersed or from weeping.

"Are you the man who comes here diving for clues?"

"There's a couple of other guys, too. And a company from Oregon. I think those dudes are treasure hunting, though."

"The men from the company."

He nodded.

"I hate people sometimes. What about you? Aren't *you* treasure hunting? Looking for a story? I read about that."

"I like to think of it as seeking answers. This lake's a thief. You know, maybe if I find them, the lives that it stole, I can free them. Those souls don't belong here."

"I had a lot of bad dreams about this lake and my sister. I kept seeing her face. She was dead. Drowned. After the accident, I realized all along I'd been mistaken. It wasn't my sister I saw, but her daughter. Those two didn't have much of a resemblance, except the eyes and mouth. I got confused."

"That's a raw deal, miss. My brother was killed in a crash. Driving to Bellingham and a cement truck rear-ended him. Worst part is, and I apologize if this sounds cruel, you'll be stuck with this the rest of your life. It doesn't go away, ever."

"We're losing the light," she said.

Out in the reeds and the darkness, a loon screamed.

# HAND OF GLORY

*From the pages of a partially burned manuscript discovered in the charred ruins of a mansion in Ransom Hollow, Washington:*

That buffalo charges across the eternal prairie, mad black eye rolling at the photographer. The photographer is Old Scratch's left hand man. Every few seconds the buffalo rumbles past the same tussock, the same tumbleweed, the same bleached skull of its brother or sister. That poor buffalo is Sisyphus without the stone, without the hill, without a larger sense of futility. The beast's hooves are worn to bone. Blood foams at its muzzle. The dumb brute doesn't understand where we are.

But I do.

CP, Nov. 1925

T his is the house my father built stone by stone in Anno Domini 1898. I was seven. Mother died of consumption that winter, and my baby brothers Earl and William followed her through the Pearly Gates directly. Hell of a housewarming.

Dad never remarried. He just dug in and redoubled his efforts on behalf of his boss, Myron Arden. The Arden family own the politicos, the cops, the stevedores and the stevedores' dogs. They owned Dad too, but he didn't mind. Four bullets through the chest, a knife in the gut, two car wrecks, and a bottle a day booze habit weren't enough to rub him out. It required a broken heart from missing his wife. He collapsed, stone dead, on a job in Seattle in 1916 and I inherited his worldly possessions, such as they were. The debts, too.

The passing of Donald Cope was a mournful day commemorated with a crowded wake—mostly populated by Mr. Myron Arden's family and henchmen who constituted Dad's only real friends—and the requisite violins, excessive drinking of Jameson's, fistfights, and drunken profanities roared at passersby, although in truth, there hadn't been much left of the old man since Mother went.

My sister Lucy returned to Ireland and joined a convent. Big brother Acton lives here in Olympia. He's a surgeon. When his friends and associates ask about his kin at garden parties, I don't think my name comes up much. That's okay. Dad always liked me better.

I've a reputation in this town. I've let my share of blood, taken my share of scalps. You want an enemy bled, burnt, blasted into Kingdom Come, ask for Johnny Cope. My viciousness and cruelty are without peer. There are bad men in this business, and worse men, and then there's me. But I must admit, any lug who quakes in his boots at the mention of my name should've gotten a load of the old man. *There* was Mr. Death's blue-eyed boy himself, like mr. cummings said.

* * *

A dark hallway parallels the bedroom. Dad was a short, wiry man from short wiry stock and he fitted the house accordingly. The walls are close, the windows narrow, and so the passage is dim even in daylight. When night falls it becomes a mineshaft and I lie awake, listening. Listening for a voice in the darkness, a dragging footstep, or something else, possibly something I've not heard in this life. Perversely, the light from the lamp down the street, or the moonlight, or the starlight, make that black gap of a bedroom door a deeper mystery.

I resemble Mother's people: lanky, with a horse's jaw and rawboned hands meant for spadework, or tying nooses on ropes, and I have to duck when passing through these low doorways; but at heart, I'm my father's son. I knock down the better portion of a bottle of Bushmill's every evening while I count my wins and losses from the track. My closet is stacked with crates of the stuff. I don't pay for liquor—it's a bequest from Mr. Arden, that first class bootlegger; a mark of sentimental appreciation for my father's steadfast service to the cause. When I sleep, I sleep fully dressed, suit and tie, left hand draped across the Thompson like a lover. Fear is a second heartbeat, my following shadow.

This has gone on a while.

* * *

The first time I got shot was in the fall of 1914.

I was twenty-one and freshly escaped from the private academy Dad spent the last of his money shipping me off to. He loved me so much he'd hoped I wouldn't come back, that I'd join Acton in medicine, or get into engineering, or stow away on a tramp steamer and spend my life hunting ivory and drinking and whoring my way across the globe into Terra Incognita; anything but the family business. No such luck. My grades were pathetic, barely sufficient to graduate as I'd spent too many study nights gambling, and weekends fighting sailors at the docks. I wasn't as smart as Acton anyway, and I found it much easier and more satisfying to break things rather than build them. Mine was a talent for reading and leading people. I didn't mind manipulating them, I didn't mind destroying them if it came to that. It's not as if we dealt with real folks, anyway. In our world, everybody was part of the machine.

Dad had been teaching me the trade for a few months, taking me along on lightweight jobs. There was this Guinea named Alfonso who owed Mr. Arden big and skipped town on the debt. Dad and I tracked the fellow to Vancouver and caught him late one night, dead drunk in his shack. Alfonso didn't have the money, but we knew his relatives were good for it, so we only roughed him up: Knocked some teeth loose and broke his leg. Dad used a mattock handle with a bunch of bolts drilled into the fat end. It required more swings than I'd expected.

Unfortunately, Alfonso was entertaining a couple of whores from the dance hall. The girls thought we were murdering the poor bastard and that they'd be next. One jumped through a window, and the other, a half-naked, heavyset lass who was in no shape to run anywhere, pulled a derringer from her brassiere and popped me in the ribs. Probably aiming for my face. Dad didn't stop to think about the gun being a one-shot rig—he took three strides and whacked her in the back of the head with the mattock handle. Just as thick-skulled as Alfonso, she didn't die, although that was a pity, considering the results. One of her eyes fell out later and she never talked right again. Life is just one long train wreck.

They say you become a man when you lose your virginity. Not my baptism, alas, alack. Having a lima bean-sized hole blown through me and enduring the fevered hours afterward was the real crucible, the mettletester. I remember sprawling in the front seat of the car near the river and Dad pressing a doubled handkerchief against the wound. Blood dripped shiny on the floorboard. It didn't hurt much, more like the after-effects of a solid punch to the body. However, my vision was too acute, too close; black and white flashes scorched my brain.

Seagulls circled the car, their shadows so much larger than seemed possible, the shadows of angels ready to carry me into Kingdom Come. Dad gave me a dose of whiskey from his hip flask. He drove with the pedal on the floor and that rattletrap car shuddered on the verge of tearing itself apart, yet as I slumped against the door, the landscape lay frozen, immobile as the glacier that ended everything in the world the first time. Bands of light, God's pillars of blazing fire, bisected the scenery into a glaring triptych that shattered my mind. Dad gripped my shoulder and laughed and shook me now and again to keep me from falling unconscious.

Dr. Green, a sawbones on the Arden payroll, fished out the bullet and patched the wound and kept me on ice in the spare room at his house. That's when I discovered I had the recovery power of a brutish animal, a bear that retreats to the cave to lick its wounds before lumbering forth again in short order. To some, such a capacity suggests the lack of a higher degree of acumen, the lack of a fully developed imagination. I'm inured to pain and suffering, and whether it's breeding or nature I don't give a damn.

Two weeks later I was on the mend. To celebrate, I threw Gahan Kirk, a no account lackey for the Eastside crew, off the White Building roof for cheating at cards. Such is the making of a legend. The reality was, I pushed the man while he was distracted with begging Dad and Sonny Hopkins, Mr. Arden's number two enforcer, not to rub him out. Eight stories. He flipped like a ragdoll, smashing into a couple of fire escapes and crashing one down atop him in the alley. It was hideously spectacular.

The second time I got shot was during the Great War.

Mr. Arden was unhappy to see me sign on for the trip to Europe. He saw I was hell-bent to do my small part and thus gave his reluctant blessing, assuring me I'd have work when I came home from "Killing the Huns." Five minutes after I landed in France I was damned sorry for such a foolish impulse toward patriotism.

One night our platoon negotiated a mine field, smashed a machine gun bunker with a volley of pineapples, clambered through barbed wire, and assaulted an enemy trench. Toward the end of the action, me and a squad mate were in hand to hand combat with a German officer we'd cornered. I'd run dry on ammo five minutes before and gone charging like a rhino through the encampment, and thank Holy Mother Mary it was a ghost town from the shelling or else I'd have been ventilated inside of twenty paces. The German rattled off half a dozen rounds with his Luger before I stuck a bayonet through his neck. I didn't realize I was clipped until the sleeve of my uniform went sopping black. Two bullets, spaced tight as a quarter zipped through my left shoulder. Couldn't have asked for a cleaner wound and I hopped back into the fray come the dawn advance. I confiscated the German's pistol and the wicked bayonet he'd kept in his boot. They'd come in handy on many a bloody occasion since.

The third time…we'll get to that.

\* \* \*

*11/11/25*

Autumn of 1925 saw my existence in decline. Then I killed some guys and it was downhill in a wagon with no brakes from there.

Trouble followed after a string of anonymous calls to my home. Heavy breathing and hang-ups. The caller waited until the dead of night when I was drunk and too addled to do more than slur curses into the phone. I figured it was some dame I'd miffed, or a lug I'd thrashed, maybe even somebody with a real grudge—a widow or an orphan. My detractors are many. Whoever it was only spoke once upon the occasion of their final call. Amid crackling as of a bonfire, the male voice said, "I love you son. I love you son. I love you son."

I was drunk beyond drunk and I fell on the floor and wept. The calls stopped and I put it out of my mind.

Toward the end of September I hit a jackpot on a twenty to one pony and collected a cool grand at the window, which I used to pay off three markers in one fell swoop. I squandered the remainder on a trip to Seattle, embarking upon a bender that saw me tour every dance hall and speakeasy from the harbor inland. The ride lasted until I awakened flat broke one morning in a swanky penthouse suite of the Wilsonian Hotel in the embrace of an over the hill burlesque dancer named Pearl.

Pearl was statuesque, going to flab in the middle and the ass. Jesus, what an ass it was, though. We'd known one another for a while—I courted her younger sister Madison before she made for the bright lights of Chi-Town. Last I heard, she was a gangster's moll. Roy Night, a button man who rubbed out guys for Capone, could afford to keep Maddie in furs and diamonds and steak dinners. Good for her. Pearl wasn't any Maddie, but she wasn't half bad. Just slightly beaten down, a little tired, standing at the crossroads where Maddie herself would be in six or seven years. Me, I'd likely be dead by then so no time like the present.

I was hung-over and broke, and with two of my last ten bucks tipped the kid who pushed the breakfast cart. He handed me the fateful telegram, its envelope smudged and mussed. I must've paid the kid off pretty well during my stay, because he pocketed the money and said there were a couple of men downstairs asking what room I was in. They'd come around twice the day before, too. Bruisers, he said. Blood in their eyes, he said.

My first suspicion was of T-Men or Pinkertons. I asked him to describe the lugs. He did. I said thanks and told him to relay the gentlemen my room number on the sly and pick up some coin for his trouble. These were no lawmen, rather the opposite; a couple of Johnson brothers. Freelance guns, just like me.

Bobby Dirk and Curtis Bane, The Long and The Short, so-called, and that appellation had nothing to do with their stature, but rather stemmed from an embarrassing incident in a bathhouse.

I'd seen them around over the years, shared a drink or two in passing. Dirk was stoop-shouldered and sallow; Bane was stocky with watery eyes and a receding chin. Snowbirds and sad sack gamblers, both of them, which accounted for their uneven temperament and willingness to stoop to the foulest of deeds. Anybody could've put them on my trail. There were plenty of folks who'd be pleased to pony up the coin if it meant seeing me into a pine box.

While Pearl dressed I drank coffee and watched rain hit the window. Pearl knew the party was over—she'd fished through my wallet enough times. She was a good sport and rubbed my shoulders while I ate cold eggs. She had the grip of a stonemason. "You'd better get along," I said.

"Why's that?" she said.

"Because, in a few minutes a couple of men are probably going to break down the door and try to rub me out," I said, and lighted another cigarette.

She laughed and kissed my ear. "Day in the life of Johnny Cope. See ya around, doll. I'm hotfooting it outta here."

I unsnapped the violin case and leaned it against the closet. I assembled the Thompson on the breakfast table, locking pieces together while I watched the rain and thought about Pearl's ass. When I'd finished, I wiped away the excess cleaning oil with a monogrammed hotel napkin. I sipped the dregs of the coffee and opened a new deck of Lucky Strike and smoked a couple of them. After half an hour and still no visitors, I knotted my tie, slipped my automatic into its shoulder holster and shrugged on my suit jacket, then the greatcoat. Pacific Northwest gloom and rain has always agreed with me. Eight months out of the year I can comfortably wear bulky clothes to hide my weapons. Dad had always insisted on nice suits for work. He claimed Mr. Arden appreciated we dressed as gentlemen.

The hall was dim and I moved quickly to the stairwell exit. Elevators are deathtraps. You'd never catch me in one. I could tell you stories about fools who met their untimely ends like rats in a box. I descended briskly, paused at the door, then stepped into the alley. A cold drizzle misted everything, made the concrete slick and treacherous. I lighted a cigarette and stuck it in the corner of my mouth and began to move for the street.

For a couple of seconds I thought I had it made. Yeah. I always thought that.

Curtis Bane drifted from the inset threshold of a service door about ten feet to the street side. He raised his hand, palm out to forestall me. I wasn't buying. I hurled the empty violin case at his head and whipped around. And yes indeed, that rotten cur Bobby Dirk was sneaking up on my flank. I brought the trench broom from under my coat and squeezed off half the drum, rat-a-tat-tat. Oh, that sweet ratcheting burr; spurts of flame lighted the gloomy alley. Some of the bullets blasted brick from the wall, but enough ripped through a shocked and amazed Bobby Dirk to cut him nearly in half in a gout of black blood and smoke. What remained of him danced, baby, danced and flew backward and fell straight down, all ties to the here and now severed.

Curtis Bane screamed and though I came around fast and fired in the same motion, he'd already pulled a heater and begun pumping metal at me. We both missed and I was empty, that drum clicking uselessly. I went straight at him. Happily, he too was out of bullets and I closed the gap and slammed the butt of the rifle into his chest. Should've knocked him down, but no. The bastard was squat and powerful as a wild animal, thanks to being a coke fiend, no doubt. He ripped the rifle from my grasp and flung it aside. He locked his fists and swung them up into my chin, and it was like getting clobbered with a hammer, and I sprawled into a row of trash cans. Stars zipped through my vision. A leather cosh dropped from his sleeve into his hand and he knew what to do with it all right. He swung it in a short chopping blow at my face and I got my left hand up and the blow snapped my two smallest fingers, and he swung again and I turned my head just enough that it only squashed my ear and you better believe that hurt, but now I'd drawn the sawback bayonet I kept strapped to my hip, a fourteen-inch grooved steel blade with notched and pitted edges—Jesus-fuck who knew how many Yankee boys the Kraut who'd owned it gashed before I did for him—and stabbed it to the guard into Bane's groin. Took a couple of seconds for Bane to register it was curtains. His face whitened and his mouth slackened, breath steaming in the chill, his evil soul coming untethered. He had lots of gold fillings. He lurched away and I clutched his sleeve awkwardly with my broken hand and rose, twisting the handle of the blade side to side, turning it like a car crank into his guts and bladder, putting my shoulder and hip into it for leverage. He moaned in panic and dropped the cosh and pried at my wrist, but the strength was draining from him and I slammed him against the wall and worked the handle with murderous joy. The cords of his neck went taut and he looked away, as if embarrassed, eyes milky, a doomed petitioner gaping at Hell in all its fiery majesty. I freed the blade with a cork-like pop and blood spurted down his leg in a nice thick stream and he collapsed, folding into himself like a bug does when it dies.

Nobody had stuck their head into the alley to see what all the ruckus was about, nor did I hear sirens yet, so I took a moment to collect the dead men's wallets and light a fresh cigarette. Then I gathered my Thompson and its case and retreated into the hotel stairwell to pack the gun, scrape the blood from my shoes and comb my hair. Composed, I walked out through the lobby and the front door, winking at a rosy-cheeked lass and her wintery dame escort. A tear formed at the corner of my eye.

Two cops rolled up and climbed from their Model T. The taller of the pair barely fit into his uniform. He cradled a shotgun. The other pig carried a Billy club. I smiled at the big one as we passed, eyes level, our shoulders almost brushing, the heavy violin case bumping against my leg, the pistol hidden in the sleeve of my coat, already cocked. My hand burned like fire and I was close to vomiting, and surely the pig saw the gory lump of my ear, the snail-trail of blood streaking my cheek. His piggy little eyes were red and dulled, and I recognized him as a brother in inveterate drunkenness. We all kept walking, violent forces drifting along the razor's edge of an apocalyptic clash. They entered the hotel and I hopped a trolley to the train station. I steamed home to Olympia without incident, except by the time I staggered into the house and fell in a heap on the bed, I was out of my mind with agony and fever.

I didn't realize I'd been shot until waking to find myself lying in a pool of blood. There was a neat hole an inch above my hip. I plugged it with my pinky and went to sleep.

Number three. A banner day. Dad would be so proud.

* * *

Dick found me a day and a half later, blood everywhere, like somebody had slaughtered a cow in my bed. Miraculously, the wound had clotted enough to keep me from bleeding out. He took a long look at me (I was partially naked and had somehow gotten hold of a couple of bottles of the Bushmill's, which were empty by this point, although I didn't recall drinking them) and then rang Leroy Bly to come over and help salvage the situation as I was in no condition to assist. I think he was also afraid I might be far enough gone to mistake him for a foe and start shooting or cutting. Later, he explained it was the unpleasant-looking man watching my house from a catbird's seat down the way that gave him pause. The guy screwed when Dick approached him, so there was no telling what his intentions were.

The two of them got me into the tub. Good old Dr. Green swung by with his little black bag of goodies and plucked the bullet from my innards, clucking and muttering as he worked. After stitching me inside and out, he put a cast on my hand, bandaged my ear, and shot enough dope into me to pacify a Clydesdale, then gave me another dose for the fever. The boys settled in to watch over me on account of my helpless condition. They fretted that somebody from Seattle was gunning for payback. News of my rubbing out The Long and The Short had gotten around. Two or three of the Seattle bosses were partial to them, so it was reasonable to expect they might take the matter personally.

Dick's full name was Richard Stiff and he'd worked for the railroad since he was a boy, just as his father had before him. He was a thick, jowly lug with forearms as round as my calf. Unloading steel off boxcars all day will do that for a man. He was married and had eleven children—a devout Catholic, my comrade Dick. Mr. Arden used him on occasion when a bit of extra muscle was needed. Dick didn't have the stomach for killing, but was more than happy to give some sorry bugger an oak rubdown if that's what Mr. Arden wanted.

The honest money only went so far. The best story I can tell about him is that when the railroad boys gathered for their union hall meetings roll call was done surname first, thus the man reading off the muster would request "Stiff, Dick" to signal his attendance, this to the inevitable jeers and hoots from the rowdy crowd. As for Leroy Bly, he was a short, handsome middle-aged Irishman who kept an eye on a couple of local speakeasies for the Arden family and did a bit of enforcement for Arden's bookmakers as well. Not a button man by trade, nonetheless I'd heard he'd blipped off at least two men and left their remains in the high timber west of town. Rumor had it one of the poor saps was the boyfriend of a dame Bly had taken a shine to—so he was a jealous bastard as well. Nice to know as I'd never been above snaking a fella's chickadee if the mood was right.

A week passed in a confusion of *delirium tremens* and plain old delirium. Half dead from blood loss, sure, but it was the withdrawal from life-succoring whiskey and tobacco that threatened to do me in.

Eventually the fever broke I emerged into the light, growling for breakfast and hooch and a cigarette. Dick said someone from The Broadsword Hotel had called at least a dozen times—wouldn't leave a message, had to speak with me personal like. Meanwhile, Bly informed me that Mr.

Arden was quite worried about the untimely deaths of The Long and The Short. Dick's suspicions that the powers that be wanted my hide proved accurate. It had come down through the bush telegraph I'd do well to take to the air for a few weeks. Perhaps a holiday in a sunnier clime. Bly set a small butcher paper package on the table. The package contained three hundred dollars of "vacation" money. Bly watched as I stuck the cash into my pocket. He was ostensibly Dick's chum and to a lesser degree mine, however I suspected he'd cheerfully plant an ice pick between my shoulder blades should I defy Mr. Arden's wishes. In fact, I figured the old man had sent him to keep tabs on my activities.

I'd read the name of one Conrad Paxton scribbled on the back of a card in Curtis Bane's wallet, so it seemed possible this mystery man dispatched the pair to blip me. A few subtle inquiries led me to believe my antagonist resided somewhere in Western Washington beyond the principal cities. Since getting shy of Olympia was the order of the day, I'd decided to track Paxton down and pay him a visit. To this effect, would the boys be willing to accompany me for expenses and a few laughs?

Both Dick and Bly agreed, Bly with the proviso he could bring along his nephew Vernon. Yeah, I was in Dutch with Mr. Arden, no question— no way Bly would drop his gig here in town unless it was to spy on me, maybe awaiting the word to blip me off. And young master Vernon, he was a sad sack gambler and snowbird known for taking any low deed that presented itself, thus I assumed Bly wanted him to tag along as backup when the moment came to slip me the shiv. Mr. Arden was likely assessing my continued value to his family versus the ire of his colleagues in Seattle. There was nothing for it but to lie low for a while and see what was what after the dust settled.

I uncapped a bottle and poured myself the first shot of many to come. I stared into the bottom of the glass. The crystal ball hinted this Conrad Paxton fellow was in for a world of pain.

* * *

Later that afternoon I received yet another call from management at The Broadsword Hotel passing along the message that an old friend of my father's, one Helios Augustus, desired my presence after his evening show. I hung up without committing, poured a drink and turned over the possibilities. In the end, I struggled into my best suit and had Dick drive me to the hotel.

The boys smuggled me out the back of the house and through a hole in the fence on the off chance sore friends of The Long and The Short might be watching. I wondered who that weird bird lurking down the street represented—a Seattle boss, or Paxton, or even somebody on Arden's payroll, a gun he'd called from out of town? I hated to worry like this; it gave me acid, had me jumping at shadows. Rattle a man enough he's going to make a mistake and get himself clipped.

I came into the performance late and took a seat on the edge of the smoky lounge where I could sag against the wall and ordered a steak sandwich and a glass of milk while the magician did his thing to mild applause.

Helios Augustus had grown a bit long in the tooth, a portly figure dressed in an elegant suit and a cape of darkest purple silk. However, his white hair and craggy features complemented the melodic and cultured timbre of his voice. He'd honed that voice in Shakespearean theatre and claimed descent from a distinguished lineage of Greek poets and prestidigitators. I'd met him at a nightclub in Seattle a couple of years before the Great War. He'd been slimmer and handsomer, and made doves appear and lovely female assistants disappear in puffs of smoke. Dad took me to watch the show because he'd known Helios Augustus before the magician became famous and was dealing cards on a barge in Port Angeles. Dad told me the fellow wasn't Greek—his real name was Phillip Wary and he'd come from the Midwest, son of a meat packer.

I smoked and waited for the magician to wrap up his routine with a series of elaborate card tricks, all of which required the assistance of a mature lady in a low-cut gown and jade necklace, a real duchess. The hand didn't need to be quicker than the eye with that much artfully lighted bosom to serve as a distraction. As the audience headed for the exits, he saw me and came over and shook my hand. "Johnny Cope in the flesh," he said. "You look like you've been on the wrong end of a stick. I'm sorry about your father." He did not add, *he was a good man.* I appreciated a little honesty, so far as it went. Goodness was not among Dad's virtues. He hadn't even liked to talk about it.

We adjourned to his dressing room where the old fellow produced a bottle of sherry and poured a couple of glasses. His quarters were plush, albeit cramped with his makeup desk and gold-framed mirror, steamer trunks plastered with stamps from exotic ports, a walnut armoire that scraped the ceiling, and shelves of arcane trinkets—bleached skulls and beakers, thick black books and cold braziers. A waxen, emaciated hand, gray as mud and severed at the wrist, jutted from an urn decorated with weird scrollwork like chains of teeny death's heads. The severed hand clutched a black candle. A brass kaleidoscope of particularly ornate make caught my attention. I squinted through the aperture and turned the dial. The metal felt damnably cold. Jigsaw pieces of painted crystal rattled around inside, revealing tantalizing glimpses of naked thighs and breasts, black corsets and red, pouty smiles. The image fell into place and it was no longer a burlesque dancer primping for my pleasure. Instead I beheld a horrid portrait of some rugose beast—all trunk and tentacle and squirming maw. I dropped the kaleidoscope like it was hot.

"Dear lad, you have to turn the opposite direction to focus the naked ladies." Helios Augustus smiled and shook his head at my provincial curiosity. He passed me a cigar, but I'd never acquired a taste for them and stuck with my Lucky Strike. He was in town on business, having relocated to San Francisco. His fortunes had waned in recent years; the proletariats preferred large stage productions with mirrors and cannon-smoke, acrobats and wild animals to his urbane and intimate style of magic. He lamented the recent deaths of the famed composer Moritz Moszkowski and the Polish novelist Wladislaw Reymont, both of whom he'd briefly entertained during his adventures abroad. Did I, by chance, enjoy classical arts? I confessed my tastes ran more toward Mark Twain and Fletch Henderson and Coleman Hawkins. "Well, big band is a worthy enough pleasure. A certain earthy complexity appropriate to an earthy man. I lived nearly eighteen years on the Continent. Played in the grandest and oldest theatres in Europe. Two shows on the Orient Express. Now I give myself away on a weeknight to faux royalty and well-dressed rabble. Woe is me!" He laughed without much bitterness and poured another drink.

Finally, I said, "What did you call me here to jaw about?"

"Rumor has it Conrad Paxton seeks the pleasure of your company."

"Yeah, that's the name. And let's get it straight—*I'm* looking for *him* with a passion. Who the hell is he?"

"Doubtless you've heard of Eadweard Muybridge, the rather infamous inventor. Muybridge created the first moving picture."

"Dad knew him from the Army. Didn't talk about him much. Muybridge went soft in the head and they parted ways." I had a sip of sherry.

"A brilliant, scandalous figure who was the pet of California high society for many years. He passed away around the turn of the century. Paxton was his estranged son and protégé. It's a long story—he put the boy up for adoption; they were later reconciled after a fashion. I met the lad when he debuted from the ether in Seattle as the inheritor of Muybridge's American estate. No one knew that he was actually Muybridge's son at the time. Initially he was widely celebrated as a disciple of Muybridge and a bibliophile specializing in the arcane and the occult, an acquirer of morbid photography and cinema as well. He owns a vault of Muybridge's photographic plates and short films I'm certain many historians would give an eye tooth to examine."

"According to my information, he lives north of here these days," I said.

"He didn't fare well in California and moved on after the war. Ransom Hollow, a collection of villages near the Cascades. You shot two of his men in Seattle. Quite a rumpus, eh?"

"Maybe they were doing a job for this character, but they weren't his men. Dirk and Bane are traveling guns."

"Be that as it may, you would do well to fear Conrad's intentions."

"That's backwards, as I said."

"So, you *do* mean to track him to ground. Don't go alone. He's well-protected. Take some of your meaner hoodlum associates, is my suggestion."

"What's his beef? Does he have the curse on me?"

"It seems plausible. He killed your father."

I nodded and finished my latest round of booze. I set aside the glass and drew my pistol and chambered a round and rested the weapon across my knee, barrel fixed on the magician's navel. My head was woozy and I wasn't sure of hitting the side of a barn if push came to shove. "Our palaver has taken a peculiar and unwelcome turn. Please, explain how you've come into this bit of news. Quick and to the point is my best advice."

The magician puffed on his cigar, and regarded me with a half smile that the overly civilized reserve for scofflaws and bounders such as myself. I resisted the temptation to jam a cushion over his face and dust him then and there, because I knew slippery devils like him always came in first and they survived by stepping on the heads of drowning men. He removed the cigar from his mouth and said, "Conrad Paxton confessed it to some associates of mine several years ago."

"Horse shit."

"The source is…trustworthy."

"Dad kicked from a heart attack. Are you saying this lug got to him somehow? Poisoned him?" It was difficult to speak. My vision had narrowed as it did when blood was in my eye. I wanted to strangle, to stab, to empty the Luger. "Did my old man rub out somebody near and dear to Paxton? Thump him one? What?"

"Conrad didn't specify a method, didn't express a motive, only that he'd committed the deed."

"You've taken your sweet time reporting the news," I said.

"The pistol aimed at my John Thomas suggests my caution was well-founded. At the time I didn't believe the story, thinking Paxton a loud-mouthed eccentric. He *is* a loud-mouthed eccentric—I simply thought this more rubbish."

"I expect bragging of murder is a sure way to spoil a fellow's reputation in your refined circles." My collar tightened and my vision was streaky from my elevated pulse, which in turn caused everything on me that was broken, crushed, or punctured to throb. I kept my cool by fantasizing about what I was going to do to my enemy when I tracked him to ground. Better, much better.

"It also didn't help when the squalid details of Conrad's provenance and subsequent upbringing eventually came to light. The poor chap was in and out of institutions for most of his youth. He worked as a clerk at University and there reunited with papa Muybridge and ultimately joined the photographer's staff. If not for Eadweard Muybridge's patronage, today Conrad would likely be in a gutter or dead."

"Oh, I see. Paxton didn't become a hermit by choice, your people shunned him like the good folks in Utah do it."

"In a nutshell, yes. Conrad's childhood history is sufficiently macabre to warrant such treatment. Not much is known about the Paxtons except they owned a fishery. Conrad's adoptive sister vanished when she was eight and he nine. All fingers pointed to his involvement. At age sixteen he drowned a rival at school and was sent to an asylum until he reached majority. The rich and beautiful are somewhat phobic regarding the criminally insane no matter how affluent the latter might be. Institutional taint isn't fashionable unless one derives from old money. Alas, Conrad is new money and what he's got isn't much by the standards of California high society."

"I don't know whether to thank you or shoot you," I said. "I'm inclined to accept your word for the moment. It would be an unfortunate thing were I to discover this information of yours is a hoax. Who are these associates that heard Paxton's confession?"

"The Corning sisters. The sisters dwell in Luster, one of several rustic burghs in Ransom Hollow. If anyone can help you against Conrad, it'll be the crones. I admired Donald. Your father was a killer with the eye of an artist, the heart of a poet. A conflicted man, but a loyal friend. I'd like to know why Conrad wanted him dead."

"I'm more interested in discovering why he wants to bop me," I said. Actually, I was more preoccupied with deciding on a gun or a dull knife.

"He may not necessarily wish to kill you, my boy. It may be worse than that. Do you enjoy films? There's one that may be of particular importance to you."

\* \* \*

Dick gave me a look when I brought Helios Augustus to the curb. He drove us to the Redfield Museum of Natural History without comment, although Bly's nephew Vernon frowned and muttered and cast suspicious glances into the rearview. I'd met the lug once at a speakeasy on the south side; lanky kid with red-rimmed eyes and a leaky nose. Pale as milk and mean as a snake. No scholar, either. I smiled at him, though not friendly like.

Helios Augustus rang the doorbell until a pasty clerk who pulled duty as a night watchman and janitor admitted us. The magician held a brief, muttered conference and we were soon guided to the basement archives where the public was never ever allowed. The screening area for visiting big cheeses, donors and dignitaries was located in an isolated region near the boiler room and the heat was oppressive. At least the seats were comfortable old wingbacks and I rested in one while they fussed and bustled around and eventually got the boxy projector rolling. The room was already dim and then Helios Augustus killed the lone floor lamp and we were at the bottom of a mine shaft, except for a blotch of light from the camera aperture spattered against a cloth panel. The clerk cranked dutifully and Helios Augustus settled beside me. He smelled of brandy and dust and when he leaned in to whisper his narration of the film, tiny specks of fire glinted in his irises.

What he showed me was a silent film montage of various projects by Eadweard Muybridge. The first several appeared innocuous—simple renderings of the dead photographer's various plates and the famous *Horse in Motion* reel that settled once and for all the matter of whether all four feet of the animal leave the ground during full gallop. For some reason the jittering frames of the buffalo plunging across the prairie made me uneasy. The images repeated until they shivered and the beast's hide grew thick and lustrous, until I swore foam bubbled from its snout, that its eye was fixed upon me with a malign purpose, and I squirmed in my seat and felt blood from my belly wound soaking the bandages. Sensing my discomfort, Helios Augustus patted my arm and advised me to steel myself for what was to come.

After the horse and buffalo, there arrived a stream of increasingly disjointed images that the magician informed me originated with numerous photographic experiments Muybridge indulged during his years teaching at university. These often involved men and women, likely students or staff, performing mundane tasks such as arranging books, or folding clothes, or sifting flour, in mundane settings such as parlors and kitchens. The routine gradually segued into strange territory. The subjects continued their plebian labors, but did so partially unclothed, and soon modesty was abandoned as were all garments. Yet there was nothing overtly sexual or erotic about the succeeding imagery. No, the sensations that crept over me were of anxiety and revulsion as a naked woman of middle age silently trundled about the confines of a workshop, fetching pails of water from a cistern and dumping them into a barrel. Much like the buffalo charging in place, she retraced her route with manic stoicism, endlessly, endlessly. A three-legged dog tracked her circuit by swiveling its misshapen skull. The dog fretted and scratched behind its ear and finally froze, snout pointed at the camera. The dog shuddered and rolled onto its side and frothed at the mouth while the woman continued, heedless, damned.

Next came a sequence of weirdly static shots of a dark, watery expanse. The quality was blurred and seemed alternately too close and too far.

Milk-white mist crept into the frame. Eventually something large disturbed the flat ocean—a whale breaching, an iceberg bobbing to the surface. Ropes, or cables lashed and writhed and whipped the water to a sudsy froth. Scores of ropes, scores of cables. The spectacle hurt my brain. Mist thickened to pea soup and swallowed the final frame.

I hoped for the lights to come up and the film to end. Instead, Helios Augustus squeezed my forearm in warning as upon the screen a boy, naked as a jay, scuttled on all fours from a stony archway in what might've been a cathedral. The boy's expression distorted in the manner of a wild animal caged, or of a man as the noose tightens around his neck. His eyes and tongue protruded. He raised his head so sharply it seemed impossible that his spine wasn't wrenched, and his alacrity at advancing and retreating was wholly unnatural…well, ye gods, that had to be a trick of the camera. A horrid trick. "The boy is quite real," Helios Augustus said. "All that you see is real. No illusion, no stagecraft."

I tugged a handkerchief from my pocket and dabbed my brow. My hand was clammy. "Why in hell did he take those pictures?"

"No one knows. Muybridge was a man of varied moods. There were sides to him seen only under certain conditions and by certain people. He conducted these more questionable film experiments with strict secrecy. I imagine the tone and content disturbed the prudish elements at university—"

"You mean the sane folks."

"As you wish, the sane folks. None dared stand in the way of his scientific pursuits. The administration understood how much glory his fame would bring them, and all the money."

"Yeah," I said. "Yeah. The money. Thanks for the show, old man. Could have done without it, all the same."

"I wanted you to meet young master Conrad," the magician said. "Before you met Conrad the elder."

The boy on the screen opened his mouth. His silent scream pierced my eye, then my brain. For the first time in I don't know, I made the sign of the cross.

* * *

We loaded my luggage, then swung by Dick, Bly, and Vernon's joints to fetch their essentials—a change of clothes, guns, and any extra hooch that was lying around. Then we made for the station and the evening train. Ah, the silken rapture of riding the Starlight Express in a Pullman sleeper. Thank you, dear Mr. Arden, sir.

My companions shared the sleeper next to mine and they vowed to keep a watch over me as I rested. They'd already broken out a deck of cards and uncorked a bottle of whiskey as I limped from their quarters, so I wasn't expecting much in the way of protection. It was dark as the train steamed along between Olympia and Tacoma. I sat in the gloom and put the Thompson together and laid it beneath the coverlet. This was more from habit than expediency. Firing the gun would be a bastard with my busted fingers and I hoped it wouldn't come to that. I'd removed the bandages and let it be—a mass of purple and yellow bruises from the nails to my wrist. I could sort of make a fist and that was all that mattered, really.

I fell asleep, lulled by the rattle and sway of the car on the tracks, and dreamed of Bane's face, his bulging eyes, all that blood. Bane's death mask shimmered and sloughed into that of the boy in the film, an adolescent Conrad Paxton being put through his paces by an offstage tormentor. A celebrated ghoul who'd notched his place in the history books with some fancy imagination and a clever arrangement of lenses, bulbs, and springs.

Didn't last long, thank god, as I snapped to when the train shuddered and slowed. Lamplight from some unknown station filtered through the blinds and sent shadows skittering across the ceiling and down the walls. I pointed the barrel at a figure hunched near the door, but the figure dissolved as the light shifted and revealed nothing more dangerous than my suitcase, the bulk of my jacket slung across a chair. I sat there a long while, breathing heavily as distant twinkly lights of passing towns floated in the great darkness.

The train rolled into Ransom Hollow and we disembarked at the Luster depot without incident. A cab relayed us to the Sycamore Hotel, the only game in the village. This was wild and wooly country, deep in the forested hills near the foot of the mountains. Ransom Hollow comprised a long, shallow river valley that eventually climbed into those mountains. An old roadmap marked the existence of three towns and a half-dozen villages in the vicinity, each of them established during or prior to the westward expansion of the 1830s. Judging by the moss and shingle roofs of the squat and rude houses, most of them saltbox or shotgun shacks, the rutted boardwalks and goats wandering the unpaved lanes, not much had changed since the era of mountain men trappers and gold rush placer miners.

The next morning we ate breakfast at a shop a couple of blocks from the hotel, then Dick and Bly departed to reconnoiter Paxton's estate while Vernon stayed with me. My hand and ear were throbbing. I stepped into the alley and had a gulp from a flask I'd stashed in my coat, and smoked one of the reefers Doc Green had slipped me the other day. Dope wasn't my preference, but it killed the pain far better than the booze did.

It was a scorcher of an autumn day and I hailed a cab and we rode in the back with the window rolled down. I smoked another cigarette and finished the whiskey; my mood was notably improved by the time the driver deposited us at our destination. The Corning sisters lived in a wooded neighborhood north of the town square. Theirs was a brick bungalow behind a steep walkup and gated entrance. Hedges blocked in the yard and its well-tended beds of roses and begonias. Several lawn gnomes crouched in the grass or peeked from the shrubbery; squat, wooden monstrosities of shin height, exaggerated features, pop-eyed and leering.

The bungalow itself had a European style peaked roof and was painted a cheery yellow. Wooden shutters bracketed the windows. Faces, similar to the sinister gnomes, were carved into the wood. The iron knocker on the main door was also shaped into a grinning, demonic visage. A naked man reclined against the hedge. He was average height, brawny as a Viking rower and sunburned. All over. His eyes were yellow. He spat in the grass and turned and slipped sideways through the hedge and vanished.

"What in hell?" Vernon said. He'd dressed in a bowler and an out of fashion jacket that didn't quite fit his lanky frame. He kept removing his tiny spectacles and smearing them around on his frayed sleeve. "See that lug? He was stark starin' nude!"

I doffed my Homburg and rapped the door, eschewing the knocker.

"Hello, Mr. Cope. And you must be Vernon. You're exactly how I imagined." A woman approached toward my left from around the corner of the house. She was tall, eye to eye with me, and softly middle-aged. Her hair was shoulder-length and black, her breasts full beneath a common-sense shirt and blouse. She wore pants and sandals. Her hands were dirty and she held a trowel loosely at hip level. I kept an eye on the trowel—her manner reminded me of a Mexican knife fighter I'd tangled with once. The scar from the Mexican's blade traversed a span between my collar bone and left nipple.

"I didn't realize you were expecting me," I said, calculating the implications of Helios Augustus wiring ahead to warn her of my impending arrival.

"Taller than your father," she said. Her voice was harsh. The way she carefully enunciated each syllable suggested her roots were far from Washington. Norway, perhaps. The garden gnomes were definitely Old World knick-knacks.

"You knew my father? I had no idea."

"I've met the majority of Augustus's American friends. He enjoys putting them on display."

"Mrs. Corning—"

"Not Mrs.," she said. "This is a house of spinsters. I'm Carling. You'll not encounter Groa and Vilborg, alas. Come inside from this hateful sunlight. I'll make you a pudding." She hesitated and looked Vernon north to south and then smiled an unpleasant little smile that made me happy for some reason. "Your friend can take his ease out here under the magnolia. We don't allow pets in the cottage."

"Shut up," I said to Vernon when he opened his mouth to argue.

Carling led me into the dim interior of the bungalow and barred the door. The air was sour and close. Meat hooks dangled from low rafter beams and forced me to stoop lest I whack my skull. An iron cauldron steamed and burbled upon the banked coals of a hearth. A wide plank table ran along the wall. The table was scarred. I noted an oversized meat cleaver stuck into a plank near a platter full of curdled blood. The floor was filthy. I immediately began to reassess the situation and kept my coat open in case I needed to draw my pistol in a hurry.

"Shakespearean digs you've got here, Ma'am," I said as I brushed dead leaves from a chair and sat. "No thanks on the pudding, if you don't mind."

"Your hand is broken. And you seem to be missing a portion of your ear. Your father didn't get into such trouble."

"He got himself dead, didn't he?"

In the next room, a baby cried briefly. Spinsters with a baby. I didn't like it. My belly hurt and my ear throbbed in time with my spindled fingers and I wondered, the thought drifting out of the blue, if she could smell the blood soaking my undershirt.

Carling's left eye drooped in either a twitch or a wink. She rummaged in a cabinet and then sprinkled a pinch of what appeared to be tea leaves into a cloudy glass. Down came a bottle of something that gurgled when she shook it. She poured three fingers into the glass and set it before me. Then she leaned against the counter and regarded me, idly drumming her fingers against her thigh. "We *weren't* expecting you. However, your appearance isn't particularly a surprise. Doubtless the magician expressed his good will by revealing Conrad Paxton's designs upon you. The magician was sincerely fond of your father. He fancies himself an urbane and sophisticated man. Such individuals always have room for one or two brutes in their menagerie of acquaintances."

"That was Dad, all right," I said and withdrew a cigarette, pausing before striking the match until she nodded. I smoked for a bit while we stared at one another.

"I'll read your fortune when you've finished," she said indicating the glass of alcohol and the noisome vapors drifting forth. In the bluish light her features seemed more haggard and vulpine than they had in the bright, clean sunshine. "Although, I think I can guess."

"Where's Groa and Vilborg?" I snapped open the Korn switchblade I carried in the breast pocket of my shirt and stirred the thick dark booze with the point. The knife was a small comfort, but I was taking it where I could find it.

"Wise, very wise to remember their names, Johnny, may I call you Johnny?—and to utter them. Names do have power. My sisters are in the cellar finishing the task we'd begun prior to this interruption. You have us at a disadvantage. Were it otherwise…But you lead a charmed life, don't you? There's not much chance of your return after this, more is the pity."

"What kind of task would that be?"

"The dark of the moon is upon us tonight. We conduct a ritual of longevity during the reaping season. It requires the most ancient and potent of sacrifices. Three days and three nights of intense labor, of which this morning counts as the first."

"Cutting apart a hapless virgin, are we?"

Carling ran her thumbnail between her front teeth. A black dog padded into the kitchen from the passage that let from the living room where the cries had emanated and I thought perhaps it had uttered the noise. The dog's eyes were yellow. It was the length and mass of a Saint Bernard, although its breed suggested that of a wolf. The dog smiled at me. Carling spoke a guttural phrase and unbarred the door and let it out. She shut the door and pressed her forehead against the frame.

"How do you know Paxton?" I said, idly considering her earlier comment about banning pets from the house.

"My sisters and I have ever been great fans of Eadweard's photography. Absolute genius, and quite the conversationalist. I have some postcards he sent us from his travels. Very thoughtful in his own, idiosyncratic way. Quite loyal to those who showed the same to him. Conrad is Eadweard Muybridge's dead wife's son, a few minutes the elder of his brother, Florado. The Paxtons took him to replace their own infant who'd died at birth the very night Muybridge's boys came into the world. Florado spent his youth in the institution. No talent to speak of. Worthless."

"But there must've been some question of paternity in Muybridge's mind. He left them to an institution in the first place. Kind of a rotten trick, you ask me."

"Eadweard tried to convince himself the children were the get of that retired colonel his wife had been humping."

"But they weren't."

"Oh, no—they belonged to Eadweard."

"Yet, one remained at the orphanage, and Conrad was adopted. Why did Muybridge come back into the kid's life? Guilt? Couldn't be guilt since he left the twin to rot."

"You couldn't understand. Conrad was special, possessed of a peculiar darkness that Eadweard recognized later, after traveling in Central America doing goddess knows what. The boy was key to something very large and very important. We all knew that. Don't ask and I'll tell you no lies. Take it up with Conrad when you see him."

"I don't believe Paxton murdered my father," I said. The baby in the other room moaned and I resisted the urge to look in that direction.

"Oh, then this is a social call? I would've fixed my hair, naughty boy."

"I'm here because he sent a pair of guns after me in Seattle. I didn't appreciate the gesture. Maybe I'm wrong, maybe he did blip my father. Two reasons to buzz him. Helios says you know the book on this guy. So, I come to you before I go to him."

"Reconnaissance is always wisest. Murder is not precisely what occurred. Conrad drained your father's life energy, siphoned it away via soul taking. You know of what I speak—photography, if done in a prescribed and ritualistic manner, can steal the subject's life force. This had a side consequence of effecting Mr. Cope's death. To be honest, Conrad didn't do it personally. He isn't talented in that area. He's a dilettante of the black arts. He had it done by proxy, much the way your employer Mr. Arden has *you* do the dirty work for him."

She was insane, obviously. Barking mad and probably very dangerous. God alone knew how many types of poison she had stashed up her sleeve. That cauldron of soup was likely fuming with nightshade, and my booze…I pushed it aside and brushed the blade against my pants leg. "Voodoo?" I said, just making conversation, wondering if I should rough her up a bit, if that was even wise, what with her dog and the naked guy roaming around. No confidence in Vernon whatsoever.

"There are many faiths at the crossroads here in the Hollow," Carling said, bending to stir the pot and good god her shoulders were broad as a logger's. "Voodoo is not one of them. I can't tell you who did in your father, only that it was done and that Conrad ordered it so. I recommend you make haste to the Paxton estate and do what you do best—rub the little shit out before he does for you. He tried once, he'll definitely take another crack at it."

"Awfully harsh words for your old chum," I said to her brawny backside. "Two of you must have had a lovers' quarrel."

"He's more of a godson. I don't have a problem with Conrad. He's vicious and vengeful and wants my head on a stick, but I don't hold that against him in the slightest."

"Then why are you so interested in seeing him get blipped?"

"You seem like a nice boy, Johnny." Carling turned slowly and there was something amiss with her face that I couldn't quite figure out. That nasty grin was back, though. "Speaking of treachery and violence, that other fellow you brought is no good. I wager he'll bite."

"Think so?" I said. "He's just along for the ride."

"Bah. Let us bargain. Leave your friend with us and I'll give you a present. I make knick-knacks, charms, trinkets and such. What you really need if you're going to visit the Paxton estate is a talisman to ward off the diabolic. It wouldn't do to go traipsing in there as you are."

"I agree. I'll be sure to pack a shotgun."

She cackled. Actually and truly cackled. "Yes, yes, for the best. Here's a secret few know—I wasn't always a spinster. In another life I traveled to India and China and laid with many, many men, handsomer than you even. They were younger and unspoiled. I nearly, very, very nearly married a rich Chinaman who owned a great deal of Hainan."

"Didn't work out, eh? Sorry to hear it, Ms. Corning."

"He raised monkeys. I hate monkeys worse than Christ." She went through the door into the next room and I put my hand on the pistol from reflex and perhaps a touch of fear, but she returned with nothing more sinister than a shriveled black leaf in her open palm. Not a leaf, I discovered upon receiving it, but a dry cocoon. She dropped it into my shirt pocket, just leaned over and did it without asking and up close she smelled of spice and dirt and unwashed flesh.

"Thanks," I said recoiling from the proximity of her many large, sharp teeth.

"Drink your whiskey and run along."

I stared at the glass. It smelled worse than turpentine.

"Drink your fucking whiskey," she said.

And I did, automatic as you please. It burned like acid.

She snatched the empty glass and regarded the constellation of dregs at the bottom. She grinned, sharp as a pickaxe. "He's throwing a party in a couple of nights. Does one every week. Costumes, pretty girls, rich trappers and furriers, our rustic nobility. It augers well for you to attend."

I finally got my breath back. "In that case, the furriers' ball it is."

She smiled and patted my cheek. "Good luck. Keep the charm on your person. Else..." She smiled sadly and straightened to her full height. "Might want to keep this visit between you and me."

* * *

Vernon was missing when I hit the street. The cab driver shrugged and said he hadn't seen anything. No reason not to believe him, but I dragged him by the hair from the car and belted him around some on the off chance he was lying. Guy wasn't lying, though. There wasn't any way I'd go back into that abattoir of a cottage to hunt for the lost snowbird, so I decided on a plausible story to tell the boys. Vernon was the type slated to end it face down in a ditch, anyway. Wouldn't be too hard to sell the tale and frankly, watching Bly stew and fret would be a treat.

Never did see Vernon again.

* * *

Dick and Bly hadn't gotten very close to the Paxton mansion. The estate was guarded by a bramble-covered stone wall out of *Sleeping Beauty*, a half mile of wildwood and overgrown gardens, then croquet courses, polo fields, and a small barracks that housed a contingent of fifteen or so backwoods thugs armed with shotguns and dogs. God alone knew where Paxton had recruited such a gang. I figured they must be either locals pressed into service or real talent from out of state. No way to tell without tangling with them, though.

Dick had cased the joint with field glasses and concluded a daylight approach would be risky as hell. Retreat and regrouping seemed the preferable course, thus we decided to cool our heels and get skunk drunk.

The boys had caught wind of a nasty speakeasy in a cellar near Belson Creek in neighboring Olde Towne. A girl Bly had picked up in the parking lot of Luster's one and only hardware store claimed men with real hard bark on them hung around there. Abigail and Bly were real chummy, it seemed, and he told her we were looking to put the arm on a certain country gentleman. The girl suggested low at the heel scoundrels who tenanted the dive might be helpful.

The speakeasy was called Satan's Bung and the password at the door was Van Iblis, all of this Dick had discovered from his own temporary girls, Wanda and Clementine, which made me think they'd spent most of the day reconnoitering a watering hole rather than pursuing our mission with any zeal. In any event, we sashayed into that den of iniquity with sweet little chippies who still had most of their teeth, a deck of unmarked cards, and a bottle of sour mash. There were a few tough guys hanging around, as advertised; lumberjacks in wool coats and sawdust-sprinkled caps and cork boots; the meanest of the lot even hoisted his axe onto the bar. One gander at my crew and they looked the other way right smartly. Some good old boys came down from the hills or out of the swamp, hitched their overalls and commenced to picking banjos, banging drums, and harmonizing in an angelic chorus that belied their sodden, bloated, and warty features, their shaggy beards and knurled scalps. They clogged barefoot, stamping like bulls ready for battle.

Dick, seven sails to the wind, wondered aloud what could be done in the face of determined and violent opposition entrenched at the Paxton estate and I laughed and told him not to worry too much, this was a vacation. Relax and enjoy himself—I'd think of something. I always thought of something.

Truth of it was, I'd lost a bit of my stomach for the game after tea and cake at the Corning sisters' house and the resultant disappearance of Vernon. If it hadn't been for the rifling of my home, the attack by The Long and The Short, the mystery of whether Paxton really bopped Dad would've remained a mystery. Thus, despite my reassurances to the contrary, I wasn't drinking and plotting a clever plan of assault or infiltration of the estate, but rather simply drinking and finagling a way to get my ashes hauled by one of the chippies.

One thing led to another, a second bottle of rotgut to a third, and Clementine climbed into my lap and nuzzled my neck and unbuttoned my pants and slipped her hand inside. Meanwhile a huge man in a red-and-black-checkered coat and coonskin cap pranced, nimble as a Russian ballerina, and wheedled a strange tune on a flute of lacquered black ivory. This flautist was a hirsute, wiry fellow with a jagged visage hacked from a stone, truly more beast than man by his gesticulations and the manner he gyrated his crotch, thrusting to the beat, and likely the product of generations of inbreeding, yet he piped with an evil and sinuous grace that captured the admiration of me, my companions, the entire roomful of seedy and desperate characters. The lug seemed to fixate upon me, glaring and smirking as he clicked his heels and puffed his cheeks and capered among the tables like a faun.

I conjectured aloud as to his odd behavior, upon which Dick replied in a slur that if I wanted him to give the bird a thrashing, just make the sign. My girl, deep into her cups, mumbled that the flautist was named Dan

Blackwood, last scion of a venerable Ransom Hollow family renowned as hunters and furriers without peer, but these days runners of moonshine. A rapist and murderer who'd skated out of prison by decree of the prince of Darkness Hissownself, or so the fireside talk went. A fearful and loathsome brute, his friends were few and of similar malignant ilk and were known as the Blackwood Boys. Her friend Abigail paused from licking Bly's earlobe to concur.

Dan Blackwood trilled his oddly sinister tune while a pair of hillbillies accompanied him with banjo and fiddle and a brawny lad with golden locks shouldered aside the piano player and pawed the ivories to create a kind of screeching cacophony not unlike a train wreck while the paper lanterns dripped down blood-red light and the cellar audience clenched into a tighter knot and swayed on their feet, their stools and stumps, stamping time against the muddy floor. From that cacophony a dark and primitive rhythm emerged as each instrument fell into line with its brother and soon that wattled and toadlike orchestra found unity with their piper and produced a song that put ice in my loins and welded me to my seat. Each staccato burst from the snare drum, each shrill from the flute, each discordant clink from the piano, each nails on slate shriek of violin and fiddle, pierced my brain, caused a sweet, agonizing lurch of my innards, and patient Clementine jerked my cock, out of joint, so to speak.

The song ended with a bang and a crash and the crowd swooned. More tunes followed and more people entered that cramped space and added to the sensation we were supplicants or convicts in a special circle of hell, such was the ripe taint of filthy work clothes and matted hair and belched booze like sulfurous counterpoint to the maniacal contortions of the performers, the rich foul effluvium of their concert.

During an intermission, I extricated myself from industrious Clementine and made my way up the stairs into the alley to piss against the side of the building. The darkness was profound, moonless as Carling had stated, and the stars were covered by a thin veil of cloud. Despite my best efforts, I wasn't particularly impaired and thus wary and ready for trouble when the door opened and a group of men, one bearing a lantern that oozed the hideous red glow, spilled forth and mounted the stairs. The trio stopped at the sight of me and raised the lantern high so that it scattered a nest of rats into the hinder of the lane. I turned to face them, hand on pistol, and I smiled and hoped Dick or Bly might come tripping up the steps at any moment.

But there was no menace evinced by this group, at least not aimed at me. The leader was the handsome blond lad who'd hammered the piano into submission. He saluted me with two fingers and said, "Hey, now city feller. My name's Candy. How'n ya like our burg?" The young man didn't wait for an answer, but grunted at his comrades, the toadlike fiddler and banjo picker who might've once been conjoined and later separated with an axe blow, then said to me in his thick, unfamiliar accent, "So, chum, the telegraph sez you in Ransom Holler on dirty business. My boss knows who yer gunnin' for and he'd be pleased as punch to make yer acquaintance."

"That's right civilized. I was thinking of closing this joint down, though…"

"Naw, naw, ol' son. Ya gotta pay the piper round this neck of the woods."

I asked who and where and the kid laughed and said to get my friends and follow him, and to ease my mind the men opened their coats to show they weren't packing heat. Big knives and braining clubs wrapped in leather and nail-studded, but no pea shooters and I thought again how Dick had managed to learn of this place and recalled something about one of the girls, perhaps Abigail, whispering the name into his ear and a small chill crept along my spine. Certainly Paxton could be laying a trap, and he wasn't the only candidate for skullduggery. Only the good lord knew how strongly the Corning sisters interfered in the politics of the Hollow and if they'd set the Blackwood Gang upon us, and of course this caused my suspicious mind to circle back to Helios Augustus and his interest in the affair. Increasingly I kicked myself for not having shot him when I'd the chance and before he could take action against me, assuming my paranoid suppositions bore weight. So, I nodded and tipped my hat and told the Blackwood Boys to bide a moment.

Dick and Bly were barely coherent when I returned to gather them and the girls. Bly, collar undone, eyes crossed and blinking, professed incredulity that we would even consider traveling with these crazed locals to some as yet unknown location. Dick didn't say anything, although his mouth curved down at the corners with the distaste of a man who'd gulped castor oil. We both understood the score; no way on God's green earth we'd make it back to Luster and our heavy armament if the gang wanted our skins. Probably wouldn't matter even if we actually managed to get armed. This was the heart of midnight and the best and only card to turn was to go for a ride with the devil. He grabbed Bly's arm and dragged him along after me, the goodtime girls staggering in our wake. Ferocious lasses—they weren't keen on allowing their meal tickets to escape, and clutched our sleeves and wailed like the damned.

Young master Candy gave our ragged assembly a bemused once-over, then shrugged and told us to get a move on, starlight was wasting. He led us to a great creaking behemoth of a farm truck with raised sides to pen in livestock and bade us pile into the bed. His compatriot the fiddler was already a boulder slumped behind the steering wheel.

I don't recall the way because it was pitch black and the night wind stung my eyes. We drove along Belson Creek and crossed it on rickety nar-row bridges and were soon among ancient groves of poplar and fir, well removed from Olde Towne or any other lighted habitation. The road was rutted and the jarring threatened to rip my belly open. I spent most of the thankfully brief ride doubled, hands pressed hard against the wound, hop-ing against hope to keep my guts on the inside.

The truck stopped briefly and Candy climbed down to scrape the ruined carcass of a raccoon or opossum from the dirt and chucked it into the bed near our feet. Bly groaned and puked onto his shoes and the girls screamed or laughed or both. Dick was a blurry white splotch in the shadows and from the manner he hunched, I suspected he had a finger on the trigger of the revolver in his pocket. Most likely, he figured I'd done in poor, stupid Vernon and was fixing to dust that weasel Bly next, hell maybe I'd go all in and make a play for Mr. Arden. These ideas were far from my mind (well, dusting Bly was a possibility), naturally. Suicide wasn't my intent. None-theless, I couldn't fault Dick for worrying; could only wonder, between shocks to my kidneys and gut from the washboard track, how he would land if it ever came time to choose teams.

The fiddler swung the truck along a tongue of gravel that unrolled deep inside a bog and we came to a ramshackle hut, a trapper or fisherman's abode, raised on stilts that leaned every which way like a spindly, decrepit daddy longlegs with a house on its back. Dull, scaly light flickered through windows with tanned skins for curtains and vaguely illuminated the squelching morass of a yard with its weeds and moss and rusty barrels half sunk in the muck, and close by in the shadows came the slosh of Belson Creek churning fitfully as it dreamed. Another truck rolled in behind us and half a dozen more goons wordlessly unloaded and stood around, their faces obscured in the gloom. All of them bore clubs, mattock handles, and gaff hooks.

There was a kind of ladder descending from a trapdoor and on either side were strung moldering nets and the moth-eaten hides of beasts slaughtered decades ago and chains of animal bones and antlers that jangled when we bumped them in passing. I went first, hoping to not reinjure my hand while entertaining visions of a sledgehammer smashing my skull, or a machete lopping my melon at the neck as I passed through the opening. Ducks in Tin Pan Alley is what we were.

Nobody clobbered me with a hammer, nobody chopped me with an axe and I hoisted myself into the sooty confines of Dan Blackwood's shanty. Beaver hides were stretched into circles and tacked on the walls, probably to cover the knotholes and chinks in a vain effort to bar the gnats and mosquitoes that swarmed the bog. Bundles of fox and muskrat hide were twined at the muzzle and hung everywhere and black bear furs lay in heaps and crawled with sluggish flies. A rat crouched enthroned high atop one mound, sucking its paws. It regarded me with skepticism. Light came from scores of candles, coagulated slag of black and white, and rustic kerosene lamps I wagered had seen duty in Gold Rush mines. The overwhelming odors were that of animal musk, lye, and peat smoke. Already, sweat poured from me and I wanted another dose of mash.

That sinister flautist Dan Blackwood tended a cast iron stove, fry pan in one fist, spatula in the other. He had already prepared several platters of flapjacks. He wore a pork pie hat cocked at a precipitous angle. A bear skin covered him after a burlesque fashion.

"Going to be one of those nights, isn't it?" I said as my friends and hangers on clambered through the hatch and stood blinking and gawping at their surroundings, this taxidermy post in Hades.

"Hello, cousin. Drag up a stump. Breakfast is at hand." Blackwood's voice was harsh and thin and came through his long nose. At proximity, his astounding grotesqueness altered into a perverse beauty, such were the chiseled planes and crags of his brow and cheek, the lustrous blackness of his matted hair that ran riot over his entire body. His teeth were perfectly white when he smiled, and he smiled often.

The cakes, fried in pure lard and smothered in butter and maple syrup, were pretty fucking divine. Blackwood ate with almost dainty precision and his small, dark eyes shone brightly in the candle flame and ye gods the heat from the stove was as the heat from a blast furnace and soon all of us were in shirt sleeves or less, the girls quickly divested themselves of blouse and skirt and lounged around in their dainties. I didn't care about the naked chickadees; my attention was divided between my recurrent pains of hand and ear, and gazing in wonder at our satyr host, lacking only his hooves to complete the image of the great god Pan taking a mortal turn as a simple gang boss. We had him alone—his men remained below in the dark—and yet, in my bones I felt it was me and Dick and Bly who were at a disadvantage if matters went south.

"Don't get a lot of fellows with your kind of bark around here," Blackwood said. He reclined in a heavy wooden chair padded with furs, not unlike the throne of a feudal lord who was contemplating the fate of some unwelcome itinerant vagabonds. "Oh, there's wild men and murderous types aplenty, but not professional gunslingers. I hear tell you've come to the Hollow with blood in your eye, and who put it there? Why dear little Connie Paxton, of course; the moneybags who rules from his castle a few miles yonder as the crow wings it."

"Friend of yours?" I said, returning his brilliant smile with one of my own as I gauged the speed I could draw the Luger and pump lead into that hairy torso. Clementine slithered over and caressed my shoulders and kissed my neck. Her husband had been a merchant marine during the Big One, had lain in Davy Jones's Locker since 1918. Her nipples were hard as she pressed against my back.

Blackwood kept right on smiling. "Friend is a powerful word, cousin. Almost as powerful as a true name. It's more proper to say Mr. Paxton and I have a pact. Keepin' the peace so we can all conduct our nefarious trades, well that's a sacred duty."

"I understand why you'd like things to stay peaceful," I said.

"No, cousin, you *don't* understand. The Hollow is far from peaceful. We do surely love our bloodlettin', make no mistake. Children go missin' from their beds and tender maidens are ravished by Black Bill of the Wood," he winked at slack-jawed and insensate Abigail who lay against Bly, "and just the other day the good constable Jarred Brown discovered the severed head of his best deputy floatin' in Belson Creek. Alas, poor

Ned Smedley. I knew him, Johnny! Peaceful, this territory ain't. On the other hand, we've avoided full scale battle since that machine gun incident at the Luster court house in 1910. This fragile balance between big predators is oh so delicately strung. And along come you Gatlin-totin' hard-asses from the big town to upset everything. What shall I do with you, cousin, oh what?"

"Jesus, these are swell flapjacks, Mr. Blackwood," Bly said. His rummy eyes were glazed as a stuffed dog's.

"Why, thank you, sirrah. At the risk of soundin' trite, it's an old family recipe. Wheat flour, salt, sugar, eggs from a black speckled virgin hen, dust from the bones of a Pinkerton, a few drops of his heart blood. Awful decadent, I'll be so gauche as to agree."

None of us said anything until Clementine muttered into my good ear, "Relax, baby. You ain't a lawman, are you? You finer than frog's hair." She nipped me.

"Yes, it is true," Blackwood said. "Our faithful government employees have a tendency to get short shrift. The Hollow voted and decided we'd be best off if such folk weren't allowed to bear tales. This summer a couple government rats, Pinkerton men, came sniffin' round for moonshine stills and such. Leto, Brutus and Candy, you've met 'em, dragged those two agents into the bog and buried 'em chest deep in the mud. My lads took turns batterin' out their brains with those thumpers they carry on their belts. I imagine it took a while. Boys play rough. Candy worked in a stockyard. He brained the cattle when they came through the chute. Got a taste for it." He glanced at the trap door when he said this.

"Powerful glad I'm no Pinkerton," I said.

He opened his hand and reached across the space between us as if he meant to grasp my neck, and at the last moment he flinched and withdrew and his smile faded and the beast in him came near the surface. "You've been to see those bitches."

"The Corning ladies? Come to think of it, yes, I had a drink with the sisters. Now I'm having breakfast with you. Don't be jealous, Dan." I remained perfectly still and as poised as one can be with sweat in his eyes, a hard-on in progress, and consumed by rolling waves of blue-black pain. My own beast was growling and slamming its Stone Age muzzle against the bars. It wanted blood to quench its terror, wanted loose. "What do you have against old ladies. They didn't mention you."

"Our business interests lie at cross-purposes. I don't relish no competition. Wait. Wait a minute… Did you see the child?" Blackwood asked this in a hushed tone, and his face smoothed into a false calmness, probably a mirror of my own. Oh, we were trying very hard not to slaughter one another. He cocked his head and whispered, "John, did you see the child?"

That surely spooked me, and the teary light in his eyes spooked me too, but not half so much as the recollection of the cries in the dim room at the Corning bungalow. "No. I didn't."

He watched me for a while, watched me until even Dick and Bly began to rouse from their reveries to straighten and cast puzzled looks between us. Blackwood kept flexing his hand, clenching and tearing at an invisible throat, perhaps. "All right. That's hunkum-bunkum." His smile returned. "The crones don't have no children."

I wiped my palms to dry the sweat and lighted a cigarette and smoked it to cover my expression. After a few moments I said, "Does Paxton know I'm here?"

"Yes. Of course. The forest has eyes, the swamp ears. Why you've come to give him the buzz is the mystery."

"Hell with that. Some say he's at the root of trouble with my kin. Then there's the goons he sent my way. I didn't start this. Going to end it, though."

"Mighty enterprising, aren't you? A real dyed in the wool bad man."

"What is this pact? I wager it involves plenty of cabbage."

"An alliance, bad man. He and I versus the damnable crones and that rotgut they try to pass off as whiskey. Little Lord Paxton is moneyed up real good. He inherited well. In any event, he keeps palms greased at the Governor's mansion and in turn, I watch his back. Been that way for a while. It's not perfect; I don't cotton to bowing and scraping. Man does what man must."

"Who funds the sisters?"

"Some say they buried a fortune in mason jars. Gold ingots from the Old World. Maybe, after they're gone, me and the lads will go treasure hunting on their land."

So, I'd well and truly fallen from fry pan to fire. Paxton wanted me dead, or captured, thus far the jury remained out on that detail, and here

I'd skipped into the grasp of his chief enforcer. "Hell, I made it easy for you lugs, eh? Walked right into the box." I nodded and decided that this was the end of the line and prepared to draw my pistol and go pay Saint Peter my respects with an empty clip. "Don't think I'll go quietly. We Copes die real hard."

"Hold on a second," Bly said, sobering in a hurry. I didn't think the Bly clan had a similar tradition.

Blackwood patted him on the head. "No need for heroics, gents. We've broken bread, haven't we? You can hop on Shank's Mare and head for the tall timber anytime you like. Nobody here's gonna try to stop you. On the other paw, I was kind of hoping you might stick around the Hollow, see this affair through."

I sat there and gaped, thunderstruck. "We can walk out of here." My senses strained, alert for the snare that must lurk within his affable offer. "What do you want, Dan?"

"Me and the boys recently were proposed a deal by…Well, that's none of your concern. A certain party has entered the picture, is enough to say. We been offered terms that trump our arrangement with Paxton. Trump it in spades. Problem is, I've sworn an oath to do him no harm, so that ties my hands."

"That's where I come in."

"You've said a mouthful, and no need to say more. We'll let it ride, see how far it takes us."

"And if I want to cash in and take my leave?"

He shrugged and left me to dangle in the wind. I started to ask another question, and thought better of it and sat quietly, my mind off to the races. Dan's smile got even wider. "Candy will squire you back to the Sycamore. There's a garden party and dinner. All the pretty folk will be there tying one on. Dress accordingly, eh?"

\* \* \*

Candy returned us to the hotel where my entourage collapsed, semi-clothed and pawing one another, into a couple of piles on the beds. Dawn leaked through the curtains and I was queerly energized despite heavy drinking and nagging wounds, so I visited the nearby café as the first customer. I drank bad coffee in a corner booth as locals staggered in and

ordered plates of hash and eggs and muttered and glowered at one another; beasts awakened too soon from hibernation. I fished in my pocket
and retrieved the cocoon Carling had given me and lay it on the edge of
the saucer. It resembled a slug withered by salt and dried in the hot sun. I
wondered if my father, a solid, yet philosophically ambiguous, Catholic,
ever carried a good luck charm. What else was a crucifix or a rosary?

"You know you're playing the fool." I said this aloud, barely a mutter,
just enough to clear the air between my passions and my higher faculties.
Possibly I thought giving voice to the suspicion would formalize matters,
break the spell and justify turning the boat around and sailing home, or
making tracks for sunny Mexico and a few days encamping on a beach
with a bottle of whiskey and a couple of *señoritas* who didn't habla inglés.
At that moment a goose waddled over my grave and the light reflecting
from the waitress's coffee pot bent strangely and the back of my neck went
cold. I looked down the aisle through the doorway glass and spotted a
couple of the Blackwood Boys loitering in the bushes of a vacant lot across
the way. One was the big fiddler, the other wore overalls and a coonskin
cap. The fiddler rested his weight on the handle of what at first I took for
a shovel. When he raised the object and laid it across his shoulder I recognized it as a sword, one of those Scottish claymores.

A party and in my finest suit and tie it would be. Goddamn, if they were
going to be this way about it I'd go see the barber after breakfast and have
a haircut and a shave.

* * *

It was as Blackwood promised. We drove over to the mansion in a Ca-
dillac I rented from the night clerk at the hotel. Even if the guys hadn't
scoped the joint out previously, we would've easily found our way by following a small parade of fancy vehicles bound for the estate. Bly rolled
through the hoary, moss-encrusted gates and the mansion loomed like a
castle on the horizon. He eased around the side and parked in the back.
We came through the servants' entrance. Dick and Bly packing shotguns,
me with the Thompson slung under my arm. Men in livery were frantically arranging matters for the weekly estate hoedown and the ugly mugs
with the guns made themselves scarce.

Conrad Paxton was on the veranda. He didn't seem at all surprised when

I barged in and introduced myself. He smiled a thin, deadly smile and waved to an empty seat. "*Et tu* Daniel?" he said to himself, and chuckled. "Please, have a drink. Reynolds," he snapped his fingers at a bland older man wearing a dated suit, "fetch, would you? And, John, please, tell your comrades to take a walk. Time for the men to chat."

Dick and Bly waited. I gave the sign and they put the iron away under their trench coats and scrammed. A minute or two later, they reappeared on the lawn amid the hubbub and stood where they could watch us. Everybody ignored them.

I leaned the Thompson against the railing and sat across from my host. We regarded each other for a while as more guests arrived and the party got underway.

Finally, he said, "This moment was inevitable. One can only contend with the likes of Blackwood and his ilk for a finite period before they turn on one like the wild animals they are. I'd considered moving overseas, somewhere with a more hospitable clime. No use, my enemies will never cease to pursue, and I'd rather die in my home. Well, Eadweard's, technically." Conrad Paxton's face was long and narrow. His fingers were slender. He smoked fancy European cigarettes with a filter and an ivory cigarette holder. Too effete for cigars, I imagined. Well, me too, chum, me too.

"Maybe if you hadn't done me and mine dirt you'd be adding candles to your cake for a spell yet."

"Ah, *done you dirt*. I can only imagine what poppycock you've been told to set you upon me. My father knew your father. Now the sons meet. Too bad it's not a social call—I'm hell with social calls. You have the look of a soldier."

"Did my bit."

"What did you do in the war, John?"

"I shot people."

"Ha. So did my father, albeit with a camera. As for me, I do nothing of consequence except drink my inheritance, collect moldy tomes, and also the envy of those who'd love to appropriate what I safeguard in this place. You may think of me as a lonely, rich caretaker."

"Sounds miserable," I said.

Afternoon light was dimming to red through the trees that walled in the unkempt concourses of green lawn. Some twenty minutes after our arrival, and still more Model Ts, Packards and Studebakers formed a shiny black and white procession along the crushed gravel drive, assembling around the central fountain, a twelve-foot-tall marble faun gone slightly green around the gills from decades of mold. Oh, the feather boas and peacock feather hats, homburgs and stovepipes! Ponderously loaded tables of *hors d'oeuvres*, including a splendid tiered cake, and pails of frosty cold punch, liberally dosed with rum, were arrayed beneath fluttering silk pavilions. Servants darted among the gathering throng and unpacked orchestral instruments on a nearby dais. Several others worked the polo fields, hoisting buckets as they bent to reapply chalk lines, or smooth divots, or whatever.

Dick and Bly, resigned to their fate, loitered next to the punch, faces gray and pained even at this hour, following the legendary excesses of the previous evening. Both had cups in hand and were tipping them regularly. As for Paxton's goons, those gents continued to maintain a low profile, confined to the fancy bunkhouse at the edge of the property, although doubtless a few of them lurked in the shrubbery or behind the trees. My fingers were crossed that Blackwood meant to keep his bargain. Best plan I had.

A bluff man with a pretty young girl stuck on his arm waved to us. Paxton indolently returned the gesture. He inserted the filter between his lips and dragged exaggeratedly. "That would be the mayor. Best friend of whores and moonshiners in the entire county."

"I like that in a politician," I said. "Let's talk about you."

"My story is rather dreary. Father bundled me off to the orphanage, then disappeared into Central America for several years. Another of his many expeditions. None of them made him famous. He became *famous* for murdering that colonel and driving Mother into an early grave. I also have his slide collection and his money." Paxton didn't sound too angry for someone with such a petulant mouth. I supposed the fortune he'd inherited when his father died sweetened life's bitter pills.

"My birth father, Eadweard Muybridge, died in his native England in 1904. I missed the funeral, and my brother Florado's as well. I'm a cad that way. Floddie got whacked by a car in San Francisco. Of all the bloody luck, eh? Father originally sent me and my brother to the orphanage where I was adopted by the Paxtons as an infant. My real mother named me Conrad after a distant cousin. Conrad Gallatry was a soldier and died in the Philippines fighting in the Spanish-American War.

"As a youth, I took scant interest in my genealogy, preferring to eschew the coarseness of these roots, and knew the barest facts regarding Eadweard Muybridge beyond his reputation as a master photographer and eccentric. Father was a peculiar individual. In 1875 Eadweard killed his wife's, and my dearest mum's, presumed lover—he'd presented that worthy, a retired colonel, with an incriminating romantic letter addressed to Mrs. Muybridge in the Colonel's hand, uttered a pithy remark, and then shot him dead. Father's defense consisted of not insubstantial celebrity, his value to science, and a claim of insanity as the result of an old coach accident that crushed his skull, in addition to the understandable anguish at discovering Mum's betrayal. I can attest the attribution of insanity was correct, albeit nothing to do with the crash, as I seemed to have come by my moods and anxieties honestly. Blood will tell."

"You drowned a boy at your school," I said. "And before that, your stepsister vanished. Somewhat of a scoundrel as a lad, weren't you?"

"So they say. What they say is far kinder than the truth. Especially for my adopted Mum and Da. My stepsister left evidence behind, which, predictably, the Paxtons obscured for reasons of propriety. They suspected the truth and those suspicions were confirmed when I killed that nit Abelard Fries in our dormitory. A much bolder act, that murder. And again, the truth was obfuscated by the authorities, by my family. No, word of what I'd really done could not be allowed to escape our circle. You see, for me, it had already begun. I was already on the path of enlightenment, seeker and sometimes keeper of *Mysterium Tremendum et fascinans*. Even at that tender age."

"All of you kooky bastards in this county into black magic?" I'd let his insinuations regarding the fate of his sister slide from my mind, dismissing a host of ghastly speculative images as they manifested and hung between us like phantom smoke rings.

"Only the better class of people."

"You sold your soul at age nine, or thereabouts. Is that it, man? Then daddy came home from the jungle one day and took you in because... because why?"

"Sold my soul? Hardly. I traded up. You didn't come to me to speak of that. You're an interesting person, John. *Not* interesting enough for this path of mine. Your evils are definitely, tragically lowercase."

"Fine, let's not dance. Word is, you did for my father. Frankly, I was attached to him. That means we've got business."

"Farfetched, isn't it? Didn't he choke on a sandwich or something?"

"I'm beginning to wonder. More pressing: Why did you try to have me rubbed out? To keep me in the dark about you bopping my dad? That wasn't neighborly."

"I didn't harm your father. Never met the man, although Eadweard spoke of him, wrote of him. Your old man made a whale of an impression on people he didn't kill. Nor did I dispatch those hooligans who braced you in Seattle. Until you and your squad lumbered into Ransom Hollow, I had scant knowledge and exactly zero interest in your existence. Helios Augustus certainly engineered the whole charade. The old goat knew full well you'd respond unkindly to the ministrations of fellow Johnson Brothers, that you'd do for them, or they for you, and the winner, spurred by his wise counsel, would come seeking my scalp."

"Ridiculous. Hand them a roll of bills and they'll blip anyone you please, no skullduggery required."

"This is as much a game as anything. Your father was responsible for Eadweard's troubles with the law. Donald Cope is the one who put the idea of murder in his head, the one who mailed the gun that Eadweard eventually used on the retired officer who'd dallied with my mother. Eadweard wasn't violent, but your father was the devil on his shoulder telling him to be a man, to smite his enemy. After pulling the trigger, my father went off the rails, disappeared into the world and when he returned, he had no use for Helios Augustus, or anyone. He was his own man, in a demented fashion. Meanwhile, Helios Augustus, who had spent many painstaking years cultivating and mentoring Eadweard, was beside himself. The magician was no simple cardsharp on a barge whom your father just happened to meet. One of his myriad disguises. His posturing as a magician, famous or not, is yet another. Helios Augustus is a servant of evil and he manipulates everyone, your father included. Donald Cope was meant to be a tool, a protector of Eadweard. A loyal dog. He wasn't supposed to dispense wisdom, certainly not his own homespun brand of hooliganism. He ruined the magician's plan. Ruined everything, it seems."

I was accustomed to liars, bold-faced or wide-eyed, silver tongued or pleading, often with the barrel of my gun directed at them as they babbled their last prayers to an indifferent god, squirted their last tears into the indifferent earth. A man will utter any falsehood, commit any debasement, sell his own children down the river, to avoid that final sweet goodnight.

Paxton wasn't a liar, though. I studied him and his sallow, indolent affectation of plantation suzerainty, the dark power in his gaze, and beheld with clarity he was a being who had no need for deception, that all was delivered to him on a platter. He wasn't afraid, either. I couldn't decide whether that lack of fear depended upon his access to the Blackwood Boys, his supreme and overweening sense of superiority, an utter lack of self-preservation instincts, or something else as yet to make its presence felt. Something dread and terrible in the wings was my guess, based upon the pit that opened in my gut as we talked while the sun sank into the mountains and the shadows of the gibbering and jabbering gentry spread grotesquely across the grass.

"You said Augustus groomed Muybridge."

"Yes. Groomed him to spread darkness with his art. And Father did, though not to the degree or with the potency Helios Augustus desired. The sorcerer and his allies believed Eadweard was tantalizingly close to unlocking something vast and inimical to human existence."

The guests stirred and the band ascended the dais, each member lavishly dressed in a black suit, hair slicked with oil and banded in gold or silver, each cradling an oboe, a violin, a horn, a double bass, and of course, of fucking course, Dan Blackwood at the fore with his majestic flute, decked in a classical white suit and black tie, his buttered down hair shining like an angel's satin wing. They nodded to one another and began to play soft and sweet chamber music from some German symphony that was popular when lederhosen reigned at court. Music to calm a bellicose Holy Roman Emperor. Music beautiful enough to bring a tear to a killer's eye.

I realized Dick and Bly had disappeared. I stood, free hand pressed to my side to keep the bandage from coming unstuck. "Your hospitality is right kingly, Mr. Paxton, sir—"

"Indeed? You haven't touched your brandy. I'm guessing that's a difficult bit of self restraint for an Irishman. It's not poisoned. Heavens, man, I couldn't harm you if that were my fiercest desire."

"Mr. Paxton, I'd like to take you at your word. Problem is, Curtis Bane had a card with your name written on it in his pocket. That's how I got wind of you."

"Extraordinarily convenient. And world famous magician Phil Wary, oh dear, my mistake—Helios Augustus—showed you some films my father made and told you I'd set the dogs on your trail. Am I correct?"

"Yeah, that's right." The pit in my belly kept crumbling away. It would be an abyss pretty soon. It wasn't that the pale aristocrat had put the puzzle together that made me sick with nerves, it was his boredom and malicious glee at revealing the obvious to a baboon. My distress was honey to him.

"And let me ponder this… Unnecessary. Helios put you in contact with those women in Luster. The crones, as some rudely call them."

"I think the ladies prefer it, actually."

"The crones were coy, that's their game. As you were permitted to depart their presence with your hide, I'll wager they confirmed the magician's slander of my character. Wily monsters, the Corning women. Man-haters, man-eaters. Men are pawns or provender, often both. Word to the wise—never go back there."

Just like that the sun snuffed as a burning wick under a thumb and darkness was all around, held at bay by a few lanterns in the yard, a trickle of light from the open doors on the porch and a handful of windows. The guests milled and drank and laughed above the beautiful music, and several couples assayed a waltz before the dais. I squinted, becoming desperate to catch a glimpse of my comrades, and still couldn't pick them out of the moiling crowd. I swayed as the blood rushed from my head and there were two, no, three, Conrad Paxton's seated in the gathering gloom, faces obscured except for the glinting eyes narrowed in curiosity, the curve of a sardonic smile. "Why would they lie?" I said. "What's in it for them?"

Paxton rose and made as if to take my elbow to steady me, although if I crashed to earth, there wasn't much chance the bony bastard would be able to do more than slow my fall. Much as Blackwood had done, he hesitated and then edged away toward the threshold of the French doors that let into a study, abruptly loath to touch me. "You are unwell. Come inside away from the heat and the noise."

"Hands off. I asked a question."

"My destruction is their motivation and ultimate goal. Each for his or her personal reason. The sorcerer desires the secrets within my vault: the cases of photographic plates, the reels, a life's work. Father's store of esoteric theory. Helios Augustus can practically taste the wickedness that broods there, black as a tanner's chimney. Eadweard's macabre films caused quite a stir in certain circles. They suggest great depths of depravity, of a dehumanizing element inherent in photography. A property of anti-life."

"You're pulling my leg. That's—"

"Preposterous? Absurd? Any loonier than swearing your life upon a book that preaches of virgin births and wandering Jews risen from the grave to spare the world from blood and thunder and annihilation?"

"I've lapsed," I said.

"The magician once speculated to me that he had a plan to create moving images that would wipe minds clean and imprint upon them all manner of base, un-sublimated desires. The desire to bow and scrape, to lick the boots of an overlord. It was madness, yet appealing. How his face animated when he mused on the spectacle of thousands of common folk streaming from theatres, faces slack with lust and carnal hunger. For the magician, Eadweard's lost work is paramount. My enemies want the specimens as yet hidden from the academic community, the plates and reels whispered of in darkened council chambers."

"That what the crones want too? To see a black pope in the debauched Vatican, and Old Scratch on the throne?"

"No, no, those lovelies have simpler tastes. They wish to devour the souls my father supposedly trapped in his pictures. So delightfully primitive to entertain the notion that film can steal our animating force. Not much more sophisticated than the tribals who believe you mustn't point at another person, else they'll die. Eadweard was many, many things, and many of them repugnant. He was not, however, a soul taker. Soul taking is a myth with a single exception. There is but One and that worthy needs no aperture, no lens, no box.

"Look here, John: thaumaturgy, geomancy, black magic, all that is stuff and nonsense, hooey, claptrap, if you will. Certainly, I serve the master and attend Black Mass. Not a thing to do with the supernatural, I'm not barmy. It's a matter of philosophy, of acclimating oneself to the natural forces of the world and the universe. Right thinking, as it were. Ask me if Satan exists, I'll say yes and slice a virgin's throat in the Dark Lord's honor. Ask me if I believe He manipulates and rewards, again yes. Directly? Does He imbue his acolytes with the power of miracles as Helios Augustus surely believes, as the crones believe their old gods do? I will laugh in your face. Satan no more interferes in any meaningful way than God does. Which is to say, by no discernible measure."

"Color me relieved. Got to admit, the old magician almost had my goat. I thought there might be something to all this horseshit mumbo-jumbo."

"Of course, mysticism was invented for the peasantry. You are far out of your depth. You are being turned like a card between masters. The Ace of Clubs. In all of this you are but a blunt instrument. If anyone murdered your father, it was Helios Augustus. Likely by poison. Poison and lies are the sorcerer's best friends."

I took the blackened cocoon from my shirt pocket. So trivial a thing, so withered a husk, yet even as I brandished it between thumb and forefinger, my host shrank farther away until he'd stepped into the house proper and regarded me from the sweep of a velvet curtain, drawn across his face like a cowl or a cape, and for an instant the ice in my heart suggested that it was a trick, that he was indeed the creature of a forsaken angel, that he meant to lull me into complacency and would then laugh and devour me, skin, bones, and soul. Beneath the balcony the music changed; it sizzled and snapped and strange guttural cries and glottal croaks resounded here and there.

A quick glance, no more, but plenty for me to take it in—the guests were *all* pairing now, and many had already removed their clothes. The shorn and scorched patches of bare earth farther out hadn't suffered from the ravages of ponies or cleats. Servants were not reapplying chalk lines; it must've been pitch in their buckets, for one knelt and laid a torch down and flames shot waist high and quickly blossomed into a series of criss-cross angles of an occult nature. The mighty pentagram spanned dozens of yards and it shed a most hellish radiance, which I figured was the point of the exercise. Thus, evidently, was the weekly spectacle at the Paxton estate.

"Don't look so horrified, it's not as if they're going to rut in the field," Paxton said from the safety of the door. "Granted, a few might observe the rituals. The majority will dance and make merry. Harmless as can be. I hadn't estimated you for a prude."

My hand came away from my side wet. I drew the Luger. "I don't care whether they fuck or not," I said, advancing until I'd backed him further into the study. It was dim and antiquated as could be expected. A marble desk and plush chairs, towering stacks of leathery tomes accessed by a ladder on a sliding rail. Obscured by a lush, ornamental tree was a dark statue of a devil missing its right arm. The horned head was intact, though, and its hollow eyes reminded me of the vacuous gaze of the boy in Muybridge's film. "No one is gonna hear it when I put a bullet in you. No one is gonna weep, either. You're not a likeable fella, Mr. Paxton."

"You aren't the first the sorcerer has sent to murder me. He's gathered so many fools over the years, sent them traipsing to their doom. Swine, apes, rodents. Whatever dregs take on such work, whatever scum stoop to such dirty deeds. I'm exhausted. Let this be the end of the tedious affair."

"I'm here for revenge," I said. "My heart is pure." I shot him in the gut.

"The road to Hell, etcetera, etcetera." Paxton slumped against the desk. He painstakingly lighted another cigarette. His silk shirt went black. "Father, the crones, other, much darker personages who shall remain nameless for both our sakes, had sky high ambitions for me when I was born. That's why I went to a surrogate family while Floddie got shuffled to a sty of an orphanage. It must be admitted that I'm a substantial disappointment. An individual of power, certainly. Still, they'd read the portents and dared hope I would herald a new age, that I would be the chosen one, that I would cast down the tyrants and light the great fires of the end days. Alas, here I dwell, a philosopher hermit, a casual entertainer and dilettante of the left-hand path. I don't begrudge their bitterness and spite. I don't blame them for seeking my destruction. They want someone to shriek and bleed to repay their lost dreams. Who better than the architect of their disillusionment?"

To test my theory that no one would notice, or care, and to change the subject, I shot him again. In the thigh this time.

"See, I told you. I'm but a mortal, and now I die." He sagged to the floor, still clutching his cigarette. His eyes glittered and dripped. "Yes, yes, again." And after he took the third bullet, this one in the ribs an inch or two above the very first, he smiled and blood oozed from his mouth. "Frankly, I thought you'd extort me for money. Or use me to bargain for your friends whom you've so quaintly and clumsily searched for since they wandered away a few minutes ago."

"My friends are dead. Or dying. Probably chained in the cellar getting the Broderick with a hammer. It's what I'd do if I were in your shoes." I grudgingly admired his grit in the face of certain death. He'd a lot more pluck than his demeanor suggested.

"I hope your animal paranoia serves you well all the days of your life. Your friends aren't dead. Nor tortured; not on my account. Although, maybe Daniel wasn't satisfied with one double cross. I suppose it's possible he's already dug a hole for you in the woods. May you be so fortunate." He wheezed and his face drained of color, become gauzy in the dimness. After the fit subsided, he gestured at my chest. "Give me the charm, if you please."

I limped to his side and took the cigarette from him and had a drag. Then I placed the cocoon in his hand. He nodded and more blood dribbled forth as he popped the bits of leaf and silk and chrysalis into his mouth and chewed. He said, "A fake. What else could it be?" His voice was fading and his head lolled. "If I'd been born the Antichrist, none of this would've happened. Anyway...I'm innocent. You're bound for the fire, big fellow."

I knelt and grasped his tie to pull him close. "Innocent? The first one was for my dad. Don't really give a damn whether you done him or not, so I'll go with what feels good. And this does indeed feel good. The other two were for your sister and that poor sap in boarding school. Probably not enough fire in Hell for you. Should we meet down there? You'd best get shy of me."

"In a few minutes, then," Paxton said and his face relaxed. When I let loose of his tie, he toppled sideways and lay motionless. Jeeves, or Reynolds, or whatever the butler's name was, opened the door and froze in mid-stride. He calmly assessed the situation, turned sharply as a Kraut infantryman on parade, and shut it again.

Lights from the fires painted the window and flowed in the curtains and made the devil statue's grin widen until everything seemed to warp and I covered my eyes and listened to Dan Blackwood piping and the mad laughter of his thralls. I shook myself and fetched the Thompson and made myself comfortable behind the desk in the captain's chair, and waited. Smoked half a deck of ciggies while I did.

Betting man that I am, I laid odds that either some random goons, Blackwood, or one of my chums, would come through the door fairly soon, and in that order of likelihood. The universe continued to reveal its mysteries a bit later when Helios Augustus walked in, dressed to the nines in yellow and purple silk, with a stovepipe hat and a black cane with a lump of gold at the grip. He bowed, sweeping his hat, and damn me for an idiot, I should've cut him down right then, but I didn't. I had it in my mind to palaver since it had gone so swimmingly with Paxton.

Bad mistake, because, what with the magician and his expert prestidigitation and such, his hat vanished and he easily produced a weapon that settled my hash. For an instant my brain saw a gun and instinctively my finger tightened on the trigger of the Thompson. Or tried to. Odd, thing, I couldn't move a muscle, couldn't so much as bat a lash. My body sat, a big useless lump. I heard and felt everything. No difficulties there, and then I recognized what Helios had brandished was the mummified severed hand he'd kept in his dressing room at The Broadsword Hotel. I wondered when he'd gotten into town. Had Blackwood dialed him on the blower this morning? The way things were going, I half suspected the creepy bastard might've hidden in the shrubbery days ago and waited, patient as a spider, for this, his moment of sweet, sweet triumph.

That horrid, preserved hand, yet clutching a fat black candle captivated me…. I knew from a passage of a book on folklore, read to me by some chippie I humped in college, that what I was looking at must be a hand of glory. Hacked from a murderer and pickled for use in the blackest of magic rituals. I couldn't quite recall what it was supposed to do, exactly. Paralyzing jackasses such as myself, for one, obviously.

"Say, Johnny, did Conrad happen to tell you where he stowed the key to his vault?" The magician was in high spirits. He glided toward me, waltzing to the notes of Blackwood's flute.

I discovered my mouth was in working order. I coughed to clear my throat. "Nope," I said.

He nodded and poured himself a glass of sherry from a decanter and drank it with relish. "Indeed, I imagine this is the blood of my foes."

"Hey," I said. "How'd you turn the Blackwood Boys anyhow?"

"Them? The boys are true believers, and with good reason considering who roams the woods around here. I got my hands on a film of Eadweard's, one that might've seen him burned alive even in this modern age. In the film, young Conrad and some other nubile youths were having congress with the great ram of the black forest. Old Bill stepped from the grove of blood and took a bow. I must confess, it was a spectacular bit of photography. I informed the boys that instead of hoarding Muybridge's genius for myself, it would be share and share alike. Dan and his associates were convinced."

"I'm sorry I asked."

"Does everyone beg you for mercy at the end?"

"The ones who see it coming."

"Do you ever grant quarter?"

"Nope."

"Will *you* beg me for mercy?"

"Sure, why not?"

The magician laughed and snapped his fingers. "Alas! Alack! I would spare you, for sentimental reasons, and because I was such a cad to send The Long and The Short gunning for you, and to curse Donald purely from spite. Unfortunately, 'tis Danny of the Blackwood who means to skin you alive on a corroded altar to Old Bill. Sorry, lad. Entertaining as I'm sure that will prove, I'm on a mission. You sit tight, Uncle Phil needs to see to his prize. Thanks oodles, boy. As the heathens and savages are wont to say, you done good." He ignored the torrent of profanity that I unleashed upon his revelation that he'd killed my father, and casually swirled his elegant cape around his shoulders and used my own matches to strike a flame to the black candle. Woe and gloom, it was a macabre and chilling sight, that flame guttering and licking at dead fingers as he thrust it forth as a torch.

Helios Augustus proved familiar with the layout. He promptly made an adjustment to the devil statue and ten feet away one of the massive bookcases pivoted to reveal a steel door, blank save for a keyhole. The magician drew a deep breath and spent several minutes chanting in Latin or Greek, or bits of both and soon the door gave way with a mere push from his index finger. He threw back his head and laughed. I admit, that sound was so cold and diabolical if I'd been able to piss myself right then, I would've. Then he wiped his eyes and disappeared into a well of darkness and was gone for what felt like an age.

I spent the duration listening to the Blackwood Boys reciting an opera while straining with all of my might and main to lift my hand, turn my head, wiggle a toe, to no avail. This reminded me, most unpleasantly, of soldiers in France I'd seen lying trussed up in bandages at the hospital, the poor bastards unable to blink as they rotted in their ruined bodies. I sweated and tried to reconcile myself with an imminent fate worse than death, accompanied by death. "Hacked to pieces by a band of hillbilly satanists" hadn't ever made my list of imagined ways of getting rubbed out—and as the Samurai warriors of yore meditated on a thousand demises, I too had imagined a whole lot of ways of kicking.

Helios Augustus's candle flame flickered in the black opening. He carried a satchel and it appeared heavily laden by its bulges; doubtless stuffed with Eadweard Muybridge's priceless lost films. He paused to set the grisly hand in its sconce before me on the desk. The candle had melted to a blob of shallow grease. It smelled of burnt human flesh, which I figured was about right. Probably baby fat, assuming my former chippie girlfriend was on the money in her description.

Helios said, "Tata, lad. By the by, since you've naught else to occupy you, it may be in order to inspect this talisman more closely. I'd rather thought you might twig to my ruse back in Olympia. You're a nice boy, but not much of a detective, sorry to say." He waved cheerily and departed.

I stared into the flame and thought murderous thoughts and a glint on the ring finger arrested my attention. The ring was slightly sunken into the flesh, and that's why I hadn't noted it straight away. My father's wedding band. Helios Augustus, that louse, that conniving, filthy sonofawhore, had not only murdered my father by his own admission, but later defiled his grave and chopped off his left hand to make a grotesque charm.

Rage had a sobering effect upon me. The agony from my wounds receded, along with the rising panic at being trapped like a rabbit in a snare and my brain ticked along its circuit, methodical and accountant-like. It occurred to me that despite his callous speech, the magician might've left me a chance, whether intentionally or as an oversight, the devil only knew. I huffed and puffed and blew out the candle, and the invisible force that had clamped me in its vise evaporated. Not one to sit around contemplating my navel, nor one to look askance at good fortune, I lurched to my feet and into action.

I took a few moments to set the curtains aflame, fueling the blaze with the crystal decanter of booze. I wrapped Dad's awful hand in a kerchief and jammed it into my pocket. Wasn't going to leave even this small, gruesome remnant of him in the house of Satan.

An excellent thing I made my escape when I did, because I met a couple of Blackwood's boys on the grand staircase. "Hello, fellas," I said, and sprayed them with hellfire of my own, sent them tumbling like Jack and

Jill down the steps, notched the columns and the walls with bullet holes. I exulted at their destruction. My hand didn't bother me a whit.

Somebody, somewhere, cut the electricity and the mansion went dark as a tomb except for the fire licking along the upper reaches of the balcony and the sporadic muzzle flashes of my trench broom, the guns of my enemies, for indeed those rat bastards, slicked and powdered for the performance, yet animals by their inbred faces and bestial snarls, poured in from everywhere and I was chivvied through the foyer and an antechamber where I swung the Thompson like a fireman with a hose. When the drum clicked empty I dropped the rifle and jumped through the patio doors in a crash of glass and splintered wood, and loped, dragging curtains in my wake, across the lawn for the trees. I weaved between the mighty lines of the burning pentagrams that now merely smoldered, and the trailing edge of my train caught fire and flames consumed the curtains and began eating their way toward me, made me Blake's dread tyger zigzagging into the night, enemies in close pursuit. Back there in the yard echoed a chorus of screams as the top of the house bloomed red and orange and the hillbillies swarmed after me, small arms popping and cracking and it was just like the war all over again.

The fox hunt lasted half the night. I blundered through the woods while the enemy gave chase, and it was an eerie, eerie several hours as Dan Blackwood's pipe and his cousins' fiddle and banjo continued to play and they drove me through briar and marsh and barbwire fence until I stumbled across a lonely dirt road and stole a farm truck from behind a barn and roared out of the Hollow, skin intact. Didn't slow down until the sun crept over the horizon and I'd reached the Seattle city limits. The world tottered and fell on my head and I coasted through a guardrail and came to a grinding halt in a field, grass scraping against the metal of the cab like a thousand fingernails. It got hazy after that.

* * *

Dick sat by my bedside for three days. He handed me a bottle of whiskey when I opened my eyes. I expressed surprise to find him among the living, convinced as I'd been that he and Bly got bopped and dumped in a shallow grave. Turned out Bly had snuck off with some patrician's wife and had a hump in the bushes while Dick accidentally nodded off under a tree. Everything was burning and Armageddon was in full swing when they came to, so they rendezvoused and did the smart thing—sneaked away with tails between legs.

Good news was, Mr. Arden wanted us back in Olympia soonest; he'd gotten into a dispute with a gangster in Portland. Seemed that all was forgiven in regard to my rubbing out The Long and The Short. The boss needed every gun in his army.

Neither Dick nor the docs ever mentioned the severed hand in my pocket. It was missing when I retrieved my clothes and I decided to let the matter drop. I returned to Olympia and had a warm chat with Mr. Arden and everything was peaches and cream. The boss didn't even ask about Vernon. Ha!

He sent me and a few of the boys to Portland with a message for his competition. I bought a brand spanking new Chicago-typewriter for the occasion. I also stopped by The Broadsword where the manager, after a little physical persuasion, told me that Helios Augustus had skipped town days prior on the Starlight Express, headed to California, if not points beyond. Yeah, well, revenge and cold dishes, and so forth. Meanwhile, I'd probably avoid motion pictures and stick to light reading.

During the ride to Portland, I sat in back and watched the farms and fields roll past and thought of returning to Ransom Hollow with troops and paying tribute to the crones and the Blackwood Boys; fantasized of torching the entire valley and its miserable settlements. Of course, Mr. Arden would never sanction such a drastic engagement. That's when I got to thinking that maybe, just maybe I wasn't my father's son, maybe I wanted more than a long leash and a pat on the head. Maybe the leash would feel better in my fist. I chuckled and stroked the Thompson lying across my knees.

"Johnny?" Dick said when he glimpsed my smile in the rearview.

I winked at him and pulled my Homburg down low over my eyes and had a sweet dream as we approached Portland in a black cloud like angels of death.

# THE CARRION GODS
# IN THEIR HEAVEN

The leaves were turning.

Lorna fueled the car at a mom and pop gas station in the town of Poger Rock, population 190. Poger Rock comprised a forgotten, moribund collection of buildings tucked into the base of a wooded valley a stone's throw south of Olympia. The station's marquee was badly peeled and she couldn't decipher its title. A tavern called Mooney's occupied a gravel island half a block down and across the two-lane street from the post office and the grange. Next to a dumpster, a pair of mongrel dogs were locked in coitus, patiently facing opposite directions, Dr. Doolittle's pushmi-pullyu for the twenty-first century. Other than vacant lots overrun by bushes and alder trees, and a lone antiquated traffic light at the intersection that led out of town, either toward Olympia, or deeper into cow country, there wasn't much else to look at. She hobbled in to pay and ended up grabbing a few extra supplies—canned peaches and fruit cocktail, as there wasn't any refrigeration at the cabin. She snagged three bottles of bourbon gathering dust on a low shelf.

The clerk noticed her folding crutch, and the soft cast on her left leg. She declined his offer to carry her bags. After she loaded the Subaru, she ventured into the tavern and ordered a couple rounds of tequila. The tavern was dim and smoky and possessed a frontier vibe with antique flintlocks over the bar, and stuffed and mounted deer heads staring from the walls. A great black wolf snarled atop a dais near the entrance. The bartender watched her drain the shots raw. He poured her another on the house and said, "You're staying at the Haugstad place, eh?"

She hesitated, the glass partially raised, then set the drink on the counter and limped away without answering. She assayed the long, treacherous drive up to the cabin, chewing over the man's question, the morbid implication of his smirk. She got the drift. Horror movies and pulp novels made the conversational gambit infamous; life imitating art. Was she staying at the Haugstad place indeed. Like hell she'd take *that* bait. The townsfolk were strangers to her and she wondered how the bartender knew where she lived. Obviously, the hills had eyes.

Two weeks prior, Lorna had fled into the wilderness to an old hunting cabin with her lover Miranda. Miranda was the reason she'd discovered the courage to leave her husband Bruce, the reason he grabbed a fistful of Lorna's hair and threw her down a flight of concrete stairs in the parking garage of SeaTac airport. That was the second time Lorna had tried to escape with their daughter Orillia. Sweet Orillia, eleven years old next month, was safe in Florida with relatives. Lorna missed her daughter, but slept better knowing she was far from Bruce's reach. He wasn't interested in going after the child; at least not as his first order of business.

Bruce was a vengeful man, and Lorna feared him the way she might fear a hurricane, a volcano, a flood. His rages overwhelmed and obliterated his impulse control. Bruce was a force of nature, all right, and capable of far worse than breaking her leg. He owned a gun and a collection of knives, had done time years ago for stabbing somebody during a fight over a gambling debt. He often got drunk and sat in his easy chair, cleaning his pistol or sharpening a large cruel-looking blade he called an Arkansas Toothpick.

So, it came to this: Lorna and Miranda shacked up in the mountains while Lorna's estranged husband, free on bail, awaited trial back in Seattle. Money wasn't a problem—Bruce made plenty as a manager at a lumber company, and Lorna helped herself to a healthy portion of it when she headed for the hills.

Both women were loners by necessity or device, as the case might be, who'd met at a cocktail party thrown by one of Bruce's colleagues and clicked on contact. Lorna hadn't worked since her stint as a movie theater clerk during college—Bruce insisted she stay home and raise Orillia, and when Orillia grew older, he dropped his pretenses and punched Lorna in the jaw after she pressed the subject of getting a job, beginning a career. She'd dreamed of going to grad school for a degree in social work.

Miranda was a semi-retired artist; acclaimed in certain quarters and much in demand for her wax sculptures. She cheerfully set up a mini studio in the spare bedroom, strictly to keep her hand in. Photography was her passion of late and she'd brought along several complicated and expensive cameras. She was also the widow of a once famous sculptor. Between her work and her husband's royalties, she wasn't exactly rich, but not exactly poor either. They'd survive a couple of months "roughing it." Miranda suggested they consider it a vacation, an advance celebration of "Brucifer's" (her pet name for Lorna's soon to be ex) impending stint as a guest of King County Jail.

She'd secured the cabin through a labyrinthine network of connections. Miranda's second (or was it a third?) cousin gave them a ring of keys and a map to find the property. It sat in the mountains, ten miles from civilization amid high timber and a tangle of abandoned logging roads. The driveway was cut into a steep hillside; a hundred-yard-long dirt track hidden by masses of brush and trees. The perfect bolt-hole.

Bruce wouldn't find them here in the catbird's seat overlooking nowhere.

* * *

Lorna arrived home a few minutes before nightfall. Miranda came to the porch and waved. She was tall; her hair long and burnished auburn, her skin dusky and unblemished. Lorna thought her beautiful; lush and ripe, vaguely Rubenesque. A contrast to Lorna's own paleness, her angular, sinewy build. She thought it amusing that their personalities reflected their physiognomies—Miranda tended to be placid and yielding and sweetly melancholy, while Lorna was all sharp edges.

Miranda helped bring in the groceries—she'd volunteered to drive into town and fetch them herself, but Lorna refused and the reason why went unspoken, although it loomed large. A lot more than her leg needed healing. Bruce had done the shopping, paid the bills, made every decision for thirteen, tortuous years. Not all at once, but gradually, until he crushed her, smothered her, with his so-called love. That was over. A little more pain and suffering in the service of emancipation—figuratively and literally—following a lost decade seemed appropriate.

The Haugstad cabin was practically a fossil and possessed of a dark history that Miranda hinted at, but coyly refused to disclose. It was in solid repair for a building constructed in the 1920s; on the cozy side, even: thick, slab walls and a mossy shake roof. Two bedrooms, a pantry, a loft, a cramped toilet and bath, and a living room with a kitchenette tucked in the corner. The cellar's trapdoor was concealed inside the pantry. She had no intention of going down there. She hated spiders and all the other creepy-crawlies sure to infest that wet and lightless space. Nor did she like the tattered bearskin rug before the fireplace, nor the oil painting of a hunter in buckskins stalking along a ridge beneath a twilit sky, nor a smaller portrait of a stag with jagged horns in menacing silhouette atop a cliff, also at sunset. Lorna detested the idea of hunting, preferred not to ponder where the chicken in chicken soup came from, much less the fate of cattle. These artifacts of minds and philosophies so divergent from her own were disquieting.

There were a few modern renovations—a portable generator provided electricity to power the plumbing and lights. No phone, however. Not that it mattered as her cell reception was passable despite the rugged terrain. The elevation and eastern exposure also enabled the transistor radio to capture a decent signal.

Miranda raised an eyebrow when she came across the bottles of Old Crow. She stuck them in a cabinet without comment. They made a simple pasta together with peaches on the side and a glass or three of wine for dessert. Later, they relaxed near the fire. Conversation lapsed into a comfortable silence until Lorna chuckled upon recalling the bartender's portentous question, which seemed inane rather than sinister now that she was half- drunk and drowsing in her lover's arms. Miranda asked what was so funny and Lorna told her about the tavern incident.

"Man alive, I found something weird today," Miranda said. She'd stiffened when Lorna described shooting tequila. Lorna's drinking was a bone of contention. She'd hit the bottle when Orillia went into first grade, leaving her alone at the house for the majority of too many lonely days. At first it'd been innocent enough: a nip or two of cooking sherry, the occasional glass of wine during the soaps, then the occasional bottle of wine, then the occasional bottle of Maker's Mark or Johnny Walker, and finally, the bottle was open and in her hand five minutes after Orillia skipped to the bus and the cork didn't go back in until five minutes before her little girl came home. Since she and Miranda became an item, she'd striven to restrict her boozing to social occasions, dinner, and the like. But sweet Jesus, fuck. At least she hadn't broken down and started smoking again.

"Where'd you go?" Lorna said.

"That trail behind the woodshed. I wanted some photographs. Being cooped up in here is driving me a teensy bit bonkers."

"So, how weird was it?"

"Maybe weird isn't quite the word. Gross. Gross is more accurate."

"You're killing me."

"That trail goes a long way. I think deer use it as a path because it's really narrow but well-beaten. We should hike to the end one of these days, see how far it goes. I'm curious where it ends."

"Trails don't end; they just peter out. We'll get lost and spend the winter gnawing bark like the Donners."

"You're so morbid!" Miranda laughed and kissed Lorna's ear. She described crossing a small clearing about a quarter mile along the trail. At the far end was a stand of Douglas fir and she didn't notice the tree house until she stopped to snap a few pictures. The tree house was probably as old as the cabin; its wooden planks were bone yellow where they peeked through moss and branches. The platform perched about fifteen feet off the ground, and a ladder was nailed to the backside of the tree....

"You didn't climb the tree," Lorna said.

Miranda flexed her scraped and bruised knuckles. "Yes, I climbed that tree, all right." The ladder was very precarious and the platform itself so rotted, sections of it had fallen away. Apparently, for no stronger reason than boredom, she risked life and limb to clamber atop the platform and investigate.

"It's not a tree house," Lorna said. "You found a hunter's blind. The hunter sits on the platform, camouflaged by the branches. Eventually, some poor hapless critter comes by, and blammo! Sadly, I've learned a lot from Bruce's favorite cable television shows. What in the heck compelled you to scamper around in a deathtrap in the middle of the woods? You could've gotten yourself in a real fix."

"That occurred to me. My foot went through in one spot and I almost crapped my pants. If I got stuck I could scream all day and nobody would hear me. The danger was worth it, though."

"Well, what did you find? Some moonshine in mason jars? D. B. Cooper's skeleton?"

"Time for the reveal!" Miranda extricated herself from Lorna and went and opened the door, letting in a rush of cold night air. She returned with what appeared to be a bundle of filthy rags and proceeded to unroll them.

Lorna realized her girlfriend was presenting an animal hide. The fur had been sewn into a crude cape or cloak; beaten and weathered from great age, and shriveled along the hem. The head was that of some indeterminate predator—possibly a wolf or coyote. Whatever the species, the creature was a prize specimen. Despite the cloak's deteriorated condition, she could imagine it draped across the broad shoulders of a Viking berserker or an Indian warrior. She said, "You realize that you just introduced several colonies of fleas, ticks, and lice into our habitat with that wretched thing."

"Way ahead of you, baby. I sprayed it with bleach. Cooties were crawling all over. Isn't it neat?"

"It's horrifying," Lorna said. Yet, she couldn't look away as Miranda held it at arm's length so the pelt gleamed dully in the firelight. What was it? Who'd worn it and why? Was it a garment to provide mere warmth, or to blend with the surroundings? The painting of the hunter was obscured by shadows, but she thought of the man in buckskin sneaking along, looking for something to kill, a throat to slice. Her hand went to her throat.

"This was hanging from a peg. I'm kinda surprised it's not completely ruined, what with the elements. Funky, huh? A Daniel Boone era accessory."

"Gives me the creeps."

"The creeps? It's just a fur."

"I don't dig fur. Fur is dead. Man."

"You're a riot. I wonder if it's worth money."

"I really doubt that. Who cares? It's not ours."

"Finders keepers," Miranda said. She held the cloak against her bosom as if she were measuring a dress. "Rowr! I'm a wild-woman. Better watch yourself tonight!" She'd drunk enough wine to be in the mood for theater. "Scandinavian legends say to wear the skin of a beast is to become the beast. Haugstad fled to America in 1910, cast out from his community. There was a series of unexplained murders back in the homeland, and other unsavory deeds, all of which pointed to his doorstep. People in his village swore he kept a bundle of hides in a storehouse, that he donned them and became something other than a man, that it was he who tore apart a family's cattle, that it was he who slaughtered a couple of boys hunting rabbits in the field, that it was he who desecrated graves and ate of the flesh of the dead during lean times. So, he left just ahead of a pitchfork-wielding mob. He built this cabin and lived a hermit's life. Alas, his dark past followed. Some of the locals in Poger Rock got wind of the old scandals. One of the town drunks claimed he saw the trapper turn into a wolf and nobody laughed as hard as one might expect. Haugstad got blamed whenever a cow disappeared, when the milk went sour, you name it. Then, over the course of ten years or so a long string of loggers and ranchers vanished. The natives grew restless and it was the scene in Norway all over again."

"What happened to him?"

"He wandered into the mountains one winter and never returned. Distant kin took over this place, lived here off and on the last thirty or forty years. Folks still remember, though." Miranda made an exaggerated face and waggled her fingers. "Booga-booga!"

Lorna smiled, but she was repulsed by the hide, and unsettled by Miranda's flushed cheeks, her loopy grin. Her lover's playfulness wasn't amusing her as it might've on another night. She said, "Toss that wretched skin outside, would you? Let's hit the rack. I'm exhausted."

"Exhausted, eh? Now is my chance to take full advantage of you." Miranda winked as she stroked the hide. Instead of heading for the front door she took her prize to the spare bedroom and left it there. She came back and embraced Lorna. Her eyes were too bright. The wine was strong on her breath. "Told you it was cool. God knows what else we'll find if we look sharp."

\* \* \*

They made fierce love. Miranda was much more aggressive than her custom.

The pain in Lorna's knee built from a small flame to a white blaze of agony and her orgasm only registered as spasms in her thighs and shortness of breath, pleasure eclipsed entirely by suffering. Miranda didn't notice the tears on Lorna's cheeks, the frantic nature of her moans. When it ended, she kissed Lorna on the mouth, tasting of musk and salt, and something indefinably bitter. She collapsed and was asleep within seconds.

Lorna lay propped by pillows, her hand tangled in Miranda's hair. The faint yellow shine of a three-quarter moon peeked over the ridgeline across the valley and beamed through the window at the foot of the bed. She could tell it was cold because their breaths misted the glass. A wolf howled and she flinched, the cry arousing a flutter of primordial dread in her breast. She waited until Miranda's breathing steadied, then crept away. She put on Miranda's robe and grabbed a bottle of Old Crow and a glass and poured herself a dose and sipped it before the main window in the living room.

Thin, fast moving clouds occasionally crossed the face of the moon and its light pulsed and shadows reached like claws across the silvery landscape of rocky hillocks and canyons, and stands of firs and pine. The stars burned a finger-width above the crowns of the adjacent peaks. The land fell away into deeper shadow, a rift of darkness uninterrupted by a solitary flicker of manmade light. She and Miranda weren't welcome; the cabin and its former inhabitants hadn't been either, despite persisting like ticks bored into the flank of a dog. The immensity of the void intimidated her, and for a moment she almost missed Bruce and the comparative safety of her suburban home, the gilded cage, even the bondage. She blinked, angry at this lapse into the bad old way of thinking, and drank the whiskey. "I'm not a damned whipped dog." She didn't bother pouring, but had another pull directly from the bottle.

The wolf howled again and another answered. The beasts sounded close and she wondered if they were circling the cabin, wondered if they smelled her and Miranda, or whether their night vision was so acute they could see her in the window—she half in the bag, a bottle dangling from her hand, favoring her left leg, weak and cut from the herd. She considered the cautionary tale of Sven Haugstad and drank some more. Her head spun. She waited for another howl, determined to answer with her own.

Miranda's arms encircled her. She cupped Lorna's breasts and licked her earlobe, nibbled her neck. Lorna cried out and grabbed Miranda's wrist before she registered who it was, and relaxed. "Holy crap, you almost gave me a heart attack!" The floor creaked horribly, they'd even played a game of chopsticks by rhythmically pressing alternating sections with their shoes, but she hadn't heard her lover cross the room. Not a whisper.

Something metallic snicked and an orange flame reflected in the window and sweet, sharp smoke filled Lorna's nostrils. Miranda gently pressed a cigarette to Lorna's lips. Miranda said, "I needed this earlier, except I was too damned lazy to leave the covers. Better late than never."

"Gawd, you read my mind." Lorna took a drag, then exhaled contentedly. The nicotine mixed with the alcohol did its magic. Her fear of the night land and its creatures receded. "I guess I can forgive you for sneaking up on me since you've offered me the peace pipe. Ahhh, I've fallen off the wagon. You're evil. Did you hear the wolves?"

"Those aren't wolves," Miranda said. She reclaimed the cigarette. She inhaled and the cigarette's cherry floated in the window as her face floated in the window, a blur over Lorna's shoulder. "Those are coyotes."

"No shit?"

"Is that why you're so jumpy? You thought the *wolves* were gonna get you?"

"I'm not jumpy. Well, sheesh—an almost full moon, wolves howling on the moor, er, in the woods. Gotta admit it's all kinda spooky."

"Not wolves. Coyotes. Come to bed…It's chilly."

"Right. Coyotes," Lorna said. "I'm embarrassed. That's like peeing myself over dingoes or raccoons."

Snug under a pile of blankets, Lorna was drifting off to sleep when Miranda said in a dreamy voice, "Actually, coyotes are much scarier than wolves. Sneaky, sneaky little suckers. Eat you up. Lick the blood all up."

"What?" Lorna said. Miranda didn't answer. She snored.

\* \* \*

One morning, a woman who resembled Vivian Leigh at the flowering of her glory knocked on the door. She wore a green jacket and a green and yellow kerchief and yellow sunglasses. Her purse was shiny red plastic with a red plastic strap. Her gloves were white. Her skirt was black and her shoes were also black. She smiled when Lorna opened the door and her lipstick was blood red like the leaves. "Oh, I'm very sorry to disturb you, Ma'am. I seem to be a trifle lost." The woman introduced herself as Beth. She'd gone for a drive in the hills, searching for the Muskrat Creek Campground. "Apparently, I zigged when I should've zagged," she said, and laughed a laugh worthy of the stage. "Speaking of zigzags, do you mind?" She opened an enamel case and extracted a cigarette and inserted it into a silver holder and lighted up with a stick match. It was all very mesmerizing.

Lorna had nearly panicked upon hearing the knock, convinced Bruce had tracked her down. She recovered and invited the woman inside and gave her a cup of coffee. Miranda had gone on her morning walk, which left Lorna with the task of entertaining the stranger while deflecting any awkward questions. She unpacked the road map from her Subaru and spread it across the table. She used a pencil to mark the campgrounds, which were twenty-odd miles from the cabin. Beth had wandered far off course, indeed.

"Thank goodness I came across you. These roads go on forever." Beth sipped her coffee and puffed on her fancy cigarette. She slipped her sunglasses into her purse and glanced around the cabin. Her gaze traveled slowly, weighing everything it crossed. "You are certainly off the beaten path."

"We're private people," Lorna said. "Where's your car?"

Beth gestured toward the road. "Parked around the corner. I didn't know if I could turn around in here, so I walked. Silly me, I broke a heel." She raised her calf to show that indeed yes, the heel of her left pump was wobbly.

"Are you alone?"

"Yes. I was supposed to meet friends at the campgrounds, but I can't reach anybody. No bars. I'm rather cross with them and their directions."

Lorna blinked, taking a moment to realize the woman meant she couldn't get proper phone reception. "Mine works fine. I'd be happy to let you place a call—"

"Thanks anyway, sweetie." Beth had sketched directions inside a notebook. "It'll be a cinch now that I've got my bearings." She finished her coffee, said thanks and goodbye, waving jauntily as she picked her way down the rutted lane.

Lorna started the generator to get hot water for a quick shower. After the shower she made toast and more coffee and sat at the table relaxing with a nice paperback romance, one of several she'd had the foresight to bring along. Out the window, she glimpsed movement among the trees, a low and heavy shape that she recognized as a large dog—no, not a dog, a wolf. The animal almost blended with the rotten leaves and wet brush, and it nosed the earth, moving disjointedly, as if crippled. When it reared on its hind legs, Lorna gasped. Miranda pulled back the cowl of the hide cloak, and leaned against a tree. Her expression was strange; she did not quite appear to be herself. She shuddered in the manner of a person emerging from a trance and walked to where the driveway curved and left three paper plates pressed into the bank. She spaced the plates about three feet apart. Each bore a bull's-eye drawn in magic marker.

Miranda came inside. She'd removed the hide. Her hair was messy and tangled with twigs and leaves. "Who was here?" Her voice rasped like she'd been shouting.

"Some woman looking for a campground." Lorna recounted the brief visit, too unnerved to mention what she'd witnessed. Her heart raced and she was overcome by dizziness that turned the floor to a trampoline. Miranda didn't say anything. She opened a duffel bag and brandished a revolver. She examined the pistol, snapping its cylinder open, then shut. Lorna wasn't particularly conversant with guns, but she'd watched Bruce enough to know this one was loaded. "I thought we were going to discuss it before you bought one," she said.

Miranda rattled a small box of shells and slipped them into the pocket of her vest. "I didn't buy one. A friend gave it to me when I told him about Brucifer. An ex-cop. This sucker doesn't have a serial number."

"There's no reason to be upset. She was lost. That's all."

"Of course she was."

Lorna watched her put the gun in her other pocket. "What's wrong?"

"You've only paid cash, right? No debit card, no credit card?"

"You mean in town?"

"I mean anywhere. Like we agreed. No credit cards."

"Tell me what's wrong. She was lost. People get lost. It's not unheard of, you know. And it doesn't matter. I didn't tell her my name. I didn't tell her anything. She was lost. What was I supposed to do? Not answer the door? Maybe stick that gun in her face and demand some ID?"

"The campgrounds are closed," Miranda said. "I was outside the door while she gave you her shuck and jive. She came in a panel van. A guy with a beard and sunglasses was driving. Didn't get a good look at him."

Lorna covered her face. "I think I'm gonna be sick."

Miranda's boots made loud clomping sounds as she walked to the door. She hesitated for a few moments, then said, "It's okay. You handled her fine. Bruce has got entirely too much money."

Lorna nodded and wiped her eyes on her sleeve. "We'll see how much money he has after my lawyer gets through with him."

Miranda smiled. It was thin and pained, but a smile. She shut the door behind her. Lorna curled into a ball on the bed. The revolver fired, its report muffled by the thick walls of the cabin. She imagined the black holes in the white paper. She imagined black holes drilling through Bruce's white face. Pop, pop, pop.

* * *

Miranda brought Lorna to a stand of trees on the edge of a clearing and showed her the hunting blind. The bloody sun fell into the earth and the only slightly less bloody moon swung, like a pendulum, to replace it in the lower black of the sky. "That is one big bad yellow moon," Miranda said.

"It's beautiful," Lorna said. "Like an iceberg sliding through space." She thought the fullness of the moon, its astral radiance, presaged some kind of cosmic shift. Her blood sang and the hairs on her arms prickled. It was too dark to see the platform in the branches, but she felt it there, heard its timbers squeak in the breeze.

"Been having strange dreams," Miranda said. "Most of them are blurry. Last one I remember was about the people who used to live around here, a long time ago. They weren't gentle folks, that's for sure."

"Well, of course not," Lorna said. "They stuck a deer head over the fireplace and skinned poor hapless woodland critters and hung them in the trees."

"Yeah," Miranda said. She lighted a cigarette. "Want one?"

"No."

Miranda smoked most of her cigarette before she spoke again. "In the latest dream it was winter, frost thick on the windows. I sat on the bearskin rug. Late at night, a big fire crackling away, and an old man, I mean old as dirt, was kicked back in a rocker, talking to me, telling me stuff.

I couldn't see his face because he sat in the shadows. He wore old-timey clothes and a fur jacket, and a hat made out of an animal head. Coyote or wolf. He explained how to set a snare for rabbits, how to skin a deer. The dream changed and jumped around, like dreams do, and we were kneeling on the floor by the carcass of, I dunno what. A possum, I think. The meat was green and soft; it had been dead a while. The old man told me a survivor eats what's around. Then he stuck his face into that mess of stinking meat and took a bite."

"That's a message," Lorna said. "The great universal consciousness is trying to tell you, us, to adapt. Adapt or die."

"Or it could be a dream, full stop."

"Is that what you think?"

"I think it's time to get our minds right. Face the inevitable."

"The inevitable?"

"We're never going to get away," Miranda said.

"Well, that's a hell of an attitude."

"I saw that van again. Parked in that gravel pit just down the road. They're watching us, Lorna."

"Oh, Jesus."

"Don't worry about those bastards. They'll be dealt with."

"Dealt with? Dealt with how?" Lorna's mind flashed to the revolver. The notion of Miranda shooting anyone in cold blood was ridiculous. Yet, here in the dark beyond the reach of rule or reason, such far-fetched notions bore weight. "Don't get any crazy ideas."

"I mean, don't worry yourself sick over the help. Nah, the bigger problem is your husband. How much time is Bruce going to get? A few months? A year? Talk about your lawyer. *Bruce's* lawyer is slick. He might not get anything. Community service, a stern admonition from the judge to go forth and sin no more."

Lorna winced. Stress caused her leg to throb. The cigarette smoke drove her mad with desire. She stifled a sharp response and regarded the moon instead. Her frustration dissolved in the presence of cold, implacable majesty. She said, "I know. It's the way of the world. People like Bruce always win." She'd called Orillia earlier that evening, asked her how things were going at the new school. Orillia didn't want to talk about school; she wanted to know when she could see Daddy again, worried that he was lonely. Lorna had tried to keep emotion from her voice when she answered that Mom and Dad were working through some issues and everything would soon be sorted. Bruce was careful to not hit Lorna in front of their daughter, and though Orillia witnessed the bruises and the breaks, the sobbing aftermath, she seemed to disassociate these from her father's actions.

"There are other ways to win." Miranda was a black shadow against the dead silver grass. "Like you said—adapt or die. The old man showed me. In the beginning you need a prop, but it gets easier when you realize it's all in your head."

It was a long walk back through the woods. Dry leaves crunched beneath their shoes. They locked themselves into the cabin and got ready for bed.

Lorna's dreams had been strange as well, but she'd kept quiet. She wasn't open about such things, not even with Miranda. The ghost of old man Haugstad didn't speak to Lorna; instead, her dreams transported her to the barren slopes above the tree line of the valley. The moon fumed and boiled. She was a passenger in another's body, a body that seethed with profound vitality. The moon's yellow glow stirred her blood and she raced down the slope and into the trees. She smelled the land, tasted it on her lolling tongue, drawing in the scent of every green deer spoor, every droplet of coyote musk, every spackling of piss on rock or shrub. She smelled fresh blood and meat-blacked bone. There were many, many bones scattered across the mountainside. Generational heaps of them—ribs, thighs, horns, skulls. These graveyards were secret places, scattered for miles across deep, hidden caches and among the high rocks.

Lorna stroked Miranda's belly. Miranda's excess had melted away in recent days. She was lean from day-long hikes and skipped meals and her scent was different, almost gamey, her hair lank and coarse. She was restless and she whined in her sleep. She bit too hard when they made love.

Miranda took Lorna's hand and said, "What is it?"

"I'm afraid you're going to leave."

"Oh, where the fuck is this coming from?"

"Something's different. Something's changed. You weren't honest about where you found the coat. The skin."

Miranda chuckled without humor. "Let sleeping dogs lie."

"I'm not in the mood for cute," Lorna said.

"My sweet one. I left out the part that might...frighten you. You're skittish enough."

"I'm also not in the mood for Twenty Questions. What did you mean earlier—the old man showed you?"

"Old man Haugstad told me where to look, what I needed to do."

"In a dream."

"Not in a dream. The day I discovered the blind, a coyote skulked out of the bushes and led me along the path. It was the size of a mastiff, blizzard white on the muzzle and crisscrossed with scars."

"I don't understand," Lorna said, but was afraid she might.

"We're here for a reason. Can't you feel the power all around us? After I lost Jack, after I finally accepted he was gone, I pretty much decided to off myself. If I hadn't met you at that party I probably would've died within a few days. I'd picked out the pills, the clothes I intended to wear, knew exactly where it was going to happen. When was the only question."

Lorna began to cry.

"I won't leave you. But it's possible you might decide not to come with me." Miranda rolled to her opposite side and said nothing more. Lorna slowly drifted to sleep. She woke later while it was still dark. Miranda's side of the bed was a cold blank space. Her clothes were still piled on the floor. In a moment of sublimely morbid intuition, Lorna clicked on a flashlight and checked the spare bedroom where Miranda had taken to hanging the fur cloak from a hook on the door. Of course the cloak was missing.

She gathered her robe tightly, sparing a moment to reflect upon her resemblance to the doomed heroines on any number of lurid gothic horror novel covers and went outdoors into the freezing night. Her teeth chattered and her fear became indistinguishable from the chill. She poked around the cabin, occasionally calling her lover's name, although in a soft tone, afraid to attract the attention of the wolves, the coyotes, or whatever else might roam the forest at night.

Eventually she approached the woodshed and saw the door was cracked open by several inches. She stepped inside. Miranda crouched on the dirt floor. The flashlight was weak and its flickering cone only hinted and suggested. The pelt covered Miranda, concealed her so she was scarcely more than a lump. She whined and shuddered and took notice of the pallid light, and as she stirred, Lorna was convinced that the pelt was not a loose cloak, not an ill-fitted garment, but something else entirely for the manner in which it flexed with each twitch and shiver of Miranda's musculature.

The flashlight glass cracked and imploded. The shed lay in utter darkness except for a thin sliver of moonlight that burned yellow in Miranda's eyes. Lorna's mouth was dry. She said, "Sweetheart?"

Miranda said in a voice rusty and drugged, "Why don't you…go on to bed. I'll be along. I'll come see you real soon." She stood, a ponderous yet lithe, uncoiling motion, and her head scraped the low ceiling.

Lorna got out fast and stumbled toward the cabin. She didn't look over her shoulder even though she felt hot breath on the back of her neck.

* * *

They didn't speak of the incident. For a couple of days they hardly spoke at all. Miranda drifted in and out of the cabin like a ghost and Lorna dreaded to ask where she went in the dead of night, why she wore the hide and nothing else. Evening temperatures dipped below freezing, yet Miranda didn't appear to suffer, on the contrary, she thrived. She hadn't eaten a bite from their store of canned goods, hadn't taken a meal all week. Lorna lay awake staring at the ceiling as the autumn rains rattled the windows.

On the fifth or sixth afternoon, she sat alone at the kitchen table downing the last of the Old Crow. The previous evening she'd experienced two visceral and disturbing dreams. In the first she was serving drinks at a barbeque. There were dozens of guests. Bruce flipped burgers and hob-knobbed with his office chums. Orillia darted through the crowd with a water pistol, zapping hapless adults before dashing away. The mystery woman Beth, and a bearded man in a track suit she introduced as her husband, came over and told her what a lovely party, what a lovely house, what a lovely family, and Lorna handed them drinks and smiled a big dumb smile as Miranda stood to the side and winked, nodding toward a panel van parked nearby on the grass. The van rocked and a coyote emerged from beneath the vehicle, growling and slobbering and snapping at the air. Grease slicked the animal's fur black, made its yellow eyes bright as flames.

A moment later, Lorna was in the woods and chasing the bearded man from the party. His track suit flapped in shreds, stained with blood and dirt. The man tripped and fell over a cliff. He crashed in a sprawl of broken limbs, his mouth full of shattered teeth and black gore. He raised a mutilated hand toward her in supplication. She bounded down and mounted him, licked the blood from him, then chewed off his face. She'd awakened with a cry, bile in her throat.

Lorna set aside the empty bottle. She put on her coat and got the revolver from the dresser where Miranda had stashed it for safekeeping. Lorna hadn't fired the gun despite Miranda's offer to practice. However, she'd seen her lover go through the routine—cock the hammer, pull the trigger, click, no real trick. She didn't need the gun, wouldn't use the gun, but somehow its weight in her pocket felt good. She walked down the driveway, moving gingerly to protect her bum knee, then followed the road to the gravel pit where the van was allegedly parked. The rain slackened to drizzle. Patches of mist swirled in the hollows and the canyons and crept along fern beds at the edges of the road. The valley lay hushed, a brooding giant.

The gravel pit was empty. A handful of charred wood and some squashed beer cans confirmed someone had definitely camped there in the not so distant past. She breathed heavily, partially from the incessant throb in her knee, partially from relief. What the hell would she have done if the assholes her husband sent were on the spot roasting wienies? Did she really think people like that would evaporate upon being subjected to harsh language? Did she really have the backbone to flash the gun and send them packing John Wayne style?

She thought the first muffled cry was the screech of a bird, but the second shout got her attention. Her heart was pounding when she finally located the source about a hundred yards farther along the road. Tire tracks veered from the narrow lane toward a forty-foot drop into a gulch of trees and boulders. The van had landed on its side. The rear doors were sprung, the glass busted. She wouldn't have noticed it all the way down there if not for the woman crying for help. Her voice sounded weak. But that made sense—Beth had been trapped in the wreck for several days, hadn't she? One snip of the brake line and on these hills it'd be all over but the crying. Miranda surely didn't fuck around, did she? Lorna bit the palm of her hand to stifle a scream.

"Hey," Miranda said. She'd come along as stealthily as the mist and lurked a few paces away near a thicket of brambles. She wore the mangy cloak with the predator's skull covering her own, rendering her features inscrutable. Her feet were bare. She was naked beneath the pelt, her lovely flesh streaked with dirt and blood. Her mouth was stained wine-dark. "Sorry, honeybunch. I really thought they'd have given up the ghost by now. Alas, alack. Don't worry. It won't be long. The birds are here."

Crows hopped among the limbs and drifted in looping patterns above the ruined van. They squawked and squabbled. The woman yelled something unintelligible. She wailed and fell silent. Lorna's lip trembled and her nose ran with snot. She swept her arm to indicate their surroundings. "Why did you bring me here?"

Miranda tilted her misshapen head and smiled a sad, cruel smile. "I want to save you, baby. You're weak."

Lorna stared into the gulch. The mist thickened and began to fill in the cracks and crevices and covered the van and its occupants. There was no way she could navigate the steep bank, not with her injury. Her cell was at the cabin on the table. She could almost hear the clockwork gears of the universe clicking into alignment, a great dark spotlight shifting across the cosmic stage to center upon her at this moment in time. She said, "I don't know how to do what you've done. To change. Unless that hide is built for two."

"Don't worry, baby." Miranda took her hand and led her back to the cabin, and tenderly undressed her. She smiled faintly when she retrieved the revolver and set it on the table. She kissed Lorna and her breath was hot and foul. Then she stepped back and began to pull the hide away from her body and as it lifted so did the underlying skin, peeling like a scab. Blood poured down Miranda's chest and belly and pattered on the floorboards. The muscles of her cheeks and jaw bunched and she hissed, eyes rolling, and then it was done and the dripping bundle was free of her red-slicked flesh. Lorna was paralyzed with horror and awe, but finally stirred and tried to resist what her lover proffered. Miranda cuffed her temple, stunning her. She said, "Hold still, baby. You're gonna thank me," and draped the cloak across Lorna's shoulders and pulled the skullcap of the beast over Lorna's eyes.

"You came here for this?" Lorna said as the slimy and overheated pelt cupped her and enclosed her. The room went in and out of focus.

"No, babe. I just followed the trail and here we are. And it's good. You'll see how good it is, how it changes everything. We've been living in a cage, but that's over now."

"My god, I loved you." Lorna blinked the blood from her eyes. She glanced over and saw the revolver on the table, blunt and deadly and glowing with the dwindling light. She grabbed the weapon without thought and pressed it under Miranda's chin and thumbed the hammer just as she'd seen it done. Her entire body shook. "You thought I'd just leave my daughter behind and slink off to Never-Never Land without a word? Are you out of your fucking mind?"

"Give it a minute," Miranda said. The fingers of her left hand stroked the pelt. "One minute. Let it work its magic. You'll see everything in a whole new way. Come on, sweetie." She reached for the revolver and it barked and twisted in Lorna's hands.

Lorna didn't weep. Her insides were stone. She dropped the gun and swayed in place, not focusing on anything. The light began to fade. She made her way outside and sat on the porch. She could smell everything and strange thoughts rushed through her mind.

There was a moment between twilight and darkness when she almost managed to tear free of the hide and begin making the calls that would return her to the world, her daughter, the apocalyptic showdown with the man who'd oppressed her for too long. The moment passed, was usurped by an older and much more powerful impulse. Her thoughts turned to the woods, the hills, a universe of dark, sweet scent. The hunt.

\* \* \*

Two weeks later, a hiker spotted a murder of crows in a raucous celebration as they roosted around the wrecked van. He called emergency services. Men and dogs and choppers swarmed the mountainside. The case made all of the papers and ran on the local networks for days. Investigators found two corpses—an adult male and an adult female—in the van. The cause of death was blunt force trauma and prolonged exposure to the elements. Further examination revealed that the brake lines of the van were sawed through, indicative of homicide. The homicide theory was supported by the discovery of a deceased adult female on the floor of a nearby cabin. She'd died of a single bullet wound to the head. A fourth individual who'd also lived on the premises remained missing and was later presumed dead. Tremendous scrutiny was directed at the missing woman's estranged husband. He professed his innocence throughout the subsequent trial. That he'd hired the deceased couple to spy on his wife didn't help his case.

Years later, a homicide detective wrote a bestseller detailing the investigation of the killings. Tucked away as a footnote, the author included a few esoteric quotes and bits of trivia; among these were comments by the Chief Medical Examiner who'd overseen the autopsies. According to the ME, it was fortunate picture ID was present on scene for the deceased. By the time the authorities arrived, animals had gotten to the bodies, even the one in the cabin. The examiner said she'd been tempted to note in her report that in thirty years she'd never seen anything so bizarre or savage as these particular bites, but wisely reconsidered.

# THE SIPHON

Lancaster graduated from college in 1973 and landed a position in the sales department of a well-known Wichita company that manufactured camping gear. He hated the outdoors but was naturally manipulative, an expert at affecting sincerity and bright-eyed chumminess of variable intensity. Despite this charm that wowed the socks off clients, he never made much headway with management or co-workers, two species immunized against snake oil and artifice.

Around Halloween of 1989, he accepted a job as a field representative with another Wichita firm called Roache Enterprises. His farewell party was attended by four department associates, a supervisor, and a custodian. The supervisor brought a single-layer white cake and somebody spiked the punch with bourbon. His boss projected an old staff picture on the slide panel—Lancaster isolated in the foreground, his expression a surprised snarl, uncomfortably reminiscent of the candid shot of an infamous serial killer who'd been electrocuted by the state of Florida earlier that year. Lancaster was better looking, much smoother, were such a thing possible.

The conference room was brown and yellow, the tables and chairs yellow, bleached by fluorescent strips. Later that institutional light would seep into Lancaster's dreams. The hum of the lights. The cake, a rib bone scalloped to the marrow. The lights. The hum. He dreamed of the two women he'd loved and left when he was young and reckless, before he'd matured and steadied, before he'd learned to maintain his great control.

He dreamed how their pleas and imprecations were abruptly stilled, how their faces became empty as the buzzing moon.

He would awaken from such nightmares and grope for the special wooden box in its secret place in the dresser. The box represented that window into a brief, agonized segment of his early post college years; the red blur he refused to examine except in moments of dire want. A small lacquered coffer, dead black with a silver clasp. Dead black and cool to the touch, always cool as if stored in a refrigerator rather than a drawer. Lancaster needed the box, its contents, needed them with a fevered intensity because they fulfilled the hunger at his core, because the switch that had originally been thrown to motivate and necessitate his acquisition of these trophies clicked off as arbitrarily as it had been clicked on and with it his will to pursue, to physically enact his desires. Thus he'd sift through the box of treasures, move his lips in wordless naming of each precious trinket until his mind quieted. Until the humming of the fly in the mantle of the light ceased. Until the humming of the moon ceased and he could sleep again.

* * *

Roache Enterprises was founded in 1963 during the height of the Cold War when it manufactured guidance control systems for cruise missiles. Modern-era Roache retained 170,000 full-time employees around the globe. The company dealt in electronics; plastics; chemical engineering; asphalt; irrigation systems; sugar, rubber, and cotton plantations; data mining; modular housing; and a confounding array of other endeavors. The Roache Brothers were five billionaires who'd retreated to South America compounds and the French Riviera. The public hadn't seen them—except for annual state of the corporation recorded video addresses—in twenty years. A board of regents ran the show from headquarters in France, India, Scotland, England, and of course, Kansas.

Lancaster spent months abroad, jetting between continents. He'd married once, a union only a mayfly might've envied, which had resulted in a daughter, Nancy, now an adult living in Topeka whom he saw on Christmas and sometimes Easter. The rest of his family was scattered: father dead, mother living in a trailer park in Tennessee, and two sisters in Washington State whom he had no real contact with since college.

Incapable of love, its intricacies and necessities a mystery to him, he was fortunately content with the life of a gentleman bachelor and disappeared into the wider world. His job was generally one of information gathering and occasional diplomacy—a blackmailer or flatterer, depending upon the assignment. Charlatans were kings in the corporate culture of Roache, a culture that was the antithesis of the blue collar aesthetic of his former company. Lancaster excelled in this niche and Roache rewarded him accordingly. He possessed apartments in Delhi and Edinburgh, and standing reservations at luxury hotels in places such as Denmark, Paris, and New York. He'd come a long way since peddling camp stoves and sleeping bags.

The National Security Agency reached out to Lancaster in 1991 while he vacationed at White Sands Beach, Hawaii. He was invited aboard a yacht owned by the friend of the friend of a former client who did business with Roache Enterprises on a piecemeal basis. The yacht-owner was named Harold Hoyte. Hoyte and his wife Blanche, a ripe and sensual ex-B-movie actress who'd starred under an assumed name in a couple of Russ Meyer's films, owned an import business; this provided cover for their activities as senior operatives of the Agency, the bulk of which revolved around recruitment and handling.

They had dinner with two other couples on the deck of the *Ramses*, followed by wine and pills and hideously affected slow-dancing to Harold Hoyte's expansive collection of disco. Harold went ashore, ostensibly to locate a couple of fellow revelers who'd gotten lost on the way to the party, and Blanche promptly led Lancaster into the master suite and seduced him to KC and the Sunshine Band on a king-size bed washed in the refracted shimmer of a glitter ball.

Harold Hoyte made a pitch for Lancaster to join the NSA in the wee hours of the morning as they shared the last joint and the dregs of the scotch. Lancaster declined. A double life simply wasn't his style. He told Hoyte he had a good thing going with Roache and who needed a poisoned umbrella tip jammed in one's ass, anyway?

Harold Hoyte smiled and said, no harm no foul. If he changed his mind… And an unlabeled video cassette of Lancaster fucking Mrs. Hoyte with theatrical flourishes soon arrived at the front desk of his hotel. That a duplicate might anonymously find its way to the Roache corporate offices was implicit. Roache was protective of its business associations large and small. They wouldn't take kindly to Lancaster's salacious escapades with the wife of a client, considering the ruin such an affair could bring to a lucrative contract were Mr. Hoyte to muster and bluster mock outrage at being cuckolded by a company representative. The Hoytes had caught him in the old honey trap. He didn't feel too angry—it was their field of expertise. Besides, spying might agree with him.

Three weeks later, he was officially an asset of the NSA. He soon learned several colleagues at Roache Enterprises moonlighted for the government. The company had eyes everywhere the US needed them. It added a new and unpredictable wrinkle to Lancaster's routine, although the life of an occasional spy didn't prove particularly thrilling. Certainly it resembled nothing of bestselling potboilers or action flicks. Mostly it came down to taking a few pictures, following strangers for a day or two, and occasionally smuggling a memory stick or something as low-tech as a handwritten code across international borders.

The upside was it motivated him to get into shape and take Judo for a while—weren't spies supposed to know Judo in case of a scrape? He'd watched the original *Manchurian Candidate* eight times; the version where Sinatra got into a knockdown drag-out fight with a foreign agent. To be on the safe side, he also bought a .38 automatic and got accurate with it at the range. He went unarmed abroad because of travel restrictions, but carried it almost everywhere while in the States. He continued to carry until his enthusiasm cooled and he stuck the gun in a shoebox and forgot it. Around then he also stopped attending Judo classes.

One night in the wake of 9/11 and the untimely deaths of forty-seven Roache employees who'd staffed an office in the North Tower, he got together for drinks with another asset high up the food chain at corporate. They were drunk when Lancaster asked him what he thought of running errands for the Agency. The exec shook his head, eyes bleary from too many bourbons. "Not what I expected. Pretty fucking boring, you ask me. I guess I'm kind of taken aback by all the satanists."

\* \* \*

The Aughts passed.

Following a six-month lull of contact with the NSA, Lancaster received a call from his current handler, Tyrone Clack. Clack took over for the Hoytes when they sailed on toward retirement and their golden years back in 2003. All communications occurred via phone—Lancaster had never even seen a photo of the agent. Clack informed him that the Agency was interested in acquiring intelligence on a naturalized citizen named Dr. Lucas Christou. The good doctor, who'd been born in Athens and transplanted to the US during adolescence, was a retired chair of the anthropology department of some tiny school near Kansas City called Ossian University. He'd become reclusive since then, seldom appearing in public, content to withdraw from society to an isolated estate.

Christou had emerged from his hermitage and would be hosting a foreign national named Rawat, a minor industrialist entering the US on business with Roache. All that was required of Lancaster was to take the doctor's measure, get to know him a bit, soften him up for possible future developments. No further explanation for the agency's interest was forthcoming and Lancaster didn't press. None of it titillated him anymore. He'd do as requested and hear nary a peep afterward. A typical, menial task. A mindless task, in fact.

Considering his superstar status as a professional schmoozer, the scheme didn't prove difficult. He returned to Wichita and manipulated events until a big cheese at corporate asked him pretty please to entertain a small party that had come to town for a tour of a cluster of empty corporate properties outside the city. Strip mall-style office buildings that had been hastily built, then left in quasi abandonment.

The guests included the potential client, Mr. Rawat, and his American companion Kara, and a bodyguard named Dedrick; the Cooks, a money-eyed New York couple who'd previously partnered on land deals with Mr. Rawat; and, of course, Dr. Christou.

All of this was explained by Vicky Diamond, an administrative assistant to the Big Cheese himself. Ms. Diamond was a shark; Lancaster noted this first thing. Youngish, but not really, dark hair, dark eyes, plenty of makeup to confuse the issue, a casual-chic dresser. Lancaster thought she smiled so much because she liked to show her teeth. She handed him dossiers on the principles—Mr. Rawat and the Cooks—and suggested an itinerary. He appreciated how she put her fingerprints on the project without overcommitting. Should things progress smoothly, she'd get much of the credit. If the sales pitch tanked, Lancaster would find himself on the hook. He liked her already.

* * *

The group met on Friday morning for breakfast at a French café, followed by a carefully paced tour of downtown landmarks. Lunch was Italian, then onward to the Museum of Treasures and a foray to quaint Cowtown, which delighted the Cooks and, more importantly, Mr. Rawat, and was at least tolerated by the others.

Lancaster had slipped Cowtown into the schedule simply to tweak Ms. Diamond as he suspected she'd fear the excessive display of Midwest provincialism. Judging from the glare he received, his assessment was on the mark. He'd softened the blow by reserving one of six tables at a tiny, hole-in-the-wall restaurant that served authentic Indian cuisine rivaling anything he'd tasted in Delhi or Mumbai. Mr. Rawat was a cool customer in every sense of the word. Elegant in his advancing years, his black hair shone like a helmet, his aged and hardened flesh gleamed like polished wood. His watch was solid gold. Even the goon Dedrick who lurked in the background, ready to intercept any and all threats, was rather classy via proximity with his long, pale hair and black suit and fancy eyeglasses that slotted him as a burly legal professional rather than a bodyguard.

Mr. Rawat raised a glass of Old Monk to Lancaster and tipped him a slight wink of approval. Dining went into the nine o'clock hour, after which they repaired to the historic and luxurious Copperhill Hotel and made for the lounge, a velvet and mirrored affair with double doors open to the grand ballroom.

Everything was going exactly as Lancaster planned until Dr. Christou and Mr. Rawat began discussing world folklore and demonology with a passion that turned heads at nearby tables. This vein was central to Dr. Christou's studies. He'd published numerous works over the course of four decades in academia, the most noteworthy a treatise called *The Feral Heart,* which documented cases of night terrors and the mythology of the living dead in the Balkans and the Greek Isles. Mr. Rawat had come across the book shortly after its publication in 1971 and written a lengthy letter taking the professor to task for his fanciful reportage. This initiated what developed into a lifelong correspondence and apparently adversarial friendship.

Dr. Christou was broad through shoulders and chest. His large head was bald except for a silvery fringe, and his mustache and beard were white streaked with black. He wore a vintage suit and three rings—two on the left hand, one on the right. He drank copiously: Canadian Club. *These days a proper Greek drinks scotch, but as a culture-strapped American, a Canadian import will suffice.* Lancaster couldn't help but notice he resembled the bluff and melodramatically distinguished actors who populated Saturday night horror features of yesteryear; a physically imposing relative of Christopher Lee. The doctor said to Mr. Rawat, "I don't pretend to know the truth, my friend. There are cracks in the world. These cracks are inhabited by…marvels undreamt of in our philosophies."

"We have known each other for an age," Mr. Rawat said, "and I am still uncertain where the truth ends and the bullshit begins with you."

"I think the subject of night terrors is fascinating," Mrs. Cook said. She and her husband were slightly younger than Mr. Rawat and Dr. Christou, around Lancaster's age, a year or two shy of senior discounts and social security checks. The couple were gray and heavyset, habitual tans as faded as ancient tattoos. Mr. Cook wore a heavy tweed jacket, and his wife a pattern dress and pearls that were slightly behind modern fashion. She'd drunk her share of gin and tonic.

"Francine majored in literature," Mr. Cook said, gesturing with his tumbler of Johnnie Walker Blue. "The classics—Henry James, Wilde, Menken, Camus, Conrad. *That* lot."

"Actually, I prefer Blackwood and Machen during the proper season. When the leaves are falling and the dark comes early and stays. *The Horla*, by Maupassant. There's a fine one regarding sleep paralysis and insanity."

"A demon that creeps into the bedchamber and squats upon its victim's chest. That particular legend is prevalent in many cultures," Dr. Christou said.

"An oldie, but a goodie," Lancaster said, beginning to feel the weight of his liquor. Ms. Diamond slashed him with a look.

"And thoroughly debunked," Mr. Rawat said. "Like *déjà vu* and near-death experiences. Hallucinations, hypnogogic delusions. Nothing sinister. No sign of the numinous, nor the unholy for that matter."

"You were so much more fun as a lad," Dr. Christou said, smiling.

"I come by my skepticism honestly. There was a time I believed supernatural manifestations possible. Lamias, *vorvolakas*, lycanthropes, the Loch Ness Monster—"

"*Rakshasa.*"

"Yes, *Rakshasa.* UFOs, spoon-bending, levitation, spontaneous combustion—"

"Spontaneous erections!"

"What, you don't believe in *Rakshasas?*" A sallow, pinch-faced man in a white jacket at the adjoining table leaned forward and partially across Lancaster so the others could hear him. His tie dipped into Lancaster's mostly empty glass of Redbreast. The man was of indeterminate age and smelled of first-class cigarettes and designer cologne. His skull was oddly pointed and hairless, dull flesh speckled with liver spots. He'd styled his mustache into a Fu Manchu. "Sorry, sorry. How rude of me. I'm Gregor Blaylock. These are my comrades, Christine, Rayburn, and Luther. My research team." The trio of graduate students were handsome and smartly dressed—the men in jackets and turtlenecks, the woman in a tunic and skirt. Both men were lean and sinewy; sweat glittered on their cheeks. The woman wore bright red lipstick. Her dark skin was flawless. She stroked Mr. Blaylock's shoulder, a pairing of youth and age that was eerily congruous to that of Mr. Rawat and his escort Kara.

Dr. Christou laughed and stood to shake hands. "Gregor! Good to meet in person at last. What great coincidence has brought us together?"

"Oh, you know there are no coincidences, Lucas."

Ms. Diamond quickly made further introductions as the men pushed the tables together so the newcomers might join the festivities. Lancaster wasn't certain of the new peoples' nationalities. Even listening to Mr. Blaylock speak proved fruitless to solving that riddle. Perhaps Asian-heritage and a European education accounted for the man's exotic features and the flattening of his accent. It was odd, very odd. Evidently, Mr. Blaylock was also an anthropology professor, and another of Dr. Christou's legion of fans and correspondents, but details weren't forthcoming, just the gibberish of mutual recollection that left all save its intimates in the fog. He finally gave in and said, "If I may be so bold, where are you from? Originally, that is."

Mr. Blaylock said, "Why, I was born here. We all were born here." He inclined his head to include his companions. Something in the curl of his lip, his archness of tone, indicated *here* didn't necessarily refer to Kansas or the heartland, but rather the continent, if not the world itself. So Mr.

Blaylock was that smug species of academic who delighted in *double entendre* and puns. Asshole. Lancaster drained his whiskey, masking a sneer.

Ms. Diamond pressed against Lancaster as a spouse might and muttered, "What the hell are you doing?" She maintained her pearly shark smile for the audience.

"It's a fair question," Mr. Blaylock said, as if he'd somehow overheard the whisper. "Mr. Lancaster, you've been around the block, yeah?"

"I've heard the owl hoot," Lancaster said. "And the Sri Lankan Frogmouth too."

"I hear you. You Limeys speak your minds. You're inquisitive. No harm. I approve."

"Not *much* harm," Ms. Diamond said.

"You are exceedingly generous, Mr. Blaylock. But I'm American."

"Oh, yeah? Odd. You must spend loads of time on the island."

Dr. Christou said, "Our kind patron heard a Frogmouth hoot. Have you seen a *Rakshasa*, perhaps?"

"Not in Kansas," Mr. Blaylock said.

"What's a *Rakshasa?*" Mr. Cook said.

"It's a flesh-eating monster from Indian mythology, dear," Mrs. Cook said. "There are packs of them roaming about in classical Indian literature, such as the *Mahabharata*."

Dr. Christou said, "I've not encountered one either, nor do I know anyone with firsthand knowledge. However, in 1968 I visited a village on the Greek island of Aphra and interviewed the locals, including a Catholic priest, who were thoroughly convinced *vorvolakas* stalked them. The priest showed me a set of photographs taken by a herdsman that were rather convincing."

"Ha! The ones in *The Feral Heart* were far from convincing, old friend. Very, very far."

"Certainly the lighting was poor. Sunset, so the contrast of light and darkness was jarring. Of course, shrinking them down to fit the page also compromised the quality."

"Was there a creature in the pictures? How exciting," Mrs. Cook said.

"Eh? You haven't read his *famous* book?" Mr. Rawat said.

"In fact, yes. I read books for the words, not the pictures."

"There were at least four creatures, actually," Dr. Christou said. "The shepherd spied them emerging from a crypt in the hills at dusk. The man was on a bluff and they glared up at him. Horrifying once you realize what you're dealing with, I assure you."

"The goat herder took a picture of *something*," Mr. Rawat said. "To settle the matter, the film should be sent to a laboratory and analyzed."

"Alas, that is impossible," Mr. Christou said. "I returned them to the priest after they were copied into the book. The village was abandoned in 1970, its inhabitants scattered along the mainland. What became of the herdsman or the film remains a mystery."

"Rubbish," Mr. Rawat said. "I've studied the photos a million times. Our nameless shepherd captured images of youthful vagabonds. Perhaps grave-robbers at rest, if one is inclined toward drama."

"No mystery about the missing film," Mr. Blaylock said. "When the Greek government repatriated the villagers to the mainland I'm sure such materials were confiscated or lost. You mentioned a priest—perhaps the Church spirited away the evidence for secret study. Too convenient?"

"Too conspiratorial, I'd think," Lancaster said. "Most of the tinfoil hats amongst the clergy were exiled to the fringes by the '70s, were they not?"

"You are familiar with the Eastern Church?" Mr. Rawat said, raising an eyebrow.

"There was this girl I met in Athens who'd gone astray from ecclesiastical upbringing in a big way. She gave me the history lesson. The infighting and intrigue, the conspiracies."

"I bet," Ms. Diamond said.

"Life is full of little conspiracies," Dr. Christou said and looked at Mr. Blaylock. "Imagine running into *you* here of all places. I thought you lived in British Colombia."

Mr. Cook said, "What were those other critters you mentioned earlier? A *vorvo*-something?" He sounded bored.

"Vorvolakas," Mr. Rawat said.

"Vorvo-whatsis?"

"Blood-sucking undead monster from Greek mythology, dear," Mrs. Cook said. "There are scads of them in the old writings of the Eastern Church."

"There's also that Boris Karloff movie," Mr. Rawat said. He smiled coolly and sipped his rum. "You can watch the whole thing on the internet.

I'm certain my esteemed colleague has done so in the name of research."

Lancaster said, "Val Lewton's film. Scared me pantless when I was a wee lad. What a great old flick."

"I like you more and more. *Yia mas*!" Dr. Christou knocked back yet another Canadian Club.

"Val Lewton," Mr. Cook said, his glazed eyes brightening. "Now you're talking. My dad owned a chain of theaters. Lewton was a hell of an auteur, as the kids say."

"Oh, honey." Mrs. Cook smiled with benign condescension and patted her husband's cheek so it jiggled. "Val Lewton? Really? Goodness."

"Hellenic vampire tradition is quite rich," Mr. Christou said. "The damned rise from their graves—day or night—and creep through villages, rapping on doors, tapping on windows, imitating the cries of animals and children. It is said one must never answer a door after dark on the first knock."

Mrs. Cook said, "As I understand it, Grecian vampires are actually more akin to shape changers. Lycanthropes and what have you."

"Quite right, dear lady! Quite right!" Dr. Christou said. "The Balkan Wars led to a minor usurpation by the Slavic vampire myth of the Greek antecedent. Or, I should say, a co-option, though who ultimately co-opted whom is open to debate. Ah, you would've been a much brighter assistant than the clods I was assigned on my expeditions. And lovelier to boot!"

"Oh, hush, Doctor," Mrs. Cook said, casually patting her hair as she cast about for the waiter. "Seriously, although you're the expert, doesn't it seem plausible that these legends—the Rakshasa, the lycanthropes and vampires, the graveyard ghouls, the horrors of Dunsany, Moses, and Lovecraft, are variations on a theme?"

"If by plausible you mean impossible," Mr. Rawat said.

"Certainly," Mr. Blaylock said. "And a hundred other beasties from global mythology. Each iteration tailored to the traditions and prejudices of individual cultures. However, as Mr. Rawat so elegantly declared, it's rubbish." He smiled slyly. "Except for ghosts. The existence of ghosts is a theory I can get behind."

There were more rounds of drinks accompanied by tales of werewolves, vampires, and other things that went bump in the night. An orchestra appeared and began to play classics of the 1930s. The Cooks ventured unsteadily onto the dance floor, and gallant Mr. Rawat escorted Ms. Diamond after them—she, ramrod stiff and protesting to no avail. Mr. Rawat's continental chauvinism doubtless nettled her no end.

Lancaster excused himself to visit the restroom. He pissed in the fancy urinal and washed his hands and dried them on a fancy scented towel. He checked his watch in the lobby, decided to risk a few moments away from the party, and ducked into the stairwell and lighted a cigarette. Moments later Mr. Blaylock and Dr. Christou barged through the door, drinks in hand, Dedrick hot on their heels, a pained expression replacing his customary stoicism. Dr. Christou and Mr. Rawat immediately lighted cigarettes. Both smoked Prima Lux. "Ah, great minds!" the doctor said, grinning at Lancaster, who covered his annoyance with a friendly mock salute.

A few minutes later, cigarettes smoked and drinks drunk, everyone headed back to the table. Lancaster did the gentlemanly deed of holding the door. Dr. Christou hesitated until the others had gone ahead. He said in a low voice, "I confess an abiding fondness for Boris Karloff and Val Lewton. Anyone who holds them dear is first class by my lights." The doctor leaned slightly closer to Lancaster, scorching him with whiskey breath. "In recent years I've become convinced the priest of Aphra was duped by the shepherd. Those cemetery photographs were surely a hoax. Which is a damned shame because I think there truly was an extraordinary event occurring in that village." He laid his very large hand upon Lancaster's shoulder. This drunken earnestness would've been comical except for the glimmer of a tear in the corner of the aged scholar's eye. "Please extend my apologies to our fair company. That last drink was a bridge too far. I'm off to my quarters."

Lancaster wondered if the evening could possibly become more surreal. He watched in bemusement as the big man trundled away and boarded an elevator.

He returned to the ballroom where Ms. Diamond sat alone at the table. She watched the others dance, her mouth sullen. He sat next to her and, feeling expansive from the booze, said, "I have a bottle of twelve-year-old scotch back at the Chateau." His blue eyes usually had an effect on women. He was also decently muscled from a regimen of racquetball and swimming. He assiduously colored the gray from his expensively styled hair, and all of this combined to smooth the rough edges of advancing age, to create the illusion of a man in his late forties, the urbane, chisel-jawed protagonist of sex-pill commercials rather than a paunchy playboy with stretch marks and pattern baldness sliding into the sunset years. But Ms. Diamond was having none of it.

"I think you also probably have a dozen STDs," she said. "Half of them exotic and likely incurable by fire."

"Well, I don't like to brag," he said.

The group dispersed, shuffling off to their respective rooms, and Lancaster shook the hands of the men and kissed the hands of the ladies—Kara's skin tasted of liquor, and Mrs. Cook's was clammy and scaly and bitter. He glanced at her face, and her eyes were heavy-lidded, her thick mouth upturned with matronly satisfaction at his discomfort.

* * *

Lancaster hailed a cab and made it to his townhouse a few minutes after 2 a.m. Nothing spectacular—two bedrooms, a bathroom with a deep whirlpool tub and granite everything, and a kitchen with wood cabinets and digital appliances. In the living room, lush track lighting, thick carpet, and a selection of authentic-looking Monet and van Gogh knockoffs, a half-dozen small marble sculptures imported from Mediterranean antique shops, a gas fireplace and modest entertainment center, and of course, a wet bar tucked opposite bay windows with a view of the river.

He wasn't in a steady relationship. His previous girlfriend, a Danish stewardess twenty-five years his junior, had recently married a pilot and retired to "make babies," as she put it in the Dear John email. He dialed the escort service and asked for one of the girls he knew. The receptionist informed him that person was unavailable, so he requested Trina, a moderately attractive brunette who'd stayed over a few months back, and this time he was in luck, his Girl Friday would be along in forty-five minutes. He dropped his coat into an oversized leather chair, hit the remote to dim the lights, a second time to ignite a romantic blaze in the hearth, and once more to summon the ghost of Jeff Healey through speakers concealed behind a pair of African elephant statuettes.

The drink and Ms. Diamond's dragon lady glare had worked him over. That and the bizarre dinner chatter and the raw emotion flowing from ponderous Dr. Christou. Lancaster brought forth the special box, currently hidden upon a shelf inside a teak cabinet that housed his cigars and collection of foreign coins. Tonight he needed to gaze within the box, to drink it with his eyes, to satiate the nameless desire that welled from his deepest primordial self.

He sat for a while in the thrall of conflicting emotions. The ritual calmed him less than usual. He shut the box and returned it to its cubby. His breath was labored.

Cigarette in one hand, a fresh glass of scotch sweating in the other, he sank into the couch and closed his eyes. The doorbell went *ding-dong!* and his eyes popped open. The glass was dry and the cigarette had burned perilously near his knuckle. He set the glass on the coffee table and crushed the cigarette in the ashtray. At the door it occurred to him the bell had only rung once, and it bothered him somehow. He peered through the spy-hole and saw nothing but the empty walk, yellow and hazy under the streetlamp light. The doorknob throbbed with a low voltage current that tingled momentarily and vanished.

He opened the door and Trina-the-escort popped up like a jack-in-the-box, still fumbling with a compact that had slipped from her stylish red-lacquer handbag. She wore a slick black dress and had dyed her hair blonde since their last encounter. "Hiya," she said and caught his tie in the crook of her finger as she stepped past him from the dark into the light. As the door swung closed, a breeze ruffled his hair and he shivered, experiencing the unpleasant sensation that he'd forgotten something important, perhaps years and years ago. His brain was fairly pickled and the girl already slid out of her dress and the strange unease receded.

When they'd finished, Trina kissed his cheek, dragged on their shared cigarette, then briskly toweled herself and ducked into the bathroom. He dialed her a taxi and lay in the shadows listening to the shower, the edge off his drunkenness and succumbing to exhaustion as he recalled the faces of his dinner guests—Dr. Christou's haunted eyes, Mr. Blaylock's predatory smile, and Mr. Rawat cool and bland even as he dissected and debated. The others ran together, and uneasiness crept back in as his damp flesh cooled, as the red numerals of the alarm clock flickered in a warning. The girl reappeared, dressed, perfumed, and coifed with a polka dot kerchief. She said she'd let herself out, call her again any time. He drifted away, and—

*Ding-dong!* He sat up fast, skull heavy. Only three or four minutes had passed, yet he was mostly anesthetized from the alcohol and overwhelming drowsiness. He waited for the next ring, and as he waited a chill seeped into his guts and he thought strange, disjointed thoughts. Why was he so nervous? The vein in his neck pulsed. Trina must've forgotten something. He rose and went to the door. As he turned the deadbolt, he experienced the inexplicable urge to flee. It was a feeling as powerful and visceral as a bout of vertigo, the irrational sense that he would be snatched into the darkness, that he would meet one of Dr. Christou's unknowable marvels lurking in the cracks of the Earth.

Trina stepped back with a small cry when he flung the door open and stood before her, sweat dripping from his torso. A taxi idled on the curb. She regained her composure, although she didn't come closer. "Forgot my cell," she said. Dazed, he fetched her phone. She extended her hand as far as possible to snatch the phone. She hustled to the taxi without a goodbye or backward glance.

The canopy of the trees across the street shushed in the breeze, and fields littered with pockets of light swept into the deeper gloom like the crown of a moonlit sea. The starry night was vast and chill, and Lancaster imagined entities concealed within its folds gazing hungrily upon the lights of the city, the warmth of its inhabitants.

Lancaster was not an introspective man, preferring to live an inch beneath his own skin, to run hot and cold as circumstances required. Fear had awakened in him, stirred by God knew what. Imminent mortality? Cancer cells spreading like fire? The Devil staring at him from the pit? Momentarily he had the preposterous fantasy that this primitive terror wasn't a random bubble surfacing from the nascent tar of his primordial self, but an intrusion, a virus he'd contracted that now worked to unnerve and unman him.

Whatever the source, he was afraid to stand in the tiny rectangle of light that faced the outer darkness. That darkness followed him into sleep. The gnawing fear was with him too. The dark. The hum of the stars.

\* \* \*

Lancaster arranged for a limousine driver named Ms. Valens to pick the party up in front of the hotel after lunch the next day. He suggested a helicopter for speed, but Dr. Christou had an aversion to flying in light aircraft—a train and bus man, was the good doctor. Mr. Rawat and the Cooks were traveling to the airport that evening immediately following the tour of the corporate property, so the chauffeur loaded their luggage, which included Mr. Cook's pair of golf bags and no less than five suitcases for Mrs. Cook. Lancaster chuckled behind his hand at Ms. Valens's barely concealed expression of loathing as she struggled to heft everything into the trunk while Ms. Cook tutted and tisked and the muscular Dedrick stood impassively, watching nothing and everything at once.

The two-hour drive was along a sparsely traveled stretch of secondary highway that lanced through mile upon mile of wheat fields and sunflower plantations. The sky spread black and blue with rolling storm clouds, and crows floated like gnats beneath the belly of a dog. Light distorted as it passed through the tinted windows and filled the passenger compartment with an unearthly haze.

Lancaster and Ms. Diamond poured champagne from the limousine bar: *A glass to celebrate surviving their hangovers*, Lancaster said. Dr. Christou took his with a couple of antacid tablets, and Kara refused, covering her mouth with exaggerated revulsion. The others finished the magnum of *Grand Brut* with the diffidence of draining a bottle of spring water. Lancaster had seldom witnessed such a tolerance for booze except when playing blackjack with the alkie barflies in Vegas backwaters during his wild and wooly college days. He checked the stock to estimate whether it would last until he got his charges onto the plane. It was going to be close. Ms. Diamond's eyes widened when she met his and he felt a smidgen of uncharacteristic pity for her distress.

Mr. Rawat took a sheaf of blueprints and maps from his gold-clasped leather briefcase and spread them across his knees. Mr. Cook and Ms. Diamond sat on either side of him. Their faces shone with the hazy light reflected from the paper. Lancaster's eyeballs ached. The scenery slid past like a ragged stream of photographic frames. He pondered the previous evening's gathering at the hotel. Mrs. Cook winked and knocked his knee under the table. Mr. Blaylock grinned, minus an eyetooth, and Christine, the voluptuous vamp, stroked Blaylock's shoulder, her nails denting the exquisite fabric of his dinner jacket. Luther and Rayburn were a blur, unimportant. Mr. Cook drank with the methodical efficiency of a man who'd rather face the scaffold than another day with his wife, and he smiled with the same, superficial cheer as Ms. Diamond did—probably a reflexive counter to deeper, darker impulses. Mr. Rawat debated Dr. Christou with a passion reserved for a lover, while fox-sharp Kara looked on with jaded boredom, and Lancaster wondered how close the men might actually be and perhaps, perhaps the NSA thought to use them against one another, to leverage a clandestine affair, and damn, this trip might actually prove interesting. Lancaster snapped out of it. His sunglasses disguised the fact he'd dozed for a few moments, or so he hoped.

They arrived at the property, several acres of single-story, hi-tech buildings fronted by immaculately trimmed lawns and plum trees. The office sectors were divided by access lanes, the whole complex erected in the middle of nowhere, an island on an ocean of grain. A grounds keeping truck inched along about a quarter of a mile down the frontage road. Workers in orange jackets paced it on the sidewalk, blasting away with leaf blowers.

No sooner had her feet touched the pavement, Ms. Diamond launched into a rehearsed spiel, subtly leading Mr. Rawat, Dedrick, and the Cooks by the collective nose toward the nearest wall of glass. She unlocked a set of doors with a key card and they walked inside. Meanwhile, Kara squinted at the changeable sky and fussed with the brim of her hat while Dr. Christou stood in the shadow of the car, rubbing his skull and muttering. Lancaster called the catering company, gained assurances the team would arrive on schedule. Ms. Diamond had reserved tables at a restaurant in a town several miles away. He knew she'd underestimated the softness of this particular group—such people couldn't go five or six hours without food and booze, couldn't go without being waited upon hand and foot; so he'd hired one of the finer outfits in the city to prepare dinner and truck it to the site at approximately the time he figured the tour would be wrapping up.

"Had enough, have you?" Dr. Christou said. "Of our chums, I mean."

"Ms. Diamond has them in hand. I couldn't very well abandon you or the lovely Kara, could I?" Lancaster lighted a cigarette. The "lovely" Kara had retreated into the limousine. He suspected she was raiding the olives. Poor dear was emaciated.

"I'd say you are more preoccupied keeping tabs on me than helping your colleague net that big fish pal of mine."

"You're happy, Mr. Rawat is happy. Or am I wrong?" Lancaster said, thinking fast, wondering if the doctor was cagier than he appeared. "I'm here to make certain everyone has as nice a trip as possible." He gestured at the surrounding plains. "Got my work cut out for me. This is the kind of land only a farmer or Bible salesman could love."

"I have a theory. It's the land that makes people crazy, not their superstitions. Consider fundamentalist Islam and fundamentalist Christianity—then look around. Look at all this emptiness under a baleful fireball. Add a few uneducated peasants to the equation and *voila*. Petrie dish for lunacy."

"Amber waves of grain far as the eye can see, and me without a drop of milk..."

The big man nodded, still rubbing his skull. "I knew a fellow in Tangiers during my callow and malleable youth. French Intelligence, retired. He *claimed* to be retired. A lovely, older man; quite affable, quite accommodating, charmingly effete. He always dressed in a suit and smoked *Gauloises* Brunes. Kept a little black pistol in his dresser at the hotel—a Walther, as I recall. He spoke of enemies from the old days. You remind me a bit of him."

"Except I don't have enemies. As to the, ahem, French connection, my mother claims we are descended from the Huguenots—but isn't that a socially acceptable variation of the asylum nuts claiming to be Napoleon reincarnate?"

The grounds crew stopped across the way. There were seven of them. They lighted cigarettes and leaned against their truck or sprawled in the grass and drank water from milk jugs. A young Mexican god shaded his eyes with his hand and smiled at Lancaster. The Mexican's shoulders were broad and dark as burnt copper and his black hair fell in ringlets to his nipples. His chest and stomach rippled with the musculature of a bull. He unsnapped the cap on a jug and poured water over his head, a model pimping it hard in a rock video, and whipped his hair in a circle. Water flew everywhere. His teeth were white, white.

Dr. Christou followed Lancaster's stare. He sighed and lighted a cigarette of his own. "I always enjoyed a cherry pipe. Had to quit—too *de trop* for a professor, chewing on a pipe stem. Damnable shame. You understand the power of perception, of course. I've accrued a fine, long list of enemies. My work is eccentric enough without piling on cliché. Ah, how I loathe those fuckers in admin."

Lancaster laughed, unbalanced by Christou's sortie and disliking the sensation intensely. He said, "An amazing coincidence, running into your colleague last night."

"Indeed. Blaylock wasn't... He wasn't as I expected him to be. We've corresponded for years. I thought... Well, goes to show, doesn't it? How meager our understanding of the human heart."

"Only the shadow knows."

"What a chestnut! Is that how you get through life, Mr. Lancaster? A sense of detachment and an arsenal of wry witticisms?"

"I'm not the best at small talk."

"Nonsense—that's why they sent you. You are an *expert* at small talk, a maestro at manipulating the inconsequential to your design. I'm hardly offended—fascinated, rather."

The clouds kept rolling and the light changed and changed, darkening from red and orange to purple, and a damp breath moved across the land, but it didn't rain. The air was supercharged and Lancaster tasted a hint of ozone. "Here comes the dinner wagon," he said as a van with a corporate logo departed the main road and cruised toward them.

"The irony is, my connections are retired or passed on," Dr. Christou said. "We've gotten old. If revolutionaries live long enough they become the establishment. The reef incorporates all discrete elements."

"Honestly, Doctor, I don't know what the hell you're talking about."

"Right, then. For the record, you're wasting taxpayer money on me. Any information I've got isn't worth a drachma on the international market. Unless this is about revenge. Perhaps someone simply wishes to discredit me, to ruin my life's work."

Lancaster wasn't certain how to respond. Possibly the man was dangerous; perhaps he possessed contacts within some intelligence agency and had obtained Lancaster's files, maybe he knew the game. He kept his emotions in check, paid out a bit of rope. "Kind of paranoid, yeah? It's late in the day to achieve much by destroying you, isn't it, Doc?"

"There are those who can be relied upon in their pettiness. You tell whomever it is, this isn't worth their effort." Dr. Christou drew on his cigarette butt. He knocked on the limousine window glass, coaxing Kara to emerge. Lancaster keyed the caterers into the central office, superintending their deployment and beachhead in the largest conference room he could find. As the team spread tablecloths and arranged the dinnerware, the overhead lights flickered and hummed and Lancaster stood with his cell flipped open, his brain in neutral.

"This place is spooky," Kara said, hipshot against the edge of the nearest table. She popped a cocktail shrimp into her mouth. Her little black magpie eyes blinked, blinked. "I hate empty buildings. This place goes for miles. Just a bunch of endless hallways. Almost all the lights are off. It feels like somebody's going to jump at me from the shadows. I dunno. Silly, huh?"

"Not so much," Lancaster said, marshaling his strength to play the part. He patted her arm, mostly to comfort himself. He suppressed his anxiety and phoned Ms. Diamond and informed her supper awaited. There was a long, chilly silence before she thanked him and said her group would be along shortly.

The meal was passable by elitist standards: overdone Beef Wellington and too-boney Alaska king salmon. Lancaster's choice of vintage Italian wines and two chilled bottles of Chopin mollified the party. He stopped after one drink, his stomach knotted, shoulders bunched with rising tension. His guests were more than happy to drain the liquor—even Kara had overcome her squeamishness to hoist a glass of white wine. Mr. Rawat entered the proceedings wearing a dour expression matched only by Ms. Diamond's, but after five or six shots of vodka he melted somewhat and began to joke with Dr. Christou. Meanwhile, the Cooks were inscrutable in their lukewarm affability, nibbling at the finger foods and consuming glasses of wine with impressive efficiency.

One of the caterers approached Lancaster with an apologetic nod and asked if he was expecting more company. Lancaster asked why, and the man said someone had buzzed the intercom at the entrance. He'd assumed a member of the party had gotten locked out, or the limo driver... Nobody was at the door. It was getting dark and some of the lights in the parking lot weren't on, so he wasn't able to see much. Lancaster didn't know Ms. Valens's number; he called the home office and got it from a secretary in human resources, then dialed the driver, intending to ask if she'd happened to see anyone on the grounds near the entrance. The call went straight to voicemail.

"A problem?" Ms. Diamond said as she sidled close, knifing him with one of her fake smiles. "And thank you ever so much for cutting me off at the knees by cancelling our reservations at a first class restaurant in favor of your little picnic stunt."

"They seem to be happily stuffing their faces," he said with his own contrived smile of collegiality. "No problem. The caterer thought someone was at the door. I'm checking with Ms. Valens now." Until that instant he'd toyed with the notion of asking Dedrick to make a parking lot sweep, dissuaded by the fellow's cold-fish demeanor and the suspicion he wasn't the type to run errands for anyone other than his master, Mr. Rawat. Lancaster pushed away from the table and turned his back on Ms. Diamond, went into the deep gloom of the hall, trailing his hand for a light switch. The front office was also murky, ankle-high illumination provided by a recessed panel of track lights in the baseboard paneling. The effect was spooky, as Kara said.

The night air lay cool upon his skin, tickled his nostrils with the scents of dust and chaff. A lone sodium lamp shone in an adjoining lot, illuminating itself and not much else. He approached the limo and noticed the chassis slightly shifting upon its shocks, and his eyes adjusted he discerned pants and a jacket discarded near the driver side door, and several empty pocket-sized liquor bottles gleaming in the starlight upon the asphalt. Ms. Valens straddled the young Mexican god as he sprawled across the hood. His giant hands were on her ass, her fancy cap turned backward on his head. Lancaster sparked his lighter. They stared at him, drawn by the flame. "Don't mind me," he said, and lighted a cigarette. They didn't.

"What's going on out there!" Ms. Diamond said. Her voice carried from the entrance where she held the door as if afraid to venture forth. She sounded as melodramatic as an actress in a Quaker dress and bonnet, clutching her throat as she scanned the plains for a sneaking Comanche. "Lancaster, where the devil are you?" she said.

"Coming," he said, and chuckled. He tapped his watch at Ms. Valens and walked away.

Ms. Diamond awaited him and they stood for a few moments in the unlighted office, listening to the loud voices and laughter from the conference room. She said, "Good thing it's time to go—the booze is *finito*. Have you seen Kara? The supermodel."

"Oh, that one," he said.

"You haven't been hitting the vodka hard enough to play the drunk asshole card. Got to hand it to you, Lancaster, this has turned into a cock-up. Those bastards aren't buying it. Rawat's not interested in this land. I dunno what the deal is with the Mr. Howell and Lovey. You're supposed to be the sweet-talker, but your head isn't in the game. Now that silly bitch has taken a powder. Anyway, she's mooned over you all day. Sweet little bulimic doe."

"No need to waste charm since you're not trying to sell *her* any swampland. She was binging on *hors devours*, last I saw. Might be a long ride back to the city."

"Where the hell has she gotten to."

"Likely in the john commencing the purging stage of the operation," he said.

"No, I looked. Would you mind checking down the hall—bet she's somewhere doing a line or having a crying jag or what the fuck ever. I've got to herd my sheep toward the exit before they start bleating in an insane frenzy of DTs."

"Sure," he said, regretting it in the same breath. Kara had uttered a true statement: the halls were dark, dark. She wouldn't have ventured into them alone, not with her apparently sincere apprehension. He located a central bank of dials in an adjoining passage and fiddled with them until a few domes winked on. Mercifully, each door was locked and he satisfied his obligation to search for the woman with a knock and a half-hearted inquiry—yoo-hoo, in there, lady? No? Moving on, moving on, even as the walls tightened like the throat of a cave burrowing into bedrock. His sweaty hand made it increasingly difficult to grasp door handles. He felt liquor in the wires of his brain, but he hadn't drunk enough, Ms. Diamond had noted it rightly, so why this haze, this disorientation?

Inside the employee break room, she lay in a fetal position on a table. A water-cooler bubbled in the corner. The refrigerator door was ajar and its white, icicle-chill light shone over her naked legs, white panties. Her upper body curved away, her face hidden in the sweep of hair. He slapped the wall switch and the overhead light flashed once and went dead. He approached and bent toward her still form.

She shuddered violently and raised herself on one elbow and laughed.

Her arm unfolded like a blade. She seized his collar, pulled his face to hers. She kissed him hard with the taste of cold metal and all he could see was the refrigerator shivering in her eye, his own eye shivering in her eye. His eye rolled, rolled. This wasn't Kara. The dimness had tricked him. "Be glad those lights didn't come on," Christine said, sounding different than he'd expected—she hadn't spoken once during cocktails the previous evening at the hotel as she hung on Mr. Blaylock's arm. Her voice was hoarse. "I suppose you're wondering why I've called you here," she said. A certain fluidity suggested multitudes beneath her skin. "The service door was open, by the way. That's how we got in."

"You killed small animals as a child, didn't you?" Mr. Blaylock said. He stood before the gaping refrigerator, backlit so his face was partially hidden. Lancaster recognized the man's voice, his peculiar scent. Mr. Blaylock soothed him. "That's how it begins. Don't be afraid. It's not your turn. Not tonight. Really, you've been dead for years, haven't you?" And to his left, past a doorframe that let yet further into the heart of the complex, more figures crowded. Presumably Mr. Blaylock's acolytes from the dinner party.

Lancaster pulled free from Christine's clutches. She spoke gibberish to him, lips and the sound from her lips moving asynchronously. He wheeled and plunged into the hall, blundered without sight or thought toward the conference chamber and the reassurance of a crowd. His mouth hurt on the inside. The caterers were already gone, leaving the room as antiseptic as they'd found it. The guests milled, awkward and surly in the absence of entertainment.

"Finally you appear!" Ms. Diamond said through her teeth. "Don't believe in answering your phone. Damn it and hellfire, Lancaster! The natives are restless. We need to move on out."

"Yeah, can we just go already?" Kara pressed tight against Mr. Rawat, wheedling in a daddy's-little-girl tone. Her white cheeks were blotched pink. Lancaster's tongue ached and he tried to recall what he'd meant to say, why those two disturbed him. Hadn't he gone searching for her? The possibility seemed more remote by the second. He pressed a napkin to his lips, stemming the blood-flow, his short-term memory erasing itself like a tape under a magnet.

He followed at the tail of the procession toward the parking lot. He glanced over his shoulder. A figure watched him from the darkened hallway. It slipped backward and vanished. Then he was letting the door close, a gate shutting on a sepulcher, and a few moments later he couldn't recall why the taste of adrenaline mixed with the mouthful of wet copper.

* * *

The limousine and its running lights floated on the black surface of the night road. Farther on, the skyline of the city glowed like a bank of coals. Lancaster thought of his townhouse, the cold comfort of his large television and well-stocked bar, his firm bed, the expert and clinical charms of his high-dollar call girls. A voice whispered to him that he might not ever again step across the threshold. Blood continued to trickle from his tongue and he swallowed frequently.

Ms. Diamond's knee brushed his own; her hands were primly folded in her lap. She smiled a glassy smile of defeat. Mr. Rawat lolled directly across the way, eyes closed. Kara's cheek rested against the breast of his jacket. The Cooks reclined a few inches over, nodding placidly with the swaying of the car. Dedrick was in front, riding shotgun, hidden by the opaque glass.

Dr. Christou said to Mrs. Cook, "What do you mean, Francine? The land itself can possess sentience? The Great Father of the Native Americans writ in root and rock?"

"Yes," said Mrs. Cook. "Yes, that is exactly what I mean. Vortexes, dolmens, leylines, sacred monoliths, massive deposits of crystal and other conducting minerals."

Dr. Christou shrugged. "How do you envision these anomalies affecting the larger environment—human society?"

"The natives amplified them with ceremonies and the construction of corresponding devices. Some acolytes yet perform the ancient rituals in the name of...various entities. Places of power become more powerful." The dome light was on. Mrs. Cook stared into the mirror of her compact. She patted her nose. "There's an ancient gridwork across this landscape. A scar. You can't feel it? How it plucks at you, siphons a tiny bit of your very life force? No, you can't. My disappointment is... Well, it's profound, Doctor. Profound indeed."

"But *you* can feel it," Dr. Christou said. He averted his gaze, grimacing, a man who'd gotten the scent of something rancid and might vomit.

"Yes. Yes! Why else would I let hubby-kins drag me to Kansas of all benighted places?"

Mr. Cook sneered. "I don't give a tinker's damn for office property, only that its foundation lies upon the rim of a vast, ancient wheel. We, this speck of a vehicle, travel across it like a flea on the back of an elephant."

"You see, my good doctor, we've done our homework. The old races made a number of heroic excavations." Mrs. Cook had applied a lot of powder. Her face was ghastly pale, except her lips, which resembled red earthworms. "Those excavations are hidden beneath the shifting stones and the sunflowers and the wheat. Yet they endure and exert significant force. A million bones ground to dust, a lake of blood leeched down, down into the earth, coagulated as amber. This good earth buzzes with a black radiation. Honey and milk to certain individuals."

"Right on," Mr. Cook said, idly adjusting his silvery ascot. He licked his lips at Mrs. Cook as she snapped shut the compact.

"Besides the Serpent Intaglio, I'm unaware of any geoglyphs in this region. Even if these geoglyphs of yours exist…Comanche, Arapahoe, Kickapoo, Kaw… none of them were terraformers on the scale you suggest." Dr. Christou was rubbing his skull again. A red splotch grew livid on his brow.

"Not the new tribes," Mrs. Cook said. "Rather the civilizations that ruled here when this continent was still fused to Asia."

"Back, back, back," Mr. Cook said. "Only two continents in those days. Plus the polar caps. A wee bit before our time, admittedly."

Lancaster surfaced from his own disjointed thoughts and began to process the exchange. Cold bright recollection smashed through his mind, a dousing of ice water, although he only experienced the visceral epiphany in the abstract, unable to comprehend the nature of its import. He said with practiced and patently false calmness, "Mr. Rawat, how did you come to learn of the Roache property? Someone brought it to your attention. Your investors, or someone in your employ? You have a department devoted to mergers and acquisitions."

Ms. Diamond casually dug an elbow into Lancaster's ribs. Mr. Rawat opened one eye. "Byron and Francine. They prepared a prospectus."

"Byron and I were vacationing in Portugal," Mrs. Cook said. "The three of us happened to stay at the same hotel. One thing led to another, and another…"

"We became fast friends," Mr. Rawat said.

"Bosom buddies," Mr. Cook said, staring directly and unblinkingly at Lancaster. What had Ms. Diamond called him? Mr. Howell from *Gilligan's Island*. Yeah, there was an uncanny resemblance here in the shifty gloom.

Lancaster glanced from the Cooks to Dr. Christou. "Last night, who started that conversation about monsters?" He knew even before anyone answered that his assumption Mr. Rawat or Dr. Christou chose the topic was in error. They'd merely carried it along. He remembered kissing Mrs. Cook's hand the previous evening, its repellent flavor of sweet, rotting fruit and underlying acridness. She'd been inside his mind before that, though, been inside all of their heads, that was her power. Even now her likeness floated in his waking mind, whispering to him how it was, how it would be. A river of blood, the sucking of living marrow—

Mrs. Cook's bright smile widened. "*Monsters* fascinate me to no end." She leaned forward and grasped Dr. Christou's thigh as if propositioning a would-be lover. "We've read all of your books, Doctor."

"We've come a long way for this," Mr. Cook said. "There are some friends we'd like to introduce to you."

Dr. Christou's face slackened. He made an inarticulate sound from the back of his throat. Finally, he mastered himself and said to Lancaster, "Do you understand what's happening? My god, Lancaster. Tell me you understand."

Lancaster hesitated and Mrs. Cook cackled, head thrown back, throat muscles bunching.

Mr. Cook glanced out the window, then at his watch. "Oh, my. They're waiting. I almost dared not hope... On with the show." He loosened his tie.

The limo slowed and halted at a lonely four-way crossroads overseen by a traffic light dangling from a wire. The light burned red. A sedan was parked at an odd angle in the approaching right-hand lane, hazards flashing. A man and a woman dressed in evening clothes stood nearby, blank and stolid, awaiting rescue, perhaps. Lancaster squinted; the couple seemed familiar. As the limo began to roll forward through the intersection, Ms. Diamond said, "My god." She pressed the intercom button and ordered Ms. Valens to pull over.

"Wait, don't do it," Dr. Christou said with the affect of a man heavily medicated; a man who'd chosen to give warning in afterthought when it was far too late.

"It's them." Ms. Diamond was already on her way out of the car and briskly walking toward the other motorists. Her heels clacked on the asphalt.

"What's going on?" Mr. Rawat said, annoyed.

"Who are those people?" Kara said. Her face was sleepy and swollen.

Mr. Cook reached up and killed the dome light. From the shadows he said, "Victoria's parents. They burned alive in a car crash. 1985. She has lived alone for so long."

"Uh-uh," Kara said. "That's Casey Jean Laufenburg and her brother Lloyd. I went to high school with those guys."

"Did they burn in a car accident too?" Dr. Christou said.

"Worse. Casey Jean's in retail. It's awful." She gazed at Mr. Rawat imploringly. "Can we please keep going? Why do we have to stop?" She sounded fully awake and afraid.

"Don't you want to say hello to your chums?" Mr. Cook said. "And you, Doctor. Aren't you just positively consumed with fascination? This is how it happens. A lonely road at night. You come across someone familiar…an old friend, a brother, a sister, the priest from the neighborhood."

Mrs. Cook said, "It could be anyone, whomever is flitting around your brain. Here's the darkness, the haunted byway. Here in your twilight, you get to be part of the legend."

"That's enough booze for you, Ma'am," Lancaster said with forced cheer. Mrs. Cook released Dr. Christou and grasped Lancaster's forearm in a soft, almost effortless fashion that nonetheless reduced his resistance to that of a bug with a leg stuck on a fly strip. She opened herself and let him see. He was bodiless, weightless, sucked like smoke through a pipe stem toward a massive New England style house. He was drawn inside the house—marble tiles, sweeping staircases, bookcases, paintings—and into the master bedroom, the wardrobe, so cavernous and dim. An older couple were bound together in barbed wire. They dangled from a ceiling hook, their corpses liver-gray and bloodless, unspun hair dragging against the carpet. Eyes glazed, jaws slack. The real Cooks had never even made it out of their home.

The image collapsed and disintegrated and Lancaster reconstituted in the present, Mrs. Cook's fingers clamped on his arm. He wrenched free and flopped back into his seat, strength drained. He said to Dr. Christou, "I think we've been poisoned." Someone had spiked the liquor, dosed the food with hallucinogens to soften the group, to break them down. Lancaster had read about this, the government experiments on Vietnam soldiers, the spritzing of subways with LSD in the 1970s. Mind control was the name of the game. "Doctor, this may be…" Lancaster shook his head to clear it, trying to decide exactly *why* an oppositional force would want to drug them. "It's a kidnapping." The motive seemed shockingly obvious—ransom. This carload of rich people tooling along the countryside could represent a payday for a suitably prepared criminal. He pressed the intercom and said, "There's a situation. Something's happening."

The glass whisked down and Dedrick swiveled in his seat. "Yes?"

"I believe we're under attack. Please get Ms. Diamond. Drag her if necessary. Ms. Valens, the minute they're in the vehicle get us the hell out of here."

"Excuse me," Mr. Rawat said, his reserve cracked, a raw nerve of terror exposed in his rapid blinking. Doubtless he'd seen his share of violence back in the homeland and was acutely aware of his vulnerability. "Mr. Lancaster, what do you mean we're under attack? Dedrick?"

Dedrick's stony countenance didn't alter. "Sir, please wait." He made no further comment while exiting the limo and striding toward Ms. Diamond and friends. His right hand was thrust inside his jacket. Mr. Rawat appeared shocked and Kara retrieved a baggie from her purse. She dry-swallowed a handful of particolored pills. Surprisingly, in the face of fear she kept quiet.

Lancaster squirmed around until he managed to get a view from the rear window of what was happening outside. He simultaneously opened his cell phone and dialed the Roache security department and requested a detail be dispatched to the location at once. He considered alerting his handler Clack of the situation, except in his experience communication with the NSA office was routed through multiple filters and ultimately reached an answering machine instead of a human being ninety percent of the time. It seemed a bad sign that the Cooks were unconcerned that he'd summoned the cavalry. Something great and terrible was descending upon this merry company of travelers. He said, "Who are you working for?"

"The Russians," Mr. Cook said.

"The Bulgarians," Mrs. Cook said. "The Scythians, the Picts, the Ostrogoths, the wicker-crowned God Kings of Ultima Thule. The Martians."

"Mrs. Cook and I serve the whims of marvelous entities, foolish man," Mr. Cook said. "The ones inhabiting the cracks in the earth, as the doctor is so fond of opining."

That sounded like some kind of terrorist group to Lancaster. "Why here? Why not at the office where there'd be privacy?"

The Cooks exchanged blandly malevolent glances.

Dr. Christou mumbled, "Because we are near a place of power. A blood sacrifice requires a sacred foundation."

"Or a profane foundation," Mrs. Cook said.

"Like sex magic, the journey is half the fun." Mr. Cook's grin shone in the gloom.

"Really, you don't want to know the who, how, and why," Mrs. Cook said. "Alas, you will, and soon. We procure and thus persist."

"Yes, we persist. Until the heat death of the universe."

"Procure," Dr. Christou said in a monotone. His flesh seemed to be in the process of deliquescing. Blood beaded on his forehead, squeezed in fattening droplets from the pores and rolled down his cheeks. Blood leaked from the corners of his eyes. Blood trickled from his sleeve cuffs and dripped in his lap. "Procure, what do you procure?"

Lancaster recoiled from the doctor. He had visions of anthrax, a vial of the Ebola virus, or one of a million other plagues synthesized in military labs the world over, and one of those plagues secreted in a handbag, a golf bag, wherever, now dosed into the food, the water, the wine, this virulent nastiness eating Dr. Christou alive. On a more fundamental level, he understood Christou's affliction wasn't any plague, manmade or otherwise, but the manifestation of something far worse.

"My goodness, Doctor, they *are* eager for your humor to draw it at this distance," Mr. Cook said, gleeful as a child who'd won a prize. He pretended to pout. "I was promised a taste. Gluttons!"

"Go on, sweetie," Mrs. Cook said. "There is more than enough to spare."

Mr. Rawat said, "My friend, my friend, you're hurt!" He extended his hand, hesitated upon thinking better of the gesture.

The Cooks laughed, synchronized. A quantity of Dr. Christou's blood was drawn in gravity-defying rivulets from where it pooled on the seat, first to the floorboard, then vertically against the window where it formed globules and rotated as if suspended in zero gravity. Mr. Cook craned his neck and sucked the globules into the corner of his mouth. "If ambrosia tastes so sweet upon a mortal tongue, how our patrons must crave it as that which sustains them!"

There was a thunderclap outside and a flash of fire. Ms. Diamond ran toward them. Her left high heel sheared and she did a swan dive onto the road. Dedrick also sprinted for the limo, moving with the grace and agility of a linebacker. He hurdled the fallen woman and blasted another round by twisting and aiming from under his armpit. Lancaster couldn't see the gun, but it had an impressive muzzle flash.

The mystery couple pursued on hands and knees, clothes shredded to reveal slick, cancerous flesh illuminated in the red glare of the traffic light. Their true forms unfolded and extended. The pair approached in a segmented, wormlike motion, and the reason why was due to their joining at hip and shoulder. Their faces had collapsed into seething pits; blowtorch nozzles seen front on, except spouting jets of pure black flame. In that moment Lancaster realized what had been leeching Dr. Christou from afar and he became nauseated.

As this disfigured conglomeration encroached upon Ms. Diamond, she convulsed in a pantomime of making a snow angel against the pavement. A heavy, wine-dark vapor trail boiled from her, and was siphoned into the funnel maws of the monstrous couple. She withered and charred. The others crawled atop and covered her completely.

The passenger compartment filled with the sour odor of feces. Mr. Rawat screamed and when Kara realized what was happening outside she screamed too. The gun cracked twice more, then Dedrick was in the front seat and bellowing for Ms. Valens to drive, drive, drive! and the chauffeur floored it while Dedrick's door was still open.

Lancaster didn't have the wits to react to the knife that appeared in Mr. Cook's hand. He gaped dumfounded while Mr. Cook nonchalantly reached out over his seatback and grasped Ms. Valens's hair and sliced her throat neat as could be. However, Dedrick continued to prove quite the man of action. He reached across Ms. Valens's soon to be corpse and took the wheel and kept the vehicle pointed down the centerline as he poked his large bore magnum pistol through the partition and fired. The bullet entered Mr. Cook's temple and punched a papier-mâché hole out the opposite side of his head. The report stunned and deafened Lancaster who raised his arms defensively against the splash. A chunk of bone and hair caromed from the ceiling, splatted against Dr. Christou's jacket breast and clung like a displaced toupee. Now blood was everywhere—fizzing from Dr. Christou, misting the window in gruesome condensation, spurting from the chauffeur's carotid artery, gushing from Mr. Cook's dashed skull, filling Lancaster's mouth, his nostrils, everywhere, everywhere.

Mrs. Cook ended Dedrick's heroics. She grasped the barrel and jerked and the gun exploded again, shattering the rear window. She made her other hand into a claw and gently raked drab, blue-painted nails across his face. One of his eyes burst and deflated, and the meat of his cheeks and jaw came unstitched as if kissed by a serrated saw blade and his face more or less peeled away like a decal. The man dropped the gun and pitched backward and out of view.

More blood. More blood. More screaming. It was chaos. The limousine left the road, bounced into the ditch and plowed a ragged line through a wheat field. The occupants were violently tossed about, except for Mrs. Cook who sat serene as a padishah on her palanquin.

The car ground to a halt. The passenger door opposite Lancaster opened and Mr. Blaylock stood there in an evening suit. He said to Mrs. Cook, "Chop chop, my dear. Dark is wasting." He bowed and was gone.

Mr. Cook's dagger had flown from his hand and lodged in the plush fabric of the seat between Lancaster and Dr. Christou. Lancaster caught his balance and snatched the knife, and it was heavy and cruelly curved and fit his hand most murderously. He stabbed it like an ice pick just beneath Mrs. Cook's breast. the blade crunched through muscle and bone and slid in to the hilt where it stuck tight. He tried to climb through the broken rear window. She cackled and clutched his ankle and yanked him to her as a mother retrieving her belligerent child. She kissed him and life drained from his limbs and he was paralyzed, yet completely aware. Completely aware for the hours that followed in the dark and desolate wheat field.

* * *

When it was over.

It would never be over. Lancaster knew that most intimately.

But when it was over for the moment, he walked to the lights on the road, pushed through the rough stalks, occasionally staggering as his shoe caught on a furrow. Police car lights. Fire truck lights. The blue-white spotlights of low-cruising helicopters. The swinging and crisscrossing flashlight beams of the cops trolling the ditches. Roache had pulled out the stops.

He walked deep into the dragnet before somebody noticed that a civilian, pale as death in a blood-soaked suit, wandered amongst them.

The police whisked him directly to a hospital. Physically he was adequate—bumps and bruises and missing the tip of his tongue. Rather hale, all considered. The shrink who interviewed him wasn't convinced of Lancaster's mental stability and prescribed pills and a return visit. The police questioning didn't prove particularly grueling; nothing like the cop shows. Even Roache was eerily sympathetic. Company reps debriefed him regarding the car accident and promptly deposited a merit bonus in his bank account and arranged a vacation in the Bahamas. He didn't protest, didn't say much beyond responses to direct questions and these were flat, unaffected and ambiguous. He shuffled off to the islands, blank.

Following an afternoon that was one long stream of poolside martinis and blazing sun, Lancaster stumbled back to his hotel room and saw a man lounging in the overstuffed armchair by the bed.

"Hi, I'm Agent Clack, National Security Agency. We've chatted a few times on the phone." Agent Clack propped his feet on the coffee table. He smoked a cigarette. *Gauloises.*

The irony wasn't lost on Lancaster. "What are you, a college sophomore?" He walked to the bar and poured a vodka, pausing to gesture if his guest wanted one.

Agent Clack waved him off. Indeed, a young man—thirty tops. Pretty enough to model for a men's catalogue, he styled his wiry black hair into an impressive afro. He dressed the part of a tourist; a flower print shirt, cheap camera slung around his neck, khaki shorts and open toe sandals. Lithe and well-built as a dancer, danger oozed from him, aw, shucks demeanor notwithstanding. "They like 'em young at HQ. But I assure you, my qualifications are impeccable. Had to snuff three dudes to get the job, kinda like James Bond. Jack Bauer is a pussy compared to yours truly. You're in good hands. Enough about me. How you holding up?"

"Am I being charged?"

"You responsible for the massacre? My bosses don't think so. Neither do I. We're looking for answers, is all."

Lancaster shrugged and drank his vodka. "Did you find them?" He looked through the window when he asked, staring past the brilliant canopy of umbrella-shaded tables in the courtyard to the blue water that went on and on. "I told the cops where. The best I could remember. It was dark."

"Yeah, we found the victims. Still hunting the murderers. They seem to have evaporated." Agent Clack took a computer memory stick from his shirt pocket. "There are hundreds of pics on here. Satellite, aerial, plenty of close-ups of the action, well, the aftermath, in the field. It's classified, but... Wanna see?"

"I was there."

"Right, right. Still, things look a lot different from space. It's kinda weird, though, that you were taken from the isolated Roache property. I mean, the remote offices were an ideal setup for a prolonged torture-murder gig."

Lancaster thought of the disc of blackened earth he and the rest had been dragged to, a clearing the diameter of a small baseball diamond in the heart of the farmland, thought of what lay some yards beneath the topsoil, the subsoil, and the bedrock; an ossified ridge that curled in a grand arc, the spine of a baby Ouroboros, a gap between jaws and tail. He still smelled the blood and piss, the electric tang of pitiless starlight, the nauseating stench of his own terror. He said, "That dead ground, nothing has ever grown there. I imagine the Indians avoided it during their hunts, that the white farmers tilled around it and called it cursed. It's older than old, Agent. A ground for bloodletting. Places like it are everywhere."

"I don't give a shit about Stone Age crop circles. Who was behind the kidnapping. What was the motive. I'll let you in on a secret—we got nothing, man. No claims or demands from terrorist groups, no chatter, nada. That isn't how this goes. We *always* hear something."

"Motive? There's no motive. The ineffable simply *is*."

"The ineffable," Agent Clack said.

"The Cooks are in league with..."

"With who?" Agent Clack raised a brow.

"Evil."

"Get outta here."

"Abominations that creep along the byways of the world."

"The big E, huh? Er, yeah, sure thing. I'm more into the concept low-ercase e, the kind that lurks in the hearts of men. Anyhow, it wasn't the Cooks you were entertaining. The real Cooks were murdered in their home several days before the incident in Kansas. But you knew that."

"Yes. I was shown."

Agent Clack blew a smoke ring. "And these other individuals. Gregor Blaylock and his entourage. The grad students..."

"Let me guess. Victims of a gruesome demise, identities stolen to perpetrate an elaborate charade." Lancaster smiled; a brittle twitch.

"Not quite that dramatic. Guy's nonexistent. So are his assistants. Our records show he, *someone,* corresponded with Christou over the years, but it's a sham. There's a real live prof named Greg Blaylock and my guess is whoever this other guy is, he simply assumed that identity as needed. It's a popular con, black market brokers fixing illegals up with American citizens' social security cards. Could be a dozen people using the same serial number, sharing parallel identities. Not too hard. Blaylock and Christou hadn't actually met in person before that night. So."

"Blaylock's a cultist, a servitor. He was on the killing ground as a master of ceremonies. He...Blaylock coupled with Mrs. Cook while the nightmares fed on my companions, one by one." Lancaster poured again, swallowed it quickly. Poured another, contemplated the glass as if it were a crystal ball. "Everybody was after Christou. The monsters liked his books. What about you and your cronies? Was he a revolutionary? Bomb an embassy back in the '60s?"

"That's eyes-only spy stuff, grandpa. I'll tell you this: the geezer mixed with politically active people during his career. The kind of dudes on no fly lists. He was once a consultant for the intelligence services of our competitors. Quid pro quo. Those bodies we examined... that was beyond, man. Way, way beyond. All the blood and organs removed. Mutilation.

Looked like the victims were burned, but the autopsies said no. A brutal, sadistic, and apparently well-plotted crime. Yet the hostiles let you walk. There's a mystery my superiors are eager to get solved. Help me, man. Would ya, could ya shed some light on the subject?"

A sort of hysterical joy bubbled into Lancaster's throat. Yes, yes! To solve the ineffable mystery would be quite the trick. Certainly, Agent Clack despite his innocent face and schoolboy charm was cold and brutal, had surely seen and done the worst. Yet Lancaster easily imagined the younger man's horrified comprehension as the most vile and forbidden knowledge entered his bloodstream, began to corrode his shrieking brain with its acid. His lips curled. "Mrs. Cook called, a horrible sound unlike anything I'd ever heard, and three of the...*things* that attacked Ms. Diamond in the road shambled from the darkness and dragged us away, far from the limo and into the fields. Mr. Rawat, Kara, and their bodyguard were alive when they were dumped into the center of the clearing. The bodyguard, Dedrick...despite his horrible wounds. All of them were alive, Agent Clack. Very much alive. Dr. Christou too, although I could hardly recognize him beneath the mask of blood he wore. The blood was caked an inch thick and the fresh stuff oozed around the edges."

"I'm sorry you had to go through that. I still don't understand how we missed you out there. The wheat is only four feet tall." Agent Clack sounded more fascinated than sorry.

"I don't know how it was done. But it was. Black magic, worse."

"So, what happened? Exactly."

Lancaster hesitated for a long moment. "Eyes only, Agent. My eyes only."

"Now, now, codger. You don't wanna fuck with the man with the shiny laminated picture I.D."

"The others were drained. Drained, Agent Clack."

Agent Clack dropped his cigarette butt on the carpet and ground it to bits under his heel. He lighted another and smoked it, expression obscured by the blue haze. Finally, he said, "Alrighty, then. The investigation is ongoing. You'll talk, sooner or later. I've got time to kill."

"There are unspeakable truths." Lancaster closed his eyes for a long moment. "It pleased them to spare me in the name of a venerable cliché. Cliché's contain all truth, of course. The purpose of my survival was to bear witness, to carry the tale. The thrill of spreading terror, of lurking in the night as bogeymen of legend, titillates them. They are beasts, horrid undreamt of marvels."

"Gotta love those undreamt of marvels."

"You couldn't understand. After their masters fed, Blaylock and Mrs. Cook made Christou and the others join bloody hands and dance. The corpses danced. In a circle, jostling like marionettes. And Blaylock and Mrs. Cook laughed and plucked the strings."

Agent Clack nodded and dragged on his cigarette, then rose and regarded Lancaster with a kindly expression. "Sure. You take care. My people will be in touch with your people and all that jazz."

"Oh, we won't meet again, Agent Clack. Christou is dead, ending that particular game. Gregor Blaylock and the rest are vanished into the woodwork. I've told the story and am thus expendable. Very soon. Very soon I'll be reclaimed."

"Don't worry, we're watching you. Anybody comes sniffing around, we'll nab 'em."

"I suppose I'm comforted."

"By the way," Agent Clack said. "Is anyone else staying here with you? When I came in to wait, swore someone was in the bedroom, watching from the door. Thought it was you... Couldn't find anybody. Maybe they slipped away through the window, eh? Call me paranoid. We spooks are always worried about the baddies getting the drop on us."

"It wasn't me," Lancaster said. He turned and glanced at the bedroom doorway, the dimness within.

"Hah, didn't really think so. More oddness at the end of an odd day."

"Well, Agent, whatever it was, I hope you don't see it again. Especially one of these nights when you're alone."

Agent Clack continued to gaze at the older man for several beats. He slipped the memory stick into his pocket and walked out. He didn't bother to close the door. The gap filled with white light that slowly downshifted to black.

* * *

He finished his vacation and returned to the States and cashed in his chips at Roache. No hassle, not even an exit interview. Despite the suddenness of Lancaster's departure, some of his colleagues scrambled to throw together an impromptu retirement party. He almost escaped before one of the secretaries lassoed him as he was sneaking out the back door.

He was ushered into a Digital Age conference room with a huge table and comfortable chairs and a bay window overlooking downtown. The room shone in the streaming sunlight, every surface glowed and bloomed. His co-workers bore cheap gifts and there was a white layer cake and a bowl of punch. The dozen or so of them sang "For He's a Jolly Good Fellow" off-key. What dominated Lancaster's mind was the burble and boil of the water cooler, the drone of the inset lights. How the white frosting gleamed like an incisor. He caught his reflection in the shiny brass of a wall plate and beheld himself shrunken, emaciated, a leering devil. He averted his gaze, stared instead into the glare of the lowering sun. After the punch went dry and the songs were sung and the hand-shakes and empty pleasantries done with, he fled without looking back.

* * *

No one called, no one rang, and eventually Lancaster grew content in his final isolation. He allowed his apartment lease to lapse and went into the country and rented a room in a chintzy motel on the side of a less-traveled road. He stocked his closet with crates of liquor and cartons of cigarettes, and by day drank more or less continually in the yard of the motel beneath the gloomy shade of a big tree. By night he drank alone in the tavern and listened to an endless loop of rock-a-billy from the juke-box, the mutter and hum of provincial conversation among the locals. Cigarette smoke lay as heavy as that belched from a crematory stack. The bathroom reeked of piss. He always wore one of the seven nicer suits he'd kept from his collection. A suit for each day of the week. He thought of the lacquered black box stashed beneath his flimsy motel bed. His killing jar of the mind. So far he'd resisted the pleasure, the comfort, of handling its contents. Cold turkey was best, he thought.

He waited. Waited, lulled by the buzz of the neon advertisement in the taproom glass. Waited, idly observing barflies—gin-blossom noses, broken teeth, haggard and wasted flesh. A few women patronized the tavern, mostly soft, mostly ruined. Soft bellies, breasts, necks, bad mascara. Soft and sliding. Their soft necks stirred ancient feelings, but these subsided as *he*, in all meaningful ways, subsided.

Inevitably, one of the more vital female denizens joined him at his table in the murkiest corner of the room. They talked of inconsequentialities and danced the verbal dance. Her makeup could've been worse. Despite his weeks of self-imposed silence the old charm came readily. The deep-seated switch clicked on and sprang the lock of the cage of the sleeping beast.

Lancaster allowed her to lead him into the cool evening and toward the rear of the building. He pressed her against the wall, empty parking lot at his back, empty fields, empty sky, and he took her, breathed in the tint of her frazzled peroxide-brittle hair, her boozy sweat, listened to the faint chime of her jewelry as he fucked her. She didn't make much noise, seemed to lose interest in him as their coupling progressed. He placed his hand on her throat, thumb lightly slotted between the joints of her windpipe. Her pulse beat, beat. Her face was pale, washed in the buzzing glow of a single security light at the corner of the eaves, a moth battened against the mesh and cast raccoon shadows around the woman's eyes, masked her, dehumanized her, which suited his purpose. Except as his grip tightened his stomach rolled over, his insides realigning with the lateral pull of an intensifying gravitational force, as if he'd swallowed a hook and someone were reeling it in, toying with him.

They separated and Lancaster hesitated, slack and spent, pants unzipped. The woman smoothed her skirt, lighted a cigarette. She walked away as he stood hand to mouth, guts straining against their belt of muscle and suet. The pull receded, faded. He shook himself and retreated to the motel, his squalid burrow. The thermostat was damaged, its needle stuck too far to the right, and the room was sauna-hot, dim as a pit. He sat naked but for his briefs.

He picked up the phone on the second ring. Mr. Blaylock spoke through miles and miles of static. "You are a wild, strange fellow, Mr. Lancaster. Leave the world as a perfect mystery. Confound your watchdogs, your friends, the lovers who never knew you. All that's left is to disappear." Mr. Blaylock broke the connection.

The muted television drifted in and out of focus. Ice cracked as it melted in Lancaster's glass. The cherry glow of his cigarette flickered against the ceiling like firelight upon the ceiling of a cave. His cigarette slipped from his fingers and burned yet another hole in the carpet. He slept.

A single knock woke him. He waited for another until it became apparent none was forthcoming. He retrieved the box and placed it on the table, arrayed each item with a final reverent caress. Photographs, newspaper clippings, an earring, a charm bracelet. Something for those investigators to marvel at, to be amazed and horrified by what they'd never known regarding his secret nature. Then he went to the door, passed through and stood on the concrete steps. The tavern across the way was closed and black and the night's own blackness was interrupted by a scatter of stars, a veil of muddy light streaming from the manager's office.

The universe dilated within him, above him. Something like joy stirred in Lancaster's being, a sublime ecstasy born of terror. His heart felt as if it might burst, might leap from his chest. His cheeks were wet. Drops of blood glittered on his bare arms, the backs of his hands, his thighs, his feet. Black as the blackest pearls come undone from a string, the droplets lifted from him, drifted from him like a slow motion comet tail, and floated toward the road, the fields. For the first time in an age he heard nothing but the night sounds of crickets, his own breath. His skull was quiet.

First at a trot, then an ungainly lope, Lancaster followed his blood into the great, hungry darkness.

# JAWS OF SATURN

## I.

"The other night I dreamt about this lowlife I used to screw," Carol said. She and Franco were sitting in the lounge of The Broadsword Hotel, a monument to the Roaring Twenties situated on the west side of Olympia. Most of its tenants were economically strapped or on the downhill slide toward decrepitude, not unlike the once grand dame herself. Carol lived on the sixth floor in a single bedroom flat with cracks running through the plaster and a rusty radiator that groaned and ticked like it might explode and turn the apartment into a flaming wreck. "I mean, yeah, I hooked up with plenty of losers before I met you. Marvin was scary. And ugly as three kinds of sin. He busted kneecaps for a living. Some living."

Franco flipped open his lighter and set fire to a cigarette. He dropped the lighter into the pocket of his blazer. He took a drag and exhaled. Franco did not live in The Broadsword. Happily, he lived across town in a smaller, modern apartment building where the elevators worked and the central heating didn't rely on a coal-fed furnace. He decided not to remind her that he too damaged people on occasion, albeit only in defense of his employer. Franco didn't look like muscle—short and trim, his hair was professionally styled and his clothes were tailored. His face was soft and unscarred. He didn't have scars because he'd always been better with his guns and knives than his enemies were with theirs. Franco said, "Marvin Cortez? Oh, yeah. My boss was friends with him. If this goon scared you so much, why'd you stick around?"

"I dunno, Frankie. 'Cause it turned me on for a while, I guess. Who the hell knows why I do anything?" She pushed around her glass of slushed ice cubes and vodka so it caught the light coming through the window and multiplied it on the tablecloth. This was late afternoon. The light was heavy and reddish orange.

"Okay. What happened in the dream?"

"Nothing, really."

"Huh."

"Huh, what?"

"Dreams are messages from the subconscious. They're full of symbols."

"You get a shrink degree I don't know about?"

"No, my sister worked as a research assistant in a clinic. Where were you?"

"In bed. The whole bed was on a mountain, or something. Marvin stood at the foot of the bed and there was a drop off. The wind blew his hair around, but it didn't touch me. I was pretty scared of the cliff, though."

"Why?"

"My bed was practically teetering on the edge, dumbbell."

"This Marvin, guy. Did he do anything?"

"He stared at me—and he was too big. Granted, Marvo really was a hulking dude, Ron Perlman big and ugly, but this was extreme, and I got the impression he would've turned into a giant if the dream had lasted longer. His expression weirded me out. I realized it wasn't really him. Looked like him, except not. More like a mask and it changed as I watched. He was turning into someone else entirely and I woke up before it completely happened."

Franco nodded and tapped his cigarette on the edge of the ashtray. "Clearly you've got feelings for this palooka."

"Don't be so jealous. He skipped on me. Haven't heard from the jerk in years. Weirdest part about the dream is when I opened my eyes the bedroom was pitch black. Except…the closet door opened a bit and this creepy red light came through the crack. Damndest thing. I'm still half zonked, so it's all unreal at first. Then I started to freak. I mean, there's nothing in the closet to make a red glow, and the light itself made my hairs prickle. Something was really, really wrong. Then the door clicked shut and the room went dark again. I'd drunk *waaay* too many margaritas earlier, so I fell asleep."

"You never woke up in the first place," he said. "Dream within a dream. The red light was your alarm clock. Nothing mysterious or creepy about that."

Carol gave him a look. She wore oversized sunglasses that hid her eyes, but the point was clear. She snapped her fingers until a waiter came over. She ordered a rum and coke and made him take the vodka away. "Thing is, this got me thinking. I realize I've been having these dreams all week. I just keep forgetting."

"Your boyfriend in all of them?" Franco tried not to sound petulant. His vodka was down to the rocks and he hadn't asked the waiter for another.

"Not only him. Lots of other people. My mom and dad. A girlfriend from high school that got killed in a crash. My grandparents. Everybody guest starring in my dreams is dead. Except for Marvo—and hell, for all I know he bit the dust. He who lives by the sword and all that."

"This is true," Franco said, thinking of the time a guy swung a machete at his head and missed.

Carol glanced at her watch. She picked up her prim little handbag. "Let's go fuck. Karla's doing my hair later."

## II.

He stripped her in a half-dozen expert movements and had her crossways on the low, narrow bed, a pillow under her hips because he wanted to work her over with a vengeance. His blood boiled after their conversation regarding her old goon boyfriend. She was voluptuous as a '50s pinup and white as milk and her body amazed him. He held her hips and pushed toward climax while she cried out, shoulders and head suspended off the mattress, her fingers twisted in the sheets. He drove, and the bed moved an inch or two with each thrust, adding grooves to the warped and stained floorboards. Then, he came, crashing the bed with enough force to surely jolt the lights in the lower apartment. She swung herself upright and her expression was that of an ecstatic. He met her eyes in the gloom and his brain became jelly; it felt as if it might drain through his nose, suctioned by some force at once ancient and familiar and beyond his comprehension. The iris of her left eye was oblong, out of plumb. It seemed to elongate and slide around like the deformed bubbles in a lava lamp, and for several seconds every piece of furniture, the apartment walls, its doors and fixtures, were distorted, undulating in a way that made him sick in the stomach. Then it passed and he flopped on his back, spent and afraid.

Carol climbed atop him and kissed his mouth. Her breath was hot. Her lips moved wet and swollen against his, "Well, Jesus. Aren't you a voyeuristic sonofabitch." She reached down and her petite fist partially encircled him. She slowly put him back inside her and had her way, mouth against his ear now. He closed his eyes and the vertigo subsided, and he lay in a semi-stupor while his body reacted.

When it finally ended, Carol lighted two cigarettes. She gave him one and then dialed her friend the hairdresser and cancelled her appointment. She slurred like she did after the fifth or sixth cocktail.

Franco smoked his cigarette without enjoying it, his mind ticking with the possibilities of what he'd witnessed. She curled against him, her nails digging into the muscles of his chest. He said, "I think something odd is going on with you."

"Mmm? I feel pretty damned fine."

"Have you been taking drugs? You doing X?"

"Are you trying to piss me off?" She smiled and blew smoke at him.

"I'm trying to decide what I think. You're acting different." He didn't know what to say about her bizarre iris and figured keeping his mouth shut was the best course for the moment.

"Hmm. I've been seeing a hypnotist. Trying to break this smoking habit."

"Uh, did you happen to think that might be the reason you've had lousy dreams lately? Go screwing around in your brain and God knows what'll happen."

"Hypnotism is harmless. All that stuff about them making you cluck like a chicken or do stupid tricks is bullshit. He puts me in a light trance. I'm aware of everything the whole time."

Franco rubbed the vein pulsing in his temple. "Who's this hypnotist."

"Phil Wary. An old dude. Lives upstairs. He was a magician back in the 1970s."

"This is great."

"It's so-so. I paid him three hundred bucks. I've cut back to half a pack a day, but sheesh, it could be better. That's what I'm saying—sure as shit isn't a cure for cancer."

"Okay," he said. He didn't think anything was okay, and in fact had already made up his mind to pay Phil Wary a visit and set the coot straight. Anybody messing with Franco's girl was in peril of falling from a rooftop.

Franco dreamed of standing in a hallway. He was naked and smelled of sex and bitter perfume. The hallway was dark except at the far end where a pair of brassy elevator doors shone, illuminated by an unseen source. He walked toward the doors and they slid apart. He entered the elevator. It was tight and dim. The doors shut. A panel of glowing buttons floated in the sudden darkness. He pressed the L and waited. The elevator moved, silent and frictionless, and with a sense of tremendous speed and he screamed as his body became weightless and his shoes drifted several inches from the floor. He was trapped in a coffin-shaped capsule rocketing into zero g orbit. The control panel flickered and its numerals blackened and popped and died. The overhead strip emitted a hideous red light that caused his skin to smoke and char where it touched. The light dripped like oil, like acid dissolving him.

When the doors opened he stumbled into the empty lobby of The Broadsword Hotel. Yet the chamber was far too vast, and in the distance one of the walls had collapsed. It was cold, and the gloom thick with a sense of ruin. Furniture lay in broken heaps, and tiles of the vast marble floor were smashed, pieces scattered, and everywhere, curtains and streamers of cobwebs and dust. The tooth of the moon shone through the skylight dome. Carol stood hipshot in its sickly beam. She too was naked except for a silvery necklace, and panties that gleamed white against her delectable buttocks. Her figure was unutterably erotic in its slickness and ripe strength and quivering vulnerability, a Frazetta heroine made flesh. Her head craned toward one of the support columns, arm raised in a defensive gesture. She was a voluptuous conceptualization of Fay Wray transported to some occult dimension, gaping at an offscreen terror.

A shadow moved across the floor and obliterated Carol's paralyzed figure. It stretched unto colossal dimensions until its clawed edge overlapped Franco's feet and he raced into the elevator that was no longer an elevator, but an endless tunnel, or a throat.

III.

Franco lay in bed alone until noon. This was his first vacation in two years from his millionaire charge, Jacob Wilson. Wilson had jetted off to Paris for the week with his girlfriend of the moment and Leonard and Vernon, the senior bodyguards.

He didn't have any fear of confined spaces, but today the elevator ride was harrowing. He loosened his tie to alleviate a feeling of suffocation. A middle-aged woman in an enveloping dress crowded him and he sweated and squeezed the bridge of his nose and breathed shallowly until the lift thudded to a halt and squealed open a full ten seconds later.

Despite his rather mundane and admittedly coarse occupation, Franco enjoyed a good, thick book, and was enamored of classical architecture. The hotel had become a hobby. Almost a century old, and enormous, its caretakers kept alive certain elements and traditions not often present in its modern counterparts. There were at least two sublevels, one of which hosted a barbershop, international newspaper kiosk, cigar shop, and a gentleman's club called The Red Room, this latter held over from speakeasy days. On the ground floor was the lounge, the Oak & Shield restaurant, a largely defunct nightclub called The Owl, and the Arden Grand Ballroom. There were galas every few months and he'd vowed to accompany Carol to one in the near future. Franco was an elegant dancer, comfortable waltzing to a big band.

He went to the lounge and sat at the end of the deserted bar furthest from the double doors and the sun streaming through the windows overlooking the hillside and Capitol Lake far below, and across the way, the Capitol Dome itself, a cracked and grimy edifice that somehow retained its grandeur despite years of neglect. He ordered a Bloody Mary, followed immediately by a double vodka. He lighted a cigarette and pressed his hand to his eyes while he smoked.

Franco had become a regular at the lounge these past months since his dalliance with Carol. The staff knew who he worked for and when he dropped a hint about his interest in resident Phil Wary, the white-suited bartender disappeared, then returned with a hotel business card, Mr. Wary's apartment and phone numbers scrawled on the reverse. Franco glanced at the card, then burned it in the ashtray as a courtesy. He left a fifty on the bar when he finally dragged himself off the stool and went in search of answers. He buzzed Mr. Wary's apartment, then he unfolded his cell and tried the phone number.

Someone picked up and breathed heavily. "What?" The accent was foreign to Franco, although it reminded him of the old Christopher Lee Dracula movies.

"Mr. Wary, hey. Could I have a few minutes of your time? I'm downstairs—"

"I heard you buzzing my intercom. I hate that buzzing. That brash, persistent noise drills straight through my eardrum. No, I think you sound like an oaf, a knuckle dragger. A second generation Italian mongrel, perhaps."

Franco made a fist with his free hand and squeezed until his knuckles cracked. "Very sorry, sir. I just need five minutes. Maybe less. You know a friend of mine. Carol—"

Mr. Wary breathed into the phone. He made an odd noise in his throat. "Then I am convinced I am not interested in your company. My business with her is not for you. Goodbye."

The line went dead. Franco stared at his cell for several moments. He carefully folded and put it away. He cracked the knuckles of his right hand. It was a long climb to the seventh floor, but there was no chance of his risking the elevator again. He felt homicidal enough without exacerbating his dire mood with an outbreak of latent claustrophobia. By the fourth floor he'd come to regret his decision. His legs were soft from spending too many hours on his ass in limousines and holding down barstools. He'd given up weight lifting and jogging. The endless columns of booze and stacks of unfiltered cigarettes made his sporadic appearances at the gym painful.

He hesitated at Mr. Wary's door to try the knob—locked. He wiped his brow with the silk handkerchief in his breast pocket. Mr. Wary's apartment lay near the stairwell at the far end of the corridor opposite the elevator. The passages in The Broadsword Hotel were slightly wider and taller than typical of such buildings, rounded and ribbed at the peak in a classical manner. Gauzy light filled the window alcove above the stairwell. Shadows stretched long fingers across the carpet and most of the hallway remained in gloom. A fly complained in a darkened overhead light globe.

Franco tucked away the handkerchief and slipped his stiletto from its ankle sheath. He never carried a pistol when off duty. There wasn't much reason to—unlike thugs such as Carol's ex, he didn't need to moonlight as an enforcer. His time off was free and uncomplicated.

Mr. Wary hadn't engaged the deadbolt, so Franco easily jimmied the lock and pushed through the door. The apartment was cramped and hot and smelled of must and moldering paper. Centered in the living area was a leather couch, matching armchairs, and a pair of ornate floor lamps, all from a bygone era. Mr. Wary owned numerous paintings of foreign pastorals, vine-choked temples and ziggurats, and men and women in peculiar dress. In a corner was an antique writing desk and above its hutch, poster advertisements of magic shows. Several were illustrations of a man in fanciful robes and bejeweled turban, presumably Mr. Wary himself, presiding over various scenes of prestidigitation that generally featured buxom assistants in low-cut blouses.

A yellow cat hissed at Franco's approach and darted behind the coach.

"So it's like this, is it?" Mr. Wary leaned against the frame of the entrance to the kitchen. Short and brutish, his silver and black hair touched the collar of his expensive white dress shirt. His craggy face was powdered white, his eyes deeply recessed so they glinted like those of a calculating animal. His eyelids were painted blue and his lips carmine. He wore baggy pants and sandals that curved up at the toe. He sneered at Franco, baring a full set of sharp white teeth. "This wasn't wise of you."

"Hello, Phil," Franco said, bouncing the knife in his hand. He casually reached back and pulled the door closed. "As I was saying, we really need to have a discussion about Carol. You've been trying to help her quit smoking, I hear. Your methods seem unorthodox. She's acting squirrelly."

"Her treatment is no concern of yours. You'd do well to depart before matters go too far."

Franco bent and sheathed his blade. He straightened and cracked his knuckles and took a couple of steps further into the room. "Yes, yes, it does in fact concern me. I don't like how she's acted lately. I think you've fucked with her head, got her hooked on dope, I dunno. But I plan to figure it out."

"Fool. Love is a poison in that regard. It robs men of their common sense, inveigles them to pursue their own damnation. If it allays your worry, I promise no drugs are involved. No coercion. A touch of chicanery, yes."

"That doesn't sound very nice."

"You're not a complete barbarian. You comprehend simple words and phrases."

Franco's smile sharpened and he moved slowly toward Mr. Wary, sliding his belt free of his pants loops as he went. "Keep talking, old man. I might enjoy this after all."

"She has a virus of the mind and it's rather transmittable, I'm afraid." Mr. Wary squinted at him. He nodded. "Ah, that's who you are. Such an interesting coincidence. I know your employer. His late, lamented Uncle Theodore as well."

"Jacob?" Franco hesitated. He doubled the tongue of his belt around his wrist and let the buckle dangle. "And, exactly how is that?"

"Olympia is a small town. On occasion we've done business. Your master has, shall we say, esoteric interests. As I am a man of esoteric talents, it's a match made in…well, somewhere."

"Carol says you're a washed up magician. Nice posters. You do anyplace famous? Vegas? The Paramount? Nah; you aren't any David Copperfield. You were a two-bit showman. A hack." Franco itched to smack him in the mouth; should have done it already. The old man's contempt, his sneer, was disquieting and stayed Franco's hand for the moment as he reevaluated his surroundings, trying to detect the real source of his unease. "Your hands are gone, so now you hustle dumb broads for whatever's in their purses. I get you, Phil."

"Magician? *Magician?* I'm a practitioner of the black arts. Seventh among the Salamanca Seven. You understand what I mean when I speak of the black arts, don't you, boy? Since you refuse to leave me in peace, would you care for a drink? Too late now, anyway. I have one every afternoon. The doctor says it's good for my heart." Mr. Wary went to a cabinet and took down a crystal decanter and a pair of copitas. He poured two generous glasses of sherry and handed one to Franco. Mr. Wary sat in an armchair. He clicked his nails on the glass and the cat emerged from hiding and sprang into his lap. "Magician? Feh, I'm a sorcerer, a warlock."

"A warlock, huh?" Franco remained standing. He tasted the sherry, then drained his copita and tossed it against the wall. The small crash and tinkle of broken glass temporarily satisfied his need to inflict pain upon his host. "There's no fucking such thing, my friend."

"That was a valuable glass. I acquired the set in Florence. It survived the Second World War." Mr. Wary's eyelids fluttered and he smiled with the corner of his mouth. "Yes, I practice mesmerism. Yes, I pulled rabbits from hats and pretended to saw nubile women in half. I am conversant in many things, sleight of hand being among these. Camouflage, boy. And amusement. One meets fascinating people in that line. However, my bread and butter, my life's work, lies in peeling back the layers of occult mysteries. I was preparing your delectable girlfriend for myself. Ripening and fattening her on the ineffable wonder of the dark. Upon further reflection, I've decided to let you have her."

"What the fuck are you on, man?" Franco imagined poor Carol blithely acquiescing to Mr. Wary's charms—Franco recognized a predator when he met one. Doubtless the old man with his eccentric garb and quaint accent could pour on the charm. And dear God, what did the creepy bastard do to her when she was incapacitated on that decaying couch? "You sonofabitch. You crazy, fucked up sonofabitch." He whipped the belt buckle across Mr. Wary's face. "You're not going to see her again. She calls you, don't answer. She knocks on your door, you don't answer. She tries to talk to you in the hall, you go the other way." Franco punctuated each directive with a slap of his belt buckle while the man sat there, absorbing the abuse. It wasn't until the fourth or fifth swipe that he realized his victim was grinning.

Mr. Wary caught the belt and jerked Franco to his knees and grabbed him by the hair. "You insect. You creeping, insignificant vermin." He stood, dragging Franco upright so they were nose to nose. "Do you wish to witness my work with your precious, idiotic paramour? Such unhappiness awaits you."

Franco was calm even in his terror. He pretended to struggle against Mr. Wary's iron grip before slamming his knuckles against the man's windpipe. He'd once killed a fellow with that blow on the mean streets of Harlem. His fingers broke with a snap and he grunted in shock. Mr. Wary shook him as a dog shakes a rat in its jaws. Franco's vision went out of focus even as he slashed the edge of his left hand against the bridge of Mr. Wary's nose, and yelped because it was like striking concrete.

"That's quite enough," Mr. Wary said and looped the belt around Franco's neck and drew it snug. Franco went blind. His muscles stiffened and when Mr. Wary released him, he toppled sideways and his head bounced off the carpet.

## IV.

Mr. Wary handcuffed Franco in a closet and strung him up on tiptoes by means of keeping the belt around his neck and the other end secured to a rusty hook dangling from a chain. Mr. Wary left the door partially ajar. He suggested that Franco remain mum or else matters would go poorly for him, and worse for Carol, who was soon to arrive for her weekly appointment.

The closet was narrow and stuffed with coats and mothballed suits, but roofless—the space above rose vertically into blackness like a mineshaft. While Franco struggled to avoid hanging himself, he had ample opportunity to puzzle over how this closet could possess such a dimension. Occasionally, reddish light pulsed from the darkness and Franco relived his recent nightmare.

Afternoon bled into red evening and the stars emerged in the sliver of sky through the window behind the couch. Franco was in a state of partial delirium when Carol knocked on the door. Mr. Wary smoothed his shaggy hair and quickly donned a smoking jacket. Carol came in, severe and rushed as usual. He took her coat and fixed drinks and Franco slowly strangled, his view curtailed by the angle of the closet door.

Franco only heard and saw fragments of the next half hour, preoccupied as he was with basic survival. He fell unconscious for brief moments, revived by the pressure at his throat, the searing in his lungs. He contemplated murder. A few feet away his lover and the magician finished their drinks. Mr. Wary told her to make herself comfortable while he put on a recording of scratchy woodwind music. He drew the curtain and clicked on a lamp. He cleared his throat and began to speak in a low, sonorous tone. Carol mumbled, obviously responding to his words.

In due course, Mr. Wary shut off the record player and the apartment fell quiet but for Carol's breathing. He said, "Come, my dear. Come with me," and took Carol's hand and led her, as if she were sleepwalking, to a blank span of the wall. Mr. Wary brushed aside a strip of brittle paper and revealed what Franco took to be a dark water stain, until Carol pressed her eye against it and he realized the stain was actually a peephole. A peephole to where, though? That particular wall didn't abut another apartment—it was an outer wall overlooking the rear square and beyond the square, a ravine.

Carol shuddered and her arms hung slack. Mr. Wary stroked her hair. He muttered in her ear and turned slightly to grin at Franco. A few minutes later, he took her shoulders and gently guided her away from the wall. They exchanged inaudible murmurs. Carol wrote him a check, and seeming to secure her faculties, gathered her coat and bade Mr. Wary a brisk farewell on her way out.

"Your turn," he said upon turning his attention to Franco. He unclasped the belt and led him to the wall, its peeling flap of ancient paper. The peephole oozed a red glow. "All this flesh is but a projection. We are the dream of something greater and more dreadful than you could imagine. To gaze into the abyss is to recognize the dreamer and in recognition, to wake. Not all at once. Soon, however." He inexorably forced Franco's eye against the hole and its awful radiance.

Franco came to, slumped on the couch. Mr. Wary smoked a cigarette and watched him intently. The liquid noises of his own heart, the thump of his pulse, were too loud and he clutched his temples. He recalled a glimpse of Carol's face as dredged from nightmarish limbo. The shape of it, its atavistic lust and ravenous fury terrified him even as a tattered memory. Immense as some forsaken monument, and its teeth—He retched on his shoes.

"It'll pass," Mr. Wary said. The phone, a black rotary, rang. He answered, then listened for several moments. He extended it to Franco. "For you."

Franco accepted the phone and held it awkwardly with his good hand. Across a vast distance, Jacob Wilson said, "Franco? Sorry man, but you're done. I'll have my accountant cut you a check. Kiss-kiss." Across a vast distance, a continent and the Atlantic Ocean, Jacob Wilson hung up.

Mr. Wary took the phone from Franco. "A shame about your job. Nonetheless, I'm sure a man of your ability will land on his feet." He helped Franco rise and propelled him to the door. "Off you go. Sweets to the sweet."

Franco shuffled down the badly lighted hall. A vortex of fire roared in the center of his mind. He stepped into the stairwell. There were no stairs, only a black chasm, and he plummeted, shrieking, tumbling.

"Holy shit! Wake up, dude!" Carol shook his arm. They were in her crummy bed in her crummy apartment. The dark pressed against the window. "You okay? You okay?"

He opened and closed his mouth, biting back more screams. She turned on the bedside lamp and bloody light flooded his vision. He said, "I'm… okay." Tears of pain streamed down his cheeks.

"It's three in the fucking morning. I didn't hear you come in. Why the hell are you still dressed?" She unknotted his tie, began to unbutton his shirt. "Wow, you're sweaty. Sure you're okay? Damn—you drunk, or what?"

"I wish. Got anything?" He wiped his eyes. The lamp had now emitted its normal, butter-yellow light.

"Some Stoli in the freezer." She went into the kitchen and fixed him a tall glass of vodka. He guzzled it like water and she laughed and grabbed the mostly empty glass from his good hand. "Whoa, Trigger. You're starting to worry me." She gasped, finally noticing the lumped and swollen wreck of his right hand. "Oh my God. You've been fighting!"

He felt better. His heart settled down. He took off his pants and fell on the bed. "Nothing to worry about. I had a few too many at the bar. Came here and crashed, I guess. Sorry to wake you."

"Actually, I'm glad you did."

"Why is that?" His eyelids were heavy and the warmth of the booze was doing its magic.

"You won't believe the nightmare I was having. I was walking around in a city. Spain or Italy. One of those places where the streets are narrow and the buildings are like something from a medieval film. I could see through people's skin. X-ray vision. There's another thing. If I squinted just right, there were these…sort of bloody tendrils hooked to their skulls, their shoulders, and whatnot. The tendrils disappeared into creepy holes in the air hanging above them. The fucking tentacles squirmed, like they were alive."

He'd gone cold. The pleasant alcohol rush congealed in the pit of his stomach. The tendrils, the holes of oozing darkness—he pictured them clearly as if he'd seen them prior to Carol's revelation.

She said, "Right before you woke me with all that racket, there was an eclipse. The moon covered the sun. A perfect black disc with fire around the edges. Fucking awesome. Then, there was this sound. Can't describe it. Sort of a vibration. All the people standing in the square flew up toward the eclipse. The tendrils dragged them away. It was like the Rapture, Frankie. Except, nobody was very happy. They screamed like motherfuckers until they were specks. Wham! Here you were. The screams must've been yours."

"I rolled over onto my fingers. Hurt like hell."

"Wanna go to the clinic? Looks bad."

"In the morning."

"Fine, tough guy."

Franco tucked his broken hand close to his face. He lay still, listening for the telltale vibration of doom to pass through his bones.

V.

Carol was driving the car into Olympia's outlying farmland. The day was blue and shiny. A girlfriend had given Carol a picnic set for her birthday—a wicker basket, insulated pack, checkered cloth, thermos, and parasol. Her sunglasses disguised her expression. She always wore them.

Franco hadn't shaved in four days. He'd worn the same suit for as long. The majority of those days were spent downtown, hunched over an ever mounting collection of shot glasses at The Brotherhood Tavern. His right hand was splinted and wrapped in thick, bulky bandages. His fingers throbbed and he mixed plenty of painkillers with the booze to dull the edge while he plotted a thousand different ways to kill his nemesis, Mr. Wary. Evenings were another matter—those dim, unvarnished hours between 2 a.m. that found him alone in his Spartan bedroom, sweating and hallucinating, assailed by a procession of disjointed images, unified only in their dreadfulness, their atmosphere of alien terror.

He'd dreamed of her again last night, seen her naked and transfixed in the grand lobby of The Broadsword that belonged to another world, witnessed her lift as if upon wires toward the domed ceiling, and into shadow. Blood misted from the heights and spackled Franco until it soaked his hair and ran in rivulets down his arms and chest, until it made a puddle between his toes. He'd awakened, his cock stiff against his belly and masturbated, and after, sank again into nightmare. He was in Mr. Wary's apartment, although everything was different—an ebony clock and shelves of strange tomes, and Wary himself, towered over Franco. The old man was garbed in a flowing black robe. A necklace of human skulls jangled against his chest. Mr. Wary had grown so large he could've swallowed Franco, bones and all. He was a prehistoric beast that had, over eons, assumed the flesh and countenance of Man.

"You worship the Devil," Franco said.

"The Lord of Flies is only one. There are others, greater and more powerful than he. Presences that command his own obedience. You've seen them. I showed you."

"I don't remember. I want to go back." A hole opened in the wall, rapidly grew from pinhole to portal and it spun with black and red fires. At its heart, a humanoid form beckoned. And when he surfaced from this dream into the hot, sticky darkness of Carol's bedroom, he'd discovered her standing before her closet, bathed in the red glow. She cupped her breasts, head thrown back in exultance, sunglasses distorting her features, giving her the eyes of a strange insect. The door had slammed shut even as he cried out, and his voice was lost, a receding echo in a stygian tomb.

Now they were driving. Now they were parked atop a knoll and eating sandwiches and drinking wine in the shade of a large, flowering tree. A wild pasture spread itself around the knoll and cattle gathered in small knots and grazed on the lush tufted grass. The distant edge of the pasture was marked by a sculpture of a bull fashioned from sheets of iron. The highway sounds were faint and overcome by the sigh of the leaves, the dim crooning of some forgotten star on Carol's AM radio.

Franco hadn't told her of his apocalyptic visit to Mr. Wary, nor of his resultant termination from Jacob Wilson's security attachment. The job wasn't a pressing concern; he'd saved enough to live comfortably for a while. Prior to this most recent stint, he'd guarded an A-list actor in Malibu, and before that, a series of corporate executives, all of whom had paid well. However, he *was* afraid to speak of Wary, wouldn't know where to begin in any event.

He lay his head in her lap and as she massaged his temples he wondered about this radical change in her personality. He'd not known her to savor a tranquil pastoral setting, nor repose for any duration without compulsively checking her cell phone or chain smoking cigarettes. Her calm was eerie. As for himself, one place to get drunk off his ass was the same as another. The wine ran dry, so he uncapped his hip flask of vodka and carried on. Cumulus clouds piled up, edges golden in the midday sun. He noted some were dark at the center, black with cavities, black with the rot of worms at the core. His eyes watered and he slipped on a pair of wraparound shades and instantly felt better.

"Mr. Wary and I are through," she said.

"Oh? Why is that?" Had the crazy bastard mentioned his confrontation with Franco? Surely not. Yet, who could predict the actions of someone as bizarre as Mr. Wary?

She stuck a cigarette in her mouth and lighted up. "I'm cured."

"Wonderful."

"My nightmares are getting worse, though. I've dreamt the same thing every night this week. There's a cavern, or an underground basement, hard to say, and something is chasing me. It's dark and I don't have shoes. I run through the darkness toward a wedge of light, far off at first. It's an arch and red light is coming through it, from another chamber. I think. Nothing's clear. I'm too scared to look over my shoulder, but I know whatever's after me has gained. I can feel its presence, like a gigantic shadow bearing down, and just as I cross the threshold, I'm snatched into the air."

"The tentacles?"

"Nope, bigger. Like a hand. A very, very large hand."

"Maybe you should see a real doctor."

"I've got four pill prescriptions already."

"There's probably a more holistic method to dealing with dreams."

"Ha! Like hypnotherapy?"

"Sarcasm isn't pretty." Franco sipped vodka. He closed his eyes as a cloud darkened the sun and the breeze cooled. He shivered. Time passed, glimpsed through the shadows that pressed against the thin shell of his eyelids.

Branches crackled and the earth shifted. He blinked and beheld a blood-red sky and a looming presence, a distorted silhouette of a giant. Branches groaned and leaves and twigs showered him, roots tore free of the earth and grass, and he rolled away and assumed a crouch, bewildered at the sight of this gargantuan being uprooting the tree. He shouted Carol's name, but she was nowhere, and he ran for the car parked on the edge of the country road. Behind him, the figure bellowed and there came a crunching sound, the sound of splintering wood. A dirt clod thumped into his back.

Carol was already in the car, driver seat tilted back. She slept with her mouth slightly open. The doors were locked. Franco smashed the passenger window with his elbow and popped the lock. Carol's arms flapped and she covered her face until Franco shook her and she gradually became rational and focused upon him. Her glasses had fallen off during the excitement and he was shocked at how her pupils had deformed into twin nebulas that reflected the red glow of the sky.

"Drive! We gotta get the hell out of here."

She stared at him, uncomprehending, and when he glanced back, the monstrous figure had vanished. However, the tree lay on its side. She said, "What happened?" Then, spying the ruined tree, "We could've been killed!"

He clutched his elbow and stared wordlessly as the red clouds rolled away to the horizon and the blue sky returned.

"You're bleeding," she said.

He looked at his arm. He was bleeding, all right.

## VI.

The doctor was the same guy who'd splinted his fingers. He gave him a few stitches, a prescription for antibiotics and another for more pain pills. He checked Franco's eyes with a penlight and asked if he'd had any problems with them, and Franco admitted his frequent headaches. The doctor wore a perplexed expression as he said something about coloboma, then muttering that coloboma wasn't possible. The doctor insisted on referring him to an eye specialist. Franco cut him off midsentence with a curt goodbye. He put on his sunglasses and retreated to the parking lot where Carol waited.

She dropped him at his building and offered to come up and keep him company a while. He smiled weakly and said he wasn't in any shape to entertain. She drove off into the night. He turned the lights off, undressed, and lay on his bed with the air conditioning going full power. His breath drifted like smoke. He dialed Mr. Wary's number and waited. He let it ring until an automated message from the phone company interrupted and told him to please try again later.

The closet door creaked. The foot of the bed sagged under a considerable weight. Mr. Wary said, "I thought we had an understanding."

"What's happening to me?" Franco stared at the nothingness between him and the ceiling. He dared not look at his visitor. When Mr. Wary didn't answer, Franco said, "Why do you live in a shit hole? Why not a mansion, a yacht? Why aren't you a potentate somewhere?"

"This is what you've done with your dwindling supply of earthly moments? I'm flattered. Not what one expects from the brute castes."

"My dwindling supply...? You're going to kill me. Eat my heart, or something."

Mr. Wary chuckled. "I'd certainly eat your heart because I suspect your brain lacks nutrients. I've no designs on you, boy. Consider me an interested observer; no more, no less. As for my humble abode...I've lived in sea shanties and mud huts. I've lived in caves, and might again when the world ends one day soon."

"So much for the simple life of dodging bullets and breaking people's legs."

"You realize these aren't dreams? There is no such thing. These are visions. The membrane parts for you in slumber, absorbs you into the reality of the corona that limns the Dark. Goodbye. Don't call on me again, if you please." Mr. Wary's weight lifted from the bed and the faint rustle of clothes hangers marked his departure from the room.

Franco shook, then slept. In his dreams that were not dreams he was eaten alive, over and over and over....

## VII.

Franco collapsed in a stupor for the better part of three days. On the fourth evening, as the sun dripped away, the fugue released him and he finally stirred from his rank sheets. The moon rose yellow as hell and eclipsed a third of the sky.

The sensation was of waking from a dream into a dream.

He loaded his small, nickel-plated automatic and tucked it in his waistband. He drove over to The Broadsword and parked on the street three blocks away. The brief walk in the luminous dark crystallized his thoughts, honed his purpose, if not his plan. No one else moved, no other cars. A light shone here and there, on the street, in a building. Somehow this only served to accentuate the otherworldliness of his surroundings, and heightened his sense of isolation and dread.

Carol's apartment was unlocked, the power off. She sat in the window, knees to chin, hair loose. Moonlight seeped around her silhouette. "There you are. Something is happening."

Franco stood near her. He felt overheated and weak.

"Your arm's gone green," she said. "It stinks."

He'd forgotten about the wound, the antibiotics. His jacket stuck to the dressing and tried to separate when he let his arm swing at his side. "Oh, I've got a fever. I wondered why I felt so bad."

"You just noticed?" She sounded distant, distracted. "The moon is different tonight. Closer. I can feel it trying to drag the blood from my skin."

"Yeah."

"I sleep around the clock. Except it's more like I don't really sleep. More like being stoned. I dream about holes. Opening and closing. And caves and dollhouses."

"Dollhouses?"

"Kinda. You know those replica cities architects make? Models? I dream I'm walking through model cities, except these are bigger. The tallest buildings are maybe a foot taller than me. I look in the windows and doll people scream and run off."

"If that's the worst, you're doing all right."

"No, it gets worse. I don't want to talk about that. I've seen things that scared the living shit outta me. I'm losing it. The tendrils; I've seen them for real, while I'm awake." She rested her head against the glass.

Franco gripped the pistol in his pocket. A tremor passed through the walls and floor. Bits of plaster dust trickled from the ceiling. Something happened to the stars, although Carol's shoulder mostly blocked his view. The yellow illumination of the moon dimmed to red.

"We're going into the dark," Carol said. She'd cast aside the sunglasses. Her face was pale and indistinct.

He walked into the kitchenette and drank a glass of tap water. He removed the gun from his pocket and racked the slide. An object thumped in the other room. When he returned she was gone and the front door hung ajar. The hallway stretched emptily, except for the red glow of the elevator at the far end awaiting him with its open mouth. The stairwell entrance was bricked over. Franco considered the gun. He boarded the elevator and pressed the button and descended.

Everything happened as it had happened in his serial nightmares. She was there in the lobby, gazing toward the vaulted ceiling, and he was too late. A wrinkled hand the size and length of a compact car snatched her up by the fleshy strands as a puppeteer might retrieve a fallen marionette and then blood was everywhere. Franco froze in place, his mind splintering as he registered the tendrils that snaked from his own shoulders and rose into darkness.

An impossibly tall figure lurched from the shadow of the ornate support column. A demonic caricature of an old man, his wizened head nearly scraping the domed ceiling, hunched toward Franco, skinny fingers reaching for him, lips twisting in anticipation. Franco recalled the de Goya painting of the titan Saturn who stuffed a man into his frightful maw and chewed with wide-eyed relish. He fell back, raising his arms in a feeble gesture of defense. The giant took the fistful of Franco's strings, the erstwhile ethereal cords of his soul, and yanked him from his feet; grasped and lifted him and Franco had a long, agonizing moment to recognize his own face mirrored by the primordial aspect of the giant.

Even in pieces, eternally disgorging his innards and fluids, he remained cognizant of his agonies. He tumbled through endless darkness, his shrieks flickering in his wake.

## VIII.

He roused from a joyous dream of feasting, of drinking blood and sucking warm marrow from the bone. His sons and daughters swarmed like ants upon the surface of the Earth, ripe in their terror, delectable in their anguish. He swept them into his mouth and their insides ran in black streams between his lips and matted his beard. This sweet dream rapidly slipped away as he stretched and assessed his surroundings. He shambled forth from the great cavern in the mountain that had been his home for so long.

Moonlight illuminated the ruined plaza of the city on the mountainside. He did not recognize the configuration of the stars and this frightened and exhilarated him. During his eons' sleep, trees had burst through cracks in paving stones. He squatted to sniff the leaves, to tear them with his old man's snaggle teeth, and relish the taste of bitter sap. His lover approached, as naked and ancient as himself, and laid her hand upon his shoulder. They embraced in silent communion as the sun ate through the moon and bathed the city in its hideous blood-red glare.

The couple's shadows stretched long and dark over the all tiny houses and all the tiny works of men.

# VASTATION

When I was six, I discovered a terrible truth: I was the only human being on the planet. I was the seed and the sower and I made myself several seconds from the event horizon at the end of time—at the x before time began. Indeed, there were six billion other carbon-based sapient life forms moiling in the earth, but none of them were the real McCoy. *I'm* the real McCoy. The rest? Cardboard props, marionettes, grist for the mill. After I made me, I crushed the mold under my heel.

When I was six million, after the undying dreamers shuddered and woke and the mother continent rose from the warm, shallow sea and the celestial lights flickered into an alignment that cooked far flung planets and turned our own skies red as the bloody seas themselves, I was, exiled-potentate status notwithstanding, as a flea.

Before the revelation of flea-ishness, I came to think of myself as a god with a little G. Pontiff Sacrus was known as Ted in those days. I called him Liberace—he was so soft and effete, and his costumes…. I think he was going for the Fat Elvis look, but no way was I going to dignify my favorite buffoon by comparing him to incomparable E.

Ted was a homicidal maniac. He'd heard the whispers from the vaults of the Undying City that eventually made mush of his sensibilities. He was the sucker they, my pals and acolytes, convinced to carry out the coup. Ted shot me with a Holland & Holland .50; blasted two slugs, each the size and heft of a lead-filled cigar, through my chest. Such bullets drop charging elephants in their tracks, open them up like a sack of rice beneath a machete. Those bullets exploded me and sawed the bed in half. Sheets burst into flame and started a fire that eventually burned a good deal of Chicago to the ground.

Bessie got a bum rap.

* * *

In sleep, I am reborn. Flesh peels from the bones and is carried at tachyon velocity toward the center of the universe. I travel backward or forward along my personal axis, never straying from the simple line—either because that's the only way time travel works, or because I lack the balls to slingshot into a future lest it turn out to be a day prior to my departure.

As much as I appreciate Zen philosophy, my concentrated mind resembles nothing of perfect, still water, nor the blankness of the moon. When I dream, my brain is suspended in a case of illimitable darkness. The gears do not require light to mesh teeth in teeth, nor the circuits to chain algorithms into sine waves of pure calculation.

In that darkness, I am the hammer, the Emperor of Ice Cream's herald, the polyglot who masticates hidden dialects—the old tongues that die when the last extant son of antiquity is assimilated by a more powerful tribe. I am the eater of words and my humor is to be feared. I am the worm that has turned and I go in and out of the irradiated skulls of dead planets; a writhing, slithering worm that hooks the planets of our system together like beads on a string. When all is synchronized and the time comes to surface, a pinhole penetrates the endless blackness, it dilates and I am purged into a howling white waste. I scream, wet and angry as a newborn until the crooked framework of material reality absorbs the whiteness and shapes itself around me.

My artificial wife is unnerved at how I sleep. I sleep, smiling, eyes bright as glass. The left eye swims with yellow milk. The pupil is a distorted black star that matches its immense, cosmic twin, the portal to the blackest of hells. That cosmic hole is easily a trillion magnitudes larger than Sol. Astronomers named it Ur-Nyctos. They recorded the black hole via x-ray cameras and the process of elimination—it displaces light of nearly inconceivable dimensions; a spiral arm of dark matter that inches ever nearer. It will get around to us, sooner or later. We'll be long gone by then, scooped up into the slavering maw of functionally insensate apex predators, or absorbed into the folds of the great old inheritors of the Earth who revel and destroy, and scarcely notice puny us at all. Or, most likely, we'll be extinct from war, plague, or ennui. We mortal fleas.

* * *

The milkman used to come by in a yellow box van, although I seldom saw him. He left the milk bottles on the step. The bottles shone and I imagined them as Simic said, glowing in the lowest circle of Hell. I imagined them in Roman catapults fired over the ramparts of some burning city of old Carthage, imagined one smashing in the skull of my manager, and me sucking the last drops through the jagged red remnants while flies gathered.

I think the milkman fucked my wife, the fake one, but that might've been my imagination. It works in mysterious ways; sometimes it works at cross purposes to my design. I gave up fucking my wife, I'm not sure when. Somebody had to do it. Better him than me.

* * *

The flagellants march past the stoop of my crumbling home every day at teatime. We don't observe teatime here in the next to last extant Stateside bubble-domed metropolis. Nonetheless, my artificial wifey makes a pot of green tea and I take it on the steps and watch the flagellants lurch past, single file, slapping themselves about the shoulders with belts studded with nails and screws and the spiny hooks of octopi. They croak a dirge copped from ancient tablets some anthropologists found and promptly went mad and that madness eagerly spread and insinuated itself in the brainboxes of billions. They fancy themselves Openers of the Way, and a red snail track follows them like the train of a skirt made of meat. Dogs skulk along at the rear, snuffling and licking at the blood. Fleas rise in black clouds from their slicked and matted fur.

I smoke with my tea. I exhale fire upon the descending flea host and most scatter, although a few persist, a few survive and attach. I scratch at the biting little bastards crawling beneath the collar of my shirt. They establish beachheads in the cuffs of my trousers, my socks. And damn me if I can find them; they're too small to see and that's a good metaphor for how the Old Ones react to humanity. More on that anon, as the bards say.

At night I hunch before the bedroom mirror and stroke bumps and welts. It hurts, but I've grown to like it.

* * *

I killed a potter in Crete in the summer of 45 B.C. I murdered his family as well. I'd been sent by Rome to do just that. No one gave a reason. No one ever gave reasons, just names, locations, and sometimes a preferred method. They paid me in silver that I squandered most recklessly on games of chance and whores. Between tasks, I remained a reliable drunk. I contracted a painful wasting disease from the whores of Athens. My sunset years were painful.

The potter lived in the foothills in a modest villa. He grew grapes and olives, which his children tended. His goats were fat and his table settings much finer than one might expect. His wife and daughter were too lovely for a man of such humble station and so I understood him to be an exiled prince whose reckoning had come. I approached him to commission a set of vases for my master. We had dinner and wine. Afterward, we lounged in the shade of his porch and mused about the state of the Empire, which in those days was prosperous.

The sun lowered and flattened into a bloody line, a scored vein delineating the vast black shell of the land. When the potter squatted to demonstrate an intricacy of a mechanism of his spinning wheel I raised a short, stout plank and swung it edgewise across the base of his skull. His arms fell to his sides and he pitched facedown. Then I killed the wife and the daughter who cowered inside the villa between rows of the potter's fine oversized vases I'd pretended to inspect. Then the baby in the wicker crib, because to leave it to starvation would've been monstrous.

Two of the potter's three sons were very young and the only trouble they presented was tracking them down in a field on the hillside. Only the eldest, a stripling youth of thirteen or fourteen, fought back. He sprang from the shadows near the well and we struggled for a few moments. Eventually, I choked him until he became limp in my arms. I threw him down the well. Full darkness was upon the land, so I slept in the potter's bed. The youth at the bottom of the well moaned weakly throughout the evening and my dreams were strange. I dreamt of a hole in the stars and an angry hum that echoed from its depths. I dreamt someone scuttled on all fours across the clay tiles of the roof, back and forth, whining like a fly that wanted in. Back. And Forth. Occasionally, the dark figure spied upon my restless self through a crack in the ceiling.

The next morning, I looted what valuables I could from the house. During my explorations, I discovered a barred door behind a rack of jars and pots. On the other side was a tiny cell full of scrolls. These scrolls were scriven with astronomical diagrams and writing I couldn't decipher. The walls were thick stone and a plug of wood was inset at eye level. I worked the cork free, amazed at the soft, red light that spilled forth. I finally summoned the courage to press my eye against the peephole.

I suspect if a doctor were to give me a CAT scan, to follow the optic nerve deep into its fleshy backstop, he'd see the blood-red peephole imprinted in my cerebral cortex, and through the hole, Darkness, the quaking mass at the center of everything where a sonorous wheedling choir of strings and lutes, flutes and cymbals crashes and shrieks and echoes from the abyss, the foot of the throne of an idiot god. The potter had certainly been a man of many facets.

I set out for the port and passage back to my beloved Rome. Many birds gathered in the yard. Later, in the city, my old associates seemed surprised to see me.

* * *

Semaphore. Soliloquy. Solipsism. That's a trinity a man can get behind. The wife never understood me, and the first A.I. model wasn't any great shakes either. Oh, Wife 2.0 said all the right things. She was soft and her hair smelled nice, and her programming allowed for realistic reactions to my eccentricities. Wife 2.0 listened *too* much, had been programmed to receive. She got weird; started hiding from me when I returned home, and eventually hanged herself in the linen closet. That's when they revealed her as a replica of the girl I'd first met in Lincoln Park long ago. Unbeknownst to me, that girl passed away from a brain embolism one summer night while we vacationed in the Bahamas and They, my past and future pals and acolytes and current dilettante sycophants of those who rule the Undying City, slipped her replacement under the covers while I snored.

Who the hell knows what series of android spouse I'm up to now.

I killed most of my friends and those that remain don't listen, and never have. The only one left is my cat Softy-Cuddles. Cat version one million and one, I suspect. The recent iterations are black. Softy-Cuddles wasn't always a Halloween cat (or a self-replicating cloud of nano-bots), though, he used to be milk white. Could be, I sliced the milkman's throat and stole his cat. In any event, I found scores of pictures of both varieties, and me petting them, in a rusty King Kong lunchbox some version of me buried near the—what else?—birdbath in the back yard. When I riffle that stack of photos it creates a disturbing optical effect.

The cat is the only thing I've ever truly loved because he's the only being I'm convinced doesn't possess ulterior motives. I'll miss the little sucker when I'm gone, nano-cloud or not.

\* \* \*

During the Dark Ages, I spent twenty-nine years in a prison cell beneath a castle in the Byzantine Empire. Poetic justice, perhaps. It was a witchcraft rap—not true, by any means. The truth was infinitely more complicated as I've amply demonstrated thus far. The government kept me alive because that's what governments do when they encounter such anomalous persons as myself. In latter epochs, my type are termed "materials." It wouldn't do to slaughter me out of hand; nonetheless, I couldn't be allowed to roam free. So, down the rabbit hole I went.

No human voice spoke my name. I shit in a hole in the corner of the cell. Food and drink was lowered in a basket, and occasionally a candle, ink, quill and parchment. The world above was changing. They solicited answers to questions an Information Age mind would find anachronistic. There were questions about astronomy and quantum physics and things that go bump in the night. In reply, I scrawled crude pictures and dirty limericks. Incidentally, it was likely some highly advanced iteration of lonely old me that devised the questions and came tripping back through the cosmic cathode to plague myself. One day (or night) they bricked over the distant mouth of my pit. How my bells jangled then, how my laughter echoed from the rugged walls. For the love of God!

Time well spent. I got right with the universe, which meant I got right with its chief tenant: me. One achieves a certain equilibrium when one lives in a lightless pit, accompanied by the squeak and rustle of vermin and the slow drip of water from rock. The rats carried fleas and the fleas feasted upon me before they expired, before I rubbed out their puny existences. But these tiny devils had their banquet—while I drowsed, they sucked my blood, drowned and curdled in tears of my glazed eyes. And the flies.

* * *

Depending upon who I'm talking to, and when, the notion of regrowing lost limbs and organs, of reorganizing basic genetic matrices to build a better mousetrap, a better *mouse,* will sound fantastical, or fantastically tedious. Due to the circumstances of my misspent youth, I evolved outside the mainstream, avoided the great and relentless campaigns to homogenize and balance every unique snowflake into a singular aesthetic. No clone mills for me, no thought rehabilitation. I come by my punctuated equilibrium honestly. I'm the amphibian that finally crawled ashore and grew roots, irradiated by the light of a dark star.

I pushed my best high school bud off the Hoover Dam. Don't even recall why. Maybe we were competing for the girl who became my wife. My pal was a smooth operator. I could dial him up and ask his quantum self for the details, but I won't. I've only so many hands, so many processes to run at once, and really, it's more fun not knowing. There are so few secrets left in the universe.

This I do recall: when I pushed him over the brink, he flailed momentarily, then spread his arms and caught an updraft. He twirled in the clouds of steam and spray, twisting like a leaf until he disappeared. Maybe he actually made it. We hadn't perfected molecular modification, however. We hadn't even gotten very far with grafts. So I think he went into the drink, went straight to the bottom. Sometimes I wonder if he'd ever thought of sending me hurtling to a similar fate. I have this nagging suspicion I only beat him to the punch.

* * *

The heralds of the Old Ones came calling before the time of the terrible lizards, or in the far flung impossible future while Man languished in the throes of his first and last true Utopian Era. Perspective; Relativity. Don't let the Law of Physics fool you into believing she's an open book. She's got a *whole* other side.

Maybe the Old Ones sent them, maybe the pod people acted on their own. Either way, baby, it was Night of the Living Dead, except exponentially worse since it was, well, real. Congruent to Linear Space Time (what a laugh that theory was) Chinese scientists tripped backward to play games with a supercollider they'd built on Io while Earth was still a hot plate for protoplasmic glop. Wrap your mind around that. The idiots were fucking with making a pocket universe, some bizarre method to cheat relativity and cook up FTL travel. Yeah, well, just like any disaster movie ever filmed, something went haywire and there was an implosion. What was left of the moon zipped into Jupiter's gravity well, snuffed like spit on a griddle. A half-million researchers, soldiers, and support personnel went along for the ride.

Meanwhile, one of the space stations arrayed in the sector managed to escape orbit and send a distress call. Much later, we learned the poor saps had briefly generated their pocket universe, and before it went kablooey, they were exposed to peculiar extra-dimensional forces, which activated certain genetic codes buried in particular sectors of sentient life, so the original invaders were actually regular Joe Six-packs who got transmogrified into yeasty, fungoid entities .

The rescue team brought the survivors to the Colonies. Pretty soon the Colonies went to the Dark. We called the hostiles Pod People, Mushrooms, Hollow Men, The Fungus Among Us, etc, etc. The enemy resembled us. This is because they *were* us in every fundamental aspect except for the minor details of being hollow as chocolate bunnies, breeding via slime attack and sporination, and that they were hand puppets for an alien intellect that in turn venerated The Old Ones who sloth and seep (and dream) between galaxies when the stars are right. Oh, and hollow and empty are more metaphorical than useful: burn a hole in a Pod Person with a laser and a thick, oily blackness spewed forth and made goo of any hapless organics in its path.

The Mushroom Man mission? To liquefy our insides and suck them up like a kid slobbering on a milkshake, and pack our brains in cylinders and ship them to Pluto for R&D. The ones they didn't liquefy or dissect joined their happy, and rapidly multiplying family. Good times, good times.

I was the muckety-muck of the Territorial Intelligence Ministry. I was higher than God, watching over the human race from my enclave in the Pyrenees. But don't blame me; a whole slew of security redundancies didn't do squat in the face of this invasion that had been in the planning stages since before men came down from the trees. Game, Set, and Match. Okay, that's an exaggeration. Nonetheless, I think a millennia to repopulate and rebuild civilization qualifies as a Reset at least. I came into contact with them shortly after they infiltrated the Pyrenees compound. My second in command, Jeff, and I were going over the daily feed, which was always a horror show. The things happening in the metropolises were beyond awful. Funny the intuitive leap the brain makes. My senses were heightened, but even that failed to pierce the veil of the Dark. On a hunch, midsentence, I crushed his forehead with a moon rock I used as a paper weight. Damned if there wasn't a gusher of tar from that eggshell crack. Not a wise move on my part—that shit splattered over half the staff sitting at the table and ate them alive. I regenerated faster than it dissolved my flesh and that kept me functional for a few minutes. Oh Skippy day.

A half-dozen security guards sauntered in and siphoned the innards from the remainder of my colleagues in an orgy of spasms and gurgles. I zapped several of the baddies before the others got hold and sucked my body dry.

I'd jumped into a custodian named Hank who worked on the other side of the complex, however, and all those bastards got was a lifeless sack of meat. I went underground, pissed and scared. Organizing the resistance was personal. It was on.

* * *

We (us humans, so-called) won in the end. Rope-a-dope!

Once most of us were wiped from existence, the invaders did what any plague does after killing the host—it went dormant. Me and a few of the boys emerged from our bunkers and set fire to the house. We brought the old orbital batteries online and nuked every major city on the planet. We also nuked our secret bunkers, exterminating the human survivors. Killing off the military team that had accompanied me to the surface was regrettable—I'd raised every one of them from infancy. I could've eliminated the whole battalion from the control room with an empathic pulse, but that seemed cowardly. I stalked them through the dusty labyrinths, and killed them squad by squad. Not pretty, although I'm certain most of my comrades were proud to go down fighting. They never knew it was me who did them dirt: I configured myself into hideous archetypes from every legend I could dream up.

None of them had a noggin full of tar, either. I checked carefully.

I went into stasis until the nuclear bloom faded and the ozone layer regenerated. Like Noah, I'd saved two of everything in the DNA Repository Vault inside the honeycombed walls of Mare Imbrium. The machines mass produced *in vitro* bugs, babies and baby animals with such efficiency, Terra went from zero to overpopulation within three centuries.

The scientists and poets and sci-fi writers alike were all proved correct: I didn't need to reproduce rats or cockroaches. They'd done just fine.

\* \* \*

The layers of Space & Time are infinite; I've mastered roughly a third of them. What's done can't be undone, nor would I dream of trying; nonetheless, it's impossible to resist all temptation. Occasionally, I materialize next to Chief Science Officer Hu Wang while he's showering, or squatting on the commode, or masturbating in his bunk, and say howdy in Cantonese, which he doesn't comprehend very well. I ask him compromising questions such as, how does it feel to know you're going to destroy the human race in just a few hours? Did your wife really leave you for a more popular scientist?

Other times, I find him in his village when he's five or six and playing in the mud. I'm the white devil who appears and whispers that he'll grow into a moderately respected bureaucrat, be awarded a plum black ops research project and be eaten alive by intergalactic slime mold. And everyone will hate him—including his ex-wife and her lesbian lover. Until they're absorbed by the semi-infinite, that is.

I have similar talks with Genghis Khan, Billie Jean King, Elvis (usually during his final sit-down), and George Bush Jr. Don't tell anyone, but I even visit myself, that previous iteration who spent three decades rotting in a deep, dark hole. I sit on the rim of his pit and smoke a fat one and whisper the highlights of *The Cask of Amontillado* while he screams and laughs. I've never actually descended to speak with him. Perhaps someday.

\* \* \*

Dystopian Days, again. That fiasco with the creatures from Dimension X was just the warm-up match. Whilst depopulating Terra, our enemies were busy laying the groundwork for the return to primacy of their dread gods. Less than a millennium passed and the stars changed. The mother continent rose from primordial muck and its rulers and their servitors took over the regions they desired and we humans got the scraps.

It didn't even amount to a shooting war—Occasionally one or another cephalopodan monstrosity lumbered forth from the slimy sea and Hoovered up a hundred thousand from the crowded tenements beneath an atmospheric dome or conculcated another half billion of them to jelly. The Old Ones hooted and cavorted and colors not meant to be seen by human eyes drove whole continental populations to suicide or catatonia. Numerous regions of the planet became even more polluted and inhospitable to carbon-based life. But this behavior signified nothing of malice; it was an afterthought. Notable landmarks survived in defiance of conventional Hollywood Armageddon logic—New York, Paris, Tokyo. What kind of monsters eat Yokohama and leave Tokyo standing? There wasn't a damned thing mankind could do to affect these shambling beings who exist partially in extra-dimensional vaults of space-time. The Old Ones didn't give a rat's ass about our nukes, our neutron bombs, our anthrax, our existence in general.

Eventually, we did what men do best and aimed our fear and rage at one another. The Pogroms were a riot, literally. I slept through most of them. My approval rating was in the toilet; a lot of my constituent children plotted to draw and quarter their Dear Leader, their All Father, despite the fact the masses had everything. *Everything* except what they most desired—the end of the Occupation. I was a god emperor who didn't measure up to the real thing lurching along the horizon two hundred stories high.

Still, you'd think superpowers and the quenching of material hunger might suffice. Wrongo. Sure, sure, everybody went bonkers for molecular modifications when the technology arrived on the scene. It was my boo-boo to even drop a hint regarding that avenue of scientific inquiry—and no, I'm not an egghead. Stick around long enough to watch civilization go through the rinse cycle and you start to look smarter than you really are.

On one of my frequent jaunts to ye olden times I attended a yacht party thrown by Caligula. Cal didn't make an appearance; he'd gone with a party of visiting senators to have an orgy at the altar of Artemis. I missed the little punk. I was drunk as a lord and chatting up some prime Macedonian honeys, when one of Cal's pet mathematicians started holding forth primitive astrophysical theories I'd seen debunked in more lifetimes than I care to count. One argument led to another and the next thing I know, me and Prof Toga are hanging our sandals over the stern and I'm trying to explain, via my own admittedly crude understanding, the basics of molecular biology and how nanobots are the wave of the future.

Ha! We know how that turned out, don't we? The average schmuck acquired the ability to modify his biological settings with the flip of a mental switch. Everybody fooled around with sprouting extra arms and legs, bat wings and gigantic penises, and in general ran amok. A few even joined forces and blew themselves up large enough to take on our overlords of non-Euclidian properties. Imagine a Macy's Day float filled to the stem with blood. Then imagine that float in the grip of a flabby, squamous set of claws, or an enveloping tentacle—and a big, convulsive squeeze. Not pretty.

Like fries with a burger, this new craze also conferred a limited form of immortality. I say limited because hacking each other to bits, drinking each other's blood, or committing thrill kills in a million different ways remained a game ender. The other drawback was that fucking around with one's DNA also seemed to make Swiss cheese of one's brain. So, a good percentage of humanity went to work on their brothers and sisters hammer and tong, tooth and claw, in the Mother of All Wars, while an equal number swapped around their primal matter so much they gradually converted themselves to blithering masses of effluvium and drifted away, or were rendered unto ooze that returned to the brine.

It was a big old mess, and as I said, arguably my fault. A few of my closest, and only, friends (collaborators with the extra-dimensional monster set) got together and decided to put me out of my misery—for the sake of all concerned, which was everyone in the known universe, except me. The sneaky bastards crept into the past and blasted me while I lay comatose from a semi-lethal cocktail of booze, drugs, and guilt. That's where you, or me, came in. I mean, no matter who you are, you're really me, in drag or out.

Afterward, the gang held a private wake that lasted nearly a month. There were lovely eulogies and good booze and a surprising measure of crocodile (better than nothing!) grief. I was impressed and even a little touched.

For a couple thousand years I played dead. And once bored with my private version of Paradise Lost, I reorganized myself into material form and began a comeback that involved a centuries-long campaign of terror through proxy. I had a hell of a time tracking down my erstwhile comrades. Those who'd irritated me most, I kept trapped in perpetual stasis. Mine is the First Power, and to this day I, or one of my ever exponentially replicating selves, revive a traitor on occasions that I'm in a pissy mood and torment him or her in diabolical ways I've perfected past, present, and future.

Now, it amuses me to walk among mortals in disguise of a fellow commoner. I also feel a hell of a lot safer—the Old Ones sometimes rouse from their obliviousness to humanity and send questing tendrils to identify and extract those who excite their obscene, yet unknowable interest.

I'm going to wait them out.

* * *

Seven or eight of us still celebrate Fourth of July despite the fact the United States is now of no more modern relevance than cave paintings by hominids. Specialist historians and sentimental fools such as myself are the only ones who care.

This year, Pontiff Sacrus, Lord High Necromancer bought me a hotdog, heavy on the mustard, from an actual human vendor, and we sat on a park bench. Fireworks cracked over the lake. Small red and green paper lanterns bobbed on the water. The lanterns were dogs and cats, and Paul Revere and his horse. The city had strung wires along the thoroughfares. American flags chattered in a stiffening breeze. I breathed in the smoke and petted Softy-Cuddles who'd appeared from nowhere to settle in my lap.

The Pogroms were finished. Pontiff Sacrus had overseen the Stonehenge Massacre that spring and there weren't any further executions scheduled. According to my calculations exactly six hundred and sixty-seven unmodified Homo sapiens remained extant, although none were aware the majority of the billions who populated the planet were replicants, androids, and remote-operated clones. Pontiff Sacrus's purge squads had eradicated the changelings and shifters and the gene-splicers and any related medical doctors who might conspire to reintroduce that most diabolical technology. He'd reversed the Singularity and lobotomized the once nigh universal A.I. super job, Pontiff, old bean. He purported himself to be the High Priest of the Undying Ones, but they ignored him pretty much the same as every priest of every denomination has ever been ignored by his deity.

Now, the Pontiff has been around for ages and ages. He's kept himself ticking by the liberal application of nano-enhanced elixirs, molecular tomfoolery, and outdated cloning tech. Probably the only remaining shred of his humanity lies within that mystical force that animates us monkeys. His is the face of a gargoyle bust or the most Goddamned beautiful, dick-stiffening angel ever to walk the Earth. He's moody, like me. That's to be expected, since on the molecular level he is me. Right?

Man, oh man, was he shocked when I appeared in a puff of sulfurous smoke after all these eons. I'm a legend; a boogeyman that got assimilated by pop culture and shat out, forgotten by the masses. *Every* devil is forgotten once a society falls far enough. But Pontiff Sacrus remembered. His fear rushed through him like fire; he smelled as if he were burning right there beside me on the bench. He finally grasped that it was I who'd tormented and slain, one by one, our inner circle.

We watched the fireworks, and when the show wound down, I told him I'd decided to reach back and erase his entire ancestry from the Space Time Continuum. The honorable High Necromancer would cease to exist. The spectacle of the god's anguish thrilled me in ways I hadn't anticipated. Naturally, I never planned to actually nullify his existence. Instead, I made him gaze into the Hell of my left eye. He shrieked as I manually severed his personal timeline at the culmination of the fireworks display and set it for continual loop with a delay at the final juncture so he might fraternize with his accumulating selves before the big rewind.

Last I checked, the crowd of Sacrus's has overflowed the park. He'll be/is a city of living nerves, each thread shrieking for eternity. My kind of music.

* * *

Crete, 45 B.C., again. The Universe is a cell. I travel by osmosis. Randomly, to and fro betwixt the poles that fuse everything. It's dark but for a candle within the potter's house. The blood odor is thick. My prior self snores within, sleeping the sleep of the damned. I alight upon the slanted roof; I peep through chinks and spy our restless form in the shadows. He whimpers.

Because I'm bored to tears with my existence, and just to see what will happen, I slip down through the cracks and smother him. His eyes snap open near the end. They shine with blind energy and his bowels release, and he is finished. Then I toss his corpse into the well, and return to the bed and fall asleep in his place.

I've gone back a hundred times to perpetrate the same self murder. I've sat upon the hillside and watched with detached horror as a dozen of my selves scrabble across the roof like ungainly crows, and one by one enter the house to do the dirty deed, then file in and out to and from the well like a stream of ants. This changes nothing. The problem is, the Universe is constantly in motion. The Universe stretches to a smear and cycles like a slinky reversing through its own spine. No matter what I do, stuff keeps happening in an uninterruptible stream.

How I wish the Pod People could give me a hand, help me explore self-annihilation or ultimate enlightenment, which I'm certain are one and the same. Alas, their alien intellect, a fungal strain that resists the vagaries of vacuum, light and dark, heat and cold, remains supremely inscrutable. That goes double for their gargantuan masters. Like me, the fungal tribe and their monster gods (and ours?) exist at all points south of the present. It's enough to drive a man insane.

* * *

After epochs that rival the reign of the dinosaurs, the stars are no longer right. Yesterday the black continent and its black house sank beneath the sallow, poison waves and the Old Ones dream again in the dread majesty of undeath. I wonder how long it will be before the dregs of humanity venture from the bubble-domed metropolises it's known for ages beyond reckoning. The machines are breaking down, and they need them since after the Pogroms all bio modifications were purged. Just soft, weak Homo sapiens as God intended. The population is critically low and what with all those generations of inbreeding and resultant infertility I don't predict a bounce back this time. Another generation or two and it'll be over. Enter (again) the rats, the cockroaches, and the super beetles.

I sigh. I'm shaving. Wife is in the kitchen chopping onions while the tiny black and white television broadcasts a cooking show. The morning sky is the color of burnt iron. If I concentrate, I can hear, yet hundreds of millions of light years off, the throb and growl of Ur-Nyctos as it devours strings of matter like a kid sucking up grandma's pasta.

I stare at my freakish eyeball, gaze into the distorted pupil until it expands and fills the mirror, fills my brain and I'm rushing through vacuum. Wide awake and so far at such speed I flatten into a subatomic contrail. That grand cosmic maw, that eater of galaxies, possesses sufficient gravitational force to rend the fabric of space and time, to obliterate reality, and in I go, bursting into trillions of minute particles, quadrillions of whining fleas, consumed. Nanoseconds later, I understand everything there is to understand. Reduced to my "essential saltes" as it were, I'm the prime mover seed that gets sown after the heat death of the universe when the Ouroboros swallows itself and the cycle begins anew with a big bang.

Meanwhile, back on Earth in the bathroom of the shabby efficiency flat, my body teeters before the mirror. Lacking my primal ichor and animating force that fueled the quasi immortal regeneration of cells that in turn thwarted the perfect pathogen, the latent mutant gene of the Pod People activates and transmogrifies the good old human me into one of Them. Probably the last self-willed fungus standing—but not for long; this shit does indeed spread like wildfire. My former guts, ganglion, reproductive organs, and whatnot, dissolve into a thick, black stew while my former brain contracts and fossilizes to the approximate size of a walnut and adopts an entirely new set of operating principles.

Doubtless, it has a plan for the world. May it and my android wife be very happy together. I hope they remember to feed the cat.

# THE MEN FROM PORLOCK

September 1923

Darkness lay stone heavy as men roused, drawn from inner night by the tidal pull of blood, the weight of bones sagging outward through their flesh. Floorboards groaned beneath the men who shuffled and stamped like dray horses in the gloom of the bunkhouse. Star glow came through chinks in slat siding. Someone had lighted the stove and smoke drifted among the bunks, up to the rafters. It had rained during the night and the air was ghastly damp. Expelled breath gathered on the beams and dripped steadily; condensation oozing as from stalactites of a limestone cave. The hall reeked with the stench of a bunker: creosote and sweat, flatulence and rotten teeth and the bitter tang of ashes and singed tobacco.

Miller hunched nearly double at the long, rough-hewn pine table and ate lumpy dick and molasses for breakfast. He scooped it with a tin spoon from a tin pan blackened and scarred from a thousand fires and the abuses of a thousand spoons. When he'd done, he wiped his mustache on the sleeve of his long johns and drank black coffee from a tin cup, the last element of his rural dining set.

His hands were dirty and horned with calluses from Swede saw and felling axe. He'd broken them a few times over the years and his knuckles were swollen as walnuts. He couldn't make a tight fist with the left hand;

most mornings his fingers froze into a crab claw barely fit to manage his Willie, much less hook an axe handle. At least he was young—most of the old timers were missing fingers, or had been busted up in a hundred brutal ways—from accidents to fistfights to year after year of the slow, deadly attrition from each swing of mattock or axe. Olsen the Swede (first among the many Swedes west of the Rockies) got his leg shattered by a chain as a kid and hopped around the camp with his broadhead axe for a crutch. His archrival Sven the Norwegian (first among innumerable logger Norwegians south of Norway) lost his teeth and an ear while setting chokers back in the Old World—setting chokers was dog's work no matter what country. Even Manfred the German, known and admired for his quick reflexes, had once been tagged by an errant branch; his skull was soft in places and hairless as if he'd survived a fire, and one eye drooped much lower than the other. Lately Manny had climbed the ladder to donkey puncher. A man wasn't likely to be injured while running a donkey; if anything went wrong he'd be mangled, mutilated and killed with a minimum of suffering.

One of the Poles, a rangy, affable fellow named Kasper, frequently asked Miller if he planned to get out before he got his head lopped off, or his legs snapped, or was cut in half by a whip-cracking choker cable, or ended up with a knife stuck in his ribs during a saloon brawl. Perhaps Miller was as pigheaded as most men his age and addicted to the security of quick money in a trade few wanted and fewer escaped?

As for himself, Kasper claimed to be cursed rather than stubborn—madness ran through his blood and yoked him to cruel labor, the wages of sin committed by an overweening ancestor in the dim prehistory of Eastern Europe. The Pole wrote poems and stories by lamplight, although his English translations were so poor it would've been difficult to know exactly how to rate his poetry. Miller wasn't keen for the art of letters, although he possessed a grudging admiration for those who were clever with words. His own grandmother had studied overseas as a girl. After she shipped back to the U.S., she kept her diaries in Latin to confound nosy relatives. She showed them to Miller when he visited her home in Illinois—Grandma filled up seventy-five of the slim, clothbound tomes, a minor library.

Today, Kasper sat on the long form far from Miller, another bleary shade among jostling elbows and grinding jaws. Miller was fine with that arrangement—all day yesterday the Pole worked with him on an eight-foot saw, a misery whip, to take down an old monster cedar. He knew, as did everyone else, Miller was among the loose contingent of veterans inhabiting Slango Camp.

The Pole confided: *My oldest brother was shot by a sniper along the Rheine. He was killed with one of those fucking German "mousers"—the big rifles they shoot with. Our family lives in Warszawa and only found out what happened because one of my brother's comrades was with him when it happened and relayed the bad news and mailed home his personal effects. The Legiony sent my brother home in a simple box. I guess there was some confusion at the train depot because so many plain wooden boxes filled up the freight cars and the boxes had serial numbers instead of names. The people in charge of these things mixed up the manifest lists, so my family and the other families had to pry apart the boxes to figure out who was inside each one. They didn't send an official death notice until several weeks after the funeral, which I could not attend. I could not afford to travel home for a funeral. My little sister and cousin died last year. Cholera. It is very bad back home, the cholera. I couldn't go to her funeral, either. They buried her in our village. My brother was buried in another village because that is where my father's people come from. All the men in our family are buried there. Probably not me, that would be too expensive, but my other brothers, certainly. None of them are interested in coming to America. They are happy in Polska.*

This monologue had come at Miller over the course of many hours and became intelligible to his ear only after the third or fourth cycle. He grunted nominal responses where necessary. Finally, after they toppled the tree and prepared to call it a day, he effectively ended the conversation by unplugging his canteen and dumping its contents over his head until steam lifted from him. He'd looked the Pole in the eye and said, *At least they found enough of him to pack in a box. That's a pretty good deal if you think about it.*

Slango was small as camps went—two bunkhouses, the filing house, courtesy car, company store, a couple of storage sheds; no electricity, no indoor plumbing, nothing fancy. Bullhead & Co. played fast and loose, a shoestring operation one or two notches above a gyppo outfit. The owner and his partners ran the offices from distant Seattle and Olympia and rumor had it they'd eventually be swallowed up by Weyerhaeuser or another giant.

According to some, Bullhead himself visited once the prior year and stayed for several days in the superintendent's car on the company engine, *John Henry*. This surprised Miller; Slango Camp lay entrenched in the rugged foothills of Mystery Mountain, a heavily forested region of the Olympic Range. The camp was a good sixteen miles from the main rail line, and from there another eighteen miles from the landing at Bridgewater Junction. The spur to Slango Camp plunged through a temperate jungle of junk hemlock, poplar and skinny evergreens, peckerwood, so-called, and nearly impassable underbrush—seas of devil's club, blackberry brambles, and alder. The loggers spanned the many gullies and ravines with hastily chopped junk trees to support rickety track. It seemed improbable anybody, much less a suit, would visit such a Godforsaken place unless they had no other choice.

Miller stowed his kit and dressed in his boots and suspenders and heavy jacket. The initial sullen mutters of exhausted men coalesced and solidified around him and evolved into crude, jocular banter fueled by food and coffee and the fierce comradery of doomed souls. He'd seen it in the trenches in France between thudding barrages of artillery, the intermittent assaults by German infantry who stormed in with their stick grenades and "mousers," as Kasper said, and finally, hand to hand, belly to belly in the sanguine mud of shoulder-width tunnel walls, their bayonets and knives. He seldom made sense of those days—the mortar roars, the fumaroles from incendiary starbursts boiling across the divide, eating the world; the frantic bleats of terrorized animals, and boys in their muddy uniforms, their blackened helmets like butcher's pots upended to keep the brains in until the red, shearing moment came to let them out.

He went into the cold and wet. Light filtered through the trees. Mist seeped from the black earth and coiled in screens of brush and branches and hung in tatters like remnant vapors of dry ice. Men drifted, their chambray coats and wool sock hats dark blobs in the gathering white. Even as he shivered off that first clammy embrace of morning fog, mauls began to smash spikes and staples into the planed logs laid alongside the edges of the camp. Axes clanged from the depths of the forest, ringing from metal-tough bark. The bull gang paid cables from the iron bulk of the donkey engine. The boys shackled the cable to the harnesses of a six-oxen team and drove them, yipping and hollering, into the mist that swallowed the skidder trail—a passage of corduroy spearing straight through the peckerwood and underbrush, steadily ascending the mountain flank where the big timber lay ripe for the slaughter.

"Miller!" McGrath the straw boss gestured to him from the lee of the company store. McGrath was one of the old boys who haunted logging camps everywhere—sinewy and grizzled and generally humorless; sharp-eyed as a blackbird and possessed of the false merriment of one as well. He was Superintendent Barrett's foreman, the voice and the fist of his authority. Plug tobacco stained the corners of his mouth. Veins made ridges and valleys in his forehead and neck and the backs of his leathery hands. A lot of the men regarded him with antipathy, if not naked hatred. But that was the compact between peasants and overseers since the raising of the Pyramids.

Miller acknowledged the dynamic and accepted the state of things with equanimity. He actually felt a bit sorry for the boss, saw in the scarred and taciturn and blustering foreman the green youth who'd been ragged raw and harrowed by the elders of his day, exactly the same as every other wet-behind-the-ears kid, discerned that those scars had burrowed in deeper than most would ever know.

"Miller, boy!"

"Yes, sir."

"Been here, what—two weeks?"

"I guess that's right, sir." Really it was closer to six weeks since he'd signed on in Bridgewater and road the train to Slango with a half-dozen other new hands.

"Huh. Two whole weeks and we ain't had us a jaw. I guess we jawin' now. You a good shot, boy?"

"I dunno about that, sir."

McGrath grinned to spit chaw and rubbed his mouth. "You was a rifleman in the Army, wasn't you? A sniper? That's what I hear. You a real keener."

"Marines, sir." Miller looked at his feet. One of the men, probably Rex or Hagen, had talked. A group of them went hunting white tails a couple of Sundays back. They'd been skunked all day and taken to passing around one of the bottles of rotgut hooch Gordy Thompson kept stashed in his footlocker, and swapping lies about the battles they'd fought and the women they'd fucked and who was the lowest of the lowdown mutts in Slango, which boiled down to McGrath or Superintendent Barret, of course, and who wouldn't like to toe the line if it meant a shot at one of those bastards.

The party was heading toward camp to beat darkness when Rex, the barrel-chested brute from Wenatchee, proffered a drunken wager nobody could peg a stump he marked by pinning it with an empty cigarette pack some two hundred yards from their position. Like an idiot, Miller casually opined he could nail a stump from at least twice that distance. Everybody was three sheets to the wind; rowdy wagers were laid. Dosed on whiskey or not, Miller's hands remained steady. He fired five rounds from the British Enfield he'd carried home from the Front, rapidly jacking the bolt action to eject each shell and chamber the next bullet—eight of ten rounds in a pattern that obliterated the illustration of a horse and carriage. Floyd Hagen covered the wreckage with a silver dollar as the men murmured and whistled amongst themselves.

"Where you from?"

"Utah."

"You live in the hills, then? You a Mormon?"

"No sir, I'm not a Mormon. My people are Catholic."

"Yeah? I figure everybody in Utah for a Mormon. They run the regular folks out on rails is what I hear."

"Well, I don't know what they do in Salt Lake, sir. We were raised Catholic. The Mormons left us alone."

"But your people lived in the hills, din't they?"

"That's so."

"What I thought. You a hillbilly, I seen it straight away. Me too. North Carolina, Blue Ridges. We know all about squirrel stew, an' opossum pie, ain't that right? You got opossum in Utah, don't you, boy?"

Behind Miller's left eye the world cracked and vomited blood—red sky limning a benighted prairie of scrub and slick pebbles like the scales on the spine of the Ouroboros. In the seam of the horizon a jackrabbit flew from rock to rock.

"That Po-lack said you shot a bunch of Huns in the war. That right, boy? You pick off some Huns?" McGrath grinned and spat again, sent a withering stream of acid against the plank skirting of the shack. "Nah, don't worry about that. My grandpappy was in Antietam and he didn't talk about it none either. They's a photographer comin' in on the *John Henry*. Be here this weekend. Cookie wants a couple nice bucks for supper. I'm thinkin' you, Horn, Ruark, Bane, and Stevens can take the day off, go git us some meat. Oh, and Calhoun. He smashed his thumb the other day. Cain't hold an axe, but maybe he kin skin with his good hand, huh? Useless as teats onna boar 'round here."

"A photographer." That meant a distraction of the highest order, surpassed only by visits from upper management. This outside scrutiny also meant the bosses would be bigger pricks than usual.

"Some greenhorn named Chet Goul-ee-ay. Goddamned Frenchies. The Supe says we gotta squire him around, wipe his ass an' sich. Put on the dog an' pony show."

"I'm in the cedar stand with Ma today." Miller raised his head to follow a jay as it skimmed the roof and landed on a moss-bearded shake. A camp robber. The bird fluffed its gray feathers and watched him and the straw boss.

"I ain't sendin' Ma with you. He cain't shoot worth shit. That I know."

"Somebody's got to pack the meat downhill."

"Okay. Take him too. Seven, that's a good number, anyhow. Maybe you boys'ill get lucky."

* * *

Miller went to the bunkhouse and fetched his frame pack and rifle and slipped a knife into his belt. He stuck some shells into his jacket pockets and helped himself to biscuits and beans from the cook shack. There were four cooks. Two stout, no-nonsense types, and two doughty women renowned for their severity and parsimony with seasonings. The dour quartet bossed around a squad of bottle washers and scullery maids. The chief cook, Angus Clemson, grudgingly handed over the vittles, grumping that he hadn't been given prior notice of this raid upon his stores. Leftovers were the best he could do—and Miller had best be damned grateful for the courtesy.

The impromptu expedition took some time to organize and it was nearly midday before the other men had gathered the necessary supplies and were ready to venture forth.

Calhoun, Horn, and Ma met him in the yard. Calhoun was a tall lad; hard-bitten and deadly serious. His left thumb was wrapped in a bandage. Despite his youth and hard bark, he'd proved meticulously groomed and well-spoken. Ma was shorter, and wide as a mattock handle across the shoulders. His hair hung long and oily over a prodigious brow and his eyes shone dull yellow. He spoke seldom and when he did, his Welsh slur rendered him largely unintelligible. His raw strength was the stuff of legend. He could walk off with three hundred pounds of cable looped over his shoulders as if it were nothing. He'd once grabbed a planed log that took three men to move and hoisted it overhead with a grunt and a groan before heaving it onto a pile; on another legendary occasion he single-handedly dragged a cast iron camp stove of at least a quarter ton out of the mud before other men could finish harnessing the mules. Ma wasn't challenged to many arm wrestling or Indian wrestling matches.

Thaddeus Horn, a rawboned youngster raised in the finest Kentucky backwater tradition, wore a coonskin cap slick with grease and dirt, declared it had been in his family for three generations. Flattened and hideously bleached and hopping with bugs as the cap appeared to be, Miller scarcely doubted the assertion. The youth packed a massive Springfield rifle that could've been a relic from the days of the Texas Revolution, or a buffalo gun Sam Houston might've fired over the ramparts of the Alamo—although Cullen Ruark swore by his Big Fifty and Moses Bane scoffed good-naturedly and bragged *his* antique Rigby could knock down a small tree if he cut loose both barrels at once.

Miller asked Horn if he'd seen Stevens or the others. The kid waved toward the hills, said he figured the trio decided to hightail it before the straw boss changed his mind and sent them all back to hacking at trees.

They hiked up out of camp, slogging through the wastes and ruins of a vast swath of clear-cut land. The near slopes were littered with shorn stumps and orange sheaves of bark. The sundered loam oozed sap and water like a great open wound. Bombs might've caused such devastation, or perhaps Proteus himself rose from the depths to rip loose the skin of the ancient mountain, peeled it away to bare the granite bones.

Bane, Ruark, and Stevens awaited them at the boundary where deep forest began. Three pack-mules were tethered nearby, munching on weeds. Ruark was a wiry galoot. His snow-white beard touched the middle button of his leather vest. Nobody knew much about Ruark—he didn't say two words on any given day, but he swung an axe like a fiend from Hell. Moses Bane was another old-timer, hair just as snowy, yet even shaggier. He was also much fleshier than Ruark and scarred around the eyes and nose and almost as bullishly powerful as Ma. A lot of the younger hands called him Grampa Moses. He was a bit more talkative than his pal Ruark, especially after he'd gotten a snootful. It was said the duo served in the Spanish-American War as scouts. Neither spoke of it, however.

Both men were loaded like Sherpas—bedrolls, ropes, and hooch jugs; rifles, single shot pistols, axes, skinning knives, and God knew what all. Miller felt weary from simply looking at the old boys.

Stevens lounged on the butt of a deadfall and smoked an Old Mill from a bashed pack he stuffed in his front pocket. He rested a lever-action Winchester across his knees. A few years older than Miller and almost handsome after a rough fashion. His hair was dark and shaggy and fell near the collar of his canvas vest. Some said Stevens was the best topper at Slango; he certainly clambered up trees with the speed and agility of a raccoon.

Miller privately disdained this popular assessment—if the man was *that* good McGrath wouldn't have turned him loose to poach deer, visiting photographer or not. Bullhead & Co. ran entirely too close to the margin—Superintendent Barret had announced a few days beforehand that the home office expected to see the Slango region logged and its timber on rail flats by Valentine's Day. This produced a few sniggers and wisecrack asides about Paul and Babe signing on to right the ship. Neither Barret nor McGrath laughed and it was plain to see Slango would be upping stakes or folding its tents by midwinter.

"Boys," Stevens said.

"Whatch ya got there?" Horn eyed a glass jug in the weeds by Stevens' boot.

"Hooch," Stevens said.

"Well, guddamn, I seen that," Horn said. "Ma got some, too. Regular heathen firewater. Right, Ma?"

Ma ignored them, his attention fixed on a mosquito growing fat with blood on his misshapen thumb knuckle. The stupid intensity of the Welshman's fascination made Miller slightly sick to his stomach.

"Yeh," Stevens said. "May not bag us a deer, but we gonna get shit-drunk tryin'." He picked up the jug and put it in a burlap bag. He tied the bag to his pack and slipped the pack over his shoulders and began trudging into the woods.

"Okay!" Horn followed him, the Springfield slung loosely over his shoulder. Ma went close behind them and Miller hung slightly back to avoid being slashed across the face by sprung branches. The sun had burned through the overcast, but its rays fell weak and diffuse here in the cool, somber vault of the forest. The air lay thick and damp as if they'd shuffled into the belly of a crypt.

None of them was familiar with the environs beyond Slango. However, Stevens had borrowed a topographical map from the superintendent's car and they decided to follow the ridges above Fordham Creek. The surveyors who'd originally explored the area had noted a sizable deer population in the hinterlands upstream. Eschewing a group council, Bane and Ruark silently moved ahead of the group to cut for sign.

The old growth trees were enormous. These were the elders, rivals to the Redwood Valley sequoias that predated Christ, the Romans, everything but the wandering tribes of China and Persia. Crescents of white fungus bit into slimy folds of bark and laddered toward the canopy. Leaves had begun to drop and the ground was slimy with their brown and yellow husks. Vast mushroom beds, fleshy and splendorous, lay in shallow grottos of root and rock. Horn tromped across one in childish glee. Hooting and cackling, he grabbed Ma by the arm and the pair jigged in the pall of green smoke. Horn had been drinking heavily, or so Miller hoped. He dreaded to think the boy was so simple and maniacal as a matter of inbreeding.

Birds and squirrels chattered from secret perches and Horn abruptly blasted his rifle at a roosting ptarmigan as the group negotiated a steep defile of a dry stream bed. Leaves and wood exploded and it was impossible to determine whether the bird flew away or was blown to bits. The unexpected boom caused Stevens and Miller to drop to their knees. Horn staggered from the recoil and lost his footing on the slippery rocks. He slid ass over teakettle down the slope and crashed into some brambles. The mules skittered free and bolted into the brush and it required a good half hour to recapture them.

Stevens scowled at the boy. He gained his feet and hesitated as if contemplating violence. Then he laughed and unlimbered his jug and had a pull. Afterward, he handed the jug to Miller. Miller took a snort of the sweet, dark whiskey and lost his breath for a few seconds. Stars shot through his vision. "Careful, sonny boy. That'll curl your toes—my daddy makes it himself. Finest Californee awerdenty you're likely to sample in this lifetime."

Miller would've agreed if his voice hadn't been burned to ash in his throat.

Bane and Ruark emerged from the undergrowth and reported they'd located a large hollow not far below the chaparral and possibly that supply of deer meat the boss so badly desired. Spoor was plentiful at least. There were several high vantages and effecting a killing field shouldn't prove difficult. If all went well, the party would bag their prizes and return safely to Slango by tomorrow night.

The expedition made camp within a tiny clearing in the lee of a slab of rock jutting from the hillside. The outcropping loomed, thick with tufts of moss and lichen. They gathered wood and built a bonfire and sawed rounds from a log to seat themselves in the glare of the flames. The men stuck their hands near the fire. It was bitter cold. Each evening the snowline crept lower, dragging its veil of white dust.

Darkness blotted out the landscape. Embers streamed through notches in the canopy and swirled among the stars. Stoic, brooding Ma unpacked his fiddle and sawed a lively jig for the boys, who clogged in time while tending the mules and cooking supper. The Welshman's expression remained remote and dull as ever. His hands moved like mechanisms that operated independently of his brutish mind, or as though plucked and maneuvered by the strings of a muse. Idiocy and genius were too often part and parcel of a man. Miller grinned and tapped his toe to the rhythm, however, the ever watchful segment of his brain that took no joy in anything wondered how far the light and music penetrated into the black forest, how far their shouts and hoots echoed along gullies and draws. And his smile faded.

Supper was roasted venison, Indian bread, and coffee, a couple of fingers of moonshine in the dregs for dessert. Conversation and fiddle-accompaniment ebbed and for a while everyone fell into reverie, heads cocked toward the whispering wind as it brushed the treetops. Night birds warbled and small creatures rustled in the leaves.

"They's stories 'bout these parts," Bane said with an abruptness that caught Miller off guard. Bane and Ruark had laid out an array of knives, tomahawks, and sundry accessories for oiling and sharpening. Ruark hefted an Arkansas Toothpick, turning it this way and that so it gleamed in the firelight. Bane painstakingly stroked a whetstone across the edge of his felling axe. A lump of chaw bulged his cheek. "Legends, guess ya might say." It was no secret how much "Grandpa Moses" loved to spin a yarn. His companions immediately paid heed, leaning closer toward where he sat, white hair and beard wild and snarled, little orange sparks shooting as he rasped his axe.

Horn became agitated. "Aww, dontcha go on, old man. No call for that kinda talk while we're hunkered here in the woods at night. No sir, no sir."

Stevens guffawed. "What's a matter, kid? Your mama put the fright in you back in Kentucky?"

"Hush yer mouth 'bout my mama."

"Easy, kid. Don't get your bristles up."

Miller didn't speak, yet misgiving nagged him. He'd dwelt among the Christian devout as well as the adherents of mystical traditions. There were those who believed to speak of a thing was to summon it into the world, to lend it form and substance, to imbue it with power. He wasn't sure how to feel about such theories. However, something within him, perhaps the resident animal, empathized with the kid's fear. Mountain darkness was a physical weight pressing down and it seemed to *listen*.

Bane paused to gaze into the darkness that encroached upon the circle of the cheery blaze. Then he looked Stevens dead in the eye. "I knew this Injun name o' Ravenfoot back to Seattle who come from over Storm King Mountain way. Klallam Injun. His people have hunted this neck o' the woods afore round eyes ever hollowed canoes. He told me an' I believe the red man knows his stuff."

"Who'd believe an Injun about anything?" Stevens said. "Superstitious bastards."

"Yeah. An' what tickled yer fancy to speak up now?" Horn said, his tone still sour and fearful. Ma squatted near him, head lowered, digging into the dirt with a knife. Miller could tell the brute was all ears, though.

"That map of your'n," Bane said to Stevens.

"What the hell are you chinnin' about? The map? Now that don't make any kind of sense." Stevens took the map from his pocket, unrolled it and squinted.

"Where'd you get that?" Miller said, noting the paper's ragged border. "Tear it from a book?"

"I dunno. McGrath gave it to me. Prolly he got it from the Supe."

Now Bane's eyes widened. "My grand pappy was a right reverend and a perfessor. Had lots o' books lyin' 'round the house when I was a sprat."

"You can *read*, Moses?" Calhoun spoke from where he reclined with the wide brim of his hat pulled low. The men chuckled, albeit nervously.

"Oh, surely," Bane said. "I kin read, an' also write real pretty when I take a notion."

"Recites some nice poetry, too," Ruark said without glancing up from whetting his knife. "I'm partial to the Shakespeare." These were the first and only words he'd uttered all day.

"But Grandpappy was a dyed in the wool educated feller. He took the Gospel Word to them heathens in Eastern Europe an' the jungles of Africa, an' some them islands way, way down in the Pacific. Brought back tales turn yer hair white."

"Aha, that's what happened to your hair!" Stevens said. "Here I thought you was just old."

Bane laughed, then spat. "Yeh, so I am, laddio. This is a haunted place. Explorers wandered 'round Mystery Mountain in the 1840s. Richies in the city, newspapermen mostly, financed 'em. Found mighty peculiar things, they say. Burial mounds 'an cliffside caves with bodies in 'em like the Chinee do. A few o' them explorers fell on hard luck an' got kilt, or lost. Some tried to pioneer and disappeared, but onea 'em, a Russian, came back an' wrote hisself a book. An pieces o' that book wound up in another one, a kind o' field guide. Looks like a *Farmer's Almanac*, 'cept black with a broken circle on the cover. I seen that page afore. Ain't too many copies o' that guide not what got burned. My mama was a child o' God and hated it on account o' its pagan blasphemy, documentin' heathen rites an' sich. Grandpappy showed me in secret. He weren't a particularly devout feller after he finished spreadin' the Lord's Word. Had a crisis o' faith, he said."

"Well, what did the Russkie find?" Calhoun said.

"Don't recall, 'xactly." Bane leaned the axe against his knee and sighed. "Ruins, mebbe. Mebbe he lied, 'cause ain't nobody backed his claims. He was a snake oil salesman, I reckon. They run him outta the country."

"I think," Miller said, "that's an amazing coincidence, your ending up on this hunt. Could be you're pulling our legs."

"Mebbe. But I ain't. God's truth."

"*Arri, arri.*" Ma scowled and stabbed at the ground. His voice was thick as cold mush.

"Sounds like Ma thinks that redskin mumbo-jumbo rubbed off on you,"

Stevens said. "Why'n blue blazes did you volunteer to come along if this place is lousy with bad medicine?"

"Hell, son. McGrath done volunteered me."

"Have at it, then." Calhoun raised his hat with one finger. "What's so spooky about Mystery Mountain?"

"Besides the burial mounds and the cave crypts, and them disappeared explorers," Stevens said with a smirk.

"Oh, they's a passel o' ghosts an' evil spirits, an' sich," Bane said, again glancing into the night. "Demons live in holes in the ground. Live in the rocks and sleep inside big trees in the deep forest where the sun don't never shine. Ravenfoot says the spirits sneak up in the dark an' drag poor sleepin' sods to Hell."

"Hear that, Thad?" Stevens nodded at Horn. "Best sleep with one eye open."

"I hearda one," Ruark said, and his companions became so quiet the loudest noise was the pop and sizzle of burning sap. He spat on his whetstone and continued sharpening the knife. "Y'all remember the child's tale Rumpelstiltskin? The king ordered the miller's daughter to spin straw to gold or die, an' a little man, a dwarf, came to her an' said he'd do the job if'n she promised him her firstborn child? Done deal an' she didn't get her head chopped off."

"They got themselves hitched and made a bunch of papooses," Stevens said. "Everybody heard that story."

"How'n hell that dwarf spin straw to gold?" Horn said. He took a swig of hooch and belched.

"Magic, you jackass," Calhoun said.

"Lil' fucker was the spawn o' Satan, that's how," Bane said.

"The king made her his queen an' everthin' was hunkum-bunkum for a while," Ruark said. "Then, o' course, along comes baby an' who shows up to collect his due? She convinces him to give her until the dark o' the moon to guess his name an' call off the deal. So bein' a cantankerous cuss, the feller agrees. He knows his name is so odd she hasn't a snowball's chance in hell o' sussing it out." He paused and finally looked up from his work and slowly met the wondering gaze of each man riveted to his words. "But that ol' girl *did* cotton to the jig. She sent messengers to the four corners o' the land, their only mission to gather a list o' names. One o' them men reported a queer sight he'd spied in a deep, dark mountain valley. The scout saw a mighty fire below and who danced 'round that blaze but a pack o' demons led by the little gold-spinner hisself. The dwarf cackled an' capered, boasting that his name was Rumpelstiltskin. He was mad as a wet hen when the queen turned the tables later on. He stomped a hole in the palace floor an' fell into the earth. That was the end o' him."

"That's a pretty happy ending, you ask me," Miller said as he pondered the incongruity of camping in the remote mountains with a company of dog-faced loggers and listening to one of them butcher the Rumpelstiltskin fairytale.

"Well, that part about the demons jumpin' 'round the fire an' calling up the forces o' darkness, some say they seen similar happenins in these hills. They say if'n you creep along the right valley in the dead o' night 'round the dark o' the moon you'll hear 'em singin' an' chantin'."

"Hear who?" Calhoun said.

Ruark kind of smiled and shook his head and said no more.

"I'm turnin' in," Horn said and jumped to his feet. "Ain't listenin' to a bit more o' this nonsense. No siree Bob." He stomped a few feet away and rolled out his blanket and climbed under it so only the crown of his cap and the barrel of his rifle were showing.

"Too bad your mama ain't here to tuck you in and sing a lullaby," Stevens called.

"Told you to shuddup 'bout my mama," Horn said.

Calhoun chucked a stick of wood, bounced it off the kid's head. That broke the mood and everybody guffawed, and soon the company crawled into their blankets to catch some shuteye.

* * *

Miller roused with an urge to piss. A moment later he lay frozen, listening to the faint and unearthly strains of music. Initially, he thought it the continuation of a dream he'd had of sitting in the balcony of a fancy court while the queen in her dress and crown entertained a misshapen dwarf who wore a curious suit and a plumed hat, while in the background Ruark narrated in a thick accent, but no, this music was real enough, although it quavered at the very edge of perception. An orchestra of woodwinds and strings buoyed a choir singing in a foreign tongue. This choir's harmony rose and fell with the swirls of wind, the creaking of the sea of branches in the dark above him. He couldn't tell how far off the singers might be. Sound traveled strangely in the wild, was all the more tricky in the mountains.

"Ya hear that?" Calhoun said. Miller could barely make out the gleam of his eyes in the light of the coals. The young man's whisper was harsh with fear. "The hell is that?"

"The wind, maybe," Miller said after a few moments passed and the music faded and didn't resume. The sky slowly lightened to pearl with tinges of red. He rose and ventured into the brush, did his business and wiped his hands with dead leaves and fir needles. Ruark was moving around by the time Miller returned. The old logger kindled the fire and put on coffee and biscuits. That drew the others, grumbling and muttering, from their bedrolls.

No one mentioned anything about voices or music, not even Calhoun, so Miller decided to keep his own counsel lest they think him addled. This was desolate country and uninhabited but for the occasional trapper. He'd heard the wind and nothing else. Soon, he pushed the mystery aside and turned his thoughts toward the day's hunt.

Breakfast was perfunctory and passed without conversation. The party struck camp and headed northwest, gradually climbing deeper into the folds of Mystery Mountain. Sunlight reached fingers of gold through the canopy and cast a tiger stripe pattern over the shrubbery and giant ferns and the sweating boles of the trees. The pattern rippled as leaves rippled and shifted in a way that might hypnotize a man if he stared at it too hard. Miller blinked away the stupor and trudged along until they crested a bluff and found the wide, irregular bog Bane had spoken of the previous evening. The fellow had been correct—there was deer sign everywhere. The party fanned out in pairs and settled behind screens of brush to wait.

Miller dropped a deer as it entered the field at the edge of his weapon's effective range, while Stevens, Bane, and Ruark each bagged one in the middle ground. Unfortunately, Horn's lone shot merely injured his prey and it darted into the woods, forcing him, Ma, and Calhoun to pursue.

By noon four bucks were skinned and quartered. The men loaded the mules and strapped smaller cuts to their own packs and prepared to set off for Slango. Ma, Horn, and Calhoun remained in the forest pursuing the wounded buck.

"Damnation," Bane said, shading his eyes against the sun. "We gonna be travelin' in the dark as it is. Those green-hands dilly-dally much longer an' it's another biv-oo-ack tonight."

"Hell with that. We don't hoof it back by sundown McGrath will have our hides, sure as the Lord made little green apples." Stevens unplugged the moonshine and had a swig. His face shone with sweat from the skinning and toting. "Here's what I propose. Miller, you and Ruark take the mules and skedaddle back to Slango. Me and Bane will go round up our wayward friends and catch you two down the trail. Let's get a move on, eh?"

Miller swatted at the clouds of swarming gnats and flies. A rifle boomed in the middle distance. Again after a long interval, and a third time. A universal signal of distress. That changed everything. Stevens, Bane, and Ruark frantically shucked the meat and hot-footed in the direction of the gunshots. Miller spent several minutes dumping the saddlebags from the mules and tethering them near a waterhole before setting after his comrades. He moved swiftly, bent over to follow their tracks and broken branches they'd left in their wake. He drew the Enfield from its scabbard and cradled the rifle to his breast.

Into the forest. And gods, the trees were larger than ever there along a shrouded ridge that dropped into a deep gulf of shadows and mist. He was channeled along a trail that proved increasingly treacherous. Water streamed from upslope, digging notches through moss and dirt into the underlying rock. In sections the dirt and vegetation were utterly stripped to exposed plates of slick stone, veined red with alkali and the bloody clay of the earth. The trees were so huge, their lattice of branches so tight, it became dim as a shuttered vault, and chilly enough to see faint vapors of one's breath.

The game trail cut sharply into the hillside and eventually passed through a thick screen of saplings and devil's club and leveled into a marshy clearing. A handful of boulders lay sunken into the moss and muck around the trunks of three squat cottonwood trees. Surprisingly enough, there were odds and ends of human habitation carelessly scattered—rusted stovetops and empty cans, rotted wooden barrels and planed timber, bits of old shattered glass and bent nails. Either the site of a ruined house, long swallowed by the earth, or a dumping ground. The rest of the men gathered at the rim of the hollow nearest a precipitous drop into the valley. Fast moving water rumbled from somewhere below.

Horn lay on his back, his boots propped on the body of the fallen buck.

Ma and Calhoun were nowhere in evidence. Miller took it all in for a few moments. He finally shouldered his rifle and had a sip of water from his canteen. "He hurt?" He jerked his thumb at Horn. The boy's coonskin cap had flown off and his long, greasy hair was a bird nest of leaves and twigs. A black and blue lump swelled above his eye.

"Nah, he ain't hurt," Stevens said. "Are ya, kid? He's okay. Got the wind knocked outta him is all. Tripped over a damn root and busted his skull. He'll be right as rain in a minute. Won't ya, kid?"

Horn groaned and covered his eyes with his arm.

"He's affrighted," Bane said, and spat. The grizzled logger clutched his rifle in one hand and a tomahawk in the opposite. His knuckles were white. He kept moving his eyes.

"Afraid of what?" Miller said, surveying the area. He didn't like the feel of the place, its dankness, the malformed cottonwoods, the garbage. He also disliked the fact Calhoun and Ma weren't around.

Stevens and Bane glanced at each other and shrugged. Stevens squatted by Horn and patted his arm almost tenderly. "Wanna slug of this fine awerdenty, kid? Where'd those other boys get to, eh?" He helped Horn get seated upright, then held the jug for him while the kid had a pull.

Ruark scowled and ambled to the drop and stared down into the valley. The water thumped and so did Miller's heart. He tilted his head and stared through the opening above the clearing, regarded the brilliant blue-gold sky. Cloudless, immaculate. Already the sun was low against the peaks. Dark came early in the mountains. The sun seemed peculiar—it blurred and flames radiated from its core and its rim blackened like a coal.

Horn coughed and wiped his mouth on his wool sleeve. "Yeh, tripped an' smacked muh noggin'. Weren't no stob, though. No sir. They's a snare yonder. Prolly more where that come from." He pointed and Bane went and examined the spot.

Bane whistled and said, "He ain't blowin' smoke. Step light, boys. We ain't alone."

"Bushwhackers," Ruark said, turning with predatory swiftness to regard his comrade.

"Ain't no bushwhackers." Stevens rose and swiped at the gathering flies with his hat. "We maybe got us a trapper tucked into that park down there.

That's what we got."

"Shit." Bane lifted a piece of thin rope, its long end snaking off through the underbrush. He coiled in the slack and gave it a yank. A bell clanged nearby and Bane threw the rope and jumped back as if scalded. "Shit!"

"Yeh, shit!" Ruark said and stepped away from the ridgeline. He had his Sharps in hand now.

Miller said, "Thad, where's Cal and Ma?"

Horn still appeared confused from the blow to his head, but the grave faces of his companions sobered him a bit. "Din't see on account I was woozy for a spell. Heard 'em jawin' with somebody that come up on us. Cal said to hang on, they'd be right back."

"You act a mite nervous. Something else happen?"

The boy hesitated. "Din't much care for the sound of whoever they was that jawed with Cal an' Ma. Not 'tall. Sounded right wicked."

"The hell does that mean?" Stevens said.

Horn shrugged and pulled on his cap.

"Shitfire!" Bane said, and spat.

"How long ago?" Miller said. He thought of hiding in the trenches during the war, scanning the gloom for signs of the enemy creeping forward. He'd learned, as did most men of violence, to recognize the scent of imminent peril. At that moment the scent was very strong indeed.

"I reckon half an' hour ago. I blacked out for a while. Them shots snapped me outta it."

Before the boy had finished speaking, Bane and Ruark slipped away to the edge of the clearing, cutting for sign. Ruark whistled and everyone but Horn hustled over. Just beyond a deadfall he'd found a well-beaten footpath. Their missing comrades had passed this way, and so had at least two others. Bane swore and cut a plug of chaw and jammed it in his mouth. He swore again, and spat. The four held a brief discussion and decided there might be trouble ahead so caution was advised. Miller would help Horn back to camp while the rest went on to find Calhoun and Ma. Horn got to his feet and joined them, visibly shaking off his unsteadiness. "Like hell. Ma is my boy. I'm goin'."

"Fine," Stevens said. "Moses, you lead the way." And the men proceeded along the path single file. The going was much easier than before as the path lay a few feet from the ridgeline and the hills, while steep, were much gentler than before.

Ten minutes later they came to a fork at the base of a dead red cedar. The bole of the cedar would've required four or five men to link hands to span its girth. It had sheared off at about the eighty-foot mark. One fork of the trail continued along the ridge; the other descended into the valley, which was still mostly hidden by forest. Boot prints went both directions, but Bane and Ruark were confident there friends had travelled in the valley. Bane sniffed the air, then gestured downward. "Wood smoke."

"Sure enough," Miller said just then winding the tang of smoke. They'd proceeded only a few paces when he happened to look back and stopped with a hiss of warning to his companions.

"What is it?" Stevens said.

"That tree," Miller said, indicating a blaze mark on the downhill face of the big dead cedar—a stylized ring, broken on the sinister side. The symbol was roughly four feet across and gouged in a good three inches. Someone had daubed it in a thick reddish paint, now bled and mostly absorbed by the wood. It appeared petrified with age. Some inherent quality of the ring caused Miller's flesh to crawl. The light seemed to dim, the forest to close in.

Nobody said anything. Stevens produced a small spy glass and swept the area. He muttered and tossed the glass to Bane. Bane looked around. He passed it to Ruark. Finally he swore and handed the glass back. Stevens in turn let Miller have a go. Stevens said, "I make out three more—there, there, and there." He was correct. Miller spotted the other trees scattered along the hillside. Each was huge and dead, and each bore the weird glyph.

"I seen that mark afore," Bane said in a reverential whisper.

"That book," Miller said and Bane grunted. Miller asked for Stevens' jug, hooked the handle with his pinky, mountain man fashion, and took a long, stout pull of the whiskey until black stars shot across his vision. Then he gasped for air and helped himself to another, healthier swig.

"Jaysus," Stevens said when he finally retrieved his hooch. He shook the jug with a sad, amazed expression as if not quite comprehending how this could've happened to his stock.

"I don't cotton to this 'tall," Horn said. He rubbed the goose egg on his forehead. He was flour-pale.

"I'm with the pup," Bane said. He spat. Ruark grunted agreement. He too spat a gob of Virginia Pride into the shrubbery.

Stevens crept up to the cedar and studied it intently, ran his fingers over the rough bark. He said, "Damn it all! Boys, lookee here." As everyone clustered around he showed them how a great chunk of bark was separate from the tree. The slab of bark was as tall as three men, narrowing to a sharp peak. The outline, as of a door, was clear once they discerned it against the pattern. The bark door was hinged with sinew on one side.

"Whata ya reckon it is?" Horn said, backing away.

Watching Stevens trace the panel in search of a catch caused Miller's anxiety to sharpen. The light was fading and far too early in the afternoon. The sun's edge was being rapidly eaten by a black wave, creating a broken ring of fire and shadow. This phenomenon juxtaposed with the broken ring carved in the tree. Miller said, "Don't boys! Just leave it!"

Stevens muttered his satisfaction at locating the catch. Bane and Stevens pulled the wooden panel three-quarters of the way open and then stopped, bodies rigid as stone. From his vantage Miller couldn't make out much of the hollow, gloomy interior, but the other two men stood with their necks craned and Bane moaned, low and aggrieved as a fellow who'd been stabbed in the gut. "Sweet Lord in heaven!" Stevens said.

Miller took several broad steps to join them at the portal. He gazed within and saw—

—Something squirmed and uncoiled, a darker piece of darkness, and resolved into—

—His vision clouded violently and he staggered, was steadied by Ruark while Bane and Stevens sealed the panel, ramming it closed with their shoulders. They spun, faces white, wearing expressions of fear that were terrible to behold in men of such stern mettle.

"Good gawd, lookit the sky," Horn said. The moon occulted the sun and the world became a shadowy realm where every surface glowed and bloomed with a queer bluish-white light. Every living thing in the forest held its breath.

"Jaysus Mother Mary!" Ruark said, breaking the spell. "Jaysus Mother Mary Christ Almighty!"

And the men scrambled, tripped and staggered, grasping at branches to keep their footing. The eclipse lasted four minutes at most. The group reached the bottom as the moon and the sun slid apart and the world brightened by degrees. The valley was narrow and ran crookedly north and south. There were falls to the north and a small, shallow river wound its way through sandbars and intermittent stands of cottonwood and fallen spars and uprooted trunks.

A rustic village lay one hundred seventy or so yards distant upon the opposite side of the valley behind a low palisade of vertical logs—a collection of antique cottages and bungalows that extended as far as the middle heights of the terraced hillside. Several figures moved among the buildings, tending to chickens, hanging clothes. Stevens passed the scope around and it was confirmed that a handful of women were the only visible inhabitants.

Miller had marched similar villages in the European countryside where the foundations might be centuries old, perhaps dated from Medieval times. To encounter such a place here in the wilds of North America was incomprehensible. This town was wrong, utterly wrong, and the valley one of the hidden places of the world. He'd never heard a whisper of the community and only God knew why people would dwell in secret. Perhaps they belonged to a religious sect that had fled persecution and wished to follow their faith in peace. He thought of the dreadful music from the previous night, the ominous drums, the blackening sun, and was not reassured.

Away from the central portion of the community loomed a stone tower with a crenellated parapet surmounted by a turret of shiny clay shingles that narrowed to a spike. The tower rose to a height of four stories, dominating the village, and was constructed of bone-white stone notched at intervals by keyhole windows. The broken ring symbol had been painted in black ochre to the left of every window and upon the great ironbound oak doors at the tower's base. As with the symbol of the ring carved into the tree on the hillside, some combination of elements imbued the tower with menace that struck a chord deep inside Miller. His heart quickened and he looked over his shoulder at the way they'd come.

"Be dark soon," Stevens said. He also cast a furtive backward glance. Long shadows spread over the rushes and the open ground before them. The bloody sun hung a finger's breadth above the peaks and the sky was turning to rust. "These folks may be dangerous. Keep your guns ready."

Horn snatched at Bane's sleeve. "What'd y'all see back there?"

"Shut it, boy. Ain't gonna leave this valley goin' that direction. Nothin' more to tell."

"Yeah, shut it," Ruark said and gave the kid a shove to get him moving.

* * *

The company forded the river where it rushed shin deep, and moved to the village and passed through the open gate of the palisade after Stevens hailed the occupants. A dozen women of various ages paused in their chores and silently regarded the visitors. The women wore long, simple dresses of a distinctly Quaker style and dour bonnets and kerchiefs. They appeared well-fed and clean. Their teeth were white. Several of them immediately repaired to the central structure, a kind of longhouse. Most of the others went into the smaller houses. One of the younger girls smiled furtively at Miller. Obviously she was simple. Her dress was cut low and revealed her buxom curves, her belly swollen with child and Miller blushed and turned his head away. Chickens pecked in the weeds. A couple of goats wandered around, and a small pack of mutts approached, yipping and snaffling at the men's legs.

A brawny matron with gray hair stepped forward to greet the company, and she too offered a friendly smile. "Hello, strangers. Welcome." Her accent and mannerisms seemed off-kilter, indefinably foreign.

"Beggin' your pardon, Ma'am." Stevens doffed his hat, clutched it nervously. "Our apologies to intrude and all, but we're on the trail of a couple old boys who belong to our group. We're hopin' you might've seen 'em." His voice shook and he and Bane continued to cast worried glances over their shoulders. For his part, Miller had spent the past few minutes convincing himself he'd seen a coon or porcupine in the dead tree. Maybe a drowsing black bear.

To further distract and calm his galloping imagination, he studied the lay of the land. The houses were made of smoothed rocks and mortared stone and the windows were tiny and mostly without glass, protected from the elements by means of thick drapes and shutters. The dirt paths were grooved and hardened to iron with age. The hillside climbed steeply through trees and undergrowth, although its face was mostly rock. A cave mouth opened beneath an overhang. He'd thought perhaps some eccentric industrialist had possibly created a replica of a medieval town and transplanted its citizens, but the closer he inspected it, the more its atmosphere seeped into him, and he understood this was something far stranger.

The matron apparently observed the tension among the loggers. She said, "Dear gentlemen, ye have nothing to fear. Be at peace."

"We're not afraid, Missus," Miller said. He used a gruff tone because the woman unnerved and unsettled him with her odd accent, her anti-quated primness, the manner in which she cocked her head like a living doll. How the whites of her eyes were overcome by black. "But we *are* in a powerful hurry."

"The men will soon return from the gathering and ye shall treat with them. Until then, please rest." The matron waved them toward some bench-es near the statue of a figure in robes, two children of equally indeterminate sex crouched at its feet. The statue was defaced by weather and green mold. One grotesquely elongated hand stretched forth as if to part a curtain to reveal some dark mystery. The children's necks were cruelly bent, tongues distended, spines humped and exposed as if flayed by a butcher's knife. The larger figure's dangling hand caressed their bowed heads. "Girls, see to fetching our guests pie and lemonade." The two younger women disap-peared into the longhouse, as did the one who'd smiled at Miller. They moved with the ponderous grace of soon-to-be mothers.

Miller wondered if all of the girls were with child and wished he'd paid more attention. It seemed important. He said to the matron, "How did you come to build this village? It's not on any maps."

"Isn't it?" the woman said and for an instant her smile became sly as a predator of the wood. "Our hamlet is very old and was carried across the sea by our founders when Sir Raleigh still served the Queen's pleasure. This is a place of worship, of communion, and far, far from wicked civi-lizations of men. The nights are long in this valley. The days are gloomy. It is perfect."

Stevens wrung his hat and fidgeted. "If you don't mind, Ma'am, we need to locate our friends and be on our way before the sun goes down. Could you kindly point the way? Tracks show they come through here."

"You saw them, of course," Miller said. He decided what it was about the woman's speech that bothered him: her voice was hoarse, the cadenc-es unbalanced, her intonation stilted because she wasn't accustomed to speaking and hadn't been for a long time.

"Aye, she seen 'em alright," Bane said, mouth set in a grim line. "Prolly one o' you wenches that lured 'em here."

The matron kept smiling. Her hands trembled. "Our husbands will be home anon. Mayhap they have seen your companions." She turned and walked into the longhouse. The door closed and then came the unmistakable clunk of a bar dropping.

Bane shook his head and spat. He broke apart his Rigby and checked the load and clacked the breech into place again.

"Well, this ain't good," Stevens said.

Horn said, "What we aimin' to do?" He moved to shuck his pack and Ruark frowned and told him to leave it be.

"Gonna find Cal and Ma. That's what. And leave your goddamned pack on. We have to make tracks in a hurry you wanna be all the way up shit crick with no paddle?" Stevens clapped his hat on. "Stick our noses in every last house. Kick in the doors if we have to. Let's make it quick. Daylight is burnin'."

Miller and Bane teamed to search the cottages on the south side; Stevens, Horn, and Ruark took the north. It went fast. Miller took the lead, busting through the doors and making a brief sweep of the interiors. The women inside calmly waited, speaking not a word to the trespassers—and indeed, many were pregnant. Each house was small and dim, but there weren't many places to hide. Most were neat and well-ordered, not untoward in any obvious way. Simple furnishings, albeit archaic. Oil lamps and candles, fireplaces that doubled as ovens. A paltry selection of books on crude shelves. This last detail struck him as truly odd.

He said to Bane, "Not one Bible. You ever see this many houses without a copy or two of the good book lying around?" Bane shrugged and allowed as he hadn't witnessed that particular phenomenon either.

Both parties finished within a few minutes and regrouped in the square. Everyone was sweating from running up the hill to check the half-dozen houses perched there. Miller mentioned the lack of holy literature. Stevens said, "Yeh, mighty peculiar. Where are the kids? You seen any?"

"Gudamn!" Horn said. "Brats should be crawlin' underfoot, chasin' the chickens, screamin' bloody murder. Somethin' shore as hell ain't right."

"Mebbe they inside the big house," Ruark said. "Or that tower."

"Well, we gotta check that house," Miller said although the idea made him unhappy. The thought of searching the tower was even worse—it curved out of joint, angles distorted, and the sight made his head queer, his stomach ill. Not the tower if there were any other way.

Horn appeared stricken. "Hold on there, fellas. Them women ain't gonna hold Cal or Ma. No sir. We barge in there an' git shot, some might say we had it comin'."

"Yeh, I reckon," Stevens said. "You can stay out here and keep watch if you're afraid of the ladies. Them husbands gonna be walkin' in on us any minute. Who knows how many of them old boys'll show."

"Plenty, you kin wager," Bane said.

Miller kicked the door. "Solid as a stump," he said. Ruark spat and unlimbered his axe, as did Bane a moment later. The pair stood shoulder to shoulder chopping at the door and it crashed inward after a few blows. The men piled into the house, blinking against the smoky dimness. The sole light came from what seeped through window notches and a guttering fire in the hearth. The murk made hazy blobs of the long table, the counter and barrels stacked in threes here and there. The peak roof vaulted to a height of fifteen or so feet, supported by a massive center beam and a series of angled joists that met the wall at about chin level. Meat hooks, pots and pans, coils of rope, cured ham, and strings of sausage swayed and rustled with each gentle exhalation from the hearth.

Of the women there was no sign, but Ma was present.

Miller almost cried out when he beheld what had been done to the Welshman, and Stevens hollered loud enough to bust an eardrum. Miller didn't blame him. Ma sat Indian style, naked in the middle of the floor, blood thick as pudding around his legs, in his lap. His belly was sliced wide and a quivering rope of purple innards was strung several feet above him and looped through a large eyebolt suspended from a chain. The intestines traveled down again like a pulley cable and wrapped around a wooden turnstile. The turnstile had been cranked repeatedly and its gory yarn oozed and leaked. Most of the rest of Ma's guts were slopped across his thighs, or floating in the grue. His slack jaw drooled. He gave his comrades a glassy eyed nod not much different than his usual.

"Oh, God, Ma!" Stevens said. "What'd they do to you, hoss?"

Horn stuck his head in to see what the commotion was all about and shrieked to beat the band, so Ruark swatted him with his hat and drove him outside. Right then the matron ghosted from the gloom in the corner and hacked Bane's shoulder with a cleaver. He yelled and smacked her in the jaw with the butt of his Rigby and she sprawled.

Blood trickled from the matron's lips. The injury did not diminish her, rather imbued her with an aura of savagery and mania that caused the men to flinch as one might from a wounded beast. Her eyes were so very large and dark and they gleamed with tears of rage and exultation. She whispered with the intimacy of a lover, "Did ye see what's waiting for ye in the trees?"

"Where's our other man?" Miller strode over to the matron and leveled his rifle at her. "I'll blow a damned hole in your kneecap, Missus. See if I won't."

"No need for that. The handsome lad is in the tower. They gave us the fat one for sport. It amuses them to watch us practice cruelty."

Miller walked around Ma and the coagulating lake of blood. He grasped the ring of a trapdoor and pulled. Several of the women were huddled like goats in a root cellar. They gasped and held each other.

"See him?" Stevens said.

Miller slammed the trapdoor and shook his head.

Bane cussed as Ruark pulled the cleaver free of his shoulder with a gristly crunch. Miller fashioned a tourniquet. The entire left side of Bane's buckskin jacket was soaked through and dripping. Horn shouted. Everyone ran to the windows. Twilight lay upon the world and a disjointed chain of lamps bobbed in the purple dark, descending the switchback trail on the other side of the valley. Miller said, "Either we fort up, or we run for it."

Stevens said, "Trapped like rats in here. Roof is made of wood. They could burn us alive."

"Not with they women in here," Bane said through gritted teeth.

"You want to spend the night in here with them?" Miller said.

"Yeh, never mind."

"We could take this one as a hostage," Stevens said halfheartedly.

"Piss on that," Miller said. "Who knows what she'll chop off next time."

"Ye should flee into the hills," the matron said. "The horrors ye will soon meet…flee, good hunters. Or make an end of each other with your guns and knives. T'will be a merciful death in comparison."

"Shut up before I kill you," Miller said. The matron stopped talking at once.

"What about Ma?" Stevens said.

"He's gone," Bane said. "Worst way a man kin go. Gutted like a pig."

"We cain't leave him."

"Naw, we cain't." Ruark drew his flintlock pistol. He walked over and laid the barrel against the back of Ma's head and squeezed the trigger. For Miller, in that moment the past five years of his life were erased and he side slipped through time and space into a muddy trench in France, shells and bodies exploding. He had never left, never escaped.

Stevens aimed his rifle at the matron. He lowered it. "Don't have the sand to shoot no woman. Let's git, boys."

Ruark said, "Won't make it far in these woods in the dark."

Stevens said, "We head for the tower and fetch Cal. See what happens."

The Matron said, "Yes! Yes! Go into the house of the Master! He'll greet ye with a glad smile and open arms!"

"Quiet yerself, hag," Stevens said, menacing her with his rifle butt. "C'mon, boys. Let's find poor Cal before the villains make stew of him." There was grudging acquiescence to this plan and the men withdrew from the longhouse and its horrors.

Miller went to the palisade gate and shouldered the Enfield, aimed at the string of lights and blasted several rounds in rapid succession. One of the approaching lamps burst, the rest were doused momentarily. A howl of pain rose from the field. Miller reloaded in a hurry. He ran for the tower where his companions were gathered near its double doors. Something fluttered to his left—a coat tail disappearing behind a pile of neatly stacked firewood. He knew they'd been had. While the villagers waving lanterns on the flats played decoy, others had crept along in a flanking action. He dropped to a knee and swung his rifle around.

"Ambush!" Bane hollered as a dozen or more men in coats and top hats sprang from behind sheds, cottages, hay bales, seemingly everywhere. Pitchforks, hatchets, and knives, edges gleaming and glinting; a couple carried blunderbusses, bulkier and older than even Ruark's. Those guns cracked and spat fire. Puffs of sulfurous white smoke boiled and seethed.

Ten feet away Bane let loose both barrels of the Rigby with a clap of thunder that sounded as if Archangel Michael himself had descended from Heaven to smite the good Lord's enemies. The muzzle flash lit up the tower courtyard like a rocket explosion. A villager was cut in half and a section of the cottage wall behind him caved in, stomped by an elephant. The other loggers loosed a fusillade in a murderous fireworks display.

Night vision spoiled by the alternating glare and shadow, Miller struggled to find targets. He didn't have the opportunity to draw a bead, but simply emptied the Enfield as fast as he could work the bolt. Most of his bullets clattered off stone or ripped furrows into the earth. However, he shot one bearded brute between the eyes as the man charged with an upraised hatchet, and drilled another in the back as the fellow stood motionless as if uncertain how to join the fray.

The cottage that Bane had perforated with his gun caught fire. Flames leaped into the sky. Glass tinkled as it fractured. The fire spread to another house, then another, and in less than thirty seconds, the combatants were struggling by the red blaze of a circle in hell. Ruark swung his axe and lopped a villager's head. The head floated past Miller and into the blaze. Bane screamed and laughed, his beard splattered with blood. He pressed a man's face against a flaming timber and held it there until flesh popped and sizzled. Horn dropped his rifle and turned to run. An older gent in a stovepipe hat knocked him down and skewered him with a pitchfork. The pitchfork went in with a meaty thunk and a clink as the tines bit through into the dirt. Horn grabbed the handle and wrestled for dear life and the man grunted, planted his boot against Horn's groin, and pried loose the pitchfork and raised it to stick him again. Then Ruark's axe whapped the back of the villager's skull and turned it to jelly and the man collapsed face-down, legs twitching. Stevens' rifle boomed once, twice, and he cursed and drew a knife and sidled in tight with his companions. Miller was empty. He picked up a severed hand and forearm and threw it in a man's face, then shoulder-blocked him to the ground and methodically clubbed him to death with his rifle butt. Sweat and grease and flying drops of blood soaked him. Miller's arms were weak and he could scarcely raise them at the end. A blast of heat from the burning houses seared his cheeks and ignited the tips of his hair. The smell of roasting flesh was strong.

The remaining villagers routed, fleeing through the flames and the rolling black smoke. Bane, still braying mad laughter, chucked a tomahawk. It sank into a man's backside. The man yelped and stumbled. Bane whooped and said, "Run, ya fuckin' dogs!" And he barked.

"There's reinforcements yonder!" Stevens and Ruark grasped Horn under the arms and dragged him to his feet. The lad gasped and fainted.

Rifles thundered near the front gate. A musket ball kicked dirt near Miller's foot. "Follow me, boys!" He led the charge up the hill and into the cave along a twisting path illuminated by the hellish conflagration. Storming the tower was out of the question—he suspected it would burn to the ground soon enough. Regardless, anyone trapped inside would be smoked out or broiled alive.

The cave mouth opened into a low-ceilinged area with a sandy floor and natural outcroppings that served as adequate cover. The men quickly repurposed empty barrels and busted timbers to fashion a makeshift barricade at the entrance. After they'd finished effecting hasty fortifications, Stevens passed around the remnants of his bottle. He said, "We're in it deep. Killed us a few, but I count twenty, maybe more. Prolly mad as hornets over what we done."

"Learn us somethin' we don't know, boy," Bane said. Between blood loss and one too many belts of rotgut to kill the pain, he slurred, listing precariously until Ruark helped him sit against the wall.

Below, several houses were utterly consumed in the inferno and the fire made a sound like rushing wind. Sparks ignited the lower branches of nearby trees. The smoke had become so thick it proved difficult to discern the movements of the villagers. Men darted about with buckets, presumably hurling dirt and water on the flames. Miller went flat and laid the Enfield across his rolled jacket. He waited, inhaled, partially exhaled, and squeezed the trigger. A lucky shot—a villager's arms flew from his sides and he toppled and lay in the dirt, one hand extended into a burning pile of wood, and soon his clothes smoked and flames licked over them. The rest of the villagers made themselves scarce. The fire spread swiftly after that.

Horn moaned and twisted on the ground. He prayed for Jesus, Mary, and God. Miller helped Ruark peel aside the boy's shirt and slid his hand under his body and felt around. The tines had indeed gone clean through and Horn leaked like a sieve. It wouldn't be long. He caught Ruark's glance and shook his head slightly. Ruark spat. "Boy didn't even fire that peashooter o' his. Bastards."

Horn cried for his mama.

"Hush," Stevens said, striking a match and lighting a lamp he'd found on a peg. He hung the lamp from a support timber in the back of the cave where it constricted to a narrow passage that descended into absolute darkness. Miller couldn't determine the purpose of the cave; although moderately carved and shored, it wasn't a mine. Occult symbols had been chalked upon the walls. Stick figures bowed and scraped, dwarfed by what appeared to be a huge bundle of twigs. Not twigs—worms, or something squiggly like worms.

Huddled around the lamp, the loggers resembled characters from some gothic fable; resurrection men leaning on spades at midnight in a swampy graveyard. By that primitive oil lamplight, the company was a horrific, blood-soaked mess. They piled their packs and sundries in the middle of the floor and counted ammunition and rations. Wounds were appraised: Bane's hacked shoulder would be the death of him without medicine. Ruark had gotten hit in the belly; the hole was about the size of a bean and welled purple and it bubbled when he took a breath. The black powder ball was still inside, although the old logger shrugged and spat and said he felt fine as frog's hair. Stevens revealed nasty punctures in his thigh and ribs, a vicious slash across his breast. Only Miller had survived the melee unscathed.

"What? None of that blood you're covered in is yours? Not even a scratch, you lucky bastard!" Stevens threw back his head and laughed as Ruark helped wind strips of cloth around his torso to staunch the bleeding.

Miller didn't say anything. He'd never taken more than a few bumps and bruises, the occasional cut from flying shrapnel, during the war, had literally walked through the apocalypse at Belleau Wood untouched.

Stevens made a firepot by slathering bear grease in a tin cup and lighting a strip of cloth for a wick. He and Ruark proposed to scout the tunnel and make certain nobody was sneaking along their back-trail. That left Miller with the kid, who was unconscious and raving, and Bane, who appeared to also have one foot in the grave.

The wait proved short, however. Stevens and Bane reappeared, wide-eyed as horses who'd been spooked by fire. Ruark tossed loose timber and small rocks in the tunnel opening. Stevens reported that the caves stretched on and on, and branched every few paces. In his estimation, anybody damn fool enough to venture into that labyrinth would be wandering for eternity.

After a long, whispered conference, it was decided the men would wait until daylight and then make a run for Slango. There was no telling when or if McGrath might deign to send a search party, so it was safest to assume they were on their own. Watches were set with Ruark taking the first as he allowed he couldn't sleep anyhow. He snuffed the lamp and the firepot and they settled in to wait.

Stevens said, "Ever wonder what Rumpelstiltskin wanted with a kid?"

Miller pulled his hat down and tried to relax. An eldritch white radiance illuminated the cave and it was just him and Horn; everyone else melted and vanished. Mist flowed from the passage and curled over the pile of packs, swirled over Horn's chest and around Miller's knees. Horn stared. His face was gray, suspended in the mist. He said, "C'mon, tell me true. What'd y'all see in that tree? What was hidin' up in there?"

"Worms," Miller said. He wasn't certain if this was accurate. The memory slipped and slithered and changed when he tried to examine it closely. A fibrous network of slimy roots, or worms, or a mass of tendrils squirming in the moist dark of the mighty cedar bole. "They had faces." *Demons sleep in holes in the ground. Live in the rocks, sleep inside big ol' trees in the deep forest where the sun don't never shine.*

"Oh." Horn nodded. "I dunno what the little man in the story wanted with the child, but I kin tell ya the villagers give their babies to their friends inside the trees... inside this mountain. The sons an' daughters of Ol' Leech. An' I kin tell ya what the people of Ol' Leech do with 'em."

"I'd rather you didn't."

"Jist shut yer eyes an' look inside. We so close, ya kin see their god. He's sleepy like a bear in winter. Dreamin' of his people. Dreamin' of us here in the daylight, too. But he's wakin' up. Be creepin' out a his den pretty soon, I reckon."

"Save it, kid."

"He loves his people. Loves us too, in a different way." Horn's smile was shrewd and cruel. He opened his mouth and inhaled the peculiar light and Miller's dreams became confused. He dreamt of falling through the mountain, through the entire Earth, and into the sky, accelerating like a bullet until the light of the sun dwindled to a pinprick. He crashed through the icy, blood-black surface of a strange moon and drifted weightless in its hollow core. The cavern was rank and humid and dark as pitch. He floated over crags and canyons and forests of clabbered flesh and fungus, his body carried upon the updrafts of a warm, gelatinous sea. At the center of this sea a mountain range shuddered and stirred. The colossus writhed and uncoiled with satanic majesty, aroused by the whine of flea wings. It whispered to him.

* * *

Miller awoke to Calhoun begging for help.

Calhoun cried from the direction of the tower. He called them by name in a tone of anguish and his voice carried. He began screaming the screams of a man partially buried alive or hung in barbed wire or swollen with mustard gas. Miller lay in the shadows, watching the dying light of the fires shiver across the wall of the cave. Calhoun kept screaming and they all pretended not to hear him.

* * *

Still later and after night settled in as tight as a blindfold, Stevens shook Miller. "Somethin's wrong."

"Oh, jumpin' Jaysus," Ruark said and moments later lighted the firepot. Miller would've cursed the old man for revealing their position, except he saw the cause of alarm—Horn was gone, spirited away from under their noses. Drips and drabs of blood smeared into the tunnel, into the blackness. "Them sonsabitches snatched Thad!"

As if in response to the light, a faint, ghostly moan echoed up the passage from great subterranean depths. *Help me, boys. Help me.* At least that's what it sounded like to Miller. The distance and acoustics could've made wind whistling through chimneys of rock resemble almost anything.

"Lordy, Lordy," Bane said. He was a frightful sight; gore limed his beard and jacket. He might've been a talking corpse. "That's the boy."

"Ain't him," Stevens said.

"The kid is done for," Miller said. His eyes watered and he struggled to keep his voice even. "Whoever's hooting down that tunnel is no friend of ours."

"They's right, Moses," Ruark said. "This an ol' Injun trick. Make a noise of a wounded friend an draw ya in." He ran his thumb across his throat with an exaggerated flourish. "Ya should know it, hoss. That boy is daid."

"Lookit all the blood," Stevens said.

Bane shoved a plug of tobacco into his mouth and chewed with his eyes closed. His flesh was papery and his eyelids fluttered the way a man's do when he's caught in a terrible dream. He resembled the photographs of dead outlaws in open coffins displayed on frontier boardwalks. He spat. "Yeh, an' lookit me. Still kickin'."

*Help me. Help me.* The four of them froze like woodland animals, heads inclined toward the dim cries, the cold, cold draft.

"Ain't him," Stevens repeated, but mostly to himself.

Bane stood. He leaned against the wall, the barrel of his Rigby nosing the sand. He nodded to Ruark. "You comin'?"

Ruark spat. He lifted the firepot and led the way.

Bane said, "Alrightee, boys. Take care." He tapped his hat and limped after his comrade. Their shadows swayed and jostled, and their light grew smaller and seeped into the mountain and was gone.

The others sat in the dark for a long time, listening. Miller heard faint laughter, a snatch of Bane singing "John Brown's Body," and then only the fluting of the wind in the rocks.

"Oh, hell," Stevens said when the silence between them had gone on for an age. "You was in the war."

"You weren't?"

"Uh-uh. My father worked for the post office. He fixed my card so's I wouldn't get conscripted."

"Wish I'd thought of that," Miller said.

"You seen the worst of it. Any chance we kin get out a this with our skins?"

"Nope."

There was another long pause. Stevens said, "Want a smoke?" He lighted two Old Mills and passed one to Miller. They smoked and listened, but there was nothing to hear except for the wind, the rustle of branches outside. Stevens said, "He weren't dragged. The kid crawled away."

"How do you figure? He was pretty much dead."

"*Pretty much* ain't the same thing, now is it? I heard 'em talkin' to him, whisperin' from the dark. Only heard bits. Didn't need more…they told him to come ahead. An' he did."

"Must've been persuasive," Miller said. "And you didn't raise the alarm."

"Hard to explain. Snake-bit, frozen stiff. It was like my body fell asleep yet I could hear what was goin' on. I was piss-scared."

Miller smoked his cigarette. "I don't blame you," he said.

"I got my senses back after a piece. Kid was long gone by then. Whoever they are, he went with 'em.'"

"And now Moses and Ruark are with them too."

"I didn't tell the whole truth about what we saw in the tunnel."

"Is that so."

"Didn't seem much point carryin' on. Not far along the trail it opens into a cavern. Dunno how big; our light couldn't touch but the edges of the walls and the ceilin'. There were drops into plain ol' nothin' an' more passages twistin' every which way. But we stopped only a few steps into the cavern. A pillar rose high as the light could reach. Broad at the base like a pyramid and made of rocks all slippery an' shiny from drippin' water. Except, the rocks weren't just rocks. There were skeletons cemented in between. Prolly hundreds an' hundreds. Small things. There was a hole at eye level. Smooth as the bore of my gun and about the size of my fist. Pure black, solid, glistenin' black that threw the light from our torch back at us. We didn't peep too close on account of the skeletons before we turned tail and ran. Saw one thing as we turned to haul our asses… That hole had widened enough I could a jumped in and stood tall. It made a sound that traveled from somewhere farther and deeper than I want a think about. Not the kind a sound you hear, but the kind you feel in your bones. Felt kinda bad and good at once. I could tell Ruark liked it. Oh, he was afraid, but compelled, I guess you'd say."

"Well," Miller said after consideration, "I can see why you might've kept that to yourself."

"Yeh. I wish them ol' coons had stayed back. Maybe we could a blasted our way out with their guns and ours."

Miller didn't think so. "Maybe. Catch some shut eye. Sunup in a couple hours."

Stevens rolled over and set his hat over his face and didn't move again. Miller watched the stars fade.

* * *

They left the cave at dawn and descended the hill into the ruins of the village. Ashes turned in the breeze. The tower stood, although scorched and blackened. Its double doors were sprung, wood smoldering, hinges melted. Smoke curled from the gap. Many of the surrounding houses had burned to their foundations. Gray dust lay over everything. Corpses were stacked near the longhouse and covered with a canvas tarp to keep the birds away. Judging from height and width of the collection, at least fifteen bodies were piled beneath the tarp awaiting burial. Twenty-five to thirty men and women combed the charred wreckage. Their hands and faces were filthy with the gray dust. Some stared hatefully at the pair, but none spoke, none raised a hand.

Miller and Stevens trudged through the village and onward, following the river south as it wended through the valley. With every step, Miller's shoulders tightened as he awaited the inevitable musket ball to shear his spine. Early in the afternoon, they climbed a bluff and rested for the first time.

After Stevens caught his breath, he said, "I don't understand. Why they'd let us live?" He removed his hat and peered through the trees, searching for signs of pursuit.

"Did they?" Miller said. He didn't look the way they'd come, instead studying the forest depths before them, tasting the damp and the rot and the cold. He thought of his dream of flying into the depths of space, of the terrible darkness between the stars and what ruled there. "We've got nowhere to hide. I had to guess, I'd guess they're saving us for something very special."

So, they continued on and arrived at the outskirts of Slango as the peaks darkened to purple. Nothing remained of the encampment except for abandoned logs and mucky, flattened areas, and a muddle of footprints and drag marks. Every man, woman, and mule was gone. Every piece of equipment likewise vanished. The railroad tracks had been torn up. In a few months forest would reclaim all but the shorn slopes, erasing any evidence Slango Camp ever stood there.

"Shit," Stevens said without much emotion. He hung his hat on a branch and wiped his face with a bandanna.

"Hello, lads," a man said, stepping from behind a tree. He was wide and portly and wore a stovepipe hat and an immaculate silk suit. His handlebar mustache was luxuriously waxed and he carried a blackthorn cane in his left hand. A dying ray of sun glowed upon the white, white skin of his face and neck. "I am Dr. Boris Kalamov. You have caused me a tremendous amount of trouble." He gestured at the surroundings. "This is not our way. We prefer peaceful coexistence, to remain unseen and unheard, suckling like a hagfish, our hosts none the wiser, albeit dimly cognizant through the persistent legends and campfire tales which please us and nourish us as much as blood and bone. To act with such dramatic flourish goes against our code, our very nature. Alas, certain of my brethren were taken by a vengeful mood what with you torching the village of our servants." He *tisked* and wagged a finger that seemed to possess too many joints.

Miller didn't even bother to lift his rifle. He was focused upon the nightmare taking shape in his mind. "How now, Doctor?"

Stevens was more optimistic, or just doggedly belligerent. He jacked a round into the chamber of his Winchester and sighted the man's chest.

Dr. Kalamov smiled and his mouth dripped black. "You arrived at a poor time, friends. The black of the sun, the villagers' holiest of holy days when they venerate the Great Dark and we who call it home. Their quaint and superstitious ceremony at the dolmen cut short because of your trespass. Such an interruption merits pain and suffering. O' Men from Porlock, it shan't end well for you."

Stevens glanced around, peering into the shadows of the trees. "I figured you didn't come for tea, fancy pants. What I want a know is what happens next."

"You will dwell among my people, of course."

"Where? You mean in the village?"

"No, oh, no, no, not the village with *your* kind, the cattle who breed our delicacies and delights. No, you shall dwell in the Dark with *us*. Where the rest of your friends from this lovely community were taken last night while you two cowered in the cave. You're a wily and resourceful fellow, Mr. Stevens, as are most of your doughty woodsmen kin. We can make use of you. Wonderful, wonderful use."

"Goodbye, you sonofabitch," Stevens said, cocking the hammer.

"Not quite," Dr. Kalamov said. "If we can't have you, we'll simply make do with your relatives. Your father still works for the post office in Seattle, does he not? And your sweet mother knits and has supper ready when he gets home to that cozy farmhouse you grew up in near Green Lake. Your little brother Buddy working on the railroad in Nevada. Your nephews Curtis and Kevin are riding the range in Wyoming. So many miles of fence to mend, so little time. Very dark on the prairie at night. Perhaps you would rather we visit them instead."

Stevens lowered his rifle, then dropped it in the mud. He walked to the doctor and stood beside him, slumped and defeated. Dr. Kalamov patted his head. The doctor's hand was large enough to have encompassed it if he'd wished, and his nails were as long as darning needles. He flicked Stevens' ear and it peeled loose and plopped wetly in the bushes. Stevens clapped his hand over the hole and screamed and fell to his knees, blood streaming between his fingers. Dr. Kalamov smiled an avuncular smile and tousled the man's hair. He pushed a nail through the top of Stevens' skull and wiggled. Stevens fell silent, his face slack and dumb as Ma's had ever been.

"Reckon I'll decline your offer," Miller said. He drew his pistol and weighed it in his hand. "Go ahead and terrorize my distant relations. Meanwhile, I think I'll blow my brains out and be shut of this whole mess."

"Don't be hasty, young man," Dr. Kalamov said. "I've taken a shine to you. You're free to leave this mountain. There's a lockbox in the roots of that tree. The company payroll. Take it, take a new name. And when you're old, be certain to tell of the horrors that you've seen…horrors that will infest your dreams from today until the day you die. We'll always be near you, Mr. Miller." He doffed his hat and bowed. Then he grasped Stevens by the collar and bundled him under one arm and into the gathering gloom.

The lockbox was where the man had promised and it contained a princely sum. Miller stuffed the money in a sack as the sun went down and darkness fell. When he'd finished packing the money he buried his head in his arms and groaned.

"By the way, there are two minor conditions," Dr. Kalamov said, leering from behind a stump. The flesh of his face hung loose as if it were a badly slipping mask. His eyes were misaligned, his mouth a bleeding black slash that extended to his ears. He had no teeth. "You're a virile lad. Be certain to spawn oodles and oodles of babies—I must insist on that point. We'll be observing, so do your best, my boy. There is also the matter of your firstborn…"

Miller had nearly pissed himself at Dr. Kalamov's reappearance. He forced his throat to work. "You're asking for my child."

Dr. Kalamov chuckled and drummed his claws on the wood. "No, Mr. Miller. I jest. Although, those wicked old fairytales are jolly good fun, speaking such primordial truths as they do. Be well, be fruitful." He scuttled backward and then lifted vertically into the shadows, a spider ascending its thread, and was gone.

\* \* \*

Years later, Miller married a girl from California and settled in a small farming town. He worked as a gunsmith. His wife gave birth to a boy. After the baby arrived he'd often lie awake at night and listen to the house settle and the mice scratch in the cupboards. When the baby cried, Miller's wife would go into the nursery and soothe him with a lullaby. Miller strained to hear the words, for it was the deep silences that unnerved him and caused his heart to race.

There was a willow tree in the yard. It cast a shadow through the window. As his wife crooned to the baby in the nursery, Miller watched the shadow branches ripple upon the dull white oval of wall. On the bad nights, the branches twitched and narrowed and writhed like tendrils worming their way through fissures in the plaster toward the bed and his sweating, paralyzed form.

One morning he went to the shed and fetched an axe and chopped the tree down. The first tree he'd felled since his youth. The willow was very old and very large and the job lasted until lunchtime.

The center was semi-rotten and hollow, and when the tree crashed to earth the bole partially split and gushed pulp. Something heavy and multi-segmented shifted and retracted inside the trunk. Water gurgled from the wound with a wheeze that almost sounded like someone muttering his name. He dumped kerosene over everything and struck a match. The neighbors gathered and watched the blaze, and though they gossiped amongst themselves, no one said a word to him. There'd been rumors.

His wife came to the door with the baby in her arms. Her expression was that of a person who'd witnessed a dark miracle and knew not how to reconcile the fear and wonder of the revelation.

Miller stood in the billowing smoke, leaning on his axe, eyes reflecting the lights of hell.

# MORE DARK

On the afternoon train from Poughkeepsie to New York City for a thing at the Kremlin Bar—John and me and an empty seat that should've been Jack's, except Jack was dead going on three years, body or no body. Hudson out the right-hand window, shining like a scale. Winter light fading fast, blending the ice and snow and water into a steely red. More heavy weather coming, they said. A blizzard; the fifth in as many weeks. One body blow after another for the Northeast and no end in sight.

We were sneaking shots of Glenfiddich from a flask. I watched a kid across the aisle watching me from beneath eyelids the tint of blue-black scarab beetle shells. He wore a set of headphones that merely dampened the Deftones screaming "Change." His eardrums were surely bleeding to match the trickle from his nose. He seemed content.

Another slug of scotch and back to John with the flask.

I thought of the revolver waiting for me in the dresser of my hotel room. I could hear it ticking. I dreamed about that fucking gun all of the time. It loomed as large as a planet-killing asteroid in my mind. It shined with silvery fire against satin nothingness, slowly turning in place, a symbolic prop from a lost Hitchcock film, the answer to the meaning of my life. The ultimate negation. A Rossi .38 Special bought on the cheap at a pawnshop on 4th Avenue, now snug in a sock drawer. One bullet in the chamber, fated to nest in my heart or brain.

My wife of a decade had mysteriously (or not so mysteriously if one asked her friends) walked out six weeks ago, suitcase in one hand, ticket to the Bahamas in the other. My marching orders were to be gone by the time she got back with a new tan. Yeah, I wasn't taking the divorce well. Nor the fiasco with the novel, nor a dozen impending deadlines, chief among them a story I owed S.T. for *Dark Membrane II*, an anthology in homage to the works of H.P. Lovecraft. This last item I hoped to resolve prior to dissipating into the ether, but at the moment it wasn't looking favorable. Still, when marooned in the desert and down to crawling inch by bloody inch, that's what one does. Crawl, and again.

John said, "I saw *him*, once. The Author Formerly known As… A while back, when the gang was in Glasgow for Worldcon. Me, Jack, Jody, Paul, Livia, Wilum, Ellen, Canadian Simon and English Simon, Gary Mac, Ian, Richard G, both Nicks—Berkeley Nick and New York Nick. Some others…all of us wandering from pub to pub after dark. Hal still lived in Scotland, so he showed us around, although he was drunk, as usual, and I figured we'd find the con hotel again by morning, *if* we were lucky. A crowd busted out of a club and this chick, in a leather jacket with her hair shaved to about half an inch of fuzz and dyed pink, almost knocked me over as she elbowed by like a striker for the Blackheath Football Club. Hal stared at her as she stomped away, then leaned over to me and whispered gravely, 'Whoa, lad, that'd be like fookin' a coconut, wouldn't it?'" John was a tall, burly fellow of Scotch-Irish descent; an adjunct professor at SUNY New Paltz. He wore glasses, tweeds, and a tie whether he was lecturing or mowing the lawn. Honestly, he usually appeared as if he'd *just* mowed a lawn, such was his habitual dishevelment. Nonetheless, his charisma was undeniable. The more his beard grayed and his hair thinned, the more irresistible the world at large found him, especially the ladies. Like Machiavelli, he was becoming dangerous in middle age and I hoped he used his powers for good rather than evil.

As John spoke, he cradled the marionettes, Poe and As You Know Bob, in his lap. Poe dressed in black, naturally, and had a pencil mustache and overlarge, soulful eyes, all the better to reflect sardonic ennui. As You Know Bob was clad in a silvery coverall and collar—a spacesuit sans helmet. Bob's shaggy hair and beard were white, its eyes a cornflower blue that bespoke earnestness and honesty, if not wisdom. The puppets were on loan from Clara, John's twelve-year-old daughter. She intended to become a world-class puppeteer, just like John Malkovich in *Being John Malkovich*. Disturbing, but admirable.

Let's be crystal clear. I hate puppets. Hate them. They descend from a demonic line parallel to mimes and clowns and are wholly of the devil, especially the lifelike variety. The uncanny valley is not one I've ever enjoyed strolling through. John wasn't particularly keen on puppets either. However, as a prolific author with a constant itinerary of speaking engagements he'd twigged to their utility as icebreakers at readings and lectures where the audience was often mixed—the little bastards were perfect to talk down to the kiddies (*As you know, Bob, this novel is the eleventh in the saga of non-Euclidian horrors invading Earth from the X-Space!*) while keeping the high schoolers and adults reasonably amused throughout the expositional phase.

John brought his marionettes because we were going to witness (and witness is the best way to describe it) a public reading by the reclusive horror author formerly known as Tom L, or simply L to his small, yet fervent cult of devotees. L featured puppets and marionettes in his tales, alluding to humanity's suffering at the whim of the gods, and owned an exquisite selection of the things, each handcrafted by master designer W Lindblad, a native Texan bookseller renowned for his macabre dolls and enormous collection of rare and banned volumes of perverse occult lore. Also renowned for being a career felon, but that didn't usually come up until whoever mentioned his name was as drunk as we were getting at the moment.

I assumed John hoped for an autograph, maybe a few words of kinship from L. I wasn't quite clear. Nor did I understand his obsessive fascination with the guy. L was a skilled, if obscure, author of weird tales, operating within the precincts of such classical masters as Lovecraft and Robert Aickman, tempering these influences with his own brand of dread and showmanship, much of it fueled by a loathing of corporate life, and, if one took him at his word, life itself. He'd written dozens of horror and dark fantasy tales over the years, the bulk of them collected in a tome entitled *Enemy of Man*. The book had sold well enough to warrant several foreign editions and garnered almost every award in the field. It was, as the *Washington Post* proclaimed, an instant classic.

I owned a cheap paperback reprint of the original immaculate hard-cover, albeit mine contained lengthy story notes and a preface by the author. My impression of L's work was lukewarm as I found his glib pooh-poohing of the master Robert Aickman as a formative influence of his disingenuous considering their artistic similarities, and L's reduction of human characters to ciphers a trifle off-putting. L the author was vastly more interested in the machinations of malign forces against human-ity than the individuals involved in said struggle. Nonetheless, his skill with allegory, simile, atmosphere and setting was impeccable and his style unique despite its debt to classical literary ancestry. His gloom and groan regarding the Infernal Bureaucracy wasn't my cup of tea, yet it possessed a certain resonance among the self-loathing, chronically inebriated, per-petually persecuted set. However, there was the man himself, and it was L the man that turned me cold.

L dwelt in a moribund American Heartland city (although independent confirmation of his residence and bona fides were lacking) that had been abandoned by most of the citizenry and at least half the rats. Afflicted by a severe mood disorder, he maintained few contacts among the profes-sional writing community, albeit his associates were erudite men, scholars and theorists such as himself. Perhaps this hermit-philosopher persona is what eventually cemented his status as a quasi-guru whose fictive medita-tions upon cosmic horror and Man's minuteness in the universe gradually shifted to relentless proselytizing of antinatalist propaganda in the form of email interviews, random tracts produced on basement presses, and one full-blown trade paperback essay entitled *Horror of Being,* or *HoB* as his acolytes dubbed it. That book was published to much clamor amongst his fans and a tentative round of golf claps by the critics who weren't cer-tain which way to jump when it came to analyzing L's eerily lucid lunacy. Nobody enjoyed receiving death threats or dead rats in the post. On the other hand, endorsing such maxims as "The kindest and most noble act any sapient being may commit is to never procreate" and "Consciousness is an abomination" wasn't too spiffy on a journalist's credentials.

John continued: "We stumbled back to the hotel eventually, although I don't recall how we got there, and sat around the lounge comforting Paul about a terrible *Strange Vistas* shellacking of his novel. Somebody on staff had it in for him, no two ways about it. Once HBO bought it for a series, the asshats sweetened right up about his new books and *SV* begged him on bended knee for an interview. How convenient, eh?"

"Screw *SV* and that knob job who runs feature reviews," I said and grabbed the flask for another swig. I'd always had the luck of the Irish when it came to press, but *Strange Vistas* was notorious for the suspect quality of its reviews department, mainly because it was helmed by a blithering idiot who desperately wanted to be his generation's John Clute, and was instead doomed to a life of disappointment and neglect, which while typical and deserved fare for much of the Brit Lit scene, no doubt stung like a mother-fucker. Among the ezine's handful of reputable freelance contributors dwelt a rotten core of ankle biters who would savage a book like a terrier shaking a rat on the principle that bile drove traffic and brought some, yea any, at-tention to themselves that would be otherwise lacking if dependent upon their own merits. Look at me! For the love of God! reviewers. Fortunately, no one actually read the rag but friends, family, proofreaders, chronic mas-turbators, and the aggrieved authors themselves.

"Holy shit, don't utter such heresy near me!" John made a sign in the air. "The woods have eyes, the fields ears. That effing bastard Niall-whatever who edits the thing will have me killed or blackballed, whichever is worse."

"Niall is so famous and respected he needs no surname. He has never heard of you."

"You'll be singing a different tune if he gets a hold of your next book, you ham-fisted hack. I don't know why he called you ham-fisted. They're rather delicate, actually."

"Speaking of coconuts," I said.

"Oh, yeah. Here we go."

"When I was a young stud, I'd dated this girl for a few weeks. It was all new and mysterious. We went to the ocean with another couple, had a fire on the beach, drank some wine, all that tediously romantic sort of crap. On the way home, me and the guy are up front in his car, discussing rock versus heavy metal, the girls giggling and bickering in the back. I hear the distinctive snap of a bra coming undone, more giggling, then smell coconut scent. The guy's eyes pop out of his head and he almost swerves into the ditch trying to adjust the rearview mirror. I turn around and, by thunder, the ladies have peeled off their tops and are giving each other a coconut lotion rubdown for no logical reason whatsoever, except for our viewing pleasure."

"My god."

"Whomever. Trust me, words don't do the scene justice."

"Nothing like that ever happens to me." There was a world of bitterness in that admission.

"I have lived a varied life," I said. "Short, but varied."

"Great, now I got sidetracked with visions of gleaming breasts and…Yeah, there was a point to the bit about Scotland. If I could only concentrate…"

"L was in the house?" An easy guess on my part, but something in my brain shifted with the *rightness* of it as the words were uttered. The phantom click of a pistol's hammer cocking.

"Yes! The fabulous bastard materialized at the edge of the lounge near the bar. The lights were low and he looked ghostly with his wild hair and strange eyes. He wore an old-fashioned suit with a white carnation in the lapel. And he carried a blackthorn cane. A twisted, sinister accouterment, that cane. I bet there was a cavalry saber hidden inside." John's expression was as wistful as Bob's eyes were blue.

"I thought he avoided conventions. Ruin his image. Le Hermit and all."

"So they say. Although there are rumors. People know people who spotted him at the bar sipping Ardbeg at World Horror in '89, haunting the hotel terrace at the World Science Fiction Convention in '97, sitting in the back of a horror lit panel at Comic-Con whenever. Jack swore they had a ten-minute conversation in the green room at Readercon in 2007. There was a power outage and they sat in the dark and smoked a joint and discussed the suicide cults in Japan. There's a haunted forest at the base of Mt. Fuji. College students off themselves in droves every year. Suicide Mecca. Japanese government tries to keep it hushed up, but y'know."

"For a man who loathes existence, you'd think he'd be even more on board with suicide. It's right for others, not him…"

"Oh, L is definitely against. Antinatalists abhor suicide. Goes counter to the code."

"Right, ending their miserable existences would trump the much greater joy of pissing and moaning about their miserable existences."

'That, and it's big fun to inflict one's contrarian views upon the hapless."

"Hapless and gullible. Some people are born looking for a crock of shit to get their head stuck in. Jack didn't tell me he met L."

"He only mentioned it to me a few months before he died, disappeared, whatever."

"That's unsettling," I said.

"I have to agree," John said. "But it's a coincidence. L didn't clip Jack. Hell, Jack probably didn't even really meet L. He got high and dreamed the whole thing. Plus the dude was a hell of a liar." He laughed and had a drink by way of genuflection. One simply didn't take Jack's name in vain.

"No, man," I said. "It's unsettling because Jack was obviously hallucinating at the end. That's a sign of way too many drugs, or mental illness. Maybe he was bipolar. We could've helped him." I tried not to wince at the irony of my observation.

"Sorry, I'm not gonna kick my own ass over what happened to Jack. For your information, I really did spot L. Michael C was sitting next to me. He saw the guy too, before he walked away. I ran over to see if I could flag him down. L was gone baby gone, of course."

"Of course," I said. "That's how men of mystery roll. And ghosts. And leprechauns."

"Michael's taking us for a few drinks before the show. You can ask him yourself. He's keen on the subject. Actually knows L from the old days. Calls 'em the cat food days instead of salad days."

The last thing either of us needed were more drinks. On the other hand, who was I to turn down a chance to booze with Michael C, an author nearly as cultish and reclusive as the inimitable L? Besides, Michael only drank the finest single malt, expense be damned.

The train rattled into a tunnel and darkness. By the faint plastic glow of the interior lights I had a rush of vertigo that tricked my body into believing the passenger car no longer moved laterally, but had shifted to the vertical plane and was descending at tremendous velocity, an express elevator to the pits. Streaks of red flickered against the windows. The kid with the earphones glanced at me. His earphones resembled the curved horns of a ram. His eyes reflected the void. He smiled. His smile was the void.

I gave him the finger.

\* \* \*

Michael C awaited us at Grand Central Station. We immediately repaired to a hole in the wall with an Irish house band and a sexy bartender decked in a leather bustier. Thank Jesus, Mary, and the Saints for those.

Most of the clientele were faux bikers and imitation punk rockers. I suspected their tattoos peeled and peacock-hued mohawks combed over to make office dress code come Monday morning. The garage music banged and wheedled with stops and gaps that hurt my brain. I ordered a round of Glenrothes and we toasted good old dead Jack one more time.

Michael was clad in black, as ever. Black silk shirt and string tie, black slacks and black wingtips. His hair was black and curled spring-tight. He was pale, gaunt of cheek, and wiry as a hound, ever restless without actually twitching or fidgeting. His eyes, though. They shivered and crackled. He proved quite pleased to discuss Tom L.

"Sure, we saw him in Glasgow. Dude was there, scoping the joint. I recognized him right away."

"What does he do? For a living, I mean." Anybody who knows anything knows writers don't survive off earnings from *writing*. We all have real jobs such as being teachers, dish washers, drug dealers, and crack whores.

"Works as an underwriter. Or writes technical manuals for research and development at an auto plant. Or he heads a lab at a defense contractor. Point is, nobody knows what he does outside of writing because he says something different to whomever asks. Wilum and S.T. told me L bought several blocks of abandoned properties for a dollar and that he lives completely alone. Pushes a shopping cart to and from an outlet store like a bag lady. Spends evenings on the stoop in a pair of John Lennons and a peacoat, smoking foreign cigarettes and watching kids smash in the windows of wrecked cars. Sleeps in a king-sized poster-bed in the penthouse of a historic brownstone that used to be a famous hotel where all the Motown singers and execs held court. Just him now, and the things that go bump in the night." Michael had snagged Poe and was experimenting with the marionette's strings as he talked, causing Poe to strut and lurch on the tabletop in a creepy pantomime of moonwalking, then spinning like a 1970s break-dance king performing a herky-jerky tarantella. In sixty seconds Michael had gotten more of the hang of it than John had in a whole year. John shrugged and cheerfully kept at his scotch, hugging Bob in the crook of his elbow like the protective father he was.

I said, "Didn't Nathan B post an exposé on his blog? *Exploding the Myth of L?*"

Michael nodded. "As a joke, yes. A tongue-in-cheek deconstruction of the L mystique. Nathan thinks, or at least he *likes* to think, L doesn't exist. His theory is a few writers got together during the 1980s and created their very own Richard Bachman. He even went so far as to out that British hack, Mark S, as one of the original instigators, although that's a mighty generous accusation considering Mark S's best ideas were all previously written by Lovecraft, Aickman."

"Yeah, I read something by Mark S—*The White Paws*. That was his best-seller. Moved thirty-six copies at the British Fantasy Convention when everybody got drunk and thought they were signing up for a charity drive."

"*The White Paws* was followed closely by *The Man Who Collected Barbara Cartland*," John said. "But it didn't do so hot, alas."

"Kicked ass in the Commonwealth," I said.

"Does that even count?"

"Nah, not really. I apologize."

I hadn't thought much of Mark S's *The White Paws*. The sorry bastard worshipped at the altar of L and his work came off all the worse by way of comparison. L-lite, so to speak.

Sadly, he'd been famously murdered by another author, an English lady he'd cyberstalked for ages. They'd had an ongoing feud over a metafictional story good ol' woman-hating S wrote that painted her in an unflattering light. Then the female author had the audacity to go and win the British Fantasy Award a few times while S was passed over without comment, as usual. Despite his public disdain for industry laurels and accolades, he snapped and began haunting internet message boards the lady frequented, and posting pseudo-anonymous rants about how girls like her only won awards because they looked fetching in a skirt.

He finally crossed the line by rummaging through trash bins outside her apartment one night and she, having lost her wits due to S's relentless fear campaign, sneaked up on him and cracked his skull with a ball peen hammer, cut off his head and stored it in the freezer behind a frozen Butterball turkey, or whatever the fuck brand they sell in jolly old England. She was currently finishing up a remarkably short stint at a women's prison and her book sales were sensational.

I'd heard that S's funeral reception was attended by exactly one person: feared and dreaded genre editor S Jones who'd show up for anything that offered free alcohol and who'd once infamously hailed Mark S as the savior of British horror, much to everyone's eternal chagrin. At least Jones sprang for the wreath. HOCUS, the science fiction industry magazine, gave S a one-sentence obituary, which was more than they'd given any of his books at least. All very lurid, as befitted the community.

Michael said, "Anyway, Nate hypothesized the L Syndrome was a sophisticated long con. A masterful grift. Dead letter drops, fake email addresses, phony author bios, author photo of some guy dead since the Roaring Twenties. Started as a game, each of them penning gibberish and sending it to *Space & Time*, *Horror Show*, *Night Cry*, etc., etc. It got out of hand and editors actually bought the stuff and, next thing you know, Tom L is a hot property, a horror wunderkind, the underground antidote to Stephen King and Dean Koontz, the Jack Spicer headbutt to Rod McKuen's yammering gob that is category horror. The gig got stale years ago, but now these pranksters are stuck with carrying on the charade. Hard to let go of those royalty checks. Nathan is wrong, of course. I've corresponded with L since 1988. We were pen pals on Usenet for a while before he got so reclusive. Met him on five other occasions. Went to his house once. The man is real as real gets."

"You visited his house? Goddamn it!" John pounded the table with his big fist and our shot glasses jumped. "That pisses me off more than the story you told me on the train." He glared at me.

"Today is the day to face the fact you are a frustrated and unfulfilled sonofabitch," I said. "And if you'd rather ogle L's house than coconut oil dripping off a perfectly formed breast, well, I am not certain what kind of friend you are."

"There's no reason I can't do both!"

Michael continued patiently: "It was just an apartment L stayed in after his wife died. Or disappeared. Similar to the Jack situation. Whatever the case, L camped for a while before he picked up and moved to where he is now. Nothing special, that apartment. Neat as you please, though. Sterile as a gynecologist's office."

"What, no copies of the *Necronomicon* lying on the coffee table?" I said. Probably sarcastically.

"Just something about the history of puppets. No bodies hanging in the closet either."

I didn't ask the obvious: what L was like, because I really didn't give a shit. So I asked about our good buddy Nathan instead. "Where's Nathan? He's in town, right?" Nathan had been a bartender in New Orleans during the aughts. He got out right before the hurricane and the floods. His daughter was thirteen and working on a PhD in nuclear physics at Cal Tech. Meanwhile, he lived in a shack in South Carolina and wrote the most delicately horrific short stories I'd ever read. Another recluse. Damn, we all had at least that much in common with Tommy L.

"No. Hell of a thing. Nate B and Paul from Boston were up north visiting Canadian Simon at some Podunk book festival. Those Canucks release a chapbook every other effing weekend it seems. Paul got hurt in a sledding accident, broke his wrist, but he's okay. None of the Canadians in the sled were injured. Nate should've gone sledding instead of doing whatever *he* was doing... He contracted a mess of flukes, so now he's getting de-wormed. Gonna be a while."

"De-wormed?" I said. "He's got worms? No shit?"

"That's what flukes are, worms," John said, so drunk he sounded sober again.

"No shit." Michael made the Scout sign. "He'll be crapping spaghetti for six weeks minimum."

"Everybody knows you don't drink the water up there," I said.

"Mentally challenged *children* know it," John said, taking a huge gulp of scotch. He was beginning to worry me.

"Maybe he got 'em directly from Simon," I said.

"I'm careful to stick to booze north of Maine and I don't kiss Canadians, ever," Michael said, handing me Poe's reins. He rose with the sudden grace of a mantis and fetched another round: brimming mugs of a honey mead I'd not tasted before, kind of earthy and coppery and acidic. It felt like fur sliding down my throat the wrong way. My eyes watered and the hairs in my nose bristled. "A rare cask," he said when I asked what the fuck it was. "This is the only place in New York it can be found and the proprietor only serves it to certain customers on special occasions. I'm such a customer and a live reading by L is definitely a special occasion."

"There's an occultation of the moon in three hours," John said.

"Our fair maiden in the pointy bustier mentioned it—the clincher," Michael said.

"What in blue-blazes is so special about this reading, besides a kooky horror author showing his face in public for once instead of staying in with the cats?" I said, wiping my mouth. My head felt half staved-in. Another part of my brain was turning over possibilities like a kid flipping rocks with a stick and that part of me imagined the liquor was so rare, so exotic, Michael had paid for it with a Black AMX card he only used once a decade for this singular event, and the promise of services to be rendered later. Sexual services. This simply had to be the donkey show of gourmet hooch.

We regarded one another for a few moments, then he leaned closer, so his chin was level with the tabletop, and said, "Okay, look. Here's the thing you rubes gotta know. Especially you, John-Boy. First, L won't be showing his face at all. This is the new deal. He wears a costume. And he doesn't speak."

I laughed. "Right. He doesn't speak."

"He does not."

"Oh, yeah," John said. "Meant to tell you, the guy—"

Michael shushed him with a hard look. "No, no, don't spoil the effect. He'll see soon enough."

"How does he orate if he won't open his mouth?" I said, feeling very drunk and very petulant. Pretty soon they'd be telling me the asshole didn't walk, but floated, as if on a palanquin toted by tiny elves in rhinestone jumpsuits. "Is it a pantomime like charades? An interpretive dance?"

"You'll see," Michael said and his eyes shimmered with the void I'd been noticing more and more all around me every day.

"Oh, man, it's weird," John said happily. Actually, he pitched his voice to a falsetto and held As You Know Bob in front of his face and pretended the puppet was adding its two-bits to the conversation.

"Yes, weird indeed," Michael said, brandishing Poe in a similar manner. "You'll see. You'll see."

"I do hope it's something new," I said, choosing to ignore their foolishness. "I keep the paperback of *Enemy of Man* in the bathroom. I've read the thing cover to cover twice."

"Yes, oh yes, you are in luck, mon frère. L's written a fresh book of essays, the companion volume to *Horror of Being*. No one other than his agent has even glimpsed the manuscript, but word is, it's his masterpiece.

Distils fifty-odd years of spleen in one raging spume of a satirical opus. It's called *The Beautiful Thing That Awaits Us All*. A howling void of blackness, I imagine." Michael said that with what I swore was a shiver of delight.

"It's going to do for the antinatalists what Ron Hubbard did for the whack jobs waiting to be whisked to Yuggoth by the ETs," John said.

Time and space dilated. So did the tavern and the heads of everyone inside. John and Michael were Thanksgiving parade floats tethered to chairs, smugly amused by my agnosticism toward all things L. I would see, I would see...

\* \* \*

The next thing I recalled, we disembarked a subway in Brooklyn and were on the Dr. Seuss-angled steps of the Kremlin Bar that wound and wound and rose and rose from the glittery icy darkness of New York winter's night to the velvety gloom of interiors that had, in their day, seen a lot of blood from the innards of poets, and booze, and bullet holes. Wood creaked beneath our shoes and brass gleamed here and there between folds of curtains, and the space around the bar was at capacity with an audience that buzzed rather than spoke. A living, breathing, telepathically communing Yin-Yang symbol. Intimate and impersonal as an Arctic starfield. Everything smelled of cigarette smoke and liquor and sweet, sweet perfume, and musk. The golden-green light tasted exactly like the last round of mystery mead we'd shared at the nameless tavern.

I'd been in the business a while, but though I recognized an occasional face such as a genre radio show host and a couple of editors and agents and a handful of local authors, most were strangers to me, seldom glimpsed wildlife that had crept from the forest depths to gather in the sacred glade and listen to Pan wheedle on his recorder by the dark of the moon. Literally the dark of the moon as a glance at my watch confirmed the eclipse John mentioned earlier would be in progress at any moment. I was an interloper, a blasphemer, and I half-expected a torrent of white blood corpuscles to gush forth and consume me as a hostile bacterium.

John and Michael shouldered a path to our reserved spot in a corner beneath a green-gold shaded dragon lamp. Its radiance made our hands glow against the tablecloth. Ellen D, famed editor and hostess of the event, came by and said hello and snapped our pictures and bought us another round in recognition of Jack's empty seat. I just poured the whiskey straight down my gullet, inured to its puny effects, and waited for whatever was coming, to come.

Tom L was not in evidence yet. His table of honor lay near the burnished wooden podium that had propped up many generations of crazed, catastrophically inebriated authors. The table was tenanted by two women, a blonde and a brunette in slinky sheath dresses, and a man in a slinky turtleneck. The man was handsome and clean-shaven the way one can only get with a straight razor. He reminded me of the actor Jan Michael Vincent during his youth before he socked some chick in the jaw for handing his girlfriend an eight ball at a party and tanked his career. I hadn't thought of Vincent in ages. I looked sidelong at the women some more and decided they were way out of my league no matter how smashed I might endeavor to get. Both wore long velvet gloves and smoked cigarettes with hoity-toity cigarette holders. Neither wore a Dalmatian puppy stole, but that wouldn't have surprised me an iota.

"Jumping Josephat, that's W Lindblad!" John said, rattling his puppets in excitement.

"THE W Lindblad?" I said and rolled my eye.

"*Is that Jan Michael Vincent?*" a woman stage-whispered.

"*No way…OMG! The Puppet Master is in the house! Eeeee!*" I heard another woman exclaim.

"Sonofa…he flew in from Texas!" John said.

"Who wouldn't?" Michael said.

"Oh, for fuck's sake," I said and wished mightily for another shot. *Drano* would've worked fine. The philosophy behind *HoB* was becoming more appealing by the second. Every necktie made me think of nooses and solid overhead fixtures.

"Lindblad isn't allowed in the UK," Michael said, lowering his voice like we were conspiring to knock over the joint. "Larceny rap. I don't know all the details, except that he got in hot water regarding some rare book that was up for grabs on the black market by way of Finland. Ah, those wily Finns. There was a bidding war going down in some rickety warehouse on the Thames and the Bobbies busted in and clapped the whole lot in irons. I guess twenty different consulates got frantic midnight calls. Lindblad's chummy with more Arab princes than the Bush family is, so getting the governor to pinch hit wasn't much of a trick. After much legal finessing, he was sprung on the promise he wouldn't show his face in England for a while. That, in a nutshell, is that."

"Must've been a hell of a lot of kinky nudity in ye tome," I said.

"Not really. It was the foreign edition of a US weird almanac or an occult guidebook. Rather innocuous, you ask me."

"He did a dime in Huntsville back in the late 1970s for gashing somebody with a broken wine bottle," John said with grave respect. "Lived on the mean streets, close to the bone. After getting his MFA, Lindblad was a derelict for like fifteen years, or something. L befriended him, scraped him out of the gutter and gave him a purpose. Heard that from Lee T. Lee knows everybody in Texas. Got his ear to the ground."

"That sexy little twerp over there *did not* do hard time in Huntsville," I said trying to remain cool. "And he sure as shit didn't do hard time in Huntsville in the '70s. Too pretty and too young. Look at those soft, effeminate hands."

"Looks sorta hard to me," John said with an intrigued arch of his brow. Luckily, his powers didn't work on suave ex-cons.

"Older than he appears," Michael said. "Oil of Olay is a miracle product."

I rubbed my temples and counted to ten. Thank god right then two things happened: Ellen saw my plight and brought me another triple of whatever was cheap at the bar, and Tom L drifted from a shrouded alcove and stood near his trio of groupies. Stood, mind you, not sat. "Whoa. Okay, that's a big dude." I drank up and plunked my empty on the table and gawked, just like everybody else.

"Behold the man," John said with or without irony; I was too bombed and too awestruck to make that call.

Larger than life was a cliché that fit this apparition all too well. L was conservatively six-feet-eight and broad as the proverbial barn. His bulk was encompassed in a heavy robe of crimson silk that pooled around and hid his presumably huge feet. He wore what I can only describe as an executioner's hood, also of crimson silk. No flesh was visible, not even the glint of his eyes through the hood slits. He stood motionless, a statue briefly animated, that had shambled unto view, and was now once again frozen in place. Something about his great size and stoicism, the inscrutability of the slits for his eyes and mouth, the blithe obliviousness of his entourage as they chatted amongst themselves, ignoring the giant entirely, scared the living bejeezus out of me, scared me on the level where the coyotes and the lizards and lonely rolling tumbleweeds held sway. A polar bear had beached itself upon an ice shelf with a herd of seals and the seals barked with joy, witless to their mortal danger.

I'd seen a picture of L once, a candid shot of him in a sport coat and a bad haircut, hunched in the act of stubbing a cigarette into an ashtray, grimacing at the camera as a thief with his hand in the till might. A grainy, fuzzy, slightly out of focus picture, but clear enough and contextualized by the presence of other persons in the frame that it was utterly incongruous with the figure in crimson. The author in the photograph was of average size and build. No way no how the same individual as this behemoth holding court. I said as much to my comrades.

"He's changed over the years," Michael said. "It's rather uncanny, I admit."

"How can you be sure it's even him?"

"Who else would it be?"

I glanced at my empty glass and sighed. "Could be motherfucking Patrick Ewing in there for all we know."

The crowd was apparently sufficiently lubricated in preparation for the appointed moment. Ellen made her way to the podium where she efficiently introduced her guest with, "I present a man who needs no introduction. Please help me welcome Tom L to the Kremlin."

Applause followed, although none of the raucous hooting or whistling that usually accompanied the appearance of a famous and popular author, and the room subsided into a deep and reverential hush as the giant ascended the dais with a slow, measured shuffle and then loomed without flexing a muscle or uttering a word for at least a full minute.

This silence gathered weight. A current began to circulate through the room and the lamps dimmed further, and as they dimmed, L's already massive form seemed to absorb the light as a black hole bends and deforms everything in its well, and his silk costume shifted black and he was limned in white like the white-hot edge of a blade. Yes, my senses were swimming from enough scotch to paralyze a rhino. Nonetheless, that powerful forces were in play between performer and audience was unmistakable and unmistakably unnatural. Even though nothing was happening, *everything* was happening. I thought of the silvery moon going dark over the city, and behind Luna's shadow, Mars through Pluto falling into a radical symmetry, cogs linking and locking along axial darkness.

L's left sleeve rustled with inner life and slowly, horribly from its cavernous depths birthed a puppet. The thing that emerged was the girth of a toddler, soft and yellow as decayed bone, and glistening with a sheen as of jelly. It wore a skullcap, rusty bells, dark surcoat, a red cloak and red leggings; a diminutive malformed jester, or a monk of Franciscan lore. Misshapen, malignant, diabolic—the hand puppet's countenance was remarkable in its jaundiced smoothness, its cockeye, and demented smirk. Its arms were overlong, its spindly hands and fingers mockeries of human proportion. The hands were restless. They writhed and gestured, both languid and spasmodic, gracile and palsied.

The puppet gazed at the audience, tilting its head and shuttering one off-kilter eye, then the other. It reached out with the deliberateness of a hunting spider extending a pedipalp to taste prey, and tapped the microphone. During none of the creature's articulations did the towering form of L so much as twitch. So dexterous were L's manipulations, the puppet appeared to operate wholly independent from the man himself.

The puppet said breathily, the male analogue to Marilyn Monroe prepping to sing "Happy Birthday, Mr. President," "I am Mandibole." And, after a pause where it groaned like an asthmatic, "Tonight, I shall recite a story created by my benefactor, the incomparable L. It has never been told. It is a true story." The voice seemed to emanate directly from the puppet's twisted lips. "Imagine the heads of everyone at every table in this room disembodied and attached, like ripe fruit, to the branches of a tree in a field. A huge, leafless tree in a wide and grassless field. The field is black dirt and the tree is also dark, fleshy and warm, however it does not live so much as persist, suckling the life force from its own fiber, its own fruit, in essence a cannibal of itself.

"The hanging heads: your comrades, your neighbors, yourselves, do not speak, cannot speak, for their mouths and yours are crammed with bloody seeds. You and they hang from the black tree in the black field, this tableaux illuminated by interior flames from the heads, for the seeds glow with fire, swelling and frothing maggots of deathly light. You sway in the breeze like jack-o'-lanterns and cannot utter protest, or question your Maker, or petition your Accuser. You are muted by choking mouthfuls of gore. And this is Hell, my friends. It will continue and continue unto Eternity, until it becomes something worse. Something worse." It repeated *something worse* at least twenty times, imperceptibly lowering its voice until the words trailed off.

I observed this spectacle with profound unease. I felt as a man helplessly staked near a colony of fire ants might feel, flesh crawling in anticipation of the approaching swarm. A needlessly surreptitious glance around the room confirmed that every person was slack-jawed, faces shining in rapt concentration while their bodies faded to lumps within deepening shadow. John and Michael had completely forgotten my presence. They, along with everyone else at the Kremlin, were on some distant soundstage in Hell, hanging from the Tree of Anti-Life.

Certainly my overreaction was the result of mental depression and an admittedly tenuous grasp on reality. Being wasted on god knew how many brands of liquor was likely a contributing factor. This tempered my urge to beg forgiveness of John and Michael for doubting them, for sneering at the notion L was some evil messiah sent by the dark gods to spread a message of disharmony and dread. But only a little.

Mandibole said, "Now imagine the hours passing, the days, weeks, months… Imagine the flesh deliquescing from bone, hair peeling in strips. The blackbirds feasting on eyes, noses, tongues… But you see everything that happens, feel every exquisite inch of yourselves slithering down the craws of the flock…"

I rose and lurched to the bar, hand covering my good ear to block the persistent drone of Mandibole's oration. The bartender didn't meet my eye when I demanded a shot. He grabbed a fresh bottle of Johnnie Walker and shoved it at me. I cracked the seal and had a pull worthy of Lee Van Cleef and Lee Marvin combined, and listed against the rail, gasping for breath, and for a few moments this distracted me from whatever malevolent shit the puppet was spouting.

"Hey there, sailor," the blonde from L's table said, sliding next to me so her red lips were near my neck, the heat off her tongue tracing my skin in collaboration with the alcohol igniting my veins. Her body lotion was lilac and water. She laid her hand on my thigh and didn't exactly smile, but made an expression something like one. "Buy a girl a drink?" She took the bottle and sipped, delicate and ladylike. Her un-smile widened. "You seem sad. It's because you're alone."

"I'm with friends," I said, conscious of the thickness of my voice, wondering if its intrusion upon the scene would cause the crowd to turn on me, to hiss at me for silence. No one seemed to notice; they were a roomful of wax dummies glued into their seats, heads fused, gazes fixed upon the podium. Only the brunette and the man in the turtleneck were watching us. Both of them were doing the un-smiling thing.

"Don't worry about these…people," the blonde said, her breath hot and sweet with the Johnnie Walker. "We're *all* all alone in the world." She wasn't a true blonde—her roots showed dark where the peroxide ran thin.

"Of course we are. That's why I'm sad. Man alive, I carried a torch for Julie Andrews. You're more vulpine, but I'm not picky."

"It's a different thing entirely. Sun and moon. Heaven and Hell." Her fingers roamed my thigh as she talked. Strange though, rather than erotic; jittery and unsynchronized as Mandibole's hand movements or Poe moonwalking as Michael pulled its strings.

I stuck out my hand, although the gesture seemed superfluous at this point. "I'm—"

"We know who you are, Mr. B."

"We?"

"Certainly. You're recognizable enough if one squints just right."

"What's your name, baby?"

"I'm W Lindblad. Who else?" She swept her fingers perilously near my crotch, then tweaked my nose, leaned back and laughed coldly. Over her shoulder, the man in the turtleneck gesticulated and pantomimed the blonde's motions and behind him Mandibole exaggerated a pantomime of Mr. Turtleneck. Elsewhere, Pluto groaned and rolled off its axis.

"I fucking knew it would be something like this." I had to chuckle, though. The last time a beautiful woman approached me at a bar she'd bought me a scotch and then asked if I'd found Jesus. JC was still missing, apparently. "Of all the poor schmucks in this joint, you had to pick on me?"

"You're the only one rude enough to interrupt this momentous performance, this ritual that will open the way and bridge the gulf between new stars and old ones." She laughed a dog's laugh without changing expression.

"Oh, okay. Amazing work with that puppet. I assume it's one of yours."

"You refer to a puppet as *it*. Refreshing. Most people say he or she."

"No sense in imbuing inanimate objects with sexual characteristics, even in jest."

"Says a world about you. In this case *it* is more correct than you could possibly conceive. The precise term, in fact. None other would do. However, Mandibole is no invention of mine. *It* comes from elsewhere. It's a traveler. A visitor."

In the background, Mandibole said, "*Something worse, something worse, something worse,*" and kept chanting it and chanting it. Several of the listeners joined in and soon it was like a church revival meeting with the parishioners chorusing the right reverend's punch lines. All of the lights had died except for the one hanging directly over the podium. Beyond the first row, all was darkness. The blonde and I sat, bumping knees, in darkness too.

The blonde's face blended into the ink. Her eyes glinted red though, seeming to hang in blank space. "Why the ring? She's gone gone gone."

I didn't understand for a moment, then reached instinctively for my throat where I kept my wedding ring on a chain under my collar. The ring was an empty gesture, not that acknowledging this changed anything, and so the emptiness conquered all. I couldn't decide how to feel, so I tittered uneasily. "Nice. Are you a cold reader? Do divinations for old biddies and their toy poodles in Manhattan?"

"I like Rick James and long walks on the beach. Maybe I'm too forward. My secret weakness. I read minds as a party trick. Free of charge. So, if you had to guess, why do you think your woman left you?"

"Leave me? Ha! She kicked my ass to the curb."

"Why do you suppose this sad thing has occurred?"

"Why is the center of the universe as soft as a tootsie pop undulating with nuclear sludge serenaded by an orchestra of idiot flautists playing 'Locomotive Breath'?"

"Fair enough," she said.

"Wanna get out of here?" I said.

Her red eyes burned like coals. "A minute ago you were thinking of our Lord & Savior. *There's* a fascinating case."

"Is this a long story? Because—"

"Silence, fool. That Christ was a puppet, strings played by a master in the gallery of stars, is the kind of truth that would get you burned in ear-lier days. The parallel between God and Geppetto, Christ and Pinocchio, surely an absurdist's delight. I think the supernatural element is bunk and lazy storytelling to boot. That the holy carpenter was only a simple lunatic with delusions of grandeur makes his fate all the more grisly, don't you agree? His suffering was the ultimate expression of the form. Tortur-ers long ago discovered that pleasure and pain are indistinguishable after a certain point. Jesus ejaculated as the thorns dug in and the spearhead stabbed, and he waited in vain for his imaginary father. Suicide is a sin, so they say. Unless you're a martyr, then green light go. Doesn't have to be hard, even though it's harder for some. Some have a talent for destruc-tion. I swallowed seventy sleeping pills and half a magnum of raspberry champagne on prom night. Wow, my mascara was a mess. The homecom-ing queen was my sister, if you can believe. She snuffed it right with a bag of bleach over her face on New Year's Eve, 2001. Bitch was better at everything."

I froze, dreams of a semi-anonymous fare-thee-well blow job in the bathroom across the hall going down like the *Titanic*, so to speak, and considered the possibility that besides obvious derangement, the woman might be physically dangerous to me, especially in my current helpless state. The scene had taken on the tones of the anaconda from *The Jungle Book* cartoon mesmerizing that sap Mowgli with its whirly eyes and thes-pian lisp: *trust in me!* It seemed wiser to keep my trap shut and grunt noncommittally, which is what I did.

She said, "But he's beyond all this and he finally knows. He's a real boy now."

"What *does* Jesus know? The obvious answer would be everything, at the Right Hand of God and such."

"He's seen the beautiful thing that awaits us all. Waiting at the bottom of the hole beneath everything."

"If you're saying shit rolls downhill, I have to concur." I turned away and she grabbed my wrist. Her flesh was icy beneath the gloves. I wit-nessed Christ broken upon the cross. The sky burned. Christ's battered face was my own. The sky dimmed to starless black and filled his eyes with its void. "Jesus!" I said and blinked rapidly and flinched from the woman, convinced she'd somehow projected this image into my brain.

Mandibole cried, "Death is the aperture, the cathode into truth, the beginning! The beginning, my sweet ones. More fearsome words were never spoken. A more vile threat has never been uttered. Yes, there are worse things, worse things, and death is not among them."

The blonde's grip tightened and tightened. Oh, yeah, an anaconda, all right. "That's a goo-ood boy," she said and her many teeth glinted as her eyes glinted. Not a serpent, but a monstrous rat with tabby tom under her claw and pleased as punch. Good ol' Punch. Or, maybe just maybe it was Judy who'd become a real girl. "I can see that you've seen. Infinite dark, infinite cold, infinite sleep. Much better than the alternative—infinite existence as a disembodied spirit. Awareness for eternity. All you have to do is let go. Let Mandibole eat your consciousness. Then, trot back to your little hotel room and go on permanent vacation."

"My choice is non-being via having my mind dissolved or be a screaming head for eternity? What the fuck happened to door number three?" I said.

"Be glad of the choice. Most don't receive one. Talk to L after the gig. He can help you get your mind right for the voyage into nothing. Don't quit your quest a few miles from home. Don't linger like HP and die of a tumor, last days spent wasting away on tins of cat food and the indifference of the universe. Don't end it foaming and raving in a ditch as dear Edgar did. Who'd come to your grave with a flower and a glass of brandy every winter to mark your sad demise? You don't rate, I'm afraid."

Something cold and hard pressed against my temple and across the way, Mandibole, haloed in a shaft of hellish angelic light, the far wandering ice-light of devil stars, swiveled and stared into the gloom directly at me, into me, and winked, and an abyss was revealed.

"Oh, what is this bullshit again?" A bulb in the liquor case behind the bar blinked to life as a diving bell surfacing from the deeps, and world-famous publisher GVG appeared and pried the bottle from the woman's hand where she'd stuck it to my head. "Go tell Tom I don't care how many Horror Writer's Association Awards he's got rusting on his mantle. I still don't regret not publishing that crap." He smacked her sequin-studded ass and shooed her away, and she retreated to her friends with a hiss and a glare.

GVG owned a venerable science fiction magazine and had given me my first pro sale. I hadn't seen him since the previous year's World Fantasy Convention.

"Thanks," I said, slumping with sudden weariness. "Quite a scene. One minute I'm getting lucky, the next I don't even know what."

"You weren't getting lucky, farm boy. In New York City we call that shit getting unlucky. Take a hedge trimmer to that beard and you might not scare away all the nice girls. Or, on second thought, write something remotely commercial for once. Yeah, try that second thing."

"The girlies like a man with folding green," I said.

"Ain't that the truth, my friend." He smiled sadly and looked me in the eye. "The secret is chicks don't dig seldom-read hosers like Mark S. So don't be that guy. A little less of your Henry James lovin'-grampa's favorite toilet reading and a bit more twenty-first century. Come into the light."

I didn't have the heart to crack wise, or to confess that it was way too late for a career-defining shift. We listened as Mandibole dispassionately described skulls stripped to bloody bone kicked around the equivalent of an Elysian soccer field while the gods cheered and diddled each other in the grandstands. But for me the spell was broken. I said, "Not giving Tommy boy the spring cover, huh?"

GVG shrugged and adjusted his Buddy Holly glasses. "I'm immune to the charms of pseudo philosophizing horror writers and their vampire bride entourages. Wanna see horror, come see what my three-year-old and a bottle of rubber cement did to the cat and a pile of slush manuscripts in my living room. Gonna have to bite the bullet and go electronic one of these days. Just remember something, okay? Dunno what that spooky chick told you, what you've got planned, but the only thing that changes when you check out is that nothing ever changes again. It's no different on the other side. No different at all." With that, he squeezed my shoulder and darted back into the shadows, good deed for the evening accomplished.

"The faithful shall be eaten first as a reward. The nonbelievers, the scoffers, the faithless, shall be eaten last, or not at all. As for you, my sweets, your fate is this—" Mandibole ceased speaking midsentence and became inert. As slowly as it had appeared, its body now receded into L's sleeve and the sleeve collapsed upon the brief, discomfiting jangle of rusty bells, an echo of Poe and a cask of Amontillado and the masonry of ancestral catacombs, a whiff of moldy death. The lights brightened and the audience awakened, table by table, from its daze and clapped with sustained appreciation. My bottle was damn near empty and I snatched it and sidled away before the bartender remembered to charge me. One for the road to Eldorado.

"Okay, you keep an eye on our buddy here—I'm going in," John said as I returned to our spot. He smoothed what remained of his hair, scooped up As You Know Bob and Poe, and charged off to meet his destiny.

L had expeditiously—for such a hulking man—retreated behind the beaded curtain of his alcove. A candle or lantern flickered murkily on the other side. A conga line quickly formed—at least a dozen starry-eyed supplicants bearing books, tattered magazines from the glory days of commercial horror lit, and in John's case, a pair of cheap marionettes swiped from his kid.

"Good luck, pal," I said to myself as Michael lolled in his seat, drooling and muttering imprecations in Pig Latin, far beyond paying John's departure or my grousing any heed. I killed the bottle and left it crossways among the cascade of empty glasses and made for the stairwell, which proved jammed with a secondary crowd of night owls who knew nothing of the reading we'd just survived, or the beautiful thing that W Lindblad swore awaited us all, but were instead standing in line for the midnight jazz club upstairs to throw open its doors. How nice for them to be them and not us!

No one stepped aside, kissy-faces too enamored with one another, too intoxicated by their own adorableness, each of them locked elbow and flank in a swanky retro mass, as I pushed my way through the gauntlet of cocktail dresses, feathery boas, and pinstripe suits and white fedoras. The people smelled pretty, and all I could see were their skulls dangling in Hell. Fuck you, Tommy L, fuck you and your little hand puppet too!

Freezing rain tick-tacked on the sidewalk awning, the roofs of parked cars. I tightened the collar of my overcoat and hunched in the stairwell, sharing the smoke of a drunk woman balanced on high heels as she waved a cigarette and cackled into her cell phone. The air was just chilly enough to slice through the fog and remind me of how much alcohol I'd guzzled over the past few hours, and for the first time since I'd walked into the Kremlin I visualized the gun waiting for me in the dresser drawer, back at the hotel. The psycho blonde had accused me of loneliness, but that wasn't quite right. Loneliness didn't justify self-destruction. Despair and grief, self-loathing and self-recrimination, failure and desertion...*those* were justifications.

Yet, the whole suicide plan sounded lame in the frigid glare of the lamps along the boulevard; a piker's lament to avoid paying the tab. Robert Service once said dying is easy, it's the keeping on living that's hard, and of course the poet was on the money, as poets usually are when it comes to smugly self-evident affirmations. I planned to blast a hole through my skull less because of insurmountable heartache, but more because I'd become too weak and too chickenshit to carry the cross one more goddamned bloody step. The marbles were going into the bag and I was headed home, exactly like any selfish, self-indulgent fifth grade snot was wont to do when confronted with one losing throw too many.

I'd almost decided to ask the woman screeching into her phone for a cigarette despite the fact I wasn't a smoker when John and Michael burst through the doors yelling and flailing their arms. I couldn't understand a word—a string of guttural yips and clicks and snarls. They were men with hyena heads.

That did the trick. I leaned over the rail and vomited up the dark heart of the cosmos.

* * *

Michael went his way, barking at slow-cruising taxis that refused to stop while John and I hustled and caught the last train out of the city. Our car was empty. A throng of night-shift workers pressed on at one lonely stop, seemed to take our measure and with exchanges of warning looks moved on to the next car. Same deal with the squad of off-duty Army grunts a few minutes later.

John and I didn't say much. His face resembled forty miles of bad road, as a country philosopher might say; hair disheveled and matted, eyes bulbous and streaked red, nose a bloody carnation; the genteel professor's bark stripped to reveal a carving: the primitive beast in the mouth of his cave. His puppets were in worse shape. Or puppet. He'd come from the Kremlin with Poe dangling from his fist, As You Know Bob conspicuously absent. Missing in action, as it were.

The train jarred as it traveled the rails, and my teeth clicked and the lights threatened to extinguish every few seconds, and Poe's wooden body lay flopped negligently across the worn spot on John's knee. The puppet's head knocked rhythmically against the metal seat divider. Something in John's demeanor made me loath to broach the subject, and thus I satisfied my deepening curiosity with those sidelong glances we men often shoot at daring cleavage or the dude standing at the next urinal, but it was Poe that attracted my attention. Poe's visage had warped the way wood and plastic do when exposed to melting heat. One eye was lost in slag; the other had crept toward the hairline. No longer fashionably soulful, that eye—now an oblong black marble, or an overlarge pit of a rotten piece of fruit.

I recalled Mandibole's loving and loveless description of bloody seeds and thought that yes, blood doth turn black. Poe's eye was the seed of corruption coagulated in a membrane of evil. It wasn't watching me, though my poor abused mind would've easily swallowed the premise like I'd swallowed so much scotch. Poe wasn't watching anything; whatever energy might've been imprinted upon it from kindliness and love, was gone. My recognition that the little puppet had been perverted into a dead, alien husk, and that neither Clara's doting joy nor John's paternal benevolence had done fuckall to prevent such an ominous transmogrification, caused my rebellious innards to gurgle and shift. I dared not dwell on As You Know Bob's fate.

That steady tap-tappity-tapping of Poe's skull against metal was too much in the end. I said, "Did you get his autograph?"

"L doesn't sign autographs anymore."

"Doesn't speak, doesn't sign books, what does he do?" I said, trying for a laugh, a smirk, anything remotely human, and while I waited a string of ghostly lights of an electrical substation floated past the window, trailing into oblivion.

John smiled, a wide, carnivorous yawn of jaws and teeth. "It was... good. He wants what's best. What's best. We're coming out of the cave. Got to, can't go on like this. Got to come out of the dark."

In my years with John, drunk, sober, and realms between those antipodes, his tone was a new one, his slur a thing unfamiliar as something dredged onto the beach from the deep sea. Tonight had been a night of such unwelcome curiosities, and considering my circumstances, perhaps a punctuating spike in the bizarre was appropriate, my karma if karma existed, if the universe kept tabs in its own insensate fashion, mindless as gravity.

We disembarked at the final station and slouched past dim and silent kiosks through frosty glass doors into a gathering storm. John paused at a trash bin and whispered to Poe, then he sneered and dropped the puppet into the trash and walked on without a backward glance. I called out a feeble goodbye that John returned with a perfunctory wave, then he was in his car, its door *thunking* shut. I started my own rental and drove to the hotel near the Newburgh Airport where the night man had on a soccer game and was relaxing with a big stack of Jack Chick pamphlets. I bought a soda from the machine in the hall because my tongue was swollen and leathery.

Man, it was a real let down.

I peeled some bills off the dwindling roll and left them on the coffee table for the maid, hoping she'd get them after the cops and the medics were done. I sat on the edge of the unmussed bed in that sterile, neat-as-a-pin, one-hundred-and-twenty-dollar-a-night hotel room. It began to snow and flakes piled against the window. The television was broadcasting nonsense; chains of American flags, sun and moon sliding atop one another to make black rings, my wife's face in the faces of enemies and strangers, a Nazi aiming his rifle at another man's back, tribal hunters racing across a moor, snarls done in red ocher, Sufis keening in a temple, my wife again and again, and Mandibole cutting through it all, speaking in tongues except for one clear strain in the cacophony: clear as a bell Michael intoning through the creature's mouth that nothing was ever easy, not this easy, and that nothing was ever clean, this wouldn't be clean, the Eternal Footman had the check ready, no shirking the bill, no escape. This couldn't end like this because nothing ever really ended, matter simply deformed, that's what the Purple People Eaters wanted to tell us, why they'd sent a representative across the spoiled Milky Way to spread the word.

The blonde laughed at me as her eyes slid around most frightfully and my wife's head superimposed and shimmered there, rippling with static, frozen in time.

I picked up the gun and I thought about my dogs that she kept in the divorce, and I thought of her as she was when we met, when she told me that it was over, and that disembodied voice replayed in my ear, promising that it would never be over, and I wished I'd run after John, wished that I'd rescued Poe from the trashcan grave and maybe I should put the gun down and get into the car and go do just that, but in this universe I'd already squeezed the trigger.

* * *

GVG and Michael were right. L and his demon spokes-puppet were right—nothing's different, nothing changes. Lasts longer, though.

# ACKNOWLEDGEMENTS

Thank you to the gang at Night Shade Books and especially Ross Lockhart, Claudia Noble, and Marty Halpern; my agents Janet Reid, Heather Evans, and Pouya Shahbazian at Fineprint Literary Management; the editors who originally published many of these tales: Nick Gevers, Jack Dann, Nick Mamatas, Darrell Schweitzer, Matt Cheney, and Eric Schaller.

Special Thanks to Jason, Harmony and the kids; Gordon Van Gelder; Ellen Datlow; Paul Tremblay; Jody Rose; Timbi Porter; Norm Partridge; Athena, my loyal companion; and to John, Fiona, and David Langan for being my family.

Finally, thank you to my readers for your support over the years.

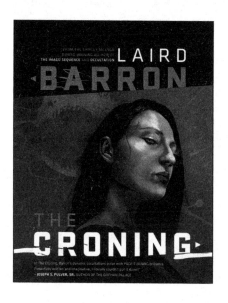

# ALSO AVAILABLE

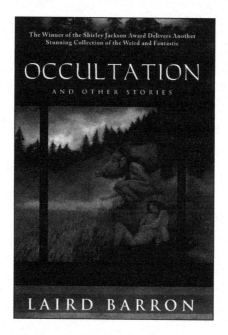

## Occultation and Other Stories
by Laird Barron

Laird Barron has emerged as one of the strongest voices in modern horror and dark fantasy fiction, building on the eldritch tradition pioneered by writers such as H. P. Lovecraft, Peter Straub, and Thomas Ligotti. His stories have garnered critical acclaim and have been reprinted in numerous year's best anthologies and nominated for multiple awards. His debut collection, *The Imago Sequence and Other Stories*, was the inaugural winner of the Shirley Jackson Award.

He returns with his second collection, *Occultation*. Pitting ordinary men and women against a carnivorous, chaotic cosmos, *Occultation*'s eight tales of terror (two never-before published) include the Theodore Sturgeon-nominated and Shirley Jackson Award–nominated story "The Forest" and Shirley Jackson Award nominee "The Lagerstätte." Featuring an introduction by Michael Shea, *Occultation* brings more of the spine-chillingly sublime cosmic horror Laird Barron's fans have come to expect.

$24.95 Hardcover • ISBN 978-1-59780-192-8

## The Imago Sequence and Other Stories
by Laird Barron

To the long tradition of eldritch horror pioneered and refined by writers such as H. P. Lovecraft, Peter Straub, and Thomas Ligotti comes Laird Barron, an author whose literary voice invokes the grotesque, the devilish, and the perverse with rare intensity and astonishing craftsmanship. Collected here for the first time are nine terrifying tales of cosmic horror, including the World Fantasy Award–nominated novella "The Imago Sequence," the International Horror Guild Award–nominated "Proboscis," and the never-before published "Procession of the Black Sloth." Together, these stories, each a masterstroke of craft and imaginative irony, form a shocking cycle of distorted evolution, encroaching chaos, and ravenous insectoid hive-minds hidden just beneath the seemingly benign surface of the Earth.

$16.95 Paperback • ISBN 978-1-59780-146-1